STONE WHISPER

A CRIMSON FANG NOVEL

STONE WHISPER

A CRIMSON FANG NOVEL

H. Y. GREGOR

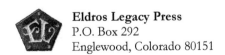

Eldros Legacy Press
P.O. Box 292
Englewood, Colorado 80151

DEDICATION

For my bear cub. May you find your own dreams and chase them, little one.

WHAT IS ELDROS LEGACY?

The Eldros Legacy is a multi-author, shared-world, mega-epic fantasy project managed by four Founders who share the vision of a new, expansive, epic fantasy world. In the coming years the Founders committed themselves to creating multiple storylines where they and many others will explore and write about a world once ruled by tyrannical giants.

The Founders are working on four different primary storylines on four different continents. Over the coming years, those four storylines will merge into a single meta story where fates of all races on Eldros will be decided.

In addition, a growing list of guest authors, short story writers, and other contributors will delve into virtually every corner of each continent. It's a grand design, and the Founders have high hopes that readers will delight in exploring every nook and cranny of the Eldros Legacy.

So, please join us and explore the world of Eldros and the epic tales that will be told by great story tellers, for Here There Be Giants!

We encourage you to follow us at www.eldroslegacy.com to keep up with everything going on. If you sign up there, you'll get our newsletter and announcements of new book releases. You can also follow up on FaceBook at:

facebook.com/groups/eldroslegacy.

Sincerely,

Todd, Marie, Mark, and Quincy
(The Founders)

ACKNOWLEDGEMENTS

Once upon a time, I committed an accidental act of violence against Quincy J. Allen. Then he gave me a book deal.

I'd be remiss if I didn't open with apologies (*again*) to Quincy for accidentally smashing his hand in my car door. Q, I'm really, *really* sorry. Thank you for your continued friendship, encouragement, and mentorship. Also, sorry.

Stonewhisper is both my first installment in the Eldros Legacy and my debut novel. There are so many people without whom this book wouldn't exist. Foremost, the founders of Eldros Legacy—Todd Fahnestock, Marie Whittaker, Mark Stallings, and Quincy J. Allen. I can never thank you enough for taking a chance on a new author. Manic, over-caffeinated appreciation for my dev editor Jonathan Miller, who praised me far too much and helped hammer out the imperfections, and copyeditor Zach Ritz, who also beat my short story into refinement in record time.

Thanks to my most excellent beta read crew: Jen Bair, Courtney Farrell, and Martin Plummer, and to Chris Mandeville, who cheered me along the whole way. Extra special thanks to Shannon Fox—drafting buddy, plot-hole spotter, and alpha-reader extraordinaire.

I wouldn't be here if I hadn't been inspired by cousins Chad Morris and Shelly Brown (proving that real people publish real books!), or without my earliest critique partners: Shley Gebert, Eliza Sanders, Daniel Quilter, Connor Olsen, Emmaline Jackson, Traci Abramson, and Allie Lyn Brady. You all deserve trophies for putting up with my rants, raves, and insane ambitions over the years.

Last but never least, to my family who sacrificed their own time and sanity to help make my dream reality.

Maps

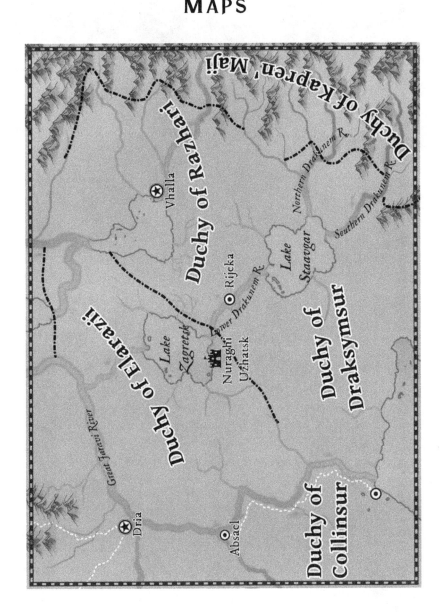

DEIHMANKOIOS

Thuroi Bakstadae os

The Wyrm Lands

CH

Strakh

Strakha H

Strakha Kleem

Strakha Khar

SOO KARI'MA
(Plains of the Dog Soldiers)

Strakha Suntin

Strakha Sundim

Strakha Raman

Cor

Strakha Vuil

Calamath

RHO KARI'MA
(Hills of the Dog Soldiers)

Strakha Tekri

Nemiassai

Var'Caspre

Iskasai

Vu

THE RIKARI NATIONS

Thookariani

The Paekkomere Ocean
(The Devil's Sea)

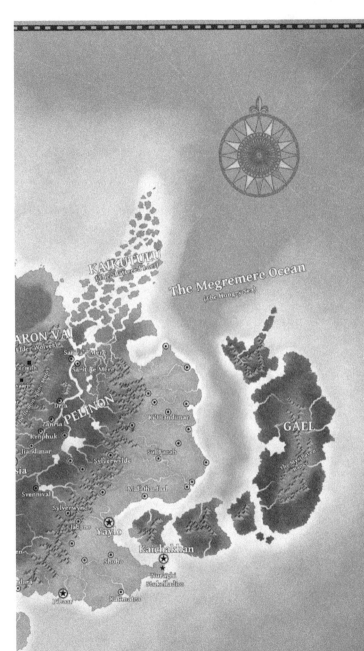

CHAPTER ONE

A STONE TOO FAR

E rion had never been so annoyed to be right. Potholes and broken earth marred the jungle trail he stood on— if the narrow smuggler's route could even be called a trail. The scent of freshly churned dirt and threatening rain weighed heavily in the air. All the damage was recent, and that could only mean one thing—Bhirtas'Drada. The pesky earth goblins had nests and burrows everywhere, and no other creatures liked to cause mischief more than they.

It was going to take forever to fix the damage in the road.

As though summoned by Erion's frustration, a gravelly chuckle sounded from somewhere within a pile of stones in the center of the trail. Erion shot a tendril of his magic toward the sound. He squinted at the offending stone—and the stone blinked back.

Giant's blood. The ground gave out beneath his feet before he could shout a warning at his companion. Mud squelched into his boots and maniacal laughter filled the air. Unbalanced, Erion crashed forward onto his forearms.

"Walk much?" A pair of black boots crunched into Erion's line of sight. Erion rolled onto his back, spat out a mouthful of grit, and glared up at his companion.

Thorne Knivhg wore his dark hair tied in a long ponytail, and Erion had never seen him wear a color that wasn't some shade of black. Thorne seemed unimposing, but his slender stature was all corded muscle. He had the latent energy of a coiled whip, and his eccentricity belied his deadly precision with the chain scythe he favored. His eyes danced with laughter as he looked down at Erion.

"*Goblins.* You going to help, or just enjoy the scenery?" Erion grumbled.

"Grinning keeps Thorne young." Thorne winked, then grabbed Erion's wrists and yanked him out of the mud.

Erion rolled his eyes at Thorne's odd cadence of speech. Maybe someday he'd get used to it. He crouched and laid his palms flat on the ground. Wind rustled through the dense network of trees lining the road, casting flickering shadows across the ruined trail. His gemajea—Land Magic—flooded through the earth. He stretched his awareness to its limits, but nothing moved within the circle of his power. The Bhirtas'Drada was quick.

Damned pests.

"Better get going, Mud Man. Road won't fix itself." A throwing knife danced across Thorne's knuckles. Corded muscles and tendons flexed in his forearms as he flipped and turned the knife in his hand.

Erion snorted. They would need an entire crew of laborers to level this road. "Won't get fixed at all until we get rid of those things."

"Boss won't like that."

A muscle in Erion's shoulder twitched at the thought of delivering the news to Isak, their crew leader in the Crimson Fang. Most members of the gang were easy enough to work with as long as Erion kept his head down. Isak went out of his way to cause trouble for him.

"Thorne has every faith in your abilities." Thorne plopped himself down on a rock with an air of casual arrogance.

Movement in the earth snagged on a tendril of Erion's magic. He bit back a grin as Thorne's rock burst into pieces and he tumbled backwards.

Erion's laughter was swallowed by a yelp as another pothole sucked him back down into the mud.

"Could have warned..." Thorne cursed. "We don't all have rock magic."

The mud squelched as Erion pulled his boots out of the hole. The goblin was laughing again, the sound like pebbles rippling down a stony slope. Erion ran after the tunneling Bhirtas'Drada, casting his magic out before him like a net.

"Kill it!" Thorne shouted.

The goblin paused, and Erion pounced. He threw a cage of stone around the creature and forced the earth upwards, revealing a cat-sized, eight-legged creature caked in mud. It squeaked with indignation. A moment later, the earth surrounding the creature exploded. The goblin raced down the road, passing over the ruined path with preternatural speed.

A second goblin popped out of the ground to his left. Erion lunged with his dagger, but it scurried away. He missed the creature by a foot or more.

Erion swore. The small ones were always hardest to catch. He gave chase. His majea grounded him, helped him find easy footing across the broken road. The creature raced into the woods.

Erion and Thorne pounded through the woods behind the retreating goblin. The Bhirtas'Drada came to an abrupt halt. Erion drew up short just as it was joined by three more of its kind. Whispers of energy radiated through the earth, catching at Erion's senses and pinpointing the creatures' location. Their digging merged to form one large tunnel beneath his feet.

Oh, daemonshite.

Erion threw himself forward as small explosions burst upwards at furious intervals, pelting them with debris. He summoned a blast of wind to sweep away the dirt, but only a whisper of breeze answered.

And then it was Erion who was running away, winding deeper into the forest with Thorne at his heels. At least he was drawing them away from the road. *A tactical retreat.*

"If Thorne knew you were going to get them, he wouldn't have bothered running all this way." Thorne drew level with Erion, breathing heavily but still grinning. Thorne seemed amused by just about everything.

"They just scattered." All trace of the Bhirtas'Drada had melted away once more. Erion frowned as a new set of steps drew his attention. He didn't need his earthwalking to sense the arrival—the ground trembled with each heavy footfall.

A rumbling growl drew their attention. They turned in time to see an enormous simiot lumbering into the clearing. The deep forest troll's eyes were tiny, and it blinked like it wasn't used to walking around in daylight. Its matted orange fur would never serve as camouflage, but who needed to hide with teeth that big?

"Made a new friend, did you?" Thorne quipped, gaping at the thing.

Erion drew his bastard sword and took a cautious step back, thinking furiously. They could try to outrun it, but he had a sneaking suspicion the Bhirtas'Drada would make it their personal mission to slow them down at any cost.

"Run, maybe?" Thorne prodded.

The simiot was still blinking at the edge of the clearing. It hadn't noticed them yet. A hasty move might tip it off to their presence—and then they'd be lunch.

He waited too long. The goblins announced their return with a flurry of tunneling beneath Erion's feet. The ground, soft from recent rain, began to sink. Within moments Erion and Thorne found themselves at the center of a sunken ring of sodden earth.

The simiot stumbled on the shifting earth and bellowed a challenge at the pair. The noise sent a flock of birds exploding into the air from the surrounding trees. And then the simiot charged.

Erion threw himself sideways, narrowly dodging the tackle. He twisted and slashed at the troll as it barreled past. Dark blood showered from the wound.

The troll rounded on him, surprisingly limber for its size. It growled and swiped at him with one enormous, clawed hand.

Erion dodged and stabbed. Dodged. Stumbled.

"Anytime you want to help!" Where the hell was Thorne? Erion shifted his sword to his right hand and made a shoving motion with his left. A wave of earth surged upwards and crashed into the troll, knocking it off its feet.

Relief flooded through Erion when the ground obeyed his will, but the effort left him gasping for breath. He'd only earned himself a moment.

The simiot snarled with rage and rolled to its feet. It staggered toward him just as Erion's sword bit into its flesh. The blade pierced deep into the simiot's flabby abdomen. The creature's momentum carried it forward, and the force wrenched the sword from Erion's hands.

A shout announced Thorne's return. He brandished a shortsword in one hand and a chain scythe in the other. Both weapons looked pitifully small next to the towering monster bearing down on them.

Erion fell back as Thorne stabbed the tip of the scythe into the simiot's back. He wrenched the blade back and forth, digging it deeper into the creature's thick hide. The simiot whirled and swiped one enormous, clawed hand at Thorne. It threw the man to the side like he was made of straw.

Thorne recovered from the fall with a neat roll, but blood stained the left side of his tunic. "Your turn!"

Erion bit back a retort and gestured for Thorne to retreat. Together, they scrambled out of the depression in the ground. Below them, the simiot turned in circles, pawing at the weapon in its back. With Erion's sword in its gut and the scythe in its back, it looked like some kind of demented, furry pincushion. The chain swung back and forth with the simiot's flailing.

"You bring your crossbow, Troll Meat?" Thorne clutched at

the wound in his side, but Erion took the snide remark as a sign that he wasn't too badly injured.

"You know I didn't. Stand back." Erion took a deep breath and focused on the ground beneath the simiot's feet.

He hadn't survived working for the Crimson Fang for so long to be stopped by some ugly simiot now.

Erion threw his will into the ground with all the force he could muster. A slab of rock jutted from the earth and smashed the simiot off its feet. It was big magic—bigger than he could have hoped for. Erion made a sweeping motion and the rock toppled onto the monster with a satisfying crunch.

"Your turn." Erion's knees gave out and he sunk to the ground. He always resorted to throwing brute force at his spells without thought to the consequences. Of course, sometimes there weren't any consequences—because sometimes the majea didn't work at all.

Someday, his lack of formal training was going to get him killed—but if there was a better way to kill a ten-foot simiot, he didn't know it.

"Come on, Stones-for-Brains. You've got to get Thorne's weapon back."

"I did not sign up for trolls." Erion rolled his wrists as he followed Thorne down the slope.

"You didn't sign up for this at all," Thorne pointed out. He reached the fallen simiot and kicked it in the ribs. It didn't move. He nodded in approval. "Nice work though."

The hilt of Erion's sword jutted out from the simiot's stomach. He summoned a sliver of his majea, urging it into the steel in the sword. Slowly, painstakingly, the blade slid out from beneath the body.

Erion stared at the bloodstained blade. He *hadn't* signed up for this—not really. He worked for the Crimson Fang, but he wasn't a member of the gang like Thorne. He wasn't even a degenerate hanging around the gang's outer circles, hoping for an invitation. But his father's debts weren't going to pay themselves, and gods knew his father wasn't capable of doing it.

Threats from the Fang piled up almost as fast as the debt—
and Erion's brother, Edric, was barely more than a kid. Now
Erion was as good as the gang's whipping boy. What else was he
supposed to have done?

At least today's job was an easy one. Clearing roads and
fighting goblins he could stomach. By recent standards, it was
practically honest work. Erion was scraping and saving every
dakkari. He might never get out of the Crimson Fang's sights,
but he'd be damned if he'd let Edric suffer the same fate.

One way or another, Erion had vowed to get his little
brother out of the city.

Erion's exhaustion was so thorough, he didn't notice the
Bhirtas'Drada return to the clearing. Thorne's curse from the
other side of the corpse was his only warning before he sank to
his knees in mud. Again.

Gallantyr's bones!

CHAPTER TWO

QUILL'S CURE

Erion and Thorne trudged into Quill's Cure three days later. The apothecary fronted some of the Crimson Fang's local business, and it was a common drop point for Erion's jobs. The shop was neat, the air ripe with a tangy blend of tinctures, potions, and herbs. Large windows let in plenty of light for the old apothecary to work by, and the worn floorboards were swept clean. Or they had been—Erion and Thorne had done their best to clean themselves up, but they still trekked mud and blood through the door with them.

Isak, the boss's right-hand man, lurked near the stairs. Blond, bearded, and hulking, he was never a sight for sore eyes. The big man jerked his thumb over his shoulder. Erion and Thorne followed the mercenary to the second-floor offices.

Officially, Isak rented the floor from the apothecary to run a thriving spices and herbs trade. Erion had always doubted the wisdom of the cover—he was surprised that Isak could even read, let alone tally sums and run a successful business. The ruse seemed to work well enough, but maybe that was because people were too terrified of the Crimson Fang to ask questions.

None of that was Erion's problem. The less he knew about the Crimson Fang's operations, the better.

Unofficially, Quill, the apothecary, inspected and verified inbound cargo. Every ingredient and piece of equipment had to be approved by him before any of the Fang's smugglers received a single dakkari.

Isak settled himself behind an enormous desk and gestured for Erion to shut the door. The mercenary didn't offer Erion or Thorne chairs.

"Road clear?" Isak made a show of scanning their filthy clothing and pursed his lips in disapproval.

"Not exactly," Thorne said as he shuffled his feet and glanced sidelong at Erion. "Thorne killed a simiot, though."

Isak snorted. "Sure. And goblins tore up the road."

"They did, actually." Erion met Isak's piercing blue eyes with a level gaze. He hadn't made a habit of letting Isak intimidate him, and he wasn't about to start now. Erion was bruised and beaten, exhausted, and had spent the last six nights sleeping on the ground. All he wanted was a hot bath and a meal big enough to feed a troll.

"And you let a bunch of vermin get the best of you." Mockery lit up Isak's eyes.

"There was also the troll," Erion pointed out.

"That Thorne killed," Thorne added helpfully.

"And you didn't fix the road," Isak said.

"Nope." Thorne poked Erion. "This one owes Thorne a new chain scythe though. That comes out of operating expenses, right?"

"Your weapons are your own problem, *Thorne*." Isak sneered at the name. "Skala, no pay on this one."

"I killed a *troll*!" Erion snapped.

"Thorne did that," Thorne whispered.

"Did you kill the Bhirtas...?" Isak raised his eyebrows.

"Drada." Of all the pests on Daemanon, Erion was convinced the earth goblins were the worst.

It was Isak's own fault that Erion hadn't been able to fix the road. Thorne had told Erion that the caravans had been complaining about trouble long before Isak had bothered to send anyone to investigate. They'd needed more men to deal with the problem.

"You'll get a partial credit against your debt once we get the next shipment. *If* we get the next shipment," Isak said.

"*My* debt?" It was a stupid technicality, but Erion fell for Isak's bait every time.

"Get out." Isak jerked his head toward the door, dismissing them.

"You have to pay me. I'll take this to Mathieu." Erion didn't move.

"I saw your father round one of the icho dens last night," Isak said. "I'm sure *he'd* be interested to know about your failure."

Erion's hand twitched toward the hilt of his sword. Everyone in the Crimson Fang knew who Erion's father was— and knew the truth of the man's drug addiction. As the baron's steward, Niklas Skala was a high-profile figure, whether he wanted to be or not.

And nobody loved abusing fallen grace like the Crimson Fang.

"Whoa, Knucklehead." Thorne knocked Erion's hand away from the sword and prodded him toward the door. "We're leaving. Thank the boss for his time."

Erion shouldered through the door without a backward glance at Isak.

"Feel free to offer your unending gratitude at any time," Thorne said as they walked down the hall.

"What?"

"For saving your stupid neck." Thorne paused, considering him for a moment. "For saving all of you? Not that your neck isn't, you know—nice, or anything."

"He can't touch me." Erion knew it was a lie as soon as the words were out of his mouth. His Land Magic—the gift enabling him to manipulate natural elements—made him valuable to the Crimson Fang. But he was also a wild card. Not a member, not a true mercenary, and not exactly a thug.

Erion was only indebted to them by proxy, and he wasn't to be trusted.

"Thorne bets he can touch you all he wants."

"Do you ever hear yourself?" Erion asked.

"Do you hear *your*self, Death Wish? Keep your head down and stick with Thorne. All the riches and none of the glory."

Erion grunted. Every member of the Crimson Fang sported a stylized fang tattoo on their forearm. The mark started out white for new recruits, but the marks were actually inked with Line Magic. Over time, the spells darkened the tattoo to blood red, then to black, as members moved higher in the ranks.

Thorne had been a member of the Crimson Fang for years, but his tattoo was still little more than a faded pink and white scar on his forearm. He'd acted as Erion's handler since they'd plundered a rotting ruin the previous year, but Erion still couldn't figure him out. He knew plenty of criminals—and Thorne just wasn't the type. The odd little man was a formidable fighter and more than handy with a lockpick or tripwire, but power hungry and malicious he was not.

Thorne paused outside a storeroom at the top of the stairs. The apothecary's testing equipment had been assembled near the windows, and the floor was crowded with stacks of crates in varying stages of unpacking.

"Keeping your head down?" Erion asked.

"Sometimes just… curious, you know?"

"No," Erion growled.

"Not even a little?"

Despite himself, Erion peeked over Thorne's shoulder. The nearest crate stood open, full of purple flowers carefully wrapped in paper. Beyond, the apothecary's scales weighed a small measure of brilliant, emerald-green powder.

"Doesn't look very tasty." Thorne wrinkled his nose.

"It's v'deru," Erion said.

"Bless you."

"Leech petals. Poison." Erion rolled his eyes. The plant was more than just poison, though. Erion had spent enough time around processed v'deru to last a lifetime. "For the icho."

"You know how they make it?" Thorne shook his head. "You should just join up already."

Erion rolled his eyes. He'd had this conversation before— with Thorne, with their crew leader Mathieu once. Even Isak had suggested it, though he made it sound more a threat than anything.

"It'd get Isak off your back. Then Thorne wouldn't have to watch out for you all the time."

"Is that what you were doing when you told him you killed the simiot?"

"Matter of pride. If Thorne hadn't stabbed the thing, you never could have smashed it."

"Call it an assist then." Erion's lips twitched into a smile. Against his better judgment, he found himself forgetting to hate working with Thorne.

Thorne shrugged. "Brains like yours, might as well be running the place."

"What happened to keeping my head down?"

"Hey, if you step up, Thorne doesn't have to."

CHAPTER THREE

THE ITHYNON

The man known as the Ithynon crossed out the equation with a vicious stab of his quill. It had to be wrong. He rubbed his eyes, cursing the poor lighting and the necessity of working in a dank, underground cell.

Across the table, his companion, Cedivar, muttered under his breath as he worked. The tip of the Line Mage's nose was stained with ink. His quill flew across the page as he drew out a line of complex symmajea. The Line Magic made the equations the Ithynon was working on look like child's play.

Not to be outdone, the Ithynon turned his attention to a wide quartz basin on his worktable. Carved symmajea encircled the basin, the inscribed spells inlaid with copper that glittered in the lantern light. Two depressions were set into either end of the oval. One held three clear crystals, each roughly the size of his palm. The Ithynon added a fourth crystal, this one black, to the empty depression on the right.

The six-sided crystal points were identical in size and shape, but that was where the similarities ended. Life energy radiated from the clear stones. Their construction was inorganic, and the magic didn't so much reside within the stone as it did cling to its structure. They were volatile—almost alive.

In contrast, the black stone was dormant to the casual observer.

The Ithynon knew better. The powerful artifact had been recovered, on his orders, from an ancient Giant stronghold. He'd taken painstaking care to unravel its secrets, then learned to harness its power.

The Ithynon held his palms over the stones and took a steadying breath. His first attempt at transferring majea between stones had almost killed him. He was a man once-bitten, and only fools refused to learn from their mistakes.

He knew about the rumors of his madness. He was not the man he'd been before his wife died, but he was no longer the animal he'd been during the early days of her loss either. The Ithynon was many things, but he was far from a fool.

"If my lord will excuse me, I have inventory to confirm." Cedivar bowed slightly and left the room with quick steps.

The Ithynon scowled. He couldn't blame the man after last time—the sudden and inexpert release of energy had blown the laboratory half to bits. But he was getting better at the transfers.

He had no other choice.

The Ithynon held his palms above the stones and tapped into the majea in his blood.

Majea in the clear crystals leapt to his left hand like sparking flames. Their energy rippled into his body. It melded with his blood and breath until he could no longer separate his own life force from the rising tide of magic. His fingertips, then his whole hand, began to burn from exposure to the raw power.

Each second counted. The Ithynon inhaled, steadying himself. *Discipline.* The majea from the stones formed into a concentrated nexus of power within him.

The burning moved to the Ithynon's heart, pumping vitality through his veins with every beat. The edges of his mind blurred as the magic surged within him. Men had killed for far less power than this.

He tapped his mind into the black crystal. The master crystal. The Life Magic inside the stone awoke like a ravenous giant; an unending void that could never be filled. It leeched onto the Ithynon's life force. Sweat beaded on his forehead as he warred with the majea in the stone.

With a determined hiss, the Ithynon thrust the raw majea at that vortex. It vanished into the void. A dizzying array of colors splashed across the Ithynon's vision. For a moment that felt like years, he stared into the depths of that incredible artifact. His mind balanced on a precipice between madness and hope.

"My lord baron!" Cedivar seized the Ithynon by the shoulder. The sudden contact severed the connection between the Ithynon and the void of majea within the stone. The men stumbled away from the worktable as one.

The Ithynon's knees trembled, and he sank to the ground. Part of him resented Cedivar for recognizing when he was overstretching his abilities and intervening. Another part of him knew he'd be lost without the Line Mage—though sometimes he resented that, too.

"I had the matter well in hand," the Ithynon snapped.

Wordlessly, Cedivar handed over a bowl of food. The Ithynon stuffed hunks of liver into his mouth, though sustenance would only help him recover so far. He needed sleep, and soon. The zomajea, his Life Magic, took more out of him every time he opened the channel of power. He glanced over at the black stone glittering in its basin. In his mind's eye, it pulsed with the majea he'd just imbued within it.

"There's a new shipment." Cedivar crouched next to his master and took his wrist, checking the Ithynon's pulse as he always did. He scowled. "You overstretched."

"Which shipment?" The Ithynon ignored Cedivar's scolding.

"The subjects, my lord."

"How many?"

"Two."

"Only two?" the Ithynon demanded.

"I'm told there was a complication with the third."

The Ithynon made a shooing motion. "I'll review their suitability before you house them. Begone."

"Yes, my lord." Cedivar rose and bowed stiffly. He left the bowl and exited without looking back.

The Ithynon ate the last of his meal and struggled to his feet. The basin on the table bore four stones—the white stones, now viridian green, newly emptied of majea and awaiting further service.

The subjects were late, and two wouldn't be enough.

Baron Drazan Voloy, the man known in the shadows as the Ithynon, glowered down at a crate by the door—overflowing with clear crystals, their majea awaiting transference. Banal duties awaited the baron in the morning. Tax ledgers to review, petitions to hear. His steward was a slovenly mess—*he* certainly wasn't going to handle matters. Another problem for another time.

His energy wasn't spent yet, and right now, the Ithynon had work to do.

CHAPTER FOUR

ICHO AND INSUBORDINATION

Erion leaned against a wall of the hazy icho lounge. The night was young, but the floor was already buzzing with patrons—with *addicts*. They sat on luxurious cushions around low tables. A glass pipe with a wide base rested on each table, topped with a large, viridian green crystal. Before night's end, the color of the stones would fade to clear. The crystals would be removed, and the men smoking from the water pipes would clamor for replacements before their icho paste could cool.

He turned at a knock on the door to his left and slid the eye slit to one side. A sallow-faced man narrowed his eyes at Erion from the hall beyond.

"Don't know you." The stranger's voice was a low growl. "Don't like new guys."

"Feeling's mutual," Erion said.

"Draxis ichor." The man spoke the passcode slowly, as though unsure of the right pronunciation.

"Chatty, aren't we?" Erion opened the door to admit the

addict. "Draxis ichor" was the name of the serum used to manufacture the icho. He didn't see the point of a passcode, but enforced the useless rule anyway. Nobody found this den unless they worked for the Crimson Fang in some capacity.

The man was heavyset, but his clothes hung from his frame as though he'd recently lost a significant amount of weight. Erion turned away from the addict and locked the door. Weight loss like that was a late sign of dependency. The man must have been spending plenty of coin at the cheaper dens to finally be admitted here. Erion turned and watched the man buy his early death at the gleaming bar in the center of the room.

It was all he could do to ignore the buzzing disquiet in his mind. He hated the icho dens—hated watching men ruin their lives and shatter their bodies, hated the reminder of how fragile people really were.

The icho rings were rampant across the entire duchy, but nowhere worse than in the Barony of Caraz. The Crimson Fang had the barony in a chokehold ever since the baroness's death. It seemed that Baron Voloy had simply quit caring after losing his wife. It had been over a year, and things had only degraded since he'd retreated within the walls of his manor. His subjects were at the mercy of an indifferent ruler and an unreliable city watch. Not even the baron's steward, Niklas Skala, was inclined to interfere with the growing crime network.

Shouts broke out in the corner. Dense white smoke wafted around the table, so thick Erion couldn't tell how many men were there. Glass shattered as he approached.

Erion didn't bother trying to shout over the din. He charged into the cloud of icho haze and grabbed the first warm body he could reach. The man swung a wild haymaker. Erion dodged it with ease and tightened his grip on the offender's collar.

"Benin? Really?" The familiar face took Erion by surprise. "They let *you* back in here?" The table Benin was sitting at was scattered with cards and dakkari. Erion rolled his eyes. Gambling and icho never meshed.

Benin slugged Erion in the gut.

Erion doubled over in pain and lost his grip on Benin's shirt.

"*Really?*"

A scrawny man across the table lunged at Benin. They crashed to the floor.

Erion resisted the urge to let the brawl play out and waded into the fray. He grabbed Benin again. The man snarled and swung at him—high and wild. Erion blocked the blow and grabbed the man's wrist. He rammed his knuckles into Benin's inner arm, just above the elbow, then twisted his wrist backwards. Bone snapped.

Benin yowled and crumpled to the ground. Erion turned on the scrawny man. His pupils were pinpricks; he was heavily under the icho's influence.

"Name?" Erion demanded.

The man took one terrified look at Erion and bolted toward the exit.

Erion ran after the man. His quarry jumped over a table, scattering the pipe setup and leaving a trail of shouting, intoxicated men in his wake.

The guard posted at the back door jumped out of the way as the addict bore down on him at speed.

"What's the point of you?" Erion snarled at the guard as he raced past. He followed the addict down the hallway, moving too fast to hear the guard's reply. It wasn't hard to guess which direction his quarry had gone—the addict was screaming now. Erion suspected he wasn't just running from capture, but also from whatever specter the icho was haunting him with.

They were heading straight toward the Crimson Fang's private lounges. Down the corridor, doors flew open as people looked for the source of the screaming. Each threshold revealed luxurious furnishings and bewildered faces.

Erion focused on the soft breath of air in around him. *Please work.* He wove the breeze into a tight gust and sent it racing toward the fleeing man's knees. His legs buckled beneath him, and the man went sprawling.

That would have been handy against those damned goblins. Erion caught up to the addict before he could recover.

"Don't get up." Erion hauled him to his feet, and the man started babbling incoherently. Erion dragged him the rest of the way down the corridor to the back door. They'd made enough of a scene already.

"What's your name?" Erion demanded as he kicked the man out the door.

"Fredrik. Hausel. Hausel." Fredrik chanted his surname like an invocation, over and over again.

"Well, Fredrik Hausel Hausel, good riddance to you." The other guard may have let Fredrik out the door, but Erion would still be the one to get blamed for the disruption.

Fredrik started humming as Erion pushed him along the back alley. The cool night air was a reprieve from the cloying haze of a half-dozen icho pipes.

A woman's scream tore through the night. Erion tensed, looking around for the source. Fredrik lurched into a pile of refuse and wrapped his arms around his head. Erion knew that icho-induced heady, altered sensations of touch, smell, and sight. Users never quite knew what they were going to get when they took the drug.

The woman screamed again. Glancing at the man cowering by the wall, Erion decided Fredrik wasn't a flight risk. He trotted down the alley in the direction they'd come from, one hand on his belt dagger. He paused at the intersection and peered around the corner.

A pair of hulking figures stalked down the alley toward him. Two women struggled at the rear of the group. Erion winced as one of the men shoved his captive forward, sending her sprawling onto the cobblestones. Cruel laughter floated down the alley as he yanked her back to her feet.

The scuffles rumbled through the cobblestones, sweeping through Erion's earthwalking senses like an alarm. Soft moonlight illuminated the alley. Erion backed deeper into the shadows as they approached.

He was deep in Crimson Fang territory. So close to the icho

lounges, this would almost certainly be Fang business.

Not my business. Not *my business.*

The mantra hadn't steered him wrong yet, but the woman's scream clung to him like a spiderweb.

One of the women suddenly broke free from the man holding her and ran toward Erion. She skidded around the corner and crashed into a pile of refuse with a muffled gasp. The woman rolled to her forearms, her fingers scrabbling at the gag tied around her jaw. She wrenched it free with a strangled gasp. Her eyes darted around in a panic—and locked onto Erion.

"Help." The word was barely a whisper.

Erion hesitated, and hated himself for it.

One of the women's captors caught up to them and pulled her roughly to her feet.

"What did we tell you?" He slapped her. The sound was a thunderclap in the quiet street.

The woman spat in his face. Enraged, the man threw her against the wall. Her head whipped back against the stone as the thug advanced on her and drew his dagger.

Erion kicked a loose cobblestone, joining his magic to the attack to command the stone's path through the air. It darted upwards and struck the man in the back.

The man turned, his blade pressed against the woman's neck, but the distraction was enough. Erion rushed the thug.

The man's grip on the dagger slipped as Erion slammed him into the wall. Erion's forearm crushed into his throat, pinning him there. Erion drew his own dagger and pressed the flat of the blade to the man's throat. He breathed a command, and the steel flared white hot.

The thug howled with pain and fear.

Erion glanced over his shoulder. The other kidnapper hesitated in the road behind them, as though unsure what to do with his own captive—or whether his accomplice was worth saving.

The woman crouched near the wall, one hand to her throat. A line of blood trickled down to her collarbone.

"Are you—" Erion began, but she interrupted him.

"I'm fine." She took her hand away. Dark blood glistened in the moonlight, but the wound was shallow—he'd missed the artery.

"Run," Erion said.

The woman's eyes widened. "Thank—"

"Run!" Erion snarled. He'd already said too much—done too much. All he could do was hope he never saw her again.

She jumped at his shout and raced down the alley. Once he judged she was a safe distance away, Erion released his hold on her aspiring captor.

"You'll pay," the man gasped, massaging his throat.

"Not likely." Erion sheathed his dagger. "Who do you work for?"

The man sneered. "Like you don't know?"

Erion gritted his teeth. He knew.

"Who's your boss?" Erion asked. *Please don't be Isak.* He was starving for an excuse to put Erion up on the rack as it was.

The man didn't answer.

A door down the alley swung outward, spilling golden light onto the cobbled road. The other kidnapper darted inside, dragging his captive along with him.

"Let's you and I have a chat." Erion took the man's elbow and steered him toward the open door.

Searing pain sliced into Erion's side, and his left knee gave out as the man kicked his lower leg. Erion crashed to one knee with a grunt. His assailant seized a fistful of Erion's hair and shoved his head forward.

Erion's temper snapped.

He struck hard and fast, ramming his elbow into the man's gut and ribs in quick succession. The man doubled over in pain but managed to keep his grip on Erion's hair. Erion snarled against the pain and lurched to his feet, dragging his attacker up with him.

Steel flashed out of the corner of Erion's vision. He seized the man's wrist, slamming his hand into the stone wall behind them. The dagger clattered to the ground.

The hold on Erion's hair vanished as they both scrambled to recover the weapon. Erion was closer—he dove forward, listening to the whispering steel of the blade. He'd always had the strongest affinity for iron, for stone and earth—he'd never seen another Land Magician with his skill with steel.

The dagger flew toward him, and Erion caught it by the handle. He whirled, knife in hand. His assailant leapt at him just as Erion drove the blade forward. It plunged into the man's stomach.

Erion dropped the blade like it had burned him and backed away. His hands shook uncontrollably.

The thug blinked rapidly as he gripped the hilt of the knife still embedded in his gut. He was already dead—his body just didn't know it yet. The dying man choked and fell to his knees.

Erion barely noticed the footfalls padding down the alley toward them. A man shouted, and a moment later, the body was being dragged away. Someone seized Erion by the shoulder.

"*You?*" A murderous grin spread across Isak's face as he took in Erion's bedraggled state.

"Me." Erion pulled from Isak's grip and put a hand to his side where he'd been stabbed. It was high on his ribcage—smarting, but not serious.

Thank Kalistar for that much, at least.

But if there were any gods, none were with him in the alley tonight.

Erion followed Isak numbly. He stumbled across a threshold and into a dingy receiving room—the same room the woman had been dragged into mere minutes before. They were in a small apartment, but it had clearly been converted into a safehouse. Down the hall to the right, several doors were open, and curtains blocked the view of what must be the kitchen.

Erion recognized the contraband that filled the front room—he'd helped deliver some of it to the apothecary. Clear, empty icho crystals filled one large barrel in the corner. A few crates were labeled as v'deru, others with ingredients and equipment names he couldn't make out.

He did a double-take and squinted at some of the unlabeled crates. Erion thought he recognized the stamp in the corner— but it couldn't be. What would Baron Voloy's sigil be doing here?

A muffled scream dragged him back to the present, reminding him why he was here.

The woman he hadn't saved was here somewhere. Erion closed his eyes. The haunted, pleading gaze of the escaped woman stared back at him. *Help.* But he hadn't helped—not really.

He shouldn't have hesitated.

I shouldn't have intervened at all.

He glanced up at Isak. A smug smile still played on the man's lips.

Erion was dead.

He stared down at the blood on his hands. Behind him, one of Isak's men escorted Fredrik into the room. Erion blinked at him for a moment—he'd nearly forgotten about the addict. The chase through the icho den felt like a lifetime ago.

"Erion?"

Panic flashed through Erion as he turned toward the voice. Mathieu, the local ringleader of the Crimson Fang, stood in the hall. Erion's insides withered.

An abrupt banging sound shuddered its way down the hall, followed by muffled shouts from one of the open doors. Erion's stomach knotted at the sound. The conscience he tried to suppress twinged at the cruelty he was witnessing. *You can't act. It's not your business.*

"Rescue." Fredrik's eyes widened with icho-induced insanity. The addict leapt to his feet and burst past Mathieu, down the dimly lit hall. He ripped the nearest door open.

A bedraggled, dark-haired woman bolted into the hall as soon as the door was open. One of Mathieu's thugs tore out of the room behind her, knocking Fredrik off his feet.

Mathieu grabbed the captive as she tried to slip past him and shoved her back down the hall. Her guard mumbled apologies and dragged her away.

Fredrik ambled back toward Erion, his movements sedated as the drug began to slow in his system. Suddenly oblivious to the woman's plight, he started to babble again.

The room seemed to close in around Erion. He took a deep breath, trying to calm his emotions. He couldn't afford panic—couldn't allow any signs of fear or doubt to seep through the cracks. And the majea he'd used that night was already taking its toll.

Without thinking, Erion brought his hands together, trapping a pocket of air. He gathered moisture into the bubble, then slapped an invisible mask of water-dense air over Fredrik's mouth. The man choked, then fell silent. The inane sound had been one stressor too many.

At least it worked this time. Despite his best efforts, sometimes his magic failed him altogether. Now his energy resources flagged. Erion needed more practice.

"Didn't think to do that sooner?" Mathieu's voice was measured, but that couldn't mask the fury on his face.

Erion met Mathieu's gaze but didn't dare reply—the situation had long since gotten out of hand.

He called himself six different kinds of idiot as Mathieu's steely gaze dissected him. One moment of insane heroism, and now Erion's entire life was unraveling. If the Fang refused to work with him anymore, his father would be at the mercy of his debts.

Erion would still pay for it one way or another—perhaps in blood.

Worse, there was no world in which his brother got away from the situation unscathed. Every breath Edric took was Erion's to safeguard—and he'd just put everything on the line.

A half-dozen excuses flew through Erion's mind, each more pathetic and groveling than the last.

"You've just killed one of my men, Skala." Mathieu's scowl deepened the crags on his already heavily scarred face.

The room closed in on Erion again, and he forced himself to take another deep breath. *You've just killed one of my men.*

Killed. Erion had killed his fair share of monsters in his time with the Fang. He'd bashed more than his fair share of heads in the icho dens. But he'd never killed a man before.

"I didn't know who he was." Erion locked gazes with Mathieu. No signs of weakness.

"Explain."

Erion did so, speaking carefully so it didn't sound like he'd intentionally attacked a member of the Crimson Fang in their own territory. At best, they'd think him an idiot. At worst...

"So, you abandoned your charge in the alley and charged right into the middle of something that had nothing to do with you?" Mathieu's voice was flat.

"I thought they were civilians—rapists, maybe. I wasn't told there were any jobs in the area tonight." Erion winced. Spoken aloud, the excuse sounded even more pathetic than he'd thought. Like the Crimson Fang would bother giving him information about jobs he wasn't strictly hired for.

"I don't pay you to think, Skala."

You haven't been paying me at all. Erion bit back the words in the nick of time. The pay discrepancy with Isak a few days before was a thimble's worth of worries in the rising tide of trouble he found himself in now.

A weighted silence fell on the room. Mathieu crossed his arms and narrowed his eyes at Erion.

"This needs discussing," Mathieu said at last.

"Aren't we discussing it now?" Erion snapped.

"You *killed one of my men,*" Mathieu emphasized the words this time, speaking slowly like he thought Erion deaf. His quiet, even tone made the reprimand more threatening than a shout ever could.

"He attacked me."

"And this safehouse wasn't meant for your knowledge." Mathieu gestured around the room.

"What safehouse?"

Mathieu's fingers twitched. For a moment, Erion expected the man to strike him.

"I've never leaked information before," Erion said. "I've no reason to start now."

Unless you terminate our deal. Erion had more than enough information to wreak havoc on Mathieu's affairs in the city. He was suddenly more aware than ever of just how dangerous his situation was.

"You interfered and helped a woman escape."

And did she somehow earn whatever fate you'd planned for her, or was she an innocent? The same fate that awaited the terrified woman in the back room, Erion had no doubt was meant for her as well. He fought to keep his mouth shut.

"Meet me at Quill's Cure tomorrow at midday. Dismissed," Mathieu said.

Erion glanced sidelong at Fredrik.

"Leave him to me." Murder glinted in Mathieu's cold eyes.

Erion couldn't bring himself to look at Fredrik. He bowed his head slightly and turned to leave the safehouse.

"Oh, Erion? Send our regards to your father. We extended his credit at the dens last week—I'm sure he'll be pleased to hear about it."

Erion schooled his face to impassivity and left without another word. When he was certain he was out of sight of the windows, he broke into a run.

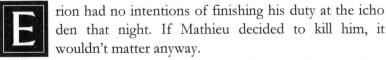

CHAPTER FIVE
CONTINGENCIES

Erion had no intentions of finishing his duty at the icho den that night. If Mathieu decided to kill him, it wouldn't matter anyway.

He slipped into the back hall of the den to retrieve his bag. His coin purse was heavier than usual, thanks to a lucky game of daggers that—with Erion's stoneburning magic—hadn't had anything to do with luck at all. The corridor was empty. Erion brushed his hand against the line of cloaks hanging on the wall, casting his magic into the fabric. He snapped his fingers when he sensed the cold metal of coin. Dakkari flowed into his palm at the summons.

The tiny exertion made his shoulders sag. That was it for his magic tonight. Erion wasn't usually so reckless, but he might be out of time.

If Mathieu was going to have me killed, he'd have done it already. But Erion wondered whether that was true. Mathieu was shrewd— he had to know that Erion would show up at the apothecary tomorrow. Maybe he just wanted Erion to panic, like a cat toying with a mouse before it pounced.

Erion had tossed Mathieu's name around casually with Isak earlier as an idiotic—and transparent—threat. The last thing Erion actually wanted was face time with Mathieu.

"Jumping ship early?" Thorne's voice lilted from a doorway as Erion left the den.

"Taking a leaf out of your book," Erion grunted.

"Thorne's book isn't very long. You've got to leave him something to work with here." Thorne trotted next to Erion.

"What do you know about Mathieu?" Erion knew Thorne had been involved with the Fang for years. Any new information was good information. What exactly had Erion stumbled onto in that hideout? Why was the Crimson Fang collecting empty icho crystals? They didn't have any other use that he knew of. He'd always assumed they were destroyed, or perhaps sold off as petty jewelry for the lower gang members to earn a quick nek.

Erion shied away from the other, more obvious questions. He didn't want to know who those women were, or what they'd done to earn that kind of treatment from the Fang. Or—more likely—what they *hadn't* done.

"Mathieu? Big man. Red hair. Lots of scars," Thorne quipped.

"Why are you even here?"

"Following you. Thought that was obvious."

"Cheers," Erion grumbled.

"Mathieu is no joke. Makes Isak look like a bunny in comparison."

"Bunny?"

"You know—twitchy nose, hops around."

Erion faltered and stared at Thorne. "Fluffy?"

Sometimes it was blatantly apparent why the Fang hadn't promoted Thorne. Trying to understand the man was like drawing blood from a stone. "What do you mean?"

"Thorne means that anyone can be an ass's ass like Isak. Takes a special kind of scary to be quiet and clever about stabbing someone in the back."

Erion paused at that. He knew Mathieu was ruthless. He'd have to be to have climbed so far up the Fang's ranks, but the man had always seemed so... *normal.* He groaned. The night had started out so simple. Why hadn't Erion just knocked Fredrik out to begin with?

Erion thought back to the man's constricted pupils and shallow breathing, and fought back the flood of memories the symptoms carried with them. One addict was more or less like another, and Erion knew them too well. If Fredrik had been knocked unconscious, or had his airway blocked for too long, he'd have died.

But now Fredrik was going to die anyway.

Erion's bloodstained hands started shaking again. He shoved them into his pockets, hoping Thorne hadn't noticed.

Thorne followed Erion like a stalking shadow. The soft scuff of boots on cobblestone accompanied them, the sound periodically displaced by a drunken song or uproarious laughter escaping from the few taverns still open at that hour.

The long walk to Erion's home at the baron's estate felt interminable. When he finally reached it, he stared up at the towering walls of Baron Voloy's estate with foreboding.

"So... does Thorne want to know?"

"I doubt it." Erion glanced sidelong at Thorne. The man's rare flashes of insight still took Erion by surprise sometimes. Thorne seemed so entrenched in his own world.

Not for the first time, he wondered how much of the man's eccentricity was a show. Thorne was a heartbender—theoretically capable of sensing and even manipulating emotions. From what Erion had seen, he wasn't very good at it, but he wasn't one to throw stones.

Erion snorted. Actually, throwing stones was about all he *could* do.

"Did I miss the joke?" Thorne asked.

Erion shook his head. "Are you coming in, or just enjoying the view?"

"And step into the lair of the enemy himself?" Thorne put a

hand to his heart. "Thorne would never dare be so reckless as to enter into the heart of the law."

"Suit yourself." Erion shrugged, but he understood. His living situation made working for the Fang—even unofficially—inherently more complex than it already was.

In another world, a just world, Erion would have taken Edric away already. They'd leave their father and his vortex of misery behind and find a quiet life. Edric would get the magic education he deserved, and Erion wouldn't spend every waking moment looking over his shoulder.

Some things were too good to hope for.

"Remember the rabbit." Thorne twitched his nose at Erion and flashed a broad grin.

"Rabbit?" Erion asked, bewildered. But Thorne was already out of earshot, dashing down the moonlit street. Then Erion remembered Thorne's bizarre comparison. He glanced around the road, half expecting Isak to melt out of the shadows, knife in hand.

Erion shivered and knocked on the servant's gate. It was locked, for once. Security seemed to grow more lax by the day. Nobody in the baron's estate—least of all Baron Voloy himself—seemed to care.

To Erion's surprise, the guard on duty actually opened the viewing window to see who stood on the other side before unlocking the gate. Erion nodded and clasped hands with the guard briefly. Hugo had joined the watch a little over a year ago, and he still seemed to take the job seriously.

"Late night," Hugo commented as he secured the gate behind Erion.

"Duty calls," Erion said. "Busy here?"

Hugo snorted. "If you call listening to the mage's hounds howling at the moon 'busy,' sure."

"I hate those things," Erion said. The two men glanced toward the back of the estate, where the baron's mage, Cedivar, had been breeding hounds for years.

"Each litter is *bigger*," Hugo agreed. "I'd hate to be on the wrong end of that scent trail."

"You and me both." Erion bade the man farewell and crossed into the yards.

He padded through the dark servants' halls, mercifully void of life. His father, Niklas, had rooms adjacent to the baron's, but Erion and Edric had long since moved to their own cramped apartments near the stables. It was a mercy—if a small one. Erion's only regret was the amount of time his brother spent alone.

The rooms were dark when he let himself in. He peeked into his brother's small room. The boy slept with his mouth slightly open, the covers knotted around him so thoroughly Erion wasn't sure how he'd extricate himself from the bed in the morning. He smiled and closed the door.

Edric was quick to remind anyone who would listen that he wasn't a child anymore. He was fifteen, and a man grown—but nothing he said would ever convince Erion. In his mind, Edric would perpetually be the baby brother tailing along at his elbow. Always wanting to be around, always wanting to help.

There was something so *good* about Edric it burned Erion's soul sometimes. Life had dealt the boy a cruel hand. The sheer injustice of it fed the quiet fires of Erion's determination. He fumbled around the bookshelf until he found quill, ink, and parchment. He'd formulated half a plan for his brother in case things ever soured with the Crimson Fang. He needed to write it out just in case... He didn't let himself finish the thought. It was just a contingency plan to get Edric away from the city. No matter what happened with Mathieu tomorrow, Erion *would* get Edric out.

⬟　⬟　⬟

Dawn broke too soon. Erion scrubbed at his eyes and blew out his candle when the gray light filtered through the window. The pittance of a letter he'd written to Edric wasn't right. The backup plan he'd cobbled together for his brother wasn't terrible though. It got Edric out of the city, if not all the way to a proper school.

Gods be good. Maybe it wouldn't be necessary.

Better Edric be miserable and safe than become another Fang pawn. He was more than old enough to take up Erion's place as the Crimson Fang's whipping boy... and his magic had just started to manifest.

Erion's fingers tapped against the narrow desk with nervous energy. He'd watched his brother with growing dread over the last year. When Edric turned fifteen, Erion had finally dared to hope that the window had passed. Edric was safer from the Fang if he was just another kid—no magic.

Then Erion had been kicked in the chest by a spooked yearling. At least one rib had cracked from the force of the kick, and breathing was an agony.

Erion thought back to the moment, feeling miserable. Edric had insisted on tending to the injury himself, and he'd laid a careful numbing poultice to ease the bruising on Erion's ribs. Warmth spread through Erion's chest like he'd swallowed a coal. Almost at once, purpling bruises faded to yellow-tinged green, and the stabbing pain on each inhale vanished.

Erion's dread was matched only by Edric's delight. It had been almost a year since the revelation. Nothing had been the same since.

Edric had to keep his magic a secret, and Erion was running out of excuses as to why.

He explained everything in the letter. The truth about their father's debts, the Crimson Fang, and the jobs that Erion kept disappearing for. They weren't all following monster bounties for the Hunter's Guild—even though Erion wished they were.

Edric already knew about their father's icho habits. It was impossible to keep that a secret. But Erion had done everything he could to shield him from the worst of it.

Footsteps padded up behind him.

"Did you ever catch that bat?" Erion asked but didn't turn around. He pocketed the letter before Edric could see it.

"It's not a bat." Edric took the empty chair and looked at Erion with serious brown eyes. Edric was barrel-chested and brawny to Erion's slender, lankier frame, though they shared their hazel eyes and sharp jawline. He was almost as tall as Erion now, and he had a feeling Edric was going to outgrow him. Little brother, indeed.

"Pigeon?" Erion grinned.

"*No.*" Edric scowled. "It's an injured fire-tail hawk, and you know it. And I *did* catch it. She's well on her way to healing up."

Erion raised his brows, impressed. Edric had been trying to coax that damn bird out of its tree for days. They still weren't sure what it was doing this far from its native habitat north of the Demonspine Mountains. "Was it you?"

Edric hesitated. "I think so? The master falconer thinks she got really lucky. He helped me with the bandages."

"Were you careful?" Erion asked.

"I'm *always* careful. But that's not what I wanted to talk to you about. I've been teaching Alwat about the horses—"

"What, the pig boy?" Erion interrupted.

Edric scowled. "The *swineherd.* He's good with animals. I thought, if he could cover a few days for me, that the next time you go on a hunt, I could come."

"We've discussed this. It's too dangerous."

"I'm learning the sword." Edric looked dubious—Erion knew he didn't have much stomach for violence or blood. He had a hard enough time even looking at injuries, let alone inflicting them.

"Don't," Erion warned. "Just don't, Edric. It's too early for this."

Edric slumped back in his chair. "I could *help* you."

"Dream bigger, little brother." The last thing Erion wanted was to crush Edric's spirits, but he wouldn't encourage him to become a bounty hunter. At least one of the Skala brothers should live up to their potential.

"Who says I can't do both?" Edric said mulishly.

"Just focus on keeping your head down and your powers

under wraps. We'll get you to the academy. I promise. But in the meantime—no bounties."

Erion pulled his brother into a hug. Edric slumped a little before returning the embrace.

"Some of us have work to do, you know," Edric muttered as the embrace went a little too long. Erion pulled away and forced a smile onto his face.

"Who's earning all the gold here?"

"I could help if you'd just let me," Edric grumbled.

"You'll have plenty of time to worry about coin when you're older."

Edric rolled his eyes.

Erion ducked into his room for his sword, then slipped the letter under his pillow on his way out. If Erion didn't come back, Edric would find the letter soon enough. He followed his brother to the yards and watched to make sure Edric entered the stables.

If Erion survived his meeting with Mathieu, he had to find a better solution. It was only a matter of time before Edric did something heroically stupid with his magic, and the Crimson Fang would entrap him just as they had Erion.

CHAPTER SIX

BONE SCOUTS

The bone scout snapped up the chunk of raw meat before it even left Cedivar's hand. He hissed and pulled his arm back. His fingers were bleeding.

"That's dinner, you feral..." Cedivar's threat descended into a string of curses.

Cedivar had long since trained himself to think of the hound's feed as *meat*. To think of them as Human remains was to court madness. *Needs must*, and Cedivar's needs were great. He watched with mingled distaste and admiration as the creature's savage fangs severed ligaments and bone with one powerful snap, and the hound swallowed it all at once.

"They're mongrels, what do you expect?" Baron Drazan Voloy joined Cedivar by the cages. Only weak sunlight filtered through narrow windows set high in the wall. The stone kennel was dim, casting the caged beasts in a shadowed light that made the hounds seem almost normal.

Almost, but not quite. They were far too large to be hellhounds, too vicious to be bloodhounds.

Not to mention the sickly orange cast to the whites of their eyes.

"*Trained* mongrels," Cedivar muttered. "They know better."

"The nature of the beast." Baron Voloy leaned closer to the cage, and one of the hounds snarled at him.

"My beasts," Cedivar reminded him. He'd trained these hounds from birth. They were far from his first litter, but he suspected they would be his last for some time—provided they lived through their trials.

Cedivar had succored countless creatures with his own experimental blends of herbs and poisons. Finally, he'd captured a pair of hellhounds. A rare enough encounter, as the female usually killed the male after mating. Even rarer that the female hadn't killed Cedivar himself, but he'd been well prepared for the encounter.

He looked down at the bone scouts, feeling pride, if not exactly fondness. They were creatures bred for a singular purpose.

"Are they ready?" Baron Voloy asked.

"Are you?"

Baron Voloy nodded. "I've ordered one to be brought up from the dungeons. He should be in the lab now."

Cedivar steeled himself and nodded. Now was his chance to prove to the baron that he hadn't been wasting time and resources just *tinkering*. He took a chain-link muzzle down from a hook on the wall. The blacksmith had balked when Cedivar had ordered the specialty piece lined with barbs on the inside of the muzzle, but he'd paid the man enough to silence his protests.

Bleeding the bone scouts was the only way to keep them under real control—not a quality he'd intended to breed into the beasts, but one he'd adjusted to.

Gods protect whatever fool opened these cages without taking proper precautions. The kennel was barred and locked and finished off with protective symmajea to discourage wanderers and saboteurs alike.

Cedivar barked a command at the bone scout he'd just fed.

The enormous hound sank onto its haunches and licked a lingering smear of blood from a paw. Its orange eyes glittered as it considered Cedivar.

He was never quite sure whether the creature saw its master or its next meal.

I am the master. Even so, Cedivar cast a glance over his shoulder at the baron.

"I'll wait outside," Voloy said.

A wise choice.

As soon as the kennel door swung shut, Cedivar opened the cage. He moved slowly, holding the muzzle out in front of him so the bone scout knew exactly what to expect from the interaction. The hound pawed the ground and lay down, unbothered by Cedivar's intrusion.

A single drop of sweat trickled down Cedivar's neck. He didn't move as he stared the hound down. *I am in control. I am alpha here.*

Then the bone scout whined as though to say *this again?* It stood, yawned, and nosed into the muzzle.

"Good boy," Cedivar whispered as he secured the links behind the hound's head and beneath its neck. Standing, the bone scout's shoulder rose to Cedivar's waist. The creature was sinewy, its fur so short that rippling muscles could be seen through its flesh with even the slightest movement.

Cedivar attached a leash to the back of the muzzle—as though something as banal as a strip of leather could control such a creature. But it wouldn't do to lead it across the yards and into the baron's labs without a visible restraint.

They took the shortest route to the manor's basement entrance. He kept the bone scout's head down, walking quickly to avoid unwanted attention.

"I'll admit to being impressed. Do we, uh—do we have to do this part?" Baron Voloy asked when Cedivar and the hound entered the subterranean chambers he'd set up as his labs.

"Only if you want it to work," Cedivar said.

"Do I have to be here?"

"Only if you want to know how it works."

Voloy fidgeted. "It's just so... *inhumane*."

Cedivar narrowly avoided a hollow laugh. Voloy's quest for knowledge had seemed innocent at first, even honorable. There was no cause more noble than love—or that was what the baron had doubtless told himself. And his research had started out harmless enough. But the baron's own methods had surpassed inhumane long ago.

Cedivar ordered the bone scout to sit and looked around the chamber. A man was chained to the far wall, everything about his appearance disheveled and screaming of neglect.

Baron Voloy stood as far away from the man as the chamber allowed.

"Who is he?" Cedivar asked.

"A murderer. I checked." And they *were* giving this man a second chance at life, after all.

A short life full of terror.

Cedivar tied the bone scout's leash to a hook on the wall and moved to a cabinet in the corner of the dimly lit lab. A wide chisel and hammer were already laid out and waiting.

"This will be fast, but I can't promise it will be pleasant," Cedivar told the killer as he advanced. "Right or left?"

The prisoner stared at Cedivar, but his eyes were unfocused.

"Right, I suppose." Cedivar laid the man's hand flat against the stone wall, then placed the tip of the chisel against the murderer's smallest finger. He crushed the hammer against the end of the chisel in one swift, brutal motion.

The man's shriek echoed through the chamber.

"*Must we?*" Baron Voloy demanded once the man's cries abated. Blood slicked down the prisoner's wrist, flowing freely from his severed finger.

"The larger the piece of bone, the more potent the trace," Cedivar said. "This should do for our purposes—but the bond fades with age."

"Meaning?" Voloy's gaze was fixed on the prisoner's blood-slicked hand.

"The older the sample, the weaker the scent."

Scent wasn't really the right word for it, but it was the best way Cedivar could describe it. The baron didn't care as long as the method worked. Cedivar put the stub of the man's finger in a bowl and washed his hands in a basin, scrubbing thoroughly until he was sure all traces of blood were gone.

"They can take him away now," Cedivar said as he dried his hands. "We'll give him a half-day head start, I think."

"That much?" Voloy asked. He was eyeing Cedivar's hound with mingled fear and curiosity.

"Make it a day." Cedivar held the bloody bowl out to the bone scout. The hound sniffed it briefly before lapping the prisoner's finger up with a barbed tongue and swallowing it whole.

The baron gagged.

Cedivar turned his attention to the murderer and untied him from the bolts latching him to the wall. He had to shout to be heard over the man's weeping.

"I suggest you run."

CHAPTER SEVEN

A RECKLESS RESCUE

Edric waited until he was certain Erion had left the manor before saddling his horse and exiting the yards through the northern gate. Worries for his brother plagued him as he rode through the forest. He could tell that something was eating away at his brother—like a parasitic growth on a tree.

He knew he couldn't heal his brother's heart, but he was going to find a way to lessen Erion's burdens. He'd find a way to take care of himself. Then Erion would have one less thing to worry about.

A wall of thorned vines rose ahead of him. Edric brushed his fingers against the foliage. Their underlying life force danced under his touch. Edric urged his horse forward, and the vines parted like a curtain to admit them.

The mare carried him into a wide circular clearing. Creating the space had taken him months—he'd gently coaxed each plant into the form he'd needed. As he learned their silent language better, he'd been able to build a living barrier around the perimeter. It was as good as any stone wall. Better, really, since Edric had some control over it. Vines crept back together as he passed through the barrier. In moments it was as though the entrance had never existed.

He dismounted and let his horse, Caz, wander. He'd had the mare since she was a foal. She never strayed far.

Edric stepped into a wide plot of rich earth. He'd spent months cultivating what had once been a barren patch of soil. To help the growth—and to bolster his strength—he'd planted kara roots around the clearing. The pale tubers were a great source of majea. He'd had to learn that from a text he'd borrowed from the baron's library, since Erion forbade him from telling anyone about his powers.

Edric pushed the bitterness of the thought away. Erion's reasons were good. They had to be.

Tender shoots of green sprung up at neat intervals, seedlings budding and thriving despite their late season planting. Edric summoned the bubbling wellspring that was his Life Magic and pushed a rivulet of power into the nearest seedling. A leaf budded at his prompting.

Within moments, other seedlings in the circle were sprouting new leaves as well. Edric had designed the plant to share a root network. To his surprise and delight, it had worked.

It was coming along well, but Edric wanted to interfere as little as possible with the natural process. He'd been breeding variations of the plant for months. He'd told the seeds what they were going to be when grown—now all he had to do was guide their progress a little. He'd designed it to be hardy, something that anyone could grow. Something so useful that everyone would *want* to grow it.

Soon, vines would start to sprawl across the clearing. Then, hopefully, the red athis flowers would bloom. Mundane healers and lifeweavers alike used the petals to stanch blood flow and quicken healing.

This athis would be better. Edric brushed his fingers over one of the vines, which was made up of tightly interwoven individual strands of fiber. Fiber that could be infused with the healing powers of the athis—and make bandages infused with majea that anyone, not just lifeweavers, could use.

If he had done it right.

Edric rolled onto his back, letting weariness from his small magic working settle over him. Untrained as he was, even small magic was sometimes overwhelming. Part of him enjoyed the heady sensation. It was proof of hard work. Honest work.

He was always careful never to overexert himself. He wasn't stupid. If something happened to him here, nobody would ever find him. Not even Erion knew about this place. His brother wouldn't understand yet.

Across the clearing, Caz's head whipped up from her grazing. Edric rolled to his feet and followed the mare to the edge of the clearing. The barrier trembled as something tried to push through the thicket.

Edric chewed on his lip. Nobody could have followed him from the baron's estate, could they? He'd been sure he was alone.

The thicket of vines and branches rustled again, farther away this time. Edric urged a sprig of leaves to the side and peeked through the small gap.

A woman crept along the barrier, stopping occasionally to press against the thicket. The hair on the back of Edric's neck rose. Not only had she figured out that it was a continuous wall, she seemed determined to break through.

Thundering hooves broke the silence—a rider coming in fast.

Edric's hideaway was well off the game trail, but apparently not well enough. He pulled back, and the gap in the wall slid closed. If he left through the opposite side of the clearing and rode fast, he could avoid the intruders.

But what were they doing here?

He climbed into the saddle and was already turning Caz's head when a scream pierced the silence.

Edric froze. The living barrier shook as the woman on the

other side fought to break through. She clawed at the thorns and the stinking, slimy glodis vines that Edric had so carefully woven together to protect his haven. This woman—whoever she was— was obviously in danger.

At least the barrier was holding up for now. Edric would have to start thickening the foliage in a wider circle around the clearing though. She never should have found the wall to begin with.

That didn't matter right now. Why was she being chased? Then he realized that didn't matter either. She needed help.

The woman whimpered as she tested the foliage's strength. The sound was almost animal—high and panicked and fearful. A horse whinnied, dangerously close.

Edric made up his mind. He drew his dagger—he *had* promised to be careful—and bid the vegetation to part. The woman tumbled through the opening into the clearing.

Edric closed the gap behind her as soon as she fell through. She rolled onto her stomach and started to crawl toward Edric. He grunted and jumped back, then commanded the glodis vines to wrap around her. In seconds, the slimy plant twisted and bound her arms to her sides. Smaller tendrils snaked around her ankles.

Edric crouched next to the woman, realizing his breathing was nearly as ragged and panicked as hers. He forced himself to take a deep, steadying breath. His captive's eyes were dilated so wide he couldn't even tell what color they were. She didn't stare at him so much as she seemed to stare *through* him.

The woman strained under the vines binding her before letting out a bloodcurdling scream.

Edric started, then stuffed a handful of grass into her mouth. The blades burst into growth and wrapped themselves around her head to form a living gag.

"I just saved your life, you idiot," Edric breathed. "Shut *up*."

Edric strained his ears for the sounds of the woman's pursuers. Did he hear hooves approaching, or was that the thundering of his own heart? If she'd found the clearing, there was every chance the horseman could too. Long moments passed before his pulse steadied and he let himself believe the immediate danger had passed.

He sat back onto his heels and held the knife in front of him. What had he been thinking? He'd let a complete stranger into his hideaway. What now?

Edric's strength was flagging. He knew his magic would get stronger, that he'd get better at wielding it as he practiced. But thanks to his duties in the stables and his promise to Erion, there had been precious little time to practice.

The woman's chest rose and fell with tiny, rapid breaths. Edric reached out hesitantly and pressed his fingers against her neck. Her pulse was almost inhumanly fast, her skin clammy despite the warm day. A knot of *wrongness* tugged at Edric's majea.

This woman was very, very sick.

Edric knew almost nothing about healing, but he could tell her life force was weak. The energy was tangled and discordant. It was almost like her body was at war with itself, trying to fight off an infection. But the infection was *all* of her.

The beds of her nails were dark. The color spread from her nails, blackening the tips of her fingers and most of her left hand. He lifted the hand. One of her fingers had been cut off. He thought the wound had mostly healed, but his majea slipped over a sense of rot there, too. Maybe it was infected.

He shook his head. None of it made any sense. He had no idea what was wrong with her, and he didn't dare try to help for fear of making things worse. She didn't respond to his touch, and her pupils were still too wide. Edric covered her eyes with his hand for five heartbeats, then removed it. No constriction at all.

Edric let out a shaky breath. He needed help, but he couldn't just leave her here like this. He put two fingers to her temple and used the only healing spell he knew would be safe.

"*Sleep,*" he whispered.

Chapter Eight

COERCION

Erion stared up at the swinging wooden sign outside of Quill's Cure. He'd taken a late breakfast with Thorne—well, Thorne had eaten. Erion watched him and nursed a weak cider. His stomach was already churning.

Thorne followed him to the apothecary. Erion knew it was part of Thorne's job to keep tabs on him. Today he was almost miserably grateful for the company. It wasn't quite midday, but the last thing Erion wanted to be was late.

The apothecary's familiarity was usually welcoming, but today the aromas of medicinal spices only served to twist his gut further. Erion looked through the window and around the room for Isak or Mathieu, but the shopfront was empty. The old healer, Quill, seemed to genuinely care about the people in Rijeka, despite squeezing every nek he could out of the Crimson Fang.

It was a common joke among Quill's patrons that his prices were criminally low but few knew they actually had crime to thank for that. The Fang gave the healer outrageous payouts to help fence their icho supplies. It was actually a good thing for the community—Quill had no need to bleed his customers for coin.

The apothecary was a walking anomaly, but he didn't seem to notice—or if he noticed, he didn't care. Erion barely knew him, but he felt a strange kinship with the shopkeeper. They'd both been caught up in forces they couldn't control. Overwhelmed by the Crimson Fang's bloody rule and striving for balance in the chaos.

Thorne shifted a throwing knife from one hand to another as they loitered outside the shop. One foot tapped on the ground. Passersby gave them a wide berth, opting to avoid Thorne and his glinting steel.

"I don't think you're invited to this meeting," Erion said. He prodded Thorne out of the street and onto the stairs leading to the shop.

"That matters?" Thorne balanced the blade on one finger for a moment as he considered this, then shrugged and flipped the blade once more. "Thorne learns new things all the time."

The door to the apothecary opened. Isak glared out at them.

"What's he doing here?" Isak demanded, pointing at Thorne.

"You're the one who assigned Thorne to watch him. Sir." He added the last as though it were an afterthought.

Isak glowered at Thorne. "You can be dealt with too, you know."

Thorne ignored him.

"He just wanted to make sure I got here safely. I hear there's gang activity in the area." Erion regretted the words as soon as he said them.

Isak practically growled at him. He jerked a thumb over his shoulder. "In."

Erion exchanged a grimace with Thorne and followed Isak inside. He'd tried to mentally prepare himself for what he might have to do. He still wasn't sure whether Mathieu meant to threaten or kill him. Maybe he'd threaten and *then* kill him. Either way, Erion wouldn't go down without a fight. He was confident he could take Mathieu on his own. Isak was another matter entirely.

He sent a prayer to whatever gods might listen that it wouldn't come to that. Erion's insides turned to jelly every time he thought about killing another man.

Mathieu had settled himself into Isak's chair in the upstairs office. He gestured for Erion to take the seat across from him, leaving a disgruntled Isak to lurk in the corner.

"Look, about last night. I—" Erion cut his prepared speech short at a severing gesture from Mathieu.

"You let it get out of hand. It happens."

Short of being attacked immediately, Erion had expected Mathieu to shout and threaten. Maybe he'd send Erion on an impossible job to the islands of Gael—somewhere he'd never return from. But this was... understanding?

Mathieu clasped his hands before him on the desk and gave Erion a hard, scrutinizing look. "You did good work with the Bhirtas'Drada the other day."

"What?" Erion blinked. He was completely lost now— probably exactly what Mathieu wanted.

"The Bhirtas'Drada. Clearing out the road? I'm told there *was* actually a simiot. The bounties on those aren't anything to sneer at."

"There wasn't a bounty."

"But you've taken out bounties from the Hunter's Guild in the past."

Erion nodded.

"The debts your father has accumulated are significant—I know you're taking work wherever you can find it. But you haven't made any cash payments against the debt, as far as I'm aware." Mathieu's brows rose, a silent invitation for Erion to counter the assertion.

Erion played dumb, choosing to ignore the unspoken question in Mathieu's words.

After a weighted pause, Mathieu gestured at Isak. "The contract?"

Isak pulled a roll of parchment from his bag and tossed it on the table. Mathieu unrolled it. He rested a paperweight on each corner, lining each square stone up with precision so the lines matched the edges of the paper perfectly.

Erion's stomach sank as he glanced over the contract. How was it possible he hadn't seen this coming? He'd been so rattled after killing the man in the alley that he'd failed to expect the most obvious outcome.

"You don't actually sign this, but I expect you know that. There are some formalities: you'll recite the oath when you get your mark, and the symmajea will bind it to your blood," Mathieu said.

They wanted Erion to join the Crimson Fang.

Erion blanched. This wasn't one of Thorne's casual suggestions or one of Isak's power moves. Mathieu's hold over the Crimson Fang in Caraz relied on his cunning—he was always thinking three steps ahead. How long had he been planning for this?

If he did this, Mathieu would have a hold over him for the rest of his life.

"I mentioned your father's credit last night," Mathieu said. "We saw him round a few days ago."

Erion nodded numbly. That made twice over the last month. It didn't sound like much; except he knew his father burned through his personal icho crystals and the v'deru paste at an alarming rate. They were expensive, and the Fang—responsible businessmen that they were—usually limited his supply. Erion had been grateful for that much at least. What credit the Fang *did* extend to his father was already going to leave Erion a criminal errand boy for the rest of his life.

Well—for the rest of his father's life, anyway.

"Have you looked at his ledger lately?" Mathieu asked.

Erion hadn't. It was just another line on the mounting list of things he didn't want to know. That list was getting awfully long.

"There are more solutions to your problems than beating your head against a brick wall and expecting it to break,"

Mathieu paused. "Though I suppose in your case, breaking walls isn't a problem."

Mathieu had struck the crux of the offer. Erion was too valuable to kill out of hand. They weren't offering membership as an act of mercy—the very thought was laughable. No—Mathieu had him backed into a corner. Erion only had to sell his soul to get out.

"It's not an option." Erion's mind strayed to the woman he'd saved last night—and the one he hadn't.

He was far from proud of the things he'd done in the name of the Crimson Fang, but he'd drawn this line in the sand long ago.

Guarding smugglers' caravans was one thing—that contraband would find its way into the Fang's hands with or without Erion's help. Fetch-and-carry errands, while degrading, were simple. When he tipped off the city guard to a rival gang's schemes or he delivered counterfeit goods to the market, nobody got hurt. Not directly, anyway.

Nothing he'd done had ever *mattered*. If those men didn't get their fix in the Fang's icho dens, they'd get it somewhere else. They made their choices.

Erion hadn't been given a choice when the Crimson Fang had raided his home to collect on his father's debts so many years ago. The terror on Edric's face had made the decision for him. Erion would have done whatever it took to protect Edric when their father failed to do so. He would do it again in an instant.

He'd been raw and untrained, but Erion's magic had been the tipping point. His skillset had intrigued the Fang enough for them to give him a trial run to pay off the debt. Then his father's addiction ensured Erion had never left.

But actually *join* the Crimson Fang? At least as things stood now, Erion had some agency over what he did for Mathieu. He'd managed to avoid the more grisly assignments, but this... Erion would sooner take on a hundred simiots than be ordered to kidnap innocent women or murder someone unfortunate enough to fall on the wrong side of Mathieu's temper.

That line was the only real choice Erion had ever made for himself.

"I won't lie, I've got plans for you," Mathieu said. "You've proved you're reliable *and* competent—Kalistar knows having one or the other is rare enough. I can use you. And you need us."

Erion just shook his head. "I'm sticking to our previous arrangement."

Mathieu tapped his fingers on the binding oath between them. "Do you know what you ran in on last night?"

Erion shook his head on instinct, but he knew. Rumors about the disappearances in the surrounding areas weren't so much whispers as they were shouts. One woman missing was an anomaly, two a coincidence...

It didn't take a great leap to connect the Crimson Fang, even before Erion had witnessed the kidnappings himself.

"Everything in that room is highly confidential. I don't even trust most of my men with what you saw in those crates tonight."

Erion prayed his bewilderment didn't show on his face. The crates? This wasn't about the kidnappings after all. It wasn't even about the murder.

"Just let me toss him in the river," Isak said.

Erion had nearly forgotten the other man was there, but now he tensed. He'd fought Isak and come out alive once before. He could do it again.

"Isak doesn't like uncertainty," Mathieu explained with a small smile. "I'm sure you've noticed."

"I don't like rats," Isak said.

"Or rats," Mathieu agreed. He turned back to Erion. "I can connect you with mages who can teach you things you'd never even imagined about your majea. You're not stupid, Erion. You'd be wasted hunting Bhirtas'Drada for the rest of your life. You're wasted paying off the debts of a half-ruined addict who was more than happy to sell you to us when given the opportunity. Don't you at least deserve to reap the full benefits of the situation you're in now?"

"It's not an option," Erion repeated.

"We can protect you. All of you." Mathieu's words were deadly quiet. "We know about that brother of yours, naturally. He'd be about fourteen now, right?"

Erion fought to keep his face impassive even as his blood ran cold. He'd known Edric would come up in this conversation, but that didn't mean he'd been prepared for it. *Be neutral. Be calm.*

Mathieu only meant he knew Edric *existed*. Nobody else knew about Edric's magic—not even their father. His brother had sworn he'd been careful to keep his power to himself. Edric wasn't stupid... he would have been careful. But was that enough if the Crimson Fang had been keeping tabs on him?

"There are worse ways that this could go for you." Mathieu's voice was a deadly rasp. "And most would say a life in the Crimson Fang is better than no life at all."

Erion didn't answer. There wasn't anything to say. It wasn't a real choice, and Mathieu knew it.

"I'm giving you three days. I suggest you weigh your options carefully, Skala."

CHAPTER NINE

A VOICE OF REASON

S omeone pounded on the door to Vandra Payuk's apartments. She glared at it and wondered whether her scribe had forgotten to tell her about a meeting. Time was her most precious resource, and she loathed interruptions.

The contracts she was writing weren't going to forge themselves.

"What?" she snapped when it was clear the visitor wasn't going away.

The lock let out a soft click, and the door swung open.

Vandra glimpsed Erion through the doorway for a half-second before the shock spell she'd drawn above the door knocked him off his feet.

"I told you I hate it when you do that." Vandra crossed the room, biting back a laugh. He'd only used his affinity with stone and steel to break into her rooms once before. He'd sworn it was a dare. Thorne had backed up his story, but even a stupid dare had been enough to convince Vandra that she needed to increase her security.

Erion propped himself up on his elbows and blinked at her from the floor. "I need your help." His chestnut hair was disheveled and badly in need of a cut, and there were dark circles under his eyes.

"I haven't changed my mind about that explosive tripwire for Thorne, if that's what you're here about." She leaned against the door frame and crossed her arms.

"What? No, listen. Mathieu and Isak want me to work for them."

Vandra raised a brow at him. "I kind of thought you already did."

"*No.* Can I just come in?"

"Can you?" Vandra asked. She peered up at the symmajea above the door and scowled. She'd have to redraw the spell after he left.

"Please, Vandra." His voice was as hollow as his eyes.

Vandra knew why he was here, but she hadn't expected him to look so ragged. Teasing him in this condition was cruel. She nodded at a cluster of chairs around a small table, across the room from the confidential records scattered atop her desk.

Erion threw himself into one of the chairs. "What the hell is going on?"

Vandra abandoned her hope that Erion would take Mathieu's offer with grace. She pursed her lips as she considered the situation.

"Tell me what happened." She knew Mathieu had offered him a contract—she'd written it up herself—but she wanted his side of the story.

Erion leaned forward, elbows on his knees. He stared at his clasped hands as he told her about the woman he'd helped to escape the night before, and the safehouse he wasn't supposed to know about.

"That's not everything," Vandra prodded.

Erion glared at her. "I killed him, all right? I tried to take him back to Mathieu and he attacked me and..."

"I think you did Mathieu a favor, honestly. He's been trying to get rid of Lucin for ages."

"What are they up to, Vandra?"

"I wouldn't know." The lie was immediate and flawless. Brokering secrets was as much a part of her job as forgeries and laundering coin.

"Don't." A warning flashed in Erion's eyes, and Vandra steeled herself for trouble. She'd never seen Erion angry before. She wanted to keep it that way.

"I'm not exactly in Mathieu's inner circle—but yes, fine. They've taken on a new contract that's gotten somewhat out of hand."

"The Reinholdt job," Erion breathed. He jumped to his feet and started pacing the room.

"You're not stupid, Erion. You know what the Crimson Fang can offer you. Why *not* join Mathieu?" He was right that the Reinholdt job had been the start of all of Mathieu's troubles. It had been the first request from the man who called himself the Ithynon, but it was far from the last. There was plenty of work to go around.

"Why haven't you joined?" Erion ceased his pacing and turned to her.

Vandra squirmed uncomfortably. It wasn't a question she wanted to answer, least of all to Erion. Her reputation relied on the common knowledge that she *wasn't* a member of the Crimson Fang. She maintained a clinical distance from all of her clients. Erion was different for more reasons than one—not least because she sympathized with the position he was in, at no fault of his own.

"How are the kidnappings related to the icho?" Erion asked.

"Does it matter?"

"I can't do what they want me to do. I couldn't do what they did to that woman."

"You've done plenty worse for them over the years." But she paused to think over the contracts she'd written for Erion in the past. The Crimson Fang called on her whenever they needed to grease the wheels on their bigger jobs. Letters with the right signatures went a long way when contraband was being smuggled over the borders of neighboring duchies, and Vandra had the best pen in the city.

Erion *hadn't* done worse—at least not for any of the jobs she'd fenced.

"Was that the first time…?" She let the question hang.

"Yes." Erion looked away from her.

Blood of gods. Had Erion really never killed anybody before?

Was she helping to corrupt one of the last good men in Rijeka?

Vandra wondered how much she should tell him. It had only been a matter of time before Mathieu pushed Erion to take the blood oath. The Fang leader already held all the right cards—he'd just needed Erion to give him the opening to force his hand.

"How are your savings coming?" Vandra asked, sensing his need to change the subject.

"Not great." Erion resumed his pacing.

"You should do it." Vandra knew what was expected of her—Mathieu had made it clear enough, and gods knew she owed most of her business to him. The gang leader knew she was on good terms with Erion. It was no accident that he'd told her the situation. She was privy to the safehouse in question, and the goods—benign and otherwise—that were kept there.

"Daemonshite, Vandra. You were supposed to be the voice of reason here. Even if my dearest wish was to slit throats for the rest of my life, I couldn't do it. It's not about me."

"That's exactly why you should do it. I do all Mathieu's contracts with the merchants *and* the Hunter's Guild, remember? I know how much more you could be making off your work."

"I won't put Edric at risk like that."

"And defying the leader of the biggest gang in Rijeka is going to protect him?" Vandra studied Erion closely. She knew he guarded what little pay he received like a dragon. He worked tirelessly, all for a thankless father that he'd be better off without.

"What's the plan for the coin?" She'd asked the question before.

"It's for Edric." He always had the same answer.

"What if I could convince Mathieu to wipe out your father's debts?"

Erion regarded her warily. "You could do that?"

"I could *try* to do that. But he wouldn't extend that kind of credit for just anyone. He wants you badly, Erion."

"Why?"

"Do you know the average mental capacity of the thugs lining up to join the Crimson Fang these days? Half the icho-addled vagrants in this city think joining up will help them score. And half the sober ones want protection so desperately they'll cuddle up to whoever has the biggest club."

"No, I mean—why are *you* so invested?" Erion asked.

"I only know what I would do in your situation. It's not the choice you wanted. But it might be the best one." She reached out and took his hand in hers.

"If I don't—I might need help." He looked down at their linked hands with a frown.

Vandra's heart sank into her stomach. "The Fang watches everything I do."

"If anyone could get us out, it's you. Don't be modest."

Vandra narrowed her eyes. "I don't want a bounty on my head any more than you do."

"I don't want a bounty on Edric's head."

"Which is *exactly* what will happen if you run. Don't you see that? I wouldn't be doing you any favors. Forget about Mathieu. With debt like yours you'll have the Fang himself on your tail."

Vandra's heart went out to him, but her hands were tied. If she helped Erion leave the city, she might as well sign his execution order herself.

The Crimson Fang always collected on its debts.

"Why do you do it?" Erion's eyes drank her in. His grip on her hand tightened, his calloused palm warm against her own. For a moment Vandra wished things were different—but there was no use in wishing.

"I made an error in judgment. We're all guilty of it, sometimes."

CHAPTER TEN

COMPLICATIONS

Erion stormed through the halls of the baron's manor. Servants cast frightened, sidelong glances at him as they scurried past. His conversation with Vandra had left his nerves frayed.

He'd thought she would be on his side—if anybody was, it would be her. Like Erion, she toed the criminal line of legitimacy with utmost care. She'd managed to stay out of the Fang's clutches, somehow.

She was no more Erion's friend than Thorne was. Erion sighed despite himself. He *liked* Thorne.

He liked Vandra.

But he'd been a fool to think he'd formed any kind of real relationship with her. He'd been reeled in by a pretty face and a few nights of flowing mead. Next time they met, he'd remember what she was: a fence, one of the best in the city. Consummately professional—consistently cool and distant with her clients.

And Vandra had told him to follow Mathieu to the slaughterhouse—where Erion was meant to be the butcher.

He didn't knock when he reached his father's chambers.

Niklas Skala rested on a divan near his windows. His rooms weren't so much dirty as they were shabby—the curtains were faded, and a tear in the corner of the lounge chair had gone untreated for so long it now stretched the length of the cushion.

"Erion?" Niklas blinked and moved to shut the door behind Erion. "To what do I owe the pleasure?"

Erion glowered at his father. It was hard to believe he'd ever looked up to him. Niklas was a shadow of the man he'd once been. The icho had stolen the color from his face and the intelligent twinkle in his eyes. The man who stood before him was gaunt, with sunken cheeks and a rapidly receding hairline.

"I had a meeting with Mathieu today," Erion breathed.

Niklas's brows drew together in a frown.

"Virath's boss." Erion threw the name at his father. Virath had been new to the Crimson Fang when he'd first started dealing icho inside the baron's estate. Now he had a comfortable position in the cellars at the manor, and a steady string of customers—of whom Niklas was first and foremost.

What little color remained in Niklas's cheeks drained from his face.

"If this is about the debts, you know I would have handled them."

"Like you handled Virath's raid?" The stone beneath Erion's boots shuddered. The motion was so faint, he doubted his father felt the tremble, but it was a warning nonetheless.

If I lose my temper, I'm no better than him. The wrong kind of rage could bring the ceiling down on top of them. Erion took a step back from his father.

"What would it take for you to release Edric to my stewardship?"

Niklas blinked, looking genuinely stunned. "What?"

Erion gritted his teeth. They'd had this conversation once before, years ago. Niklas had been adrift in a sea of icho, but his father had made it clear that he'd send a horde of the baron's soldiers after them if he took Edric away. Erion believed him.

"I don't want him to be a stable boy for the rest of his life. Edric deserves a fresh start," Erion said.

"And you deserve to run away rather than dealing with your problems, is that it?" Niklas's sudden fury would have been intimidating if Erion didn't know how frail his father had become after years of icho abuse.

"I don't deserve any of this at all. I'm offering Edric a life away from the ruins you've left us with." Erion was painfully reminded of why he spoke with his father so rarely. The conversation was rote, almost identical to the last one.

"You took up this burden yourself. You're a man grown—do as you please. But Edric is a child. He needs my protection."

"Like he needs your addiction?" Erion fought to keep his voice steady. "What kind of protection have you afforded me? Do you know what they've made me *do* since I stood up for you? Do you even care?"

The words burst from Erion without warning—a new, discordant note to the familiar conversation that dripped with heartache.

Niklas had been wasted on icho when the Crimson Fang burst into their home. He'd been unable to protest the invasion, let alone defend his children. So Erion had taken up the role of protector.

The only good turn Niklas had done since then was to move the family into the baron's home, for what scant protection that offered them. Niklas had never thanked Erion for saving his life—had never asked what deal Erion had made. As far as Erion was concerned, Niklas had never even cared.

Erion pulled back from the well of sorrow he'd suddenly uncovered. "You're welcome to step up and address the debt yourself. One word to Virath. I'm sure he'd prefer to collect your coin than my labor."

"All these years my position and loyalty to the baron have provided you and Edric with the best. A safe home. A fine education. Secure work and a lifestyle someone of our class could barely hope to dream—"

Niklas's voice rose to a shout, and Erion forced himself to disengage from his father's poisonous wrath. Niklas was all consumed by his victimization and entitlements. His convictions were just as deadly as icho—though it wasn't his life, but his honor on the precipice.

Someone knocked on the door. Erion turned just as it swung open—his father hadn't properly latched it.

Edric stood in the doorway, his face flushed with anger.

"What are you doing?" Edric's gaze flickered back and forth between Erion and their father.

"Nothing." Erion glared at Niklas. "It's *nothing.*"

"Erion was just leaving," their father said stiffly.

"You want me to leave Rijeka? Now?" Edric asked.

Erion caught his brother's eye, silently pleading with him to keep his mouth shut. So far, they'd kept Edric's magic a secret from their father. It had to stay that way.

"Erion wants to send you away." Niklas shot Erion a dark look. "I won't allow it. He knows that. You belong here. You're safe here."

Erion seethed and turned his back on his father.

"Go. Go *now.*" He dragged Edric out of the room and slammed the door on Niklas's face.

Edric tore away from Erion. "I'm not a child."

"You think I don't know that?" Erion hissed. "Do you think he *does?*"

Edric reddened again. "He wants me to train to be the next steward. He doesn't treat me like I don't know anything."

Erion almost turned back to break his father's door down. What was he playing at, trying to get Edric to take up his place as steward? Erion couldn't imagine a better way to make sure Edric fell into the Fang's grasp. The only thing better than having a steward under their control was having *two* spies inside the estate. They'd get to him young, the same way they had Erion.

There were so many things to love about Edric. If anything, the boy's heart was too big. If he found out Erion was being coerced, he'd step up in his brother's defense without a second thought.

Just like Erion had for him.

"I'm sorry, I missed the part where you decided you wanted to rot away in this manor for the rest of your life," Erion snapped.

"And I must have missed the part where you had any say!"

Erion put a hand to his head—he desperately needed sleep. "What about our plan? What about the academy?"

Edric bit his lip and stared ahead. "I could help here."

"What's happened?" Erion asked. Edric wanted to attend the magic academy in Saritu'e'Mere more than he wanted to breathe.

Edric stopped in the middle of the hall and met Erion's eyes. "You have to promise you won't get mad."

"I'm mad." Erion glowered at Edric's back as they rode down a remote game trail an hour later. He hated riding. He'd grown so accustomed to connecting with the earth beneath his boots—sensing his surroundings with his magic—that traveling without that grounding awareness was unsettling at best. But Edric said it was the fastest way, and Erion had given in.

Whatever Edric wanted to show him, it was urgent. At least the Crimson Fang's eyes wouldn't be stalking them in the woods. *Probably.*

Erion couldn't quite shake the thought. Vandra wouldn't help them escape, and part of him knew she was right to deny him—the same part of him that felt guilty for asking her at all. He had one chance in a hundred of getting away without her help. The gang had eyes everywhere.

"You promised you wouldn't get angry," Edric reminded him.

"I did no such thing."

"I didn't have to tell you."

Erion snorted. "Who else were you going to get to help you, the swineherd?"

"You should be nicer to Alwat." Edric said it earnestly, like nothing was more important to him than Erion's opinion of the swineherd. "Pigs are dangerous."

It was like Edric had forgotten he'd just confessed to practicing his magic in secret.

"Pigs? A rider almost found you doing magic in the woods, but *pigs* are dangerous?"

Edric shrugged uncomfortably. "Don't—"

"Be mad, I know." Erion was exhausted and restless. The last two days had been the longest, most agonizing days of his life.

Erion hadn't really thought his father would give his blessing to take Edric away, but he'd needed to find out for sure. Erion's calculations were mounting against him. Vandra was wary to help, and Niklas would certainly send soldiers after them if he and Edric vanished.

I could still send Edric away. Erion almost laughed at the thought. He couldn't even make Edric stay safely inside the estate's walls, let alone leave his entire life behind against his will.

Edric dismounted and picked his way to a thicket of slimy-looking vines. Erion watched the boy take a deep breath and lift his hand. The wall of vines parted. The true density of the foliage became more apparent as the plants shifted under Edric's command. They entered a wide clearing, completely encircled by a living wall.

"Fine. I'm impressed," Erion said as they dismounted.

Edric didn't seem to be listening. His eyes darted around the clearing. He muttered something under his breath and took off at a run toward the far side of the circle.

Erion followed, casting a net of magic in a wide circle around him. They were alone—the only movement in the clearing came from his and Edric's steps.

Edric drew up short, and Erion almost crashed into him. He grabbed his brother around the shoulders and skidded to a halt, then followed Edric's line of sight.

A mottled pile of cloth lay several feet ahead of them,

partially obscured by plant growth.

"She was right there."

"She?" There wasn't any movement coming from the bundle on the ground. "What do you mean, *she*?"

"She needed help."

Erion drew his sword and held out a hand to keep Edric back. He crossed the final few steps to the bundle. What he'd mistaken for a mass of soiled clothing was a *person*.

Sort of.

Erion wrinkled his nose with disgust as he considered the twisted semblance of a Human at his feet. It was a woman, or had been. Mottled skin stretched tight over hollow cheekbones and sunken eyes. Slippery glodis vines encircled the body's wrists and ankles. Woven grass gagged its mouth, baring yellowing teeth. Edric's work?

"If you've taken up grave robbing, we need to have a talk." Erion said it lightly, but panic coursed through him.

"She was alive. She screamed. I opened the barrier, and the rider charged up… I couldn't just leave her."

Erion groaned and rubbed his eyes with the back of his hand. *My little brother, the white knight.*

It was so obviously idiotic—and Erion would have been shocked if Edric had done anything else. He probably hadn't even thought about the repercussions of helping a stranger.

A screaming stranger who was being chased through the woods by gods-only-knew-what.

But none of that explained the rot before them. Edric's damsel must have escaped and—what, left a corpse behind?

Erion scanned the living barrier. There weren't any breaks in the wall of foliage that he could see. What were the chances the woman was a lifeweaver like Edric? About as likely as the woman having existed at all—or having been alive to begin with—Erion supposed. Even so…

He turned his attention back to the corpse and gave it a proper look. His stomach turned as he took in the details. She'd had long, dark hair. The weight of her braid was pulling her scalp away from her skull.

Erion grimaced and looked at the vines wrapping the body. Definitely restraints, just as the grasses were definitely a gag.

"What happened to her?" Fear had turned Edric back into that little boy Erion remembered.

"You're sure this is her?" Erion crouched to look through the woman's pockets. They were empty.

"The same clothes and—and I used the vines just like that. I left her here and I..." Edric's eyes widened and he fell silent.

Erion had seen corpses before—though they were usually fresh. This was a different kind of horror altogether. He led Edric away from the body. Edric's mare, Caz, nuzzled the boy's shoulder. He leaned into her like she was his only lifeline.

"I put her to sleep." When he finally spoke, Edric's voice was thick with unspent tears. "It's the—the only way I could help. She was mad, I think. Or sick."

"How so?" Erion handed Edric his waterskin and did his best to keep his tone even. He was rattled enough by the sight. He could only imagine Edric's panic—especially if he'd seen the woman alive mere hours earlier.

"Her eyes..." Edric shuddered. "They were dilated so wide—no color at all."

"Vampires aren't real," Erion said.

Edric's glare could have heated a forge.

"Is it possible..." Erion began.

"That I imagined it?" Edric took a deep breath, visibly steadying himself. His hand patted Caz with choppy, irregular motions. "I told her to sleep. It's the only healing I know."

Erion put his hands on his brother's shoulders.

"Breathe, Edric. Stay with me here—no, *look at me*." Erion waited until his brother's eyes locked with his before he continued. "You *did not* do this. You didn't."

"I've been practicing and—"

"This wasn't you. It wasn't." Erion repeated the words in his own head. *Edric didn't do this. He couldn't. He* wouldn't. "You said she was already sick. Maybe..."

Maybe what? A chill ran down Erion's spine. More questions he didn't want the answers to.

"We have to tell the guard." Edric's blue eyes were wide with honest, shining terror.

"*What?*" Erion literally couldn't think of a worse idea.

"A woman is dead because of me." Edric sank to the ground, looking dazed.

"She's not. You didn't. And we can't. You said someone was following her—we don't know who or why. If we tell the guard, they'll find this place, and everyone will know about your magic."

"And that I'm a murderer." Edric stared out at a circle of dirt in the center of the clearing, where tiny shoots of green were just beginning to break the surface. "I was trying to breed a new species of athis flower."

Erion barely followed the change of topic.

"For the festival." Edric took a ragged breath. "I was going to get a sponsor to Saritu'e'Mere. So you didn't have to keep working for the Hunter's Guild, if you didn't want."

Understanding cloaked Erion with guilt. The last thing he'd wanted was to burden Edric with thoughts about money, but he'd done just that by emphasizing to his brother how much he *didn't* want Edric to worry about it.

Every winter, cities all across the country of Pelinon hosted the Kuriositar—the Manifestation Festival where ambitious young magelings showcased their magical talents. Each hoped to be discovered in the hopes of expanding their skills—or moving away from the relative backwaters of Rijeka and seeing the world. To any aspiring mage, the Kuriositar represented endless possibilities. Some, the strongest and most promising, even earned sponsors to attend one of Pelinon's illustrious magic academies.

Erion couldn't let Edric participate in the Manifestation Festival. It was too risky. He wasn't going to argue about it now, though. "Let's bury her and get home. Then we'll talk."

It took Erion about a second to scoop out a shallow grave

near the edge of the clearing. He thought better of it and dug his magic deeper and deeper, shifting a small mountain of dirt aside until the hole was deeper than Erion was tall.

Edric had been careful, but somehow this woman had still found his hiding place.

And somehow, she'd died and decomposed in a matter of hours. Erion put it out of his mind as best he could—it was horrifying, mystifying, but not something he could worry about right now. *Focus on the task at hand.*

When Erion was satisfied the grave was deep enough, Edric wove a cocoon of greenery to encase the woman's body, then used the glodis vines like rope to slowly lower her into the ground. Erion's tension melted away as he covered the grave. He hadn't realized how on edge he'd been until the unknown threat was out of sight.

That's what she was—what this whole situation was. A threat. It had to have something to do with Mathieu—there was no way this was a coincidence. Who was she, and where had she come from? Would more men come searching for her now that she was dead?

He wasn't inclined to think Edric was lying. It was too insane. Short of his brother forming an icho addiction without Erion's knowledge and hallucinating enough to garble the truth of events, Edric couldn't be making this up.

What in Kalistar's name happened to her?

Edric closed his eyes, muttering under his breath, and fresh green sprouted over the filled grave. Soon all traces of the hole had vanished.

"I won't leave here," Edric said suddenly.

"Not even for the academy?"

Edric shrugged. "That's different. But I won't run away."

Erion narrowed his eyes. "What do you mean?"

"I know about the icho. I'm not stupid. I know you give Father money to keep him from…" Edric gestured vaguely. "Consequences. But I'm not leaving unless I know the plan—and I know Father is taken care of."

"You know he'd leave us for dead before he quit the icho." Erion's voice was flat, emotionless. It was a truth he'd come to terms with a long time ago.

"I don't believe that."

"Don't, or won't?"

"It doesn't matter. You can't make me just run away. I'll go to the festival. Maybe even the baron will sponsor me, if I'm good enough."

"*No.*" The word came out harsher than Erion had intended. "It's too dangerous."

Edric shuddered and looked away. "I don't—do you think it would do *that* again? That maybe I can't control it?"

Part of Erion was tempted to let his brother follow that line of thought, to convince himself that his magic was too dangerous to pursue. That he was risking hurting people. But Erion didn't have the heart. Not only was the academy in Saritu'e'Mere one of the safest places Erion could think of for Edric, it was somewhere Edric could truly learn to take care of himself before ever returning to Rijeka. The Kuriositar Festival was too risky, but Edric needed to hold onto his dreams of becoming a proper kurioi.

"That's not what I meant. It's just that… things with Father are complicated. We don't know what he'd do if he found out about you," Erion said.

"Like he makes you earn money for him?" Edric asked.

The simplification of Erion's predicament made it all the more real, somehow. For a moment, he longed for a measure of his brother's naivete. He was tired of assuming the worst about everyone.

"Who knows? Maybe you'd end up indentured to some talentless hack, working for scraps. I just want you to have the choices you deserve—and they're not *here.* You *know* that," Erion said.

Edric shrugged again, refusing to meet Erion's gaze.

"Hang on a little longer. Don't worry about the festival. I have a plan," Erion continued. Resignation rose in him. He *did* have a plan. One that he'd been spiraling toward for too long.

"And you're not going to tell me what it is," Edric said hollowly.

"Where's the fun in that?" Erion winked, but his attempt at levity wasn't catching.

"What if this happens again? If I hurt someone?"

"It won't—because you didn't do it." Erion smiled at Edric and wished with all his soul that he believed his own words.

CHAPTER ELEVEN

ADAPTATION

razan Voloy stared at his latest subject on the examination table. Despite his best efforts, the woman was still dead.

Everything had seemed so promising—he'd mixed the v'deru solution perfectly. The exact quantities of petals had been added. Cedivar's symmajea had been triple checked. Drazan himself had drained three crystals from the icho dens.

He avoided looking at the black zomajea stones. Useful they might be—but they still made his skin crawl. The relics had been retrieved from an ancient nuraghi—a Giant stronghold of legend.

Every time Drazan delved into that well of power, it was harder to pull himself back from the brink. It was safer to use the majea from the icho stones for now. There was no need to transfer majea into the relics or stare into that void of power. He could use the icho stones for his experiments for the time being. When he'd made final preparations, Drazan would fight the flood of energy in the relics. He would force them to serve his will.

For now… it was more efficient to take the majea directly from the icho crystals, when he could. *Safer.* He repeated it like a mantra. No need to expend his own energy to transfer the majea if he was going to use it immediately.

It didn't have anything to do with his fear of the Giant artifact.

I am not afraid of a stone.

Drazan turned away from the body on the examination table. His gaze fixed on the icho stones he'd drained for the ritual. He shoved the basin they rested in, scattering the stones across the table. He'd thought himself one step closer to reaching a breakthrough. Yet despite his confidence and best efforts, the experiment had still failed. *Why?*

He could study the scrolls recovered from the nuraghi again, but he already knew them by heart. Besides, one man didn't seek the same answers as another, and Drazan's procedures had extended past science and into art.

He'd pushed his mental and physical limitations. It would take several days to recover this time. If nothing else, it gave his men time to restock his supplies. More subjects. More crystals. More power.

Drazan turned away from the subject and collapsed into an armchair in the corner. He cast his mind to the problem at hand—the dead woman on the examination table.

He hadn't even bothered to cut this one open. Cedivar would probably insist. The Line Mage was too obsessive to skip such a critical step in the process. Drazan would let him do it. He already knew what they'd find—a corpse pumped full of Life Magic that had once again failed to integrate into the woman's system.

The original necromancer's records detailed all kinds of uses for his subjects, but none of them had the outcome that Drazan sought. Based on his own results, he'd begun to suspect the record-keeper had lied about his successes.

Perhaps Drazan was following the schema *too* closely.

He must have been dense not to think of it before. The days after his wife's death had been hazy—his spiral into his research even more so. But Drazan Voloy had risen from the ashes of tragedy newly empowered.

The citizens of his barony thought him mad with grief. That was true enough. The servants of his estates whispered he was just mad.

Maybe. But he knew what others did not—could not. Jolie wasn't dead. His particular affinity with Life Magic allowed him to suspend her illness. She was in a state of advanced torpor— asleep almost without breath, alive with only the sustenance he imbued into her blood from his own life force. He had never used stolen energy to keep her in stasis. The idea of sharing dirty energy—magic leeched from criminals and whores—made his skin crawl.

If the Baroness Jolie Voloy was ever to wake, she would succumb to the illness that had wasted her away. Drazan had to figure out how to bring her back before he could let that happen. He was nothing and no one without her at his side.

"Cedivar!" Drazan snapped. The man wouldn't be far away.

A key scraped in the door's lock, and Cedivar appeared in the doorway. He was disheveled after the lengthy ritual. His long silver-blond hair, usually slicked back, fell free around his shoulders in erratic tangles. The effect made him look older… and more eccentric than brilliant.

"We need a loyal erkurios. The strongest you know," Drazan said.

Cedivar hesitated. "The most loyal, my lord, or the strongest?"

"Are the requirements mutually exclusive?" Drazan asked.

"Maybe not." Cedivar cocked his head to the side, contemplating. "I'll do what I can."

"Have the servants send dinner to my chambers. No liver."

"My lord, the benefits of the iron far outweigh—"

"No liver!" Drazan said irritably. He might strangle Cedivar if the symkurios gave him one more lecture about iron. It was an uncharitable thought—Cedivar was far too valuable to kill, and he'd stayed by Drazan's side through the worst days of his life. "Go."

"Yes. My lord?"

"What?"

"It's the—the subject. From the last ritual…"

"The rabid one?" Drazan asked. She hadn't truly been rabid—at least, Drazan hadn't thought so—but she'd become nearly uncontrollable after being injected with the v'deru serum.

"She came back, my lord."

"I know that." Drazan had killed her. Twice.

"During the burial."

Drazan blinked. Now *that* was interesting. "Where is she now?"

Cedivar closed his eyes and winced.

"Where?" Drazan pounded his fist on the arm of his chair.

"She—got away. One of the diggers gave chase, but she disappeared into the forest."

"She was that fast?" Drazan's mind was split. His rage at news of the escape was split with wonder that there had been an escape at all.

"It was unexpected."

Drazan snorted. "Bring a copy of that formula to my rooms. Tomorrow night, we will—"

"We await further subjects. The last delivery was short, if my lord will recall."

Drazan grunted. It was for the best. He needed to recover his strength—but he didn't like it. The kidnappings were starting to garner unwanted attention, and the last thing he could afford was an investigation by the duke's men—or worse, a Guardian of Pelinon. The Guardians were King Saren III's sworn servants, formidable warriors and enforcers of the king's law.

"You have her sample, right?" Drazan had ordered Cedivar to take a piece of bone from each subject they experimented on. They took the same from most of his hired workers—just in case. The missing finger was becoming something of a signature.

After the mage's early demonstrations, the baron hadn't been present for any of the removals. The screams twisted his gut.

"I do," Cedivar said.

"Send the bone scouts. She can't have gotten far."

"All of them, my lord?"

"How many do you need?"

"One would suffice."

"Two, then. We can't afford to take any chances." The duke may already have men investigating the disappearances. There was no way to know for sure.

The bone scouts would find the girl before *they* could.

Drazan hadn't a clue where she might have gone—she'd been dead the last time he'd seen her. Heart silent, blood still. For months, he'd been applying the practices from the book with little success. What was different this time?

He'd known his failure the instant she'd opened her eyes. He'd revived not a woman, but a beast. Eyes dilated, movements animalistic and unpredictable. The physical form was strong— the v'deru had imbued her body with the majea, at least for a time. But her mind was gone.

A Love Magician could bring back the heart of her.

The moments after the subjects' deaths were proving more and more critical. The thump of a single heartbeat might mean the difference between victory and defeat. Drazan had to get the timing down perfectly—there would be no margin for error during the real thing.

And he could only keep the most important heart pumping—the only heart that mattered— for so long before time ran out completely.

His gaze came back to rest on the body on the table as he brooded on Cedivar's words. The last subject had come back. She was fast, and she had a mind of her own. Something had finally, *finally* gone right. Hope fluttered in his chest for the first time in weeks.

They'd need to lock this one up for a few days, just in case.

CHAPTER TWELVE

FRESHLY BLOODED

Erion nodded at Quill as he entered the apothecary. The old man smiled at him toothily, and Erion realized that Quill might just be the happiest person he knew. He filed that away for later consideration. Maybe Erion could become the man's apprentice.

He steeled himself as he approached Isak's office. Mathieu would be waiting for him—they'd be expecting him, unless Vandra had leaked Erion's slapdash attempt to leave the city. Erion could never quite pin her down. Most of her work was facilitated by the Crimson Fang these days, but he had no idea how much of her own information she chose to share with them.

If he'd ever believed she'd keep his secrets, it had been before their conversation about skipping town. Vandra was committed to her clients and her work, and that meant loyalty to the Fang over Erion, no matter what.

Erion opened the door to Isak's office. He didn't bother knocking. Erion didn't care who he pissed off—he was giving them what they wanted, and they could all hang for it.

Three faces turned toward him. Mathieu, Isak—and Vandra. Their gazes locked, and Vandra batted him a quick wink. A few locks of her raven-dark hair had escaped their intricate braids, framing her heart-shaped face. A small smile played around the corners of her lips.

What was she doing here?

"Glad to see you." Mathieu extended his hand.

"I have terms." Erion declined the handshake. Vandra's presence had given him a sudden idea.

"You're not exactly in a position to negotiate," Isak said. He cracked his knuckles as he stared at Erion.

"That act's a little tired." Erion forced himself to grin at Isak. "Pretty soon I think it will be against the rules for you to hit me, anyway."

"It's not," Isak growled. "I checked."

Erion wasn't sure what surprised him more—that there apparently *were* rules, or that Isak cared enough to follow them.

"I want my debts cleared." Erion turned back to Mathieu. If he was right, Vandra had already talked to Mathieu about this possibility. His second request would be received better if the first seemed reasonable.

"And?" Mathieu asked.

"And I want your word you'll leave my brother out of this. Do whatever you want to Niklas. I couldn't care less about him. But Edric is safe. Nobody approaches him, nobody *talks* to him. He gets left out of it."

Mathieu cocked his head as he considered this. Erion could all but see the cogs turning in the thug's head. If he refused, it almost certainly meant the Crimson Fang had found out about Edric's magic. Erion flexed his fingers and leaned slightly back. The confines of the room were tight—he'd need all the space he could get if he was going to draw his sword in a pinch.

"Easy enough, Skala. I'll clear the debt as it stands, but Niklas isn't just getting a free pass. We'll have to work something else out."

"Something that doesn't involve my brother," Erion emphasized.

Mathieu shrugged. "Have it your way."

"You swear?"

"Thief's honor." Mathieu grinned wickedly, and for the first time, Erion glimpsed his heartless, calculating core. "Deal's off if he approaches us, though."

Erion stiffened, but it was as good an answer as he could hope for. Once the Fang marked him, he wouldn't have any leverage. If he didn't push the matter, Mathieu might not suspect that Edric was anything more than he appeared; a boy unfortunate enough to have an addict for a father and a criminal for a brother.

A criminal—because that's what Erion was now.

"Let's get this over with." Erion hoped he sounded more confident than he felt. He'd only heard the ghost of a rumor about the initiation process.

"Excellent." Mathieu drew a small dagger from his belt and passed it to Vandra. "Sit."

Erion rolled up his left sleeve, sat, and laid his arm on the desk. Without warning, Vandra slit his palm with the spell dagger. Erion bit back a wince.

"Make a fist." Vandra was all business. She slipped a small bowl under Erion's hand. Rivulets of blood streamed through his fingers and dripped into the bowl.

"Here you join the guild of the Crimson Fang," Vandra said. "And so follow its laws and commit to its purpose."

Erion's heart beat faster.

"Do you submit your oath of silence to the guild?" Vandra asked.

Erion nodded.

"Say it, lad," Mathieu whispered.

"I submit." The words were a barb on Erion's tongue.

"Do you offer your loyalty to the guild?"

"Yes." *The guild.* Like it was all neat and above board.

Vandra dipped a quill into the blood. The feather's stem

turned red as it absorbed the blood, then the plumage bloomed deep crimson in kind. Erion's skin prickled with gooseflesh at the sight.

"With blood, you are bound." Vandra twisted a sharp nib onto the end of the quill. The point of the needle glittered in the sunlight.

Erion glanced at Mathieu. Was that it? He wasn't sure what he'd been expecting, but it had involved a lot more screaming in his imagination.

Then Vandra put the needle to his skin, and he *did* think about screaming. She wasn't so much tattooing ink into his skin as she was slicing his inner arm open with the spelled quill. The needle tip burned, assaulting him with flickering pain.

Ah. The newest members of the Crimson Fang weren't given white tattoos—they were given literal scars. A foundation of blood to be built upon as they proved their loyalty.

"Your position is afforded certain privileges. Bounties and benefits are based on loyalty. Prove your mettle, and you'll be rewarded for it," Mathieu said as Vandra carved a long, flowing line down Erion's inner wrist.

"What more proof do you need?" Erion grimaced. Mathieu already knew what Erion was made of.

"Your family may be rewarded for it."

"So you'll keep pumping my father with icho?" Erion didn't know what had come over him; it wasn't a great time to get mouthy with Mathieu. With each cut, Erion wondered whether Vandra was actually trying to kill him.

The scent of burning flesh filled his nostrils. Whatever symmajea Vandra had spelled onto the quill, his skin was cauterizing almost as fast as she could slice him open.

Efficient, as always.

"We'll discuss Niklas another time. Disloyalty of any kind will not be tolerated, do you understand?" Mathieu whispered.

"I'm not exactly here because I thought betraying you would be a good time."

"See that it stays that way," Mathieu said. "Thorne will be

here soon to introduce you to your new crew leader. Don't disappoint me."

"New?" Erion didn't like the sound of that.

"Some new oversight. Not that I don't trust Thorne. But he's..." Mathieu paused like he was considering his words carefully.

"An idiot?" Isak offered.

"Unique," Mathieu said.

"He was good enough before," Erion argued.

"Things change. Sadiq can deal with both of you," Mathieu said.

Erion found that strangely reassuring. Whatever they were going to make him do, it couldn't be all that bad if Thorne would be there. Erion had a hard time imagining Thorne murdering innocent women or helping a cult like the Nissrans with blood sacrifices.

Mathieu signaled to Isak and they both left the room. Erion turned his head slightly so he could see the door out of his peripheral vision. His earthwalking was useless on the second floor, and he didn't want to get caught unawares.

It was a force of habit. Mathieu and Isak had no reason to threaten him. They'd won.

The growing pain in Erion's arm drew his mind away from brooding. Soon it was all he could do to keep from yanking his arm away from Vandra's ministrations. Blood welled from the lines she drew on his arm, and she had to stop periodically to wipe his skin clean so she could see the design. The mark was more elaborate than Erion had realized—she scored symbols and obscure Line Magic within the wider bands of the design.

She was imbuing the mark with Line Magic.

"I didn't know you did this part." Erion stared at the ceiling as Vandra's work crept closer to his wrist, drawing to the final point that made up the stylized fang.

"I don't." She said it matter-of-factly, like she wasn't currently slicing Erion's wrist into oblivion. "You're a special case."

"What does that mean?"

"It means you need to stop moving, or I'll slice you open on accident and you're going to bleed out all over my new dress."

The threat was enough to still Erion to silence.

Vandra blotted the rag over Erion's wrist and squinted at her handiwork. She nodded in approval.

"Don't suppose you've got a good healer lined up?" Erion asked. His arm was on fire.

"Actually, Quill's been given specific instructions *not* to help you. He knows how things work; the pain is part of the process. One more." Vandra replaced the nib on the quill in favor of a thicker needle. "This one will hurt."

"You mean worse?" Erion made a face.

"Don't be a child."

Erion made a face as Vandra took his hand in her own. She pricked the new needle into the delicate skin of his wrist, far deeper than the initial cuts. He hissed. It was like—well, like having a needle stabbed into his wrist.

"Hold *still*." Vandra made several more pinpricks. Each sent fresh shock waves of agony up Erion's arm.

He jerked his hand away as soon as she finished. Vandra slapped his palm and pulled his arm back, then wiped the final splotches of blood from his skin.

Erion peered down at her handiwork. A tiny droplet of crimson colored the veins of white scarring his wrist.

"Is this really how things work?" Erion still harbored the suspicion that something more was coming.

Vandra shook her head. "The symmajea usually comes later."

"Usually?"

"Mathieu thought it might be good if he kept tabs on you a little earlier than the others."

"Tabs?" he asked.

"They didn't tell you?" Vandra's eyes widened a fraction.

"I'm sure what they haven't told me would fill a few books."

"There's only one real spell." Vandra wrinkled her nose. "It binds you to the laws of the Fang. They don't usually bother with that until new recruits prove they're worth the investment—I don't come cheap."

"Oh, don't you?" Erion raised a brow at her.

Vandra rolled her eyes. She muttered something that sounded like "*boys*" before continuing. "It links you into the law of succession."

"The what?" Erion asked.

"It acts as a compulsion—a preventative measure. You can't commit violence against anyone bearing a stronger mark than yours, except in self-defense. But…"

"But?" Erion prompted.

"It entitles you to right of challenge. The law of succession states that if you kill another in a challenge, you assume their rank."

"Don't know why they bothered with that." He intended to bleed the Crimson Fang for every dakkari he could get, but he'd do it in his way. Climbing the ladder was the least of his concerns.

"Like I said, preventative. I'd bet Isak had a hand in convincing Mathieu to add the link early."

"You think?" Erion lifted his brows.

Vandra shrugged. "I *think* he's terrified of you."

Erion laughed, surprising himself. It felt good.

"And what's that?" He pointed to the red mark. New recruits didn't get any colors.

"Your first blood." Vandra didn't meet his eyes.

"The initiation?" The crimson drop took on a new, threatening air as he regarded it.

"Trial by combat, you could say. You earned the right to enter the moment you killed Lucin." Her eyes were suddenly serious. "Be careful, Erion."

Erion slumped back in his chair. The tip of the tattoo brushed past his wrist, the drops of crimson ending just short of his palm.

He wasn't bleeding anymore, but the skin was inflamed and

swollen around the new scarring. He'd need bandages, and an excuse to never go around in shirtsleeves again. This was just one more thing Edric could never know.

One step closer. Erion grimaced. He'd stepped into the den of hellhounds. It was time to see how bad their bite really was.

"This better be worth it."

CHAPTER THIRTEEN
A MADMAN'S QUEST

Nope." Thorne had always suspected Erion was mad, but this latest suggestion confirmed it. They lay on their stomachs at the top of a ridge. Far below them, the ground was *moving*.

"Just one." Erion's palm hovered over the ground in front of him. Tiny specks of dirt danced beneath his influence. Thorne snorted. *Stoneburners.* Always showing off.

"Nope."

"Are you telling me you're scared?" A crazed grin lit Erion's face.

"Thorne's telling you he doesn't want to die today, Madman." Thorne liked the sound of that name—*Madman*. Maybe that one would finally stick. Then again, maybe not.

"Sadiq will kill us if we come back empty handed."

"Might kill *you*. Thorne's been around too long." That, and he wasn't even supposed to be here. Thorne thought about pointing that out, then didn't.

It was a point of pride that Thorne had spent his career with the Crimson Fang drifting idly from crew to crew—never specializing in anything, rarely advancing, and certainly not proving himself trustworthy enough to lead a ring of his own. Erion had been the perfect scapegoat. Thorne could have ridden on the madman's indecisive coattails for the rest of his days.

But then Erion had joined up, and he'd started taking things seriously. Drawing attention. Now Sadiq had sent them on an insane quest where they would likely be outnumbered ten-to-one. He'd *said* it would be an easy job, but Thorne's Love Magic had cut the crew leader's intentions to the quick. It was a test—he wanted to know just how competent Erion was, and he was willing to get Erion and Thorne both killed in the telling.

Sadiq made it clear he had business of his own to attend to. He couldn't—or wouldn't—help them against the bandits. Erion and Thorne would meet him at the predetermined Fang rendezvous after they'd finished the job—or they'd be dead. Simple enough.

Erion was putting a serious chink in Thorne's plans to remain unremarkable.

"Thorne never would have made you join if he'd known you'd get all *dedicated*." He felt that was important to say. He slid a tendril of his majea toward Erion, probing the man's emotions. Erion's mind was usually a seething ball of conflict, but lately it burned with determination and steel.

"*Thorne* never made Erion do anything," Erion said, mimicking his pattern of speech.

Thorne cracked a grin. "Matter of opinion. Thorne can unhitch from this wagon anytime."

"Wagon?"

"Your gallant company."

Erion snorted. "Be my guest. Come on, I think I see it."

Thorne wrinkled his nose. People in the Sylverwylde Mountains could probably see the thing. He knew for sure they could *smell* it.

"What if—and hear Thorne out, here—what if we *didn't*."

"Where's the fun in that?" Erion crept to his feet and drew

his sword.

"Yes, where's the fun in living?" Thorne muttered. He'd come closer to dying more times in the short time he'd been working with Erion than he had in his ten years with the Fang. He'd been forced to leave the city once, thanks to his own impulsive—but necessary—actions. When it had finally been safe to return home, he'd determined to play things safer. The men who had wanted Thorne dead had finally died themselves. It had been a fresh start, one that he'd welcomed. He'd thought things would be *quiet*.

The joke was on Thorne. Maybe *he* was the mad one.

Thorne decided not to dwell on that as he followed Erion down the slope. He made sure his throwing knives were secured—he thought he checked all the sheaths, but sometimes he lost count.

"Reminding you this was supposed to be an easy job!" Thorne shouted at Erion's back.

"None of them are easy," Erion shouted back.

Sometimes Erion's sense of decency was exhausting. Shaking down a ragtag group of mercenaries? Easy. Shaking down a ragtag group of mercenaries and their pet mage? Not so easy.

And shaking down a ragtag group of mercenaries *and* their pet mage and *his* pet aster mole?

Suicide.

Erion said it was a small mole, but Thorne didn't believe him. From their vantage they could see the upturned trees and freshly churned earth disrupted by the creature's passage. Not only was it big, but it was closer to the surface than a monster without eyes had any business being.

Thorne had only seen an aster mole once before, deep in a Delver mine. Running from the creatures made sneaking around Delver territory look easy. If it hadn't been for the fail-safes in place—spelled firetraps set up at intervals along the mine shafts—he wouldn't have survived the encounter.

He sighed. *Somebody* had to keep Erion alive. He sure didn't seem inclined to do it himself these days.

Erion and Thorne crept through the dense foliage around the mercenary camp. The mercenaries really were stupid—they hadn't even bothered trying to hide.

Then again, with an aster mole that big acting as watchdog, who needed tact?

"Doesn't this thing feel you clomping all over the ground?" Thorne asked.

Erion shushed him, and Thorne rolled his eyes. "Oh, now you decide to be cautious."

Thorne unclipped his chain scythe and tested the blade against his thumb. It was probably about the same size as one of the aster mole's claws—or one of its creepy nose tendril things.

Erion knelt and pressed his palms against the ground. Since Vandra had tattooed him, he wore leather bracers all the time. The jagged scars peeking out near the crook of his elbow were the only evidence that Erion had finally joined the Crimson Fang.

The ground under Thorne's feet trembled slightly as the stoneburner worked his magic. Thorne hoped Erion knew what he was doing.

"Five on your left," Erion said a moment later. "Mole on your right."

"And the death wizard is…?" Thorne asked.

"Right. With the monster." Erion frowned. "Probably."

Thorne wound the chain portion of his weapon in a loop from palm to elbow and gripped the haft of the scythe tightly. In his experience, kurioi—magic users—came in two flavors. If they weren't devastating battle mages, they were usually sloppy and lazy. One-trick ponies who forgot they only had one trick. Thorne knew better than to hope their mage was the latter, but he hoped it anyway.

"Can you handle the men?" Erion asked.

"If you handle that murder-mole, Thorne can handle a hundred men." He made a face. "Can fight a hundred men. Not… you know… *handle*."

"I gave you the benefit of the doubt, but it's good to know

for sure."

"Ready when you are," Thorne said.

"Start running." Erion took a deep breath and pounded the ground with both fists.

Thorne bolted toward the camp. Erion's abilities as a stoneburner weren't always reliable. In fact, Thorne suspected Erion sometimes forgot he had magic altogether.

But when Erion's magic worked, it *worked.*

The ground several feet to their right exploded upward. Fragments of earth rained down on the mercenary camp. Thorne spared a moment to blink at the display before running into the camp. Erion's diversion gave them the element of surprise. Hopefully it would draw the mole away. They might both be dead men if Thorne didn't take advantage.

Thorne drew the short, single-edged butterfly sword at his hip and charged into the mercenary camp. The fighters were rolling from their bedrolls and staggering from tents in bewilderment. A second projectile of stone launched into the air. Not as high as the first, but no less impressive.

It was a nice bit of magic—bigger than anything Thorne had ever seen Erion do before. Bigger than he'd seen *anyone* do before.

Thorne struck out with his own magic. He laced together strands of fear and confusion. He reached out and touched the mind of the nearest mercenary. The man was already badly shaken by the explosion. Thorne couldn't tell if his influence had made any difference.

Thorne would have felt bad if the mercenaries had been stealing from any other gang. They must be from Elarazii— nobody in Razhari would be stupid enough to interfere with the Crimson Fang. Not since they'd practically taken over the capital.

He struck the man down before he could turn. Thorne's spelled scythe sliced through his throat like warm butter. The man didn't even scream.

Just the way Thorne liked it—clean and easy. No blood on

his hands.

The second man turned just as Thorne reached him. He was too handsome for a mercenary. Who took time to oil their beard when living like a vagrant?

Handsome let out a gurgling scream as Thorne's sword plunged into his stomach. The mercenary's fingers fumbled for a knife at his belt, and Thorne swore. Handsome was putting up a fight.

They couldn't all be easy kills. Thorne stabbed the tip of his scythe into the side of Handsome's neck and drew the sharp blade across his throat. The man's screaming died in a spray of crimson.

Thorne stepped away from the body with distaste. Maybe he should have offered to take on the mole, after all. It was easier to kill monsters than men.

The ground quaked beneath him. The aster mole was close, answering the summons of the chaos above. From the edge of his vision, Thorne glimpsed Erion darting into the small camp to his right.

Then two men jumped at him. Thorne narrowly dodged a swinging sword. He sidestepped, and his attacker's own momentum sent him stumbling. Thorne kicked him in the back, helping him to the ground. Before he could raise his weapon, the second man was swinging for him.

This guy was *big* and armed with an axe the size of a shovel. Thorne dropped into a roll, leapt to his feet, and bolted.

If Erion had just listened, they could have gotten reinforcements from Sadiq before this raid.

But why listen? Maybe Thorne should stick to calling him Death Wish.

If nothing else, Thorne was faster than Axe Man. The mercenary gave chase. Thorne sheathed his sword and unwrapped the chain around his arm as he ran. He grasped the iron weight at the end of the chain with his free hand, then slowed until the mercenary was almost on top of him.

Thorne reversed directions at the last second and threw the

end of the chain at the mercenary's head. The heavy, fist-sized weight struck his temple. The man whirled, disoriented. Thorne twitched the chain again and circled the mercenary, fast enough that the chain encircled Axe Man's feet.

The axe arced in a wide semicircle, but the thrash was as wild as the crazed look in the mercenary's eyes. The man's boot snagged on the chain, and he crashed to one knee.

Thorne charged into his opponent. They crashed to the ground in a tangle of iron and curses. Axe and scythe fell to the side, forgotten. The mercenary wrapped his enormous hands around Thorne's throat with a snarl.

Thorne grunted. His fingers scrabbled at his belt as pressure mounted in his head. He slipped a dagger from its sheath and stabbed it into his attacker's chest. The blade skidded over bone before sheathing itself between two ribs. He drew another, smaller blade from beneath his arm and jammed it into the tender flesh beneath the mercenary's jaw. It was over in a blink.

The stupid, vicious grin was the last expression the mercenary would ever make.

Rumbling filled the air. Thorne reclaimed his knives and scrambled away from the body. He reassessed the camp; a number of men were running off into the forest. Not toward Erion, but away from their own pet monster.

Five dagger-like claws surfaced on the far side of the camp. Dirt showered down as the aster mole broke through the earth. Tentacles at the tip of its nose twisted and tasted the air, showering earth down on them.

Flesh-stripping, man-eating tentacles.

Thorne glanced over his shoulder at the retreating mercenaries, considering his options. Erion *had* said he'd take care of the monster.

CHAPTER FOURTEEN

MAGES AND MONSTERS

Erion had never felt so out of his depth. He'd ignored Thorne's warnings about attacking the mercenaries because he'd wanted to impress Sadiq. The thought was laughable—just a few weeks ago he'd have done almost anything to slide under the Crimson Fang's radar for good.

He circled the aster mole with a rising sense of dread. The monster's claws were as long as his forearm. *Giant's blood.*

Erion cast his magic forward, sending a jumble of random vibrations drumming through the ground to confuse the creature. Aster moles were blind, but he knew they had enhanced senses of touch and smell that guided them around the underground. He wasn't sure what to expect from one that had been summoned by a Life Mage, though. Erion wondered how much the mercenaries had paid to put mage and mole on their payroll.

The mole's hairless tail whipped back and forth like a rudder as it circled, trying to follow Erion's false trails. It knocked trees and stones loose as it lumbered forward. Erion's gaze scoured the area around the mole. He still hadn't found the mage.

He slipped his crossbow off his back and crept forward. The damned thing was bulky and uncomfortable, but he carried it with him whenever he left the city since his run-in with the simiot. He'd learned his lesson.

The mole stood up on its hind legs, raising its head to sniff the air with its tentacles. Erion froze. A man sat astride the aster mole in a saddle of sorts. There were no reins or visible control device, just two handles affixed to the front of the seat. Erion had found his mage.

Erion readied his crossbow. He sought comfort in the familiarity of the woodgrain, but found none. He was a good shot—but he'd never fired at a Human before.

He clicked the goat's head lever into the pins on the bow's stock and cranked the bow's string back with one fluid motion, using a whisper of majea to hasten the movement of the iron. Then he rose to one knee and slipped a bolt onto the stock, snug against the string. He just needed one good shot. The sunlight should drive the mole right back into the underground without the mage compelling it, but Erion had never seen a bond like this before. There was just as much chance it would rampage across half the countryside.

Erion exhaled and steadied the stock against his shoulder. He squeezed the trigger at the same moment the aster mole reversed course. The bolt flew wide.

He swore and grabbed the lever, jerking the string back as quickly as he could, loading, and taking aim once more.

The mole charged straight for him.

Erion let the bolt fly, not bothering to check if he'd hit anything. He slung the crossbow over his shoulder and headed for the nearest tree. Wind whipped through his hair as he ran. With a puff of breath, he swept a tide of wind toward the mole, hoping to throw the monstrosity off his scent. He was scraping at the final dregs of his majea.

The aster mole had to be at least six feet tall, and twice as long. What were they *feeding* that thing?

Erion clambered into the tree's lower branches, ignoring the tacky sap clinging to his hands. The wind trick had only bought him seconds—the mage had seen Erion climbing and urged the beast onwards.

Erion straddled the largest branch he could find and steadied himself against the trunk. He cranked the crossbow and fit another bolt.

The lever slipped from his fingers and dropped to the ground. *Dammit.*

This shot had to count. Erion leaned forward, steadying the butt of the stock against his shoulder. He counted breaths as his quarry approached, and pulled the trigger just before mole and mage reached the base of the tree.

The mage let out a strangled shout as the bolt struck him. Erion grimaced at the now-useless crossbow. He really needed Vandra to help him get a spelled whipcord—one made of iron. Then he'd never need the lever again.

The mole threw itself at the trunk, and the tree swayed under its massive bulk. Erion grabbed onto the nearest branch with both hands and watched as the crossbow clattered to the ground, joining the lever.

The tree rocked again, more forcefully. In a moment, the mole would uproot Erion's safe haven.

He dropped down until he was hanging from the branch with both hands. The half-baked plan forming in his mind was *not* a good one. The slightest miscalculation and the mole's tentacles would slice him to pieces.

No thinking. Erion dropped from the branch.

It almost worked. Instead of landing just behind the mage, Erion crashed feet first onto the man's back. The fall was longer than it had looked. Erion slid sideways, but managed to grab the mage's belt at the last second to keep from falling to the ground. The mage gasped as Erion's grasping fingers found the crossbow bolt sticking from his side.

Sorry about this. Erion grabbed the bolt and wrenched it back and forth in the mage's side.

The man shrieked with pain, all color draining from his already pale face. The mole reared back onto its hind legs and let out a high-pitched keening. The sound reverberated through Erion's skull.

Erion grabbed the handles on the mage's saddle and pulled himself into a seated position. The mage slumped forward. Erion seized the man in a headlock. Dread froze him in place. He was prepared to kill this man. It would be so easy. It was why he'd come all this way. And yet...

The hesitation cost him—the mage spat out a word Erion didn't recognize and the mole bucked and twisted beneath them. Suddenly it was all Erion could do to stay astride. The creature was all bulky muscle. Not fast, but strong and enraged.

The mage drew a wicked-looking dagger from his belt and slashed at the arm Erion had still locked around his neck. The blade skidded off Erion's leather bracer, but the point stuck fast into the crook of his elbow. Erion roared with pain and dropped his hold, knocking the dagger away.

Blood glittered in the sunlight like crimson raindrops.

Instinct crowded out Erion's previous hesitation. He couldn't kill this man. He couldn't afford not to.

He grabbed for the saddle again, this time slipping his hands beneath one of the leather straps to secure his grip. Erion threw his magic forward and seized the first metal object he could find—the mage's belt buckle.

The mole bucked, pitching them forward. Erion shoved the mage toward the mole's head with all his strength. Channeling what might be the last of his strength, Erion threw all of his magic at the belt buckle. The extra momentum was just enough to force the mage out of the saddle. He pitched over the mole's head.

Every muscle in Erion's arms screamed with exertion. A fresh wash of blood poured from the crook of his arm—then more blood spattered across his face as the mage flew into the razor-sharp barbs on the mole's nose.

The man didn't even have time to scream. Erion ducked low

over the saddle as the mole inadvertently tore its master to shreds.

It was like watching a flail strip the skin off a man's back, made a thousand times worse by the flesh-colored tentacles.

Then the creature bolted.

Erion wrapped his good hand more tightly onto the leather strap, cradling his right arm close to his chest. Without the mage, the creature was uncontrollable. He suddenly regretted splitting up with Thorne. The idea of taking on a fully-grown aster mole alone was ridiculous. Maybe he had a death wish, after all.

If I survive this, he'll never let me hear the end of it.

The aster mole showed no signs of slowing. Erion took a ragged breath. He was starting to get lightheaded. His arm needed bandaging before he lost too much blood.

For a moment, he wished Edric was there. His brother had a knack with animals—and with plants, and with healing. Edric would have an idea.

Edric's way wouldn't have involved killing the mage, either.

Erion grimaced and tried not to think about the way the man's body had been diced by the mole's tentacles. There was no loyalty amongst thieves—or, apparently, mages and their monstrous familiars.

Erion laced his injured arm through the saddle handle. The grip was weak—he'd have to be fast. He drew his sword with his left hand, wincing at every lurching footfall.

Erion drove the blade down between the mole's furry shoulder blades. The creature didn't even flinch. As he'd feared, the mage's death seemed to have thrown the creature into a mad rage.

Furious, Erion jerked the bastard sword free and slashed haphazardly, slicing into the mole's tough flesh over and over again. He channeled the jolting pain from his arm and his latent rage into each swing.

He didn't even want to be here. *Hack.* He didn't want to kill this creature—hadn't wanted to kill its master. *Slice.* Was sick of being pushed around and forced to do terrible things.

The mole bellowed and turned its head, trying to reach Erion.

The mage had known his business—Erion was perched just high enough, at just the right angle to avoid the mole's snaking appendages. Erion slashed out at the creeping tentacles, slicing one of them off. An oily, greenish substance oozed from the stump.

Enough was enough. Erion gripped the hilt of his sword with both hands and rammed it forward into the junction where the mole's head met its neck. He grunted and forced fire into the blade, increasing the heat in the steel. The searing scent of singed fur and burning flesh filled his nostrils.

Erion wrenched the sword side-to-side. Blood flowed over his leather bracer from the cut in his arm. It trickled into the gash in the mole's flesh.

The beast beneath him faltered. Its forelegs buckled. Erion leaned back at the last second, narrowly avoiding getting tossed over the creature's head just like the mage. He tumbled sideways out of the saddle and crashed to the ground. The side of his head cracked against a stone, sending spears of pain lancing through his skull.

Agony and exhaustion rooted Erion to the earth. He couldn't have moved if he'd wanted to. He blinked up at the hilt of his sword. It stuck out of the mole's neck at a haphazard angle. The steel had twisted under the heat and force until it was barely recognizable. Smoke billowed from the blade.

Damn. He'd had that sword for years.

The creature's breathing was rapid and shallow. Erion got his first clear look at the thing. Five wide, spade-like claws tipped each of the mole's paws, their edges sharp as blades. There were no eyes on the wide, triangular head.

Dimly, Erion wondered how much a kill like this would fetch from the Hunter's Guild. *Damn Crimson Fang.* That made two high-paying bounties he'd lost, thanks to his forced induction. The contract kills had been his biggest source of income.

A shadow crossed over Erion's face. He blinked and looked up at Thorne, who crouched over him.

"I think you were right." Erion attempted a smile, but the muscles in his face didn't want to work. He tried to sit up, but dizziness washed over him. He gave up the effort at once. "Should have gotten help."

"Should have gotten your head examined." For once, Thorne wasn't smiling. He poured his waterskin over the wound in Erion's arm.

"Don't," Erion protested, wincing. Thorne's face blurred in and out of focus.

"How about this—you shut up." Thorne took a swath of bandages from one of his many pockets and started wrapping Erion's arm. Erion closed his eyes to stop the world from spinning.

"How do you fit all that stuff? In your pockets?"

"How do you fit all that stupid in your head?" Thorne rolled his eyes. "I got it though." Erion managed a grin through the pain as the corners of his vision darkened. That would show Sadiq.

CHAPTER FIFTEEN

A SECOND CHANCE

rion woke to the sound of pattering rain. He blinked and tried to sit up, but a hand pushed him back down again.

"Thorne didn't save your life just for you to try and kill yourself again."

Erion's arms were pinned to his sides by several tightly wrapped blankets. He lay on bare earth, and the sky was stone above him. He shook his head and blinked. The ceiling...

No. He was in a cave.

Gods, he must have been hurt worse than he'd thought. Erion's head throbbed. He gingerly rested it back down on the rolled cloak serving as a pillow. The embers of a small fire burned between him and the mouth of the cave. The opening was draped in canvas and netting. Erion had used this hideout before—it was a blind from the outside, and nearly impossible to find if you didn't know what to look for.

Erion closed his eyes. He'd been happier when he was unconscious.

A slight breeze gusted through the cave. Erion opened his eyes to slits in time to see Sadiq settle the camouflaging back into place. His cloak was drenched.

Sadiq's gaze flickered between Erion and Thorne, darkly calculating.

"You're the biggest idiot I've ever met, Skala," he grunted at last.

Erion's lips twitched into a shadow of a smile. "But an impressive idiot."

When Erion had learned that their target had a tamed aster mole, he'd wondered whether Sadiq just wanted him dead. Then he'd realized it was a test of his abilities—and his loyalties. He'd needed to stay on Sadiq's good side; anything was better than going back to working for Isak.

"I wouldn't go so far." Sadiq pushed back the hood of his cloak and stirred the dying fire until soft flames licked at the coals. "Heavy bounty on that mole, though."

"Good thing somebody killed it. Someone might have gotten hurt." Erion didn't bother trying to hide the bitterness in his voice.

Sadiq snorted. "Don't be such an ingrate about it. You'll get your share. And nobody told you to go after the thing alone."

"In fact, Thorne recalls telling him to do exactly *not* that," Thorne grumbled.

"You still followed him," Sadiq pointed out.

Erion managed to hold his tongue, but it was a near thing. Sadiq had heavily implied there would be consequences if Erion *hadn't* handled the situation alone.

"Thorne will get part of the bounty for saving his miserable life." Thorne cocked his head and chuckled. "More like saved his death."

Erion and Sadiq stared at him, nonplussed.

"You know. *Saved* it. His death." Thorne waggled his eyebrows.

Erion shook his head and immediately regretted it as sharp pain sliced through his skull.

"Like for later?" Thorne said hopefully.

Sadiq's expression—usually schooled and stern—actually split into a grin.

Unlike Isak and Mathieu, Sadiq didn't use his status within the Crimson Fang's ranks to bully or intimidate—and unlike almost everyone in the Fang, he didn't seem to write Thorne off as some kind of idiot. It was a small thing, but it made Erion inclined to like him—against his own inclinations.

"My share?" Erion asked Sadiq, dragging the conversation back to the relevant details. He wasn't sure he'd heard the crew leader right. Sleep still held him in its groggy embrace.

"Things are different on this side of things," Sadiq said. "We'll get Vandra to write up the bounty and assign you. Mathieu takes a cut, but what you get won't be a pittance. Whine about it and he'll take a bigger percentage next time."

Whine about it? Erion hadn't ever gotten a bounty on kills for the gang before. An idea pierced through the fog in Erion's mind. Maybe he could convince Sadiq to send him on a mine raid—there were always good bounties this close to Delver territory. Their networks of ancient, abandoned tunnels were always flush with monsters that needed a good thrashing.

Prey he wouldn't mind killing.

A few quests might even be enough to get Edric off to Saritu'e'Mere before the Manifestation Festival in the spring. The kid was shaken after the woman in the woods, but Erion had a feeling Edric was still determined to make his own way to the academy.

Gravel crunched outside the cave entrance before Erion could suggest his plan.

"Incoming," Sadiq muttered. A shadow crossed his features.

Isak forced his way through the netting. He didn't have a hood, and he dripped from head to toe. A moment later, a woman followed him inside. Her hands were bound behind her back. Erion's stomach turned as he met her eyes. Hazel. Desperate.

It was the same woman he'd seen at the safehouse behind

the icho den.

So she's alive, after all. Erion's relief was short-lived. Her dark hair was matted and tangled. Bruises marred one side of her face and what was visible of her collarbone.

Fury, so close to the surface these days, rose to a boil within him. Terror and despair had aged her features, but she was barely more than a girl. Under those bruises, she might be no older than Edric.

Sadiq shot Erion a warning glance, as though reading his mind.

"What are you doing here?" Sadiq asked Isak.

"Getting out of the storm. It's raining Bhirtas'Vuoda out there, if you hadn't noticed." Isak stripped down to his shirtsleeves and lay his leather jerkin carefully by the fire.

Erion struggled to his knees. Ignoring Sadiq's hiss of warning, he crawled the few feet to the girl and offered her one of his blankets.

She looked up at him with eyes full of wild, animal fear. She snatched the blanket from him, evidently deciding it wasn't a trap—or that it was a trap worth the risk.

"Thorne?" Erion glanced over and held his hand out. Without asking, Thorne slipped a tightly wrapped package from a hidden pocket and handed it over. Erion untied the strings and revealed the cured beef inside. He placed it on the ground next to the girl.

Her fingers trembled as she snatched up the food. It was gone before Erion could drag himself back to his spot by the fire. Did she recognize him from Rijeka? His heart withered. He couldn't bring himself to look her in the eye—not again.

"I'd accuse you of going soft, but we all know you never had the stomach for this," Isak mocked.

Erion refused to answer the challenge. Not tonight—not over this. The injustice curdled his stomach. He didn't care if the girl had stolen from Isak's own mother. She hadn't asked for this, hadn't *chosen* this.

She didn't deserve whatever this fate held for her.

Silence fell, broken only by the incessant rain outside. The peaceful sound grated.

After a long while, Sadiq turned to Isak. "Were you going to Uzhastik?" His voice was dangerously soft.

Erion's heart rate spiked. Thorne shifted next to him, but the man's face was unreadable. Erion sat upright and made a show of twisting his face with the pain, determined to mask his sudden alarm.

He couldn't mean *Nuraghi* Uzhastik, could he?

But if there was another place called by that cursed name, Erion didn't know it. It wasn't a name—or a place—easy to forget. He'd been there once before, with Thorne. Erion was still haunted by the memories.

Isak grunted. "Change of plans."

Sadiq glanced at the girl. She'd fallen asleep, clutching the blanket around her like a lifeline.

"A significant one." Sadiq's brows drew down into a frown.

Erion pretended to ignore the exchange. His mind raced. The nuraghi wasn't far from here—a short trip down the river, or a few days by land depending on the route.

His skin crawled just thinking about the godless place—and what he'd done there.

Nuraghi were ancient, derelict ruins that dated back to times before record. Nobody really seemed to know what they were, or who'd built them. Each theory was more ridiculous than the last, a mill of rumors and idle gossip perpetuated by people who'd never even seen one. The myths were so impossible, Erion hadn't believed they'd existed at all—until he'd seen one.

Erion and Thorne had been hired—ordered, really—to plunder the treasury of a ruined keep in a neighboring duchy. Easy enough, until the colossal gate had opened up beneath the waters of Lake Zagretsk, and Erion had nearly been devoured by their depths.

The nuraghi were abandoned hellscapes. They deserved to rot in the myths that made them eternal.

"The Ithynon is getting serious, I see," Sadiq said.

Isak kicked him.

"Who—" Erion began. Thorne punched him in the shoulder. Erion glared at him. The man shook his head, not looking at him. An onslaught of caution suffused Erion's mind. He *knew* better than to question Isak. Like so many things, it was obviously above his pay grade.

The discomfort subsided as quickly as it had come. Erion shrugged the feeling away. He *hated* when Thorne did that. He wasn't known for being subtle with his abilities, and Erion thought he was getting a feel for when Thorne wove his ermajea upon him. He'd bet every dakkari he'd earned from the aster mole that Thorne had just manipulated him.

Of all the forms of kurioi on Daemanon, erkurioi—heartbenders, or Love Magicians—made Erion the most uneasy. Too often, Erion's mind was his only sanctuary. The idea that someone could sense, even manipulate his emotions, set his teeth on edge. Thorne's blatant use of his magic—if Erion's hunch was right—was telling. *Don't stick your nose where it doesn't belong.*

Just what—or who—was the Ithynon, and why was Isak so eager to keep quiet about it?

Erion slouched back against the wall of the cave. The rain was subsiding, and he was sure they'd be on their way back to Rijeka soon. He didn't look at the girl in the corner. At least, most of them would be going to Rijeka.

Don't be a hero.

He wasn't fooling himself. Erion was far from a hero, but he might just get away with being an idiot.

Sadiq tossed another log onto the fire, and Erion seized the opening. He let out a deep sigh, manipulating a small current to form a whirlwind in the coals. Tendrils of flame licked up the new wood and sparks flew into the air. The embers flickered in the air and drifted toward the cave entrance where Isak sat.

Erion closed his eyes, listening to the crackling music that made up the fire's essence—a song only he could hear. He knew the instant the dancing sparks landed near Isak. In his mind's eye, he imagined feeding tinder to those sparks.

Isak's bag burst into flames.

Erion's eyes snapped open at the sudden wave of heat. The shock was real. He'd hoped to singe the bag, damage it enough to buy him some time to come up with a real plan. The conflagration caught the sleeve of Isak's tunic. The big mercenary batted at the fabric, and his hand came away with angry red welts.

For the second time in as many days, the stench of burning flesh filled Erion's nose.

Erion had overblown the spell. Fire jumped from Isak's gear to the pile of neatly stacked wood by Sadiq. Isak staggered to the mouth of the cave. In his haste, his arm tangled in the netting concealing the entrance. Pockets of rain dropped from the camouflage, hissing as they struck Isak. Smoke and steam flooded the small cave.

Sadiq and Thorne fell into fits of coughs. Erion sputtered, fighting needles of pain in his head as he forced himself to his feet. He kicked the embers of the fire, scattering it.

Thorne grabbed his own bag, hesitated, then snatched Erion's as well. He cast Erion a suspicious glare before following Isak outside.

Erion crouched down by the kidnapped girl and shook her shoulder, but she didn't rouse.

She wasn't just sleeping—she was unconscious. What the hell had Isak done to her? *What could I have saved her from?*

If he'd acted differently that night in the ally. Thrown caution to the wind and saved both girls that night…

Sadiq crowded in beside him before Erion's guilt had time to manifest. "Get her other arm," he ordered.

Erion obeyed without question. Together they half-carried, half-dragged her from the cave.

Isak pummeled into Erion as soon as he reached fresh air. Erion doubled over with a gasp. He wasn't anywhere near recovered from his bout with the aster mole, and his enthusiasm with the fire had taken more energy out of him than he'd planned.

"What was that?" Isak grabbed Erion by the collar and shoved his back against the rock face.

"It's called… fire…" Erion wheezed.

"I'm sick of your games, Skala."

"Here I was thinking we were having fun." Erion glared right back at Isak.

"Let him go." Sadiq put a hand on Isak's uninjured shoulder. "We've got bigger problems."

"This rat is a pretty big problem." Isak slammed Erion against the rocks once more.

Erion's skull cracked against stone and stars filled his vision. He reached for his magic on instinct. The ground bubbled beneath Isak's feet and the crew leader sank to his knees in mud. A moment of charged silence swelled around them.

"Oh! The goblins!" Thorne said suddenly, breaking the tension. He beamed. "Nice one."

Isak swiped at Erion, intent to kill etched into the lines of his face.

Erion stepped a fraction to one side, just outside of Isak's reach. He leaned heavily against the rock behind him.

"Say you're sorry," Erion said when he caught his breath.

"I'll kill you," Isak spat.

"That threat is getting old." If Isak did decide to kill him, now would be the time. In Erion's condition, it wouldn't even be a fight.

"*Enough.*" Sadiq made a parting gesture like he was separating two brawling children. "Both of you. No damaged goods."

"Huh?" Erion squinted at Sadiq.

"The Ithynon was clear. No damaged goods. This girl isn't in any shape to travel, let alone for delivery. What were you thinking, Isak?"

Isak finally managed to wrench one boot from the mudslick Erion had trapped him in. "I was thinking that contract"—he jerked his chin toward the girl's prone figure—"isn't going to cover itself. Nobody else is stepping up."

"I'm taking her back to Rijeka," Sadiq said.

Isak froze, one leg still fixed in the mud. "You can't."

"Watch me. I'm sure Mathieu will love to see what you've done to her."

Isak muttered something unintelligible.

"She's been beaten half to death. He doesn't want them injured," Sadiq said coldly.

Erion's gaze flitted between the two men. What "he" was Sadiq referring to? Mathieu, or someone else? This Ithynon?

Isak hesitated. "That wasn't me."

"See to it you take care of the man responsible. I'd hate to see what Mathieu would do if he hears word and decides to handle the matter himself." It was clear Sadiq didn't believe Isak—and even more clear that he would personally ensure Mathieu *did* hear about the incident.

Isak yanked his foot from the pothole. The mud swallowed his boot with a squelch. He rounded on Sadiq. Isak was head-and-shoulders taller than him, but Sadiq didn't flinch. Erion found a newfound respect for his new crew leader as he eyed the exchange. Erion needed Sadiq to hold his ground. If he stepped aside, Isak would certainly maim Erion, if not kill him.

And Erion could almost believe Sadiq wanted him to live. Was there a chance he wanted the same for the girl?

"On your feet, Skala," Sadiq barked.

Erion looked pointedly down at his feet, narrowly avoiding a sarcastic comment.

"Thorne, help me with her. We're going." Sadiq glared up at Isak; a silent challenge Isak didn't answer. Erion limped after Sadiq and Thorne, hauling his and Thorne's bags behind him. After a furious moment, Isak stormed back into the cave.

Erion hoped the smoke choked him to death.

❂ ❂ ❂

They didn't make impressive progress. They trudged over

the uneven terrain, slick and muddy from the rain. Before darkness could fall, Sadiq picked a promising copse of trees. Erion stared at the girl's limp form while Sadiq and Thorne worked to clear a small campsite. The gravity of his own injuries had faded into the background for a time, but the throbbing in his arm had redoubled as though intent on reminding him he'd been ignoring the wound. He pressed one hand against the bandaged arm, applying pressure as he considered the situation.

They'd gotten her away from Isak, but that was only one small step. If only she'd wake up.

Sadiq dug through his bag and produced a small vial of muddy-looking liquid. He handed it to Erion. "Give this to her. Slowly."

"You've had this the whole time?" Erion asked.

"Any idea how expensive those things are?" Sadiq snapped back.

Erion shook his head and uncorked the healing solution. He wouldn't have minded one himself, but Sadiq wasn't exaggerating their price. Erion pried the girl's mouth open and let several drops fall onto her tongue. She began to stir at once. Her mouth closed and she swallowed the potion. Erion tipped the vial again and poured the remaining solution into her mouth.

"No!" She tore away from Erion, knocking the empty vial to the ground. "What is that? Who are you?"

"Relax," Erion said. "We're friends." He glanced at Sadiq and realized he wasn't sure if it was true or not.

"Liar," she spat. She was terrified, not stupid.

"Sit down. Eat. Tell us what happened," Sadiq said. He glanced meaningfully at Thorne and made a small gesture with his hand—so small that it would have gone unnoticed if Erion hadn't been looking for it. Sadiq wanted Thorne to calm the girl down.

She glanced all around the campsite like a caged animal, but must have realized running was a bad decision. The girl sat, and Sadiq handed her a heel of bread. She clutched it to her chest but didn't eat.

"The other guy said he was helping, too." Her voice cracked from disuse. She licked her lips. "But I don't know where he was taking me."

Erion handed her his waterskin. She hesitated, but once she'd decided it was safe, she took a large gulp.

"Thanks." She didn't give the waterskin back.

"What's your name?" Sadiq asked.

Erion watched the man carefully. What was he playing at? It was one thing for him to stop Isak from taking Erion's head off—Erion was the newest member of Sadiq's crew, after all. Letting Erion get murdered at the hands of another member of the Fang would just be neglectful.

The girl was a different matter entirely.

"What's yours?" she shot back.

Thorne chuckled, and even Erion let out a small, shaky laugh. Exhaustion was getting the better of him. Soon he'd be as nonsensical as Thorne.

"Does it matter?" Sadiq asked.

The girl kept her silence, as though illustrating Sadiq's point.

"Fine. Where are you from?" Sadiq asked instead.

"What are you going to do to me?"

Not "What are you going to do *with* me," Erion noted. "What are you going to do *to* me." Something about the distinction sent a shiver through him.

"That depends on you," Sadiq said. The girl's face paled under the mosaic of bruises.

"Leave her be."

Sadiq and Erion turned as one at Thorne's interruption. It wasn't like him to interfere with things, and even less like him to tell a superior what to do. Thorne's eyes were flat and challenging.

Then, to Erion's even greater surprise, Sadiq nodded. He drew his belt knife and leaned toward the girl. She winced and tried to squirm away, but Sadiq was too fast. He seized her wrists and slipped the dagger between her bindings, slicing them apart with a quick motion.

"We should all get some sleep," Sadiq said, dropping the knife. "Tomorrow we'll take her back to Rijeka."

"Don't take me back. Not to him," she begged.

"To who?" Sadiq asked. "Isak?"

"The big guy?" The girl shivered.

"Get some rest," Sadiq said.

And that was it. Erion gaped openly as Sadiq wrapped himself in his cloak and rolled onto his side, his back to them.

Silence closed in over the campsite like a shroud, broken only by the occasional pattering of water droplets slipping off the overhead leaves. The girl sat hunched in a ball, completely still except for her eyes. Her gaze darted around the camp as though trying to take in all three men and all possible escape routes at the same time.

Sadiq's breathing slipped into the deep, even cadences of sleep—or a convincing play of it.

Erion caught Thorne's gaze. *What the hell?* he mouthed.

Thorne stuffed a handful of pine nuts into his mouth.

It was a trap. It *had* to be a trap. Sadiq was testing him, and Thorne was in on it. The moment Erion did anything stupid, Thorne would wake Sadiq, and they'd turn Erion in.

Right?

Still clutching the uneaten heel of bread, the girl rose to the balls of her feet and snatched up Sadiq's dagger. When Sadiq didn't stir, she glared at Erion, daring him to stop her. He shrugged, bewildered, and watched her gather her skirts and bolt into the woods.

"*Thorne*," Erion hissed.

"Do it fast, Death Wish," Thorne muttered. He popped another pine nut into his mouth.

What?

But that was all the urging Erion needed. He dug through his bag and pulled out the last of his food. He wrapped his cloak around it, spared a final glance for Sadiq, then ran after the girl.

Limped off, really. She had a fair head start, but he could feel her stumbling, heavy footfalls through the ground. In the dark, he had the advantage.

"Wait!" Erion hissed when his earthwalking finally led him to her. Amazingly, she stopped and turned. She brandished the dagger in an inexpert grip. Moonlight glinted off the quivering blade.

Erion lifted his hands to show her he was unarmed. When she didn't lower the dagger, he took a half-step forward and put the bundle of food on the ground.

"Do you know the guard station in Rijeka? The big one, near the west wall of the baron's estate?"

She didn't answer.

"Are you from Rijeka?" he asked.

"I—I've been there."

"Ask for Captain Talbot. Don't talk to anyone else until they bring you to him. Make him show you his identification first. Ask him to send a message to the steward's son."

"Talbot?"

Erion ground his teeth. He was courting new and inspired levels of idiocy, but he couldn't stop himself. Niklas owed him. They'd come up with work for the girl somewhere—a safe place, away from Rijeka.

"Don't tell him anything else. Just have him send for the steward's son, you understand?" Hopefully he would beat her back to Rijeka. If not, Talbot would likely hold her somewhere safe until Erion returned.

A frown creased the girl's brow, but she nodded.

"Now run," Erion urged.

She stared at him, her feet rooted in place.

"*Run.*" Erion didn't know how much longer they had. He didn't sense Sadiq or Thorne on their tail, but he wasn't going to risk this girl's life—not again.

She turned, then swerved back and grabbed the cloak and its contents off the ground. Her eyes met his, and he saw hope glimmering there for the first time.

"It's Amelie," she whispered.

"*Amelie,*" Erion repeated. "Erion. Tell Talbot. Now go."

She vanished into the dark woods without a backwards glance.

Erion listened to the earth, followed her footsteps as she tripped and pushed through the undergrowth.

Not a simple choice—but an easy one, when it came down to it. The only choice Erion had felt good about in some time. Captain Talbot was a friend, and one of the only guards Erion was sure wasn't affiliated with the Crimson Fang. He would help.

Whatever the consequences were, Erion would accept them. He had so little say in his own life. Maybe he could help give this girl a second chance at hers.

CHAPTER SIXTEEN

FOUNDATIONS

Drazan Voloy counted his steps as he descended into the caverns. Once he'd realized the true wealth hidden in Nuraghi Uzhastik, Drazan had ordered a reliable entrance built at once. The stairway was rough-hewn, cut with haste, its steps uneven.

The rotting Giant stronghold had been lost to time and memory until Reinholdt, and then Drazan, had discovered it. What had once been a passing interest in the sciences had become an obsession after Jolie's illness. His research into Reinholdt's ruins, and the experimentation to master life itself, had drawn Drazan here like a moth to flame.

It was fate—cruel, bitter, vicious bitch that she was—and fate would bring Jolie back from the brink.

The nuraghi held its secrets jealously. Drazan had peeled them back one by one, but he'd learned from the nuraghi, too. The crews of diggers had been given up in the name of powering the zomajea stones. No loose ends. Trust no one.

The sacrifices had been harrowing—but also key to his

process. Through it, he'd learned there was a method to harvesting life force that was far superior than harvesting icho crystals.

Cedivar was the only one Drazan had trusted with the truth of the nuraghi, and his plans. He heard the Line Mage's clomping steps following him into the earth's depths. Loathe though he was to admit it, Drazan—the *Ithynon*—was lost without Cedivar.

Baron Voloy, however, was not. For the baron, Cedivar was another loose end to tie—but not just yet. First, Jolie. He had to keep his mind focused on one matter at a time.

Winter storms ravaged the world above, and Nuraghi Uzhastik was a frigid wasteland. Drazan stuffed his hands in his pockets as he waited for Cedivar to catch up. He wasn't about to cross the cursed blackness of the massive hall alone. Drazan knew what lurked in the dark, and none of it bore him goodwill.

His fingers found the crumpled parchment in his pocket. Dormant rage rekindled, warming him despite the chill. How long had this notice lay ignored in a pile before Niklas had bothered to review his letters? Even icho riddled as Niklas was, the steward should have recognized the ducal seal and opened the letter.

The steward's icho dependency had once been the leash Drazan had led him with. Now it was slowly becoming his noose.

Duke Jesper's official representatives would be here in just a few days. It scarcely gave Drazan time to prepare to receive them, let alone lay a careful trail away from the truth about the icho, the disappearances, and the Crimson Fang's unusual hold on the city. He would play the mourning widower once more.

Cedivar reached him, lugging a heavy bag that clunked with each step he took. The two men made their way across the wide hall and into the sanctum where the altar waited. Drazan waited while Cedivar lit the torches lining the protective circle in the floor.

It was fifty feet or more wide. Two concentric rings

encircled a wide dais of pitted gray stone. Every inch of the border was covered in scrawling runes and symmajea.

Reinholdt had discovered this place first, but as far as Drazan could tell, he'd only ventured into Nuraghi Uzhastik once—to collect the zomajea stones. In his desperation and mourning, Drazan had done what Reinholdt hadn't dared. He'd pierced the very heart of the nuraghi and clawed apart its secrets.

Drazan stepped up to the altar at the center of the dais. Dozens of tiny grooves split the face of the stone, each ending in a wide basin carved into one end. He eyed the hooks at each corner, and wondered how many arms and legs had been tied to this stone over the millennia. How many souls sacrificed? More indecipherable symmajea were inscribed along the grooves in the table, but its purpose was clear. Bound and prepared, each sacrifice gave up their life's blood, to be caught and guided into the basin by the meticulous grooves carved into the stone.

Drazan hated being rushed, but needs pressed. If Duke Jesper had finally decided to interfere with the chaos in Rijeka, the authorities in Corsica wouldn't be far behind.

Drazan's mind raced as he watched Cedivar drop a load of empty icho crystals into the basin at the base of the altar. There was still testing to do. The seed of a plan started to sprout in his mind.

"Just how loyal would you say Mathieu Sifet is?" Drazan asked.

Cedivar snorted. "How much are you willing to pay him?"

CHAPTER SEVENTEEN

MISGIVINGS

Vandra threw her quill onto her desk and glared up at Thorne. She worked hard to put up a neutral front for her business. It was important that she wasn't associated with criminal activity in the city—even Mathieu agreed on that point. She needed to be seen as a legitimate contractor for the Hunter's Guild, a reliable resource for the merchants and tradesmen in the city.

But lately she couldn't take a step in her own home without tripping on someone from the Crimson Fang who needed her help with something.

"Thorne is telling you *something is up.*"

"But why are you telling *me?*"

"Because of Erion," Thorne said simply.

She didn't think she'd ever heard him use Erion's name before. It was always some ridiculous nickname—Rockslide or Whipping Boy, or sometimes just "stoneburner." But his actual name?

Vandra hadn't been in Rijeka when Thorne had joined the

Crimson Fang. They'd met in Vhalla, the capital of the Duchy of Razhari, after Thorne had been driven out of Caraz. That was before Mathieu had killed his predecessor and taken over the local crews—before it had been safe for Thorne to return to Rijeka, where he'd been raised.

"What has he done now?" Vandra asked.

"Not him. Sadiq. He let a girl go. But Erion saw, and his head is more stone than brains sometimes."

"One of Isak's girls?" Vandra's mouth twisted with distaste. She refused to do anything for the brothels. Some of the girls worked there willingly, as they did in more reputable houses, but with Isak's reputation…

"No. Mathieu's." Thorne spoke calmly. For once, he wasn't bouncing on the balls of his feet or twirling a knife in his long fingers. He met her eyes with a quiet, earnest expression. A worried expression.

Thorne was taking this more seriously than anything in a long time—perhaps in the whole time Vandra had known him. He'd been the one to suggest she set up in Rijeka, and he'd eventually persuaded Mathieu to send work her way. Vandra owed her business and everything she'd built to Thorne.

She owed it to him to listen. "Tell me what happened."

Thorne did, taking fewer shortcuts and roundabout explanations than usual.

"And you're surprised Erion helped her? Where did he send her?" Vandra asked when Thorne's story came to a close. Vandra had never known Erion to shy away from a fight—he had a knack for it, whether he liked it or not. But she knew Erion's heart wasn't in most of the work he'd been forced to do lately.

"Thorne's not even surprised that Sadiq helped her. Mostly. But why was she there at all?"

Ah. The real reason for his visit came out.

"How should I know?" Vandra asked.

"You know everything, Runecaster."

Vandra snorted. "Right, well. Even if I knew, I couldn't tell you."

"Thorne knows you're hiding more than you pretend, and you pretend a lot. And Thorne knows the Ithynon is getting tired of waiting. That's two shipments now the crew has messed up."

"Yes." Two girls that Mathieu's men had failed to deliver. Vandra had refused to broker those deals, too. As far as she knew, she and Mathieu were the only two people to have actually communicated with the Ithynon—and even then, only through back channels and anonymous messengers.

She suspected she was the only person in the entire city—in the entire barony—who knew who the Ithynon really was. Staying alive meant keeping it that way.

"And since the icho trade may be dying…" Thorne said.

Vandra flinched. "What do you know about that?"

"Thorne also knows a lot more than he knows." Thorne frowned and shook his head. "Thorne knows more than people thinks he knows."

Vandra considered that. He probably did, come to think of it. The man had a knack of falling so far back in a room, people forgot he was there. It was a useful skill—especially for a heartbender.

"What do you want, Thorne?" Vandra asked.

"Thorne just wants out of it. Erion's morality is going to get Thorne killed."

"I thought you liked him."

"Thorne likes him *alive*."

Vandra arched a brow. Every time she thought she was familiar with his odd pattern of speech, he surprised her. "You like Erion alive?" she asked, trying to clarify. "While you're alive, or while Erion is?"

Thorne shrugged. "Well if Thorne's dead, he can't like anybody."

Well that was clear as mud. Vandra sighed and shook her head. "Okay. So… a new assignment? I didn't think you'd want to leave Rijeka again." She knew Thorne had good reasons for staying in the city.

"Call it a backup plan. Can't ask Mathieu." Thorne shrugged. "Would rather be killed by Isak than talk to him about it."

"And Sadiq?"

"Can't figure *him* out."

Vandra almost laughed, but the urge died in her chest. If Sadiq had really let one of Mathieu's charges escape, he could be in for worlds of hurt. It was just one more secret for the ledger.

"Have you told anyone?" she asked.

It was Thorne's turn to laugh. "Thorne lets other people have death wishes. He just wants out."

Vandra shook her head. Thorne was right—she *did* understand, better than he knew. There was no real escape—not the way any of them wanted. Some things were just too big.

"I'll just let Mathieu know that the next time he comes along to collect his bounties," Vandra said. "I'm sure he'll be happy to—"

"Hey now, Crazy Quill. Thorne doesn't come around threatening violence on your house."

Vandra gestured around them as though to say *what do you call this?*

"Usually," Thorne conceded.

"I'll see what I can do."

Thorne could easily move to Vhalla again, or anywhere else in the duchy. Mathieu would be more than happy to pack him off to another crew. But Thorne had family ties in the city. In contrast, Vandra had no ties whatsoever to Rijeka—and not a rabbit's chance in a fox den that she'd ever be allowed to leave.

She locked the door to her apartments when Thorne left and leaned against the wall, covering her face with her hands. Another of the Ithynon's subjects had escaped. How many did that make now? At least two—but were there more?

This one doesn't count. Not really. The girl had never made it.

Thorne gave Vandra too much credit. She didn't know everything. She knew just enough to keep her terrified. If she didn't do her part, she knew exactly where her next job would land her.

Tied to a bloody altar.

Whether he'd known it or not, Thorne had given Vandra a new piece of information. Why had Isak been taking the girl to the nuraghi? That was ahead of schedule.

Vandra ran over several quick theories, each more horrifying than the last. Erion had all but begged her not to deliver the artifacts he'd uncovered when the Crimson Fang had dug up the ruins near Nuraghi Uzhastik. The Ithynon had risen from the shadows like death made corporeal not long after.

It had all happened so fast. Icho became stronger and more addictive. Mathieu's monopoly on the new form of the drug strengthened his influence over the city. The baron was more reclusive than ever, and more and more people were spiraling into poverty because of the city's mismanagement.

Erion hadn't been able to give a clear reason as to why the stones made him so uncomfortable. Vandra had written off his worry as a case of cold feet—a momentary lapse of judgment in a man who knew all too well what kind of fate disobedience would earn him.

Now she knew that the Ithynon's power play was the direct result of delivery of the artifacts.

Vandra didn't work with faceless clients. It was her refusal to accept such a vulnerability that had led her to follow the trail of icho crystals to their origin. She shouldn't know who the Ithynon was. If anyone ever discovered she had such information, she'd be as good as dead.

CHAPTER EIGHTEEN
THE CRIMSON FURY

Erion shifted his chair as Thorne flopped down at the table next to him. Icy rains had forced most of the city inside for the night, and the Crimson Fury was full to bursting. Erion had managed to secure a tiny table in the corner. He'd spent most of the evening watching Thorne playing a ridiculous drinking game involving tossed daggers. It was a miracle nobody had lost a finger.

Thorne plunked a tankard of mead onto the table and pushed it toward Erion with an air of resignation.

"No thanks." Erion grinned. "You won that fair and square."

"Lost it, more like." Thorne put his head down on the table and closed his eyes. "Too much."

Erion stared at his own empty cup. Unlike Thorne, he hadn't had nearly enough to drink, and the Love Mage's antics, while amusing, weren't enough to distract him from his own problems. After reporting the raid on the mercenary camp, he'd gone straight to the guard house in the Empori District to find Talbot.

No girls had come asking after Erion, by the name of Amelie or otherwise.

"Thought you had your eyes on that Hunter's girl. Long hair, wicked smile?" Talbot had teased.

"I'm playing the long game," Erion had joked. He didn't even know where to start with Vandra. "Will you let me know if she shows up, please? It's a family matter."

Talbot had agreed, but days passed with no news of Amelie. She'd vanished into the storm, taking Erion's fading hopes of redemption with her. He was more on edge than ever before. Isak had it out for him, and his crew was getting bigger—and meaner—all the time.

Buckets of rain drowned the streets outside. The winter storm had raged on three days now. Anyone not sheltering inside was fighting the rising river with sandbags and futility. Erion had wanted to go help at the riverfront. Mathieu had ordered him here instead.

And just look at all the good I'm doing. Erion was going to go home soon if Mathieu didn't show up. He hadn't seen Edric in almost a week.

"Hey, where's your sword?" Thorne's head popped off the table and he looked at Erion with a strange intensity.

"I burned it up, remember?" It was a sore spot. Erion was loathe to part with the coin he'd need to get a decent blade, but he was worthless without one. He'd been thinking about exchanging services with the baron's blacksmith. He couldn't help with any serious crafting, but he could strengthen iron and shape horseshoes. Hell, he'd work the bellows if it meant getting a new sword for free.

"Thorne remembers you let that girl go."

Erion put a hand on Thorne's head and pushed it gently back down onto the table. "Thorne is *drunk*."

And Erion didn't need Thorne blabbing about that in a room full to the brim with restless gangsters.

"Thorne is drunk," Thorne agreed, nodding with his cheek still pressed against the wood grain. "And Erion is a fool."

Erion lifted his empty cup in mock salute. He couldn't argue with that.

"Well if it isn't the two sorriest sacks of meat I've ever had the pleasure of laying eyes on." Vandra appeared at Erion's elbow out of nowhere.

"At least we're not soggy," Erion said, eyeing her dripping cloak.

Vandra rolled her eyes and vanished again, reappearing a moment later without the cloak. She lifted her hand and snapped at the barkeep—he noticed her immediately, if only because she was the only woman in the room and wearing a dangerously low-cut red dress to top off the allure. She lifted three fingers, and the barkeep nodded.

"Looks like I'm a little late to the party," she observed as she took a seat.

"What's the occasion?" Erion asked.

"Thought the world could do with a little color, is all."

"Crimson," Erion said.

"When amongst savages." Vandra shrugged.

Erion made a face and buried himself in his mead. Drinking was easier than trying not to look at her in that dress.

Then two tankards appeared on the table, the serving boy there and gone so fast Erion would have believed the drinks had been conjured from thin air. This roused Thorne, who sat up and reached for his own drink.

"No." Erion snatched the drink away from him as Vandra laughed.

"Oh, he's fine. Remember that Elarazii pub, the one with the fish?" She mimed a long nose.

"Dashelfin," Erion said. The innkeeper claimed to have caught it himself, but Erion doubted that. The things were vicious. Erion wasn't even sure the stuffed fish had been real.

"He's nowhere near that drunk," Vandra pointed out.

"Thorne's nowhere near a dashelfin, that's for sure. If you ever see him near one, don't let him."

"Don't let him what?" Erion asked, mystified. Thorne

grabbed for the mead again. This time, Erion relented.

"Make friends." Thorne looked deadly serious. "They are *not* friendly."

"The wisdom of fools." Vandra raised her tankard in a toast.

Erion rolled his eyes, but allowed himself a drink. Thorne's nonsense was a great distraction—and a great cover for the tumult going on in Erion's mind.

"Anyway, business." Vandra leaned toward Erion.

"What—now?" Erion grimaced. "It's raining dashelfin out there. Not even Isak is working."

He pointed, and Vandra followed his movement. Isak had surrounded himself with a group of hugely muscled cronies. He'd spent the night gambling—and losing, by the sounds of it.

"Well *Isak* isn't about to get freshly blooded," Vandra said.

"He—what?" Erion said, lost.

"Mathieu wants you to get the next mark."

"So soon?" *Freshly blooded* must mean getting more marks added to his tattoo. Erion glared down at his forearm.

"I don't make the rules, I just ink them."

"So it's ink, this time?"

"Mostly."

"That does not make me feel better." In truth, the announcement was unsettling. He'd expected nothing short of a lashing after his role in helping Amelie escape. Part of him was still waiting for Sadiq to turn him in. But a promotion?

It reeked of misdirection.

Isak already thought he was a spy. Was Mathieu planning to mark Erion with some new kind of symmajea? Something that would force him to tell the truth, maybe, or track his movement so Mathieu would know if he was sneaking around against orders? Could Line Magic even do that?

"Think of it as a show of goodwill," Vandra said.

"What are you doing delivering Mathieu's messages?" Erion asked. Vandra worked so closely with the Crimson Fang, sometimes he forgot she wasn't actually a member of the gang.

"My runner didn't show up today, so I delivered the latest

batch of contracts myself. Mathieu decided he didn't want to go out in this." She shrugged and gestured vaguely at the torrent outside.

"Sounds like you missed me," Erion teased. He was finding himself strangely at ease. A year ago, he would have dreaded being trapped in a tavern and surrounded by Isak's goons. Now, though, he thought he was safer knowing where Isak was at all times. These days, a warm evening by the fire with Vandra and Thorne was as peaceful as his life might ever get.

"Believe what you want. You're buying the next round, by the way," Vandra said.

"I'm skint," Erion said.

"Not anymore you're not. Congratulations, by the way."

"On getting myself sliced open again?"

"On that bounty. A simiot *and* an aster mole." She regarded him over the top of her tankard, a slight smile curving her lips.

"Pretty soon you'll catch up to Thorne," Thorne said. He was eyeing his mead like he expected it to jump him.

"You could work on your head start," Erion said. "Sadiq seems to like you."

"Sadiq likes *Sadiq*." Thorne's face lit up with glee. "Thorne remembered. Amelie."

The tentative comfort that had been growing in Erion's chest quivered and died.

"Who?" Vandra asked, her eyes sharp.

"Drink." Erion pushed Thorne's drink into his hand. "Her name's Vandra."

Hopefully that would shut him up long enough for Erion to get him out of here.

The morning after Amelie's escape, Sadiq had struck camp and led them back to Rijeka, like nothing had happened. No comments about the girl, or the nuraghi, or the argument he'd had with Isak. Erion had spent the night dreading the conversation he'd thought inevitable—but it had never come. He'd been avoiding Sadiq ever since, going so far as to hole up in Thorne's quarters the last few nights. If Sadiq wanted to find him, he'd start looking at the baron's manor. Besides, he hadn't wanted Edric to see him until he'd recovered more fully from his injuries. Going home hadn't been an option, so he'd picked the lock on Thorne's door and helped himself to the pantry.

Thorne hadn't even asked what was going on when he staggered into his rooms to find Erion lounging on his bed. He'd pulled a spare blanket from a wardrobe—Thorne's rooms were surprisingly clean, his furnishings verging on luxurious—and thrown it at Erion. Then he'd toppled into the bed and passed out while Erion was still sitting on it.

"Let's get you home," Erion said when Thorne finished his drink.

"Not before you explain." Thorne carefully enunciated each syllable. "Why I should keep lying about the girl for you."

Erion's shock at hearing Thorne use the word "I" almost outweighed his fear of the question.

"You—what?" Erion asked. "Are you ok?" Erion glanced sidelong at Vandra, but if Thorne's admission worried or even intrigued her, she showed no sign of it. She was impassive as ever.

Thorne shook his head and seemed to gather himself. "Thorne is fine. But you won't be if you keep this up. Thorne can't leave Rijeka again."

"*Home*," Erion repeated. He didn't need Vandra asking questions.

Thorne didn't protest as Erion helped him from his chair and into his cloak. The rain would sober him up. Erion trudged up the stone steps to the road and looked around. Thorne was still standing at the below-ground entry. Then Vandra appeared. She took Thorne by the elbow and led him up the stairs.

"You know where he lives?" She had to shout for Erion to hear her over the downpour.

Erion nodded. To his dismay, she followed them down the street.

Thorne started singing—loudly, but his voice had always surprised Erion. It was low and gravelly, and entirely pleasant to listen to. The ballad seemed to have about a hundred verses, though Erion couldn't make out most of the words over the storm.

"Well, this is me." Vandra stopped at an intersection and pointed east. Her rooms were several streets away from Thorne's. "Walk me home?"

"Not sure he'll make it to your place and back," Erion said, watching Thorne's wavering progress with doubt.

"Thorne knows where he lives, don't be insulting," Thorne grumbled, but a wicked smile lit his face. "Walk the lady home."

"You sure you're—" But Thorne was walking up the street toward his own home before Erion could finish the question.

"Brilliant, thanks. I hate walking these streets alone at night." Vandra looped her arm through Erion's. "Thorne's place is just ahead, he'll be fine."

Erion let her tug him across the road, which was now masquerading as a small stream. He disengaged his arm from hers when they reached the other side. He didn't want to give her the wrong impression.

But he wasn't sure what the right impression was—not anymore.

Erion wanted her with him. He wanted her gone. He wanted her lips against his.

They walked on in silence, heads bowed against the frozen rain. Erion's teeth were chattering when they reached the hall above the bakery where Vandra lived.

"I've got wine," Vandra told him as she unlocked the door.

Erion's stomach twisted. "I should go find Thorne."

"You're an idiot if you go back out in that, Skala."

She wasn't wrong. He was still recovering from his fight with the aster mole. On one hand, yet another act of idiocy might create a neat sort of symmetry—a harmony of sorts with with recent life choices.

On another... Erion realized just how much he wanted her to insist. His resistance was crumbling by the second.

"Do I need to bribe you with one of Quill's healing

potions?"

"You know a way to a man's heart," Erion said ruefully.

"I don't actually have any—but I've got a great one that warms you up better than whiskey. You can take it back with you."

Erion gave in and followed her inside—grateful for the excuse, and hating himself for it. He hovered on the woven doormat, hesitant to drip all over her floor and unsure what to do about it.

"Just throw it anywhere." Vandra shouted from her bedchamber, reading his mind. He shucked the cloak and glanced around—her bedroom door was open. Warm, inviting light spilled onto the floor from the room.

A swath of red fabric lay on the floor in the connecting hall.

"*Anywhere*, anywhere?" Erion asked. She hadn't left the dress out on purpose—he was reading too much into it. This was her home. She was welcome to discard clothing wherever she pleased.

And leave her doors open no matter her company.

Erion swallowed and dragged his eyes away from the discarded dress. He grabbed a straight-backed chair and hung his cloak over it, then slipped out of his boots and stockings and padded over to her fireplace.

He was too wet and tired to summon even the smallest dregs of majea. Erion fumbled on the dark mantle until he found a box of long-stemmed matches, blessing Vandra for having a fire already laid in the hearth. As always, she was prepared two steps in advance. Erion had to remind himself that she had too much power and too many secrets for her own good—or for his.

The dried logs lit almost at once. Erion crouched in front of the spreading flames. A towel flopped onto his shoulders, and he turned to see Vandra perched on the low couch behind him.

"Thanks," Erion said. He scrubbed his hair with the towel. He'd see if Vandra actually had a warming potion she'd be willing to part with—he could save it for a *real* emergency—then as soon as his socks were dry, he'd go.

"You going to just stand there dripping on my rugs, or what?"

"You have a dress that fits me?"

Vandra's laugh was low and musical. She held out a robe. "You're a shivering mess. I don't want to have to remove a frozen corpse from my rooms."

"Twist my arm," Erion said—feeling twisted—and liking it. He took the robe and moved toward the bedchamber.

"Traipse your muck into my rooms and you're cleaning it up," she warned, pouring two glasses.

Erion lifted a brow. Vandra sat back with her glass, a challenge in her eyes.

Fine. But he turned his back to her before taking off his coat and shirt. He laid them across another chair, then pulled the robe over his shoulders without looking at her. He hesitated before slipping off his breeches.

What a time to get *shy.*

His pants joined the other clothing laid out to dry. Vandra moved the chairs closer to the fire, and Erion sat down on the low couch opposite her.

"We need to talk." Vandra handed him a glass of wine and fixed him with a thoughtful frown. Her eyes glittered in the firelight.

"You had to get me naked for that?"

"I'm self-employed. I make my own job perks. Nice scar, by the way."

"Which one?" Erion grunted. He'd lost count.

Vandra gestured to the crook of her own elbow. "New?"

Erion nodded. He hadn't fully recovered his grip strength in his right hand since the Life Mage's dagger had caught him there. The bracers were supposed to *prevent* injury, not encourage them.

"I heard about Sadiq. And the girl," Vandra said.

Erion grabbed for his wine and took a large gulp. "I didn't have anything to do with that."

It was true—sort of. Sadiq had cut the girl's bonds and left the dagger. All Erion had really done was give her food.

"Do you know about the icho supplier?" Vandra asked, changing subjects. She refilled both wine glasses. Even wrapped in a robe, her wet, uncombed hair pulled over one shoulder, she was beautiful.

"What about it?" Erion wasn't equipped for this conversation. Not now—late at night in Vandra's apartments, half-naked, with nothing but a bottle of wine and a half-step between them.

"Mathieu's supplier is getting cold feet. He's threatening to pull out."

"And?" That was hardly Erion's problem.

"Use that lovely brain of yours a moment. I know you've got one, or Mathieu wouldn't have pushed so hard to get you. What happens if they can't get more crystals?"

"Prices go up," Erion said.

"And Mathieu gets desperate. Starts looking for a new supplier."

"Why are you telling me this?" Erion asked.

"I don't trust Mathieu," she said simply. She filled her wine glass again and started pacing the small space.

"But I should trust you?" Her robe was shorter than the one she'd given him. He supposed he should have been grateful *he* wasn't at risk of overexposure, but maybe it would have been better if she'd taken the longer one. He was finding her bare legs distracting. Erion looked down—his second glass of wine was already empty. He didn't remember drinking it.

"Nobody trusts me," Vandra waved that away. "I know too much. And things are about to *become* too much. Mathieu is heading into dangerous waters. He can't see it. I brokered the deal, I'm the only one who knows…"

Erion waited for her to finish the thought. She took a deep breath and covered her eyes with her hand for a moment. "I need you to help me with something."

"Go on," Erion said. Vandra sighed and sat down next to him. Her leg pressed against his.

"I need eyes in Voloy's estate. I can't tell you why, but I need you to tell me if you find anything… suspicious."

"Isak already thinks I'm a spy," Erion said.

"So nothing to lose, then."

"What counts as suspicious?"

"I think the Fang has an insider there that I'm not aware of. Someone powerful."

"More powerful than Niklas?" Erion asked.

Vandra snorted. "Can he even put his own clothes on, these days?"

"He's capable of more than you think," Erion told her seriously. Niklas had built up a surprising tolerance. Erion wouldn't be surprised if the Crimson Fang was cutting Niklas's doses with fillers to keep him coming back for more. That would keep him just sharp enough to avoid getting sacked. Mathieu wouldn't risk Niklas being replaced by a competent steward. Or worse, an honest one.

"Someone else," Vandra asserted. "And I need to know who it is."

"You going to tell me why?"

"How about I tell you how much I'll pay you for the information instead?"

Erion considered it. After the bounties from the simiot and the aster mole, he would have nearly enough for Edric to start his first term at school. He didn't want to risk getting on Isak's bad side and losing out on the first steady stream of income he'd had in his life—but maybe if he could get into Sadiq's good graces, it wouldn't matter.

He glanced down at Vandra. Her lips were too close to his. Whatever her plan was, it was dangerously close to working.

Erion leaned forward as though to kiss her, calling her on her bluff. But instead of pulling back, she closed her eyes and turned her face up to his. An eternity might have passed as he took in the sweet scent of her. She'd gone out of her way to put perfume on when she'd changed.

It would be so easy. Just not simple.

Vandra's company was a pleasure he couldn't afford to risk. No matter how badly he longed to. He took her chin in his hand and guided her until their lips were nearly touching. She inhaled sharply, but didn't move.

"Is this how you get what you want?" Erion spoke each word with regret. He could just feel the outline of her lips against his.

"Apparently not." Vandra pulled back from him and crossed her arms. "Usually coin does the trick… But there's always an exception that proves the rule." Her lips twisted into a thoughtful frown.

Erion's stomach swooped at the unspoken offer in her words. "Setting your own perks?" He tried to smile to take some of the sting from his rejection. *Not easy at all.*

Vandra met his gaze. "I wouldn't call you that."

Erion swallowed and looked away from her gold-flecked eyes. He'd blame the wine, though he hadn't had nearly enough of it.

Not enough to make the mistake he was dying to seize.

"I'm not at the estate often, these days," he said.

"Your brother?" Vandra asked softly.

"What do you know about that?" Erion's pulse quickened.

Vandra's eyes widened softly at the sudden harshness in his voice. "If I had a brother, I'd want him safe, too."

Erion put his head in his hands, relieved and disgusted with himself all at once. The sooner he got Edric out, the better. He lived in terror of someone discovering the boy's magic, and who was more likely to dig up the information than Vandra? She *did* have eyes everywhere.

And now she had his, too. Even if he didn't agree to it tonight, Erion had no choice but to be on the lookout for a spy somewhere among the baron's men.

Maybe that had been her plan all along. He knew better than to try to wheedle more information out of her. She'd said her piece.

Erion took a deep breath and grabbed his clothes. They were

nowhere near dry, but he'd be soaked to the bone within seconds of stepping outside either way.

"I'll let you know what I find out, but I don't want your coin." Painful as it was to turn down the lucrative part of her offer, he couldn't bring himself to step into that world with Vandra. He could be with her, or he could take her coin.

Not even he was enough of a fool to try and balance both.

CHAPTER NINETEEN
DECEPTIVE DEALINGS

Cedivar paced the shore by the small floating dock, the silvered moonlight limiting his sight to glimmers on the gently lapping waves of Lake Zagretsk. He wasn't stepping onto the thing unless he absolutely had to. It had been designed to move in and out of cover near the shore. Calling the floating deathtrap "unstable" would be generous.

A longboat glided smoothly over the water toward him. Cedivar pulled his hood lower and made sure his mask covered his mouth and nose before going to meet the crew.

Distaste soured his mouth as he looked over the Crimson Fang men disembarking from the boat. He accepted the role the gang played in Baron Voloy's plans, but that didn't mean he liked it.

"You're late," Cedivar snapped. It was freezing out here.

"And you're ungrateful," the tall man wading toward him grumbled. "Do you have any idea what we've had to push to get this big of a haul for you? And we can't keep up with the demand unless you provide us with more crystals this time.

They're emptying faster than we can resupply."

"Why do you think I'm here?" Cedivar asked.

The newcomer reached the shore, and Mathieu Sifet's craggy features materialized from the dark. The gang leader looked around with distaste. "Not to resupply, I take it."

Cedivar rolled his eyes. So hasty. "Like I'd leave something so valuable just lying around on the shore. Your crates are up at the Reinholdt ruins. You're free to collect them yourselves."

Mathieu grunted. "So why are *you* here?"

"To negotiate. I'm sure you've been ah, working diligently, but we're not interested in prolonging the relationship."

More silence.

"My client finds the operation isn't lucrative enough to continue providing you with our supply. We'll maintain our agreed-upon terms for another month. That should give you enough time to come up with a new arrangement." Cedivar kept his tone even. More than enough time, really. He thought the baron's terms quite gracious.

Cedivar had realized the Fang's contribution was superfluous weeks ago, but he'd waited for the baron to come to his own conclusions on the matter. Cedivar was comfortable with his position and the luxuries it afforded him. The man known as the *Ithynon* was having far too much fun tinkering away in his dungeons for Cedivar to interfere.

"What exactly are you saying?" Mathieu took several menacing steps forward. Cedivar held his ground.

"I spoke quite plainly." Cedivar blinked. Was the man so stupid? "The crystals aren't integral to the icho's natural hallucinogenic properties. You shouldn't have any problems coming up with alternatives."

Of course there was no substitute as potent as the drug Baron Voloy had engineered. When topped with the zomajea crystals modeled after the Giant artifacts, each puff of an icho pipe sucked away the smallest fraction of the user's own life force. The weakening effect of that spell was what enhanced the kick on the Crimson Fang's product.

Cedivar had invented the symmajea on the crystals himself, though the baron was happy to take credit for the idea. The discovery of the stones in Nuraghi Uzhastik had opened up unimaginable possibilities. The baron had his own aims and, at least for now, it served Cedivar to aid him.

"I want a meeting with the Ithynon." Mathieu snapped a signal at his men unloading the boat. He was angry, but not perhaps angry enough. Cedivar wondered whether Mathieu had ever sampled his own product—whether he truly understood the difference in the original icho paste compared to the majea-enhanced, stone-capped version.

"I'm sure you know that's quite impossible," Cedivar said.

"And I'm sure you know we don't have to deliver these until I get that meeting. I know you need them."

Cedivar bristled. The man was bluffing—as far as Mathieu knew, the crystals he returned were useless. The Fang returned them to the Ithynon so the stones could be enhanced with whatever trade secrets he used to make icho more potent.

"So that's a no?" Mathieu spoke into the silence that had stretched between the two men. Cedivar heard the sneer in his voice.

"We don't need you," Cedivar said.

"Load it up then." Mathieu turned back to the boat, where his men had already started returning the crates to their boat.

Cedivar wished he was surprised by Mathieu's show of self-importance. With the new methods devised in the nuraghi, the baron no longer needed Mathieu's crystals. They'd found far more effective methods of acquiring the power they needed to feed the zomajea stones.

But they couldn't afford to make an enemy of Mathieu Sifet. The Crimson Fang had taken over all the dirty work that the baron's own soldiers couldn't be trusted with.

"What do you want?" Cedivar rolled his eyes and followed Mathieu.

"For your people to keep up their side of the deal, to start with."

Cedivar waited for the rest.

After a pause, Mathieu continued. "A meeting with the Ithynon. And advanced payment for the raid on Jesper's men."

"A hard bargain," Cedivar said.

"But fair, I think. The Ithynon could hire any team of thugs for the duke's men, but they'd probably botch the job."

And ask questions. It had taken trial and error to find a criminal Cedivar had been willing to liaise with on behalf of the baron, anonymously or not. Most crooks wanted coin, but a surprising number of them were too curious for their own good. Even when casual cutthroats advertised themselves as silent killers, they often weren't.

Then Cedivar had stumbled upon the woman, Vandra— almost literally—and their tenuous truce with the Crimson Fang had been born.

"Deliver the crystals to the ruins and collect your goods. I'll speak with the Ithynon. After that, we'll see what can be done about the advance pay," Cedivar said.

"Guarantee me a meeting with the Ithynon, and you have an accord."

Cedivar pretended to consider the compromise. After a moment, he nodded. "If it's within my power, I will do it."

Mathieu extended his hand, and Cedivar shook it.

Mathieu's deep-set eyes glittered as he crushed Cedivar's hand in his grip. "See that it is."

Cedivar retreated to the tree line and watched the Crimson Fang's men trudge up the hill toward the Reinholdt ruins. He wouldn't leave until he could be certain that none of Mathieu's men had lingered to follow him.

He had to give Mathieu credit for being shrewd—he wasn't particularly imaginative. It was easy to arrange a meeting with someone faceless, voiceless. The Crimson Fang leader need never know whether he'd met the Ithynon in truth.

Some things were just too easy.

CHAPTER TWENTY

THE STEWARD'S SON

Torrential rain blasted the windows in the baron's estate. Edric ducked and wove between huddled workers seeking shelter. Nobody wanted to get caught in the yards during a storm like this—the servant's halls were filled to bursting.

Edric just wanted *out*. He'd finished his work in the stables. Usually he'd go for a ride, but Caz might never forgive him if he tried to take her out in this.

He snuck into the kitchens. The long, narrow hall was one of the only rooms not filled shoulder-to-shoulder with unwanted workers. Edric suspected that was only because half of the servants were too smart to cross the cook—the other half had already done it and barely lived to tell the tale.

Edric padded between the long tables bearing the beginnings of the evening meal. The baron didn't set formal table anymore—not since the baroness's death—but there were still plenty of mouths to feed.

Sprigs of fresh herbs poked out of a row of glass jars by the window. Nobody was paying him any attention. Edric tapped each of the glass jars in turn, opening himself up to the cheerful vitality buzzing in the little plants. He smiled as the herbs sprouted new growth—just enough to tide the kitchens over for another day or two, until the rain subsided.

Something slammed down on the counter to his right. Edric jerked his hand away from the herbs. *Reckless.*

"Don't you have somewhere to be?" The cook, Runan, dusted his hands with flour and dug into the slab of dough he'd thumped on the table.

"Sorry?" Relief flooded through Edric. Runan hadn't noticed.

"The gatehouse?" Runan cut the dough into three long strips and started dotting the pieces with spiced raisins.

"You'd better get there before the steward does. It looked..." Runan frowned, thinking. "Complicated."

"Complicated?" Edric had no idea what the cook was talking about.

"I'd run," Runan said.

That was all the prompting Edric needed—he'd known Runan his entire life. If the cook thought it was serious, it probably was. Edric snatched a few raisins from the bowl. Runan swatted at his hand half-heartedly.

Edric popped one of the raisins into his mouth and grinned. "Thanks."

The gatehouse wasn't far. The guard hunched under the eaves of the building, a wide hood covering his face. He glanced up at Edric with a surly expression as he approached.

"No livestock today," he grunted.

The guard had obviously mistaken Edric for a shepherd boy looking to take animals out to pasture. Edric shook his head. "Going inside."

The man looked at him with suspicion, but unlocked the door into the gatehouse.

Edric was greeted by woodsmoke and the musty, heavy scent of wet leather. Someone had scattered rushes across the entry in an attempt to soak up the worst of the water tracked in by worn boots. The result was a trampled mess of mud.

Murmurs of conversation floated through the open door at the end of the hallway. Edric stamped his boots across the rushes, doing his best to wipe off his feet before walking down the hall to the front office.

An irritated-looking man bent over a sheaf of records at the small clerk's desk. Sodden residents of the city filled the two short rows of seats and lined the walls. A one-eared guardsman leaned toward the clerk and said something inaudible.

"The flooding, what else?" the clerk snapped. "You tell them to leave. The eastern banks near the border are overrun. Psari District."

The one-eared man laughed. "And they sent their guild heads to beg for help?"

"Seems they sent half the town." The clerk didn't bother to keep his voice down, and the townsfolk in the chairs exchanged glances of anger and discomfort at his words. "Two of 'em locked up in the back now."

"What were they arrested for? Did you tell the steward what's going on?" Edric stepped up to the desk.

"Who are *you*?" the guard asked. He grunted when the clerk kicked his shin.

Edric lifted his chin, doing his best to look the guard in the eye despite being a foot shorter than the armed man. "Edric Skala. The steward's son."

The two men exchanged a look.

"How about *you* tell the steward, then," the clerk said, "and I tell all these lovely people that *we can't help any of you today*." His voice rose as he turned and addressed the miserable petitioners. "Petitions aren't until next week! Talk to your local guard stations about sandbags, you absolute—"

"Why don't you send a runner to the Psari District?" Edric asked. "To find out whether they actually need reserves to help?" It was clear to Edric that the Psari District *did* need help, considering how many people had come to ask for it. He was trying to be diplomatic, but found his patience wearing thin. These people trusted their baron and those in his employ to take care of problems like this. The guard and the clerk weren't just being obstinate, they were being lazy.

"To go all the way out there in this?" The guard jutted his chin toward the room's only window. Rain mottled the glass, making it impossible to see through. "You volunteering? We'll send in more men when we get the official word they're needed. The guards at the river know about the flooding—seeing as they're actually *there* right now. At their posts. Doing honest work."

Edric bristled at the implication. "And are *you* doing honest work?"

"Look here, you little—"

"*Steward's son,*" the clerk reminded through gritted teeth.

"You're the runner now," Edric told the guard. "Go, or I'll report this to my father. Being an errand boy will feel like a promotion after he's finished with you." Edric knew perfectly well that his father didn't give two neks about flooding in the Psari District, but these men didn't know that.

The guard barked a curse, and the clerk kicked him in the shin again. Grumbling, the one-eared man stormed into the rain without a backwards glance.

The clerk turned his pinched face to Edric. "How can I help you?"

"By doing your job. These people came here for your help."

Edric was forcibly reminded how fortunate he was whenever he left the manor. Rijeka wasn't safe, wasn't flourishing, and its baron wasn't doing anything to help them. Living with a father addicted to icho wasn't easy, but Edric had grown up with a small circle of servants in the estate more than happy to step in and surrogate parent him—not to mention his brother. His home had always been warm and safe.

Edric looked out over the crowd. "You're all here about the flooding?"

Most of them nodded. One man in the front row stood up

and gripped his hat in trembling hands. "We've got Bhirtas'Nemus in the lumber yards, m'lord."

"Don't you work for the baron?" Edric thought he recognized the man.

"Yes, m'lord, but the bridge over the back roads collapsed, and I got sent the long way around. They won't let me in."

"You didn't provide any identification," the clerk snapped. His face began to purple as he addressed Edric again. "I'm quite capable of handling—"

"See to it that you do handle it then. I'll vouch for this man—let him through, or I'll catch one of those Bhirtas'Nemus and release it in your house."

The clerk took the threat to heart and immediately started calling names from a list. A cluster of sodden petitioners surrounded him at once.

Edric glanced around the room, wondering what he was missing. Had Runan just been looking for an excuse to get him out of the kitchens? It didn't seem likely. All the cook had to do was ask. So why did he send Edric here?

Edric's gaze rested on a woman sitting near the door. She had a hood pulled low over her face, the only visitor who didn't seem eager to get the clerk's attention.

Edric rapped his knuckles on the clerk's desk until he had the man's attention, then pointed at the woman. "Who's that?"

"How should I know?" the clerk snapped. He sighed at Edric's glare. "She asked for Captain Talbot. He's not here today, but she won't leave. Didn't say anything else."

"That wasn't so hard now, was it?" Edric said cheerily. He took several steps toward the woman. She lurched to her feet as he approached, looking up briefly at him, eyes wide with panic. Edric opened his mouth to introduce himself, but she slipped out the door before he reached her. He went to the exit and scanned the street outside.

She'd stopped on the opposite side of the street. Her hood was down, and she stared at him through the rain. Intrigued, Edric tromped through the mud to join her.

"Hullo." He came to a halt several feet away from her, worried she might run again. He realized she wasn't much older than him. "It's not my job to yell at him, really, but I'm sorry he was being such an ass. You're looking for Captain Talbot?"

Edric only knew him a little, but Talbot was close with Erion. Maybe he could help. It was as good a thing as any to do on a day like this. He didn't fancy going back to the crowded, stinking servant's halls, and his little sanctuary in the forest had lost its appeal after his visit with Erion. He hadn't gone back—not since *her.*

The girl muttered something Edric couldn't hear.

"Sorry?" he asked.

"He said to ask for Captain Talbot. Not to talk to anyone else."

"Do you want me to find him?" Edric didn't have a clue where Talbot might be. He didn't even know where Erion was.

"He called you the steward's son." It wasn't a question.

"Who? Oh. Yeah, I am." Edric stared at the strange girl, taking in her appearance properly for the first time. The deep green cloak she wore was far too big for her. The hood had swallowed her head and the edges dragged in the mud behind her. A pattern of small geometric shapes had been stitched into the collar—a pattern he recognized.

Edric took a step closer to squint at the design. The girl hissed a sharp intake of breath and backed away until she hit the stone wall of the building behind her.

Bewildered, Edric held out his hands to show they were empty. "I'm not going to hurt you."

Someone had already hurt her, that much was clear. If the fading bruises across one side of her face didn't tell that story, the fear in her eyes did.

"He said to ask for the steward's son."

"Who? Why?"

The girl was silent.

"Can I at least..." Edric floundered. Erion was better at this sort of thing—he always had a plan, and a backup plan, whenever things went wrong. "Who told you to ask for me? Was it Runan?"

"Who?" The girl's brow furrowed.

Edric grinned despite himself. "We're asking that question a lot, I guess."

The corner of her mouth twitched. It was almost a smile.

Edric looked around the mud-streaked streets. It was obvious this girl needed help—and someone had sent her to him, after all. The least he could do was get her out of the cold, right? "Can I get you a warm drink?"

She hesitated, then shook her head so forcefully it looked like she was having a fit.

Edric lifted his hands in what he hoped was a calming gesture. The last thing he wanted was for her to run again. "Somewhere public. A tavern. You can choose the table—you can leave anytime if you decide you don't trust me."

"Why are you helping me?"

Edric shrugged. "I'm the steward's son."

And she was wearing Erion's cloak.

CHAPTER TWENTY-ONE
UNSAVORY PROPOSITIONS

Erion sat with his chair propped against the back door of the icho den, the front legs balancing several inches off the ground. He glared down at his exposed forearm. He flexed his hand, watching the muscles in his arm move beneath the Crimson Fang tattoo. Three new lines in faint pink swirled down to meet the single red point on his wrist. Promotion.

"Thorne doesn't think staring at it will make it go away." Thorne kicked the front legs of Erion's chair, upending it. Erion crashed to the floor.

"Gallantyr's—what was that for?" Erion demanded. "What are you doing here?" It was late morning, and the icho den hadn't even opened yet.

Thorne stuck his hands in his pockets and looked around the empty lounge. "Boss wants you."

"Which one?" Erion asked warily.

"Does it matter?"

Erion sighed, then followed Thorne down the hall that led to the private lounges. Thorne let himself into the largest of the suites without knocking.

"Erion!" Sadiq grinned at him from a low chaise. Without the grime of the road smearing his clothing, Sadiq looked more like a lordling patronizing the icho den than one of the men running it.

Erion nodded at him, relieved it wasn't Isak. "You rang?"

"Join me. Both of you. I want to talk," Sadiq said.

Certain he knew what Sadiq wanted to talk about, Erion dragged his feet across the thick carpet, wishing he could sink into the floor. Thorne toed one of the enormous poufs, looking at it with suspicion. After a moment, he turned and left the room.

"Want me to go get him, or…" Erion pointed over his shoulder at the door where Thorne had vanished.

"Just sit," Sadiq said. "How often are you at the baron's estate these days?"

"Not often," Erion said truthfully. He camped out at Thorne's as often as possible and had done his best to return to his rooms only at odd hours. He left notes for Edric. Little, useless details about the bounties he'd been chasing, always reminding his brother to keep his magic secret and his ear to the ground. For his part, Edric rarely wrote back. There was a cold fury in the silence.

"I need you to change that," Sadiq said.

The door swung open and Thorne backed in, dragging a sturdy wooden chair from the icho den. He dropped it between Erion and Sadiq and settled in, the picture of attentiveness.

Sadiq blinked but didn't comment. "Mathieu's just ordered a hit."

"On who?" A stone of dread plummeted into Erion's stomach. If it had anything to do with the baron's estate, it was probably someone he knew. Maybe even someone he'd grown up with…

"Several, actually. It's a bit involved. We need someone familiar with the manor to get us inside." Sadiq made it sound like a request, but Erion knew it wasn't.

"Who's the target?" Erion asked again.

"When's the last time you were there?"

Erion grunted. It had been over a week.

"Duke Jesper has sent a retinue to visit Baron Voloy. I understand they've not actually arrived yet." Sadiq continued as though he hadn't expected Erion to answer.

Privately, Erion thought the duke should have intervened months ago. Surely he knew how desperate things had become. It was probably too much to hope that he'd send someone to supervise the barony's affairs. And he had to remind himself that oversight like that would be a disaster for him now.

"So Thorne's an assassin now?" Thorne's question pulled a reluctant grin from Sadiq.

"If that's what you want to call yourself. But we also have to make sure no correspondence gets back to the duke while they're here."

"How exactly are we supposed to kill an entire ducal retinue? The duke himself isn't coming, is he?" Erion asked.

What would Edric think if he saw me now? Casually discussing killing not one man, but many. Noblemen, and maybe their retainers and soldiers.

Innocent men with families and lives of their own.

"We have a contact who's set up a pinch point, we'll be alerted where we need to be and when. Until then, it's your job to handle the reports."

Erion nodded glumly. If his part of the plan stopped at intercepting messages, he'd be happy.

"Put some steel in that spine, Skala. You'll need it. Speaking of steel—have you replaced your sword yet?" Sadiq glanced at the battered shortsword at Erion's waist.

Erion twinged with embarrassment. It was one of Thorne's old weapons. Barely serviceable. He was nearly a foot taller than Thorne. The short blade looked ridiculous strapped to Erion's belt.

"I'll take that as a no. I'll see what I can do for you. In the meantime, I need you to get back to the estate and get eyes on the situation. Thorne—you'll be at the guardhouse; you'll be taking the place of a gatekeeper there."

"Which one?" Thorne asked.

"The main gate."

"No, Thorne wants to know which gatekeeper."

"What?"

"That he's impersonating? Is he tall?"

"Not a specific—nevermind." Sadiq shook his head. "There's one more thing I wanted to talk to you about, Skala. Mathieu wanted me to wait until we saw how you'd do keeping tabs on Jesper's men, but I disagreed. I think you'll do better if you know what's at stake."

Erion regarded him warily, but didn't say anything. Beside him, Thorne grumbled and shifted his chair some more.

"We need another man inside the baron's estate. Someone we can trust," Sadiq said.

"Another one?" Erion blurted.

Sadiq narrowed his eyes, and Erion regretted the outburst. Vandra had been the one to alert him to a possible spy within the ranks of the baron's servants—Erion wasn't supposed to know. If there even *was* a spy. But he trusted Vandra's instincts on those kinds of things. What was Sadiq playing at?

"I mean—besides my father?" Erion amended.

Sadiq snorted. "The only thing we trust Niklas to do is show up looking for more icho. But there are problems there, too. We're worried about supply, and we may need to… borrow… some of the baron's assets to make some changes in our favor."

"You want me to steal from him?" Erion asked.

"Not those kinds of assets. But we do need someone who can oil the gears for us."

Erion couldn't imagine what other kinds of assets Sadiq might be talking about.

"Mathieu would skewer me if he knew I told you about this—but things are getting unpredictable with our partner."

"The Ithynon."

"Yes." Sadiq leaned back and crossed his hands behind his head, considering Erion with a small frown. He glanced at Thorne. "I can trust you, Knivhyg?"

"Thorne keeps his mouth *shut*," Thorne advised.

"Funnily enough, that's precisely the opposite of my experience."

Thorne sat on his hands and sealed his lips shut by way of demonstration. Sadiq shook his head.

"If this contract goes through, it means changes. Big ones," Sadiq told them.

"Like what?" Thorne asked.

"I thought you were keeping your mouth shut?" Sadiq asked.

"Once there's things to *keep* shut, sure. What's happening?"

"Mathieu is striking preemptively. We need to secure a critical asset before there's a void in the market."

"The Ithynon is backing out... of the icho trade?" Erion mused, more to himself than anything. It wouldn't be a matter of profits. The icho trade was thriving. "Why?"

"There are a lot of factors at play. I'm not privy to most of them," Sadiq said.

"We really don't know who the Ithynon is?"

"*I* don't. Mathieu may. And..."

And Vandra, Erion realized. "What's the asset?" *And what does it have to do with me?*

"Some land, though it's likely Mathieu has more in mind down the road. It doesn't matter yet, but I wanted to warn you that the orders might be coming up."

"To keep doing what I'm already doing?"

"To work more closely with the baron's holdings."

Erion had grown up at the estate. Beyond knowing every servant, he was familiar with the baron's vassals, and the knights and landholders that sometimes visited. The Crimson Fang hadn't ever tried to utilize that knowledge before.

"To be clear," Sadiq pressed when Erion didn't speak, "your father trusts you. He has information we need, but Mathieu doesn't trust *him*. If you step up to run the barony, there's a lot of coin in it for you."

Erion drummed his fingers on the arm of his chair, pretending to consider the offer. "I'm not good at that sort of thing."

"You're not stupid, Skala. You'll learn."

"Am I being given a choice?" Erion asked.

"For now." A dangerous light glinted in Sadiq's eyes.

Edric. As far as Erion knew, they still didn't know Edric's secret—but the very existence of his brother's magic put him at risk.

"Is that all I'd be doing?" Erion had a feeling Sadiq wasn't done with him. They'd still never discussed Amelie's escape. There was something at play here that Erion didn't understand, and it twisted at his gut.

"You'd eventually take over as steward, if that's what you're asking."

The Crimson Fang was playing a long game. It shouldn't have surprised Erion, but it was the first time he'd had a glimpse at a bigger picture—grander designs beyond smuggling and turf wars with rival gangs.

There were too many things Sadiq wasn't telling him, but Erion didn't know the crew leader well enough to push him. Unlike with Isak and Thorne, he hadn't found that line—and pushing might bring up conversations he'd rather keep avoiding.

"Anything else?" Erion asked.

"Plenty," Sadiq said. "But that's enough to be getting along with for the time being. We'll be keeping a close eye on you, Skala."

"Thorne will be keeping his eyes on himself, if that's fine with everybody. He likes them where they are."

Erion stifled a laugh.

Sadiq pinched the bridge of his nose, looking pained. "And that's the end of *this* meeting. Be back here tomorrow night with what details you have on the duke's contingent."

Erion nodded curtly. His mind raced as he thought about what Sadiq was asking him to do—*ordering* him to do. They'd only told him about their plans to make him the baron's new steward to take away some of the sting of the job at hand.

He didn't want to be the steward, but he wanted to kill the duke's men even less.

... Mathieu's just ordered a hit.

Erion tapped his fist against his leg absently, thinking on the unspoken message in Sadiq's orders. *Do this once, and you'll earn our trust. Do this once, and we'll hole you up where you won't have to kill again.*

Could it really be that easy?

Erion turned to leave and nearly ran into Thorne, who had stopped dead in front of the door.

"You ready for this one?" Thorne asked.

Erion shrugged. "Getting by. I'm not trying to impress anyone."

"Fresh ink on your arm says otherwise."

"Maybe if you had a little more on yours, you wouldn't think it was exceptional."

"If Thorne had any more, his mother would kill him."

Erion cocked his head at that. Thorne had never mentioned family before.

A wave of patrons entered the lounge across the room before Erion could ask Thorne about his mother. The icho den was officially open for business. The two men separated, taking up their respective posts to keep the crowd in line and the product under close watch.

Erion leaned back in his chair again, staring but not really seeing the lounge as it began to fill with haze. A life of servitude in the baron's house... it was a position he'd been offered before, and rejected. Erion couldn't imagine working for the Crimson Fang *and* the baron would be any better.

* * *

Erion couldn't remember the last time he'd seen the baron's manor so busy. After a year or more of lethargy, suddenly every manservant and maid had tasks to complete. The receiving chambers sparkled and mouthwatering scents of cinnamon and smoked pork filled the halls.

Mercifully, the duke hadn't sent a large contingent. Two councilors, one of whom seemed to be little more than a bookkeeper, with an escort of four knights. Erion reported the numbers to Sadiq without enthusiasm. *It could be worse.*

Edric practically leapt down Erion's throat when he entered their rooms.

"Where have you *been*? What have you been doing?" Erion had expected Edric to be distant at his return—the warm reception was a welcome relief. He did his best to smile. Erion had spent most of the previous night banging heads together at the icho den. All he wanted to do was fall into bed and stay there—forever.

"You wouldn't believe me if I told you," Erion said.

"Go on." Edric fidgeted as he pestered Erion for details, and his eyes widened as Erion told him about the aster mole.

"You didn't."

Erion rolled up his right sleeve and unlaced his leather bracer—the safe arm—to show his brother the scar. He didn't mention it came from a mage's dagger and not the aster mole's claws.

"They don't grow that big," Edric argued.

But Edric wanted to believe the story, Erion could tell. He pulled a sack of coin from his pocket and tossed it to his brother. "That big?"

Edric pulled the cord and looked into the bag. "What are you going to do with it?"

"Don't be stupid," Erion said. "It's for you."

It's all for you, little brother. And then, gods forgive me, it's up to you to redeem us both.

"How much is here?" Edric asked.

"Three hundred. I told you I was getting close."

Edric screwed up his face. "I'm sorry."

"What? This is everything we've wanted."

"What about you?"

The simplicity of the question struck Erion's heart. Edric was all the good that Erion wished he himself could be.

"*I'm* going to bed. Just as soon as you catch me up on all that." Erion gestured towards the yards where he knew Edric had stabled six new horses.

"The duke sent men." Edric chewed on his lower lip. "I think father's in trouble."

"Father's always in trouble," Erion sighed. There was too much truth to the words, and he wished with all his being that Edric was ignorant of it.

"They're here to check on the baron, I think. One of the maids said they've been going through accounts."

"Which accounts?"

Edric shrugged. "Accounts. But Father's in charge of those, right?"

"Sort of." Once, Niklas had planned on Erion taking his place as the baron's steward. He'd made good on the threat a few years ago, insisting Erion start accompanying him around the estate as he went about his work. After two weeks of ink-stained hands and unending meetings, Erion's eyes had started to go cross anytime he looked at a ledger. Sums bored him to tears.

"The baron's back," Edric said.

"He was gone?"

"No. He's down from the walks," Edric clarified.

"Ah. To meet with the duke's men."

"When was the last time we actually *saw* him?" Erion asked. The baron's nightly walks across the garden walls were a common sight. Always unescorted, he ordered guards and servants alike away from his vigil—pacing above the gardens his wife had so loved. But Erion couldn't remember the last time Baron Voloy had actually left his chambers to visit the communal areas in the estate.

"Runan says a few months. And that he's mad," Edric said. "And that he's dangerous."

That piqued Erion's interest. "Why does he say that?"

"Why are you asking so many questions?"

"Nice deflection, kid."

Edric punched Erion lightly in the arm. "Why the bracers?"

"If an aster mole tried to eat you, you'd wear them too."

"I guess." Edric's demeanor fell suddenly. "Can we talk about what happened?"

"What happened?" Erion's guard rose immediately, recalling Vandra's warning that the Crimson Fang had another member planted somewhere in the baron's household. "You weren't *seen?*"

"I *told* you I'm being careful. I mean what happened in the clearing."

"Be more careful. This isn't a joke. *This,*" he pointed at the bag of coin Edric still held, "isn't easy."

Edric just stared at him.

"I'm so close. *We're* so close." Erion's oft-repeated words sounded like a prayer.

"You're that eager to get rid of me?" Edric asked.

Erion sank into a chair. How had the conversation gone so far afield? "What did you want to talk about?"

Edric jerked his head in a noncommittal gesture. "Nothing." He shouldered out the door without another word.

CHAPTER TWENTY-TWO
SWORD AND SABOTAGE

T horne kept his hood up and his head down as he crossed the yards into the baron's estate. He hated trying to follow Erion. The stoneburner always knew when someone was creeping up on him. If Erion ever figured out how to really use his majea, Thorne would be in trouble. *Everyone* would be in trouble.

He hoisted the huge sword over his back, checking that the chest strap was secure, and quickened his pace. Orders were orders, and Thorne's were to deliver them.

Orders that Erion wasn't going to like.

Thorne glanced upward and saw Erion go into the stables. He jogged a few steps and let himself in before the door could swing shut. He crouched down behind a stall and watched Erion cross the barn to a wall of shabby tack. Silver flickered in the stoneburner's hands. Thorne leaned further around the stall to see what Erion was doing.

Erion stiffened, and the knife in his hands vanished.

"You're not hiding very well, Edric."

"Thorne's not hiding Edric anywhere." Thorne huffed and stood up, pulling his hood down.

"Oh, it's you."

"Thorne was, the last time he checked. What are you doing, Sneak Thief?"

"*I'm* a sneak?" Erion glanced around the stables to make sure they were alone, then pulled out his belt knife again. He set to sawing at a strap on a particularly worn saddle.

"Thorne would leave that one alone. It's going to fall apart all by itself," Thorne said as he walked up to join Erion. "Doesn't have any life left in it."

"That's kind of the idea, as the cow's dead," Erion deadpanned.

"Thorne likes your wit, but what are you doing?"

"How did you get in here?" Erion countered.

"Thorne is an official and valued member of the honorary league of gatekeepers." Thorne puffed out his chest.

"Honorary now, are they? Does that mean they've started doing their job?"

"Nope," Thorne said proudly. "If anything, Thorne's presence has degraded their work ethic."

"Working with you isn't easy." Erion stood back from the saddle and examined his handiwork. Thorne leaned in. Both stirrups dangled by thin strips of leather.

"So... just use someone else's saddle," Thorne said. He didn't always understand Erion's thought processes, and this was no exception.

"He won't." A muscle twitched in Erion's jaw. He turned to two bridles and gave them the same treatment. Thorne fell silent as he watched Erion work. Who was he trying to stop?

"So?" Erion asked when he returned all the equipment back to their respective hooks.

"Thorne doesn't sew much."

Erion ran a hand over his face.

"Brought you these." Thorne held out a single sheaf of parchment. The seal on the letter had been broken.

"Read it for me, did you?"

"Had Thorne's name on it."

Erion turned the paper over and raised his brows. The letter wasn't addressed to anyone, let alone to Thorne.

"How are we supposed to pull this off?" Erion asked, scanning the short note. A stylized fang was the only signature at the bottom of the page.

"Sadiq has everything set up. Isak is coming to supervise."

The instructions were simple. Thorne and Erion would meet Sadiq and Isak at an ambush point some miles north of the baron's estate, near the border with the Duchy of Elarazii.

"Why are the duke's men going there?" Erion asked. "What's in Elarazii? And what exactly is Isak *supervising?*"

"If you think Isak trusts Sadiq after that play in the woods, you're paying even less attention than Thorne. And weren't you supposed to be finding the answers to all of the rest of those questions?"

"I was supposed to be intercepting mail like a mole."

"You already killed that, though."

"I'm spying on the councilors, Thorne. They haven't said anything about Elarazii in their correspondence," Erion snapped.

"They're going to inspect a field or something. Thorne doesn't care."

"Is anyone from the baron's estate escorting them?"

"*Anyone...* like the steward?" Thorne watched Erion's expression for a reaction as he brushed the man's emotions with his majea.

Thorne wasn't exactly a paragon of virtue, but reading other's emotions had gotten him into more than his fair share of messes. Prodding them along had gotten him into even more trouble, so he was careful about how he used the skill. On the upside, Thorne found that a lot of people seemed to forget he was an erkurios altogether. On the downside, he didn't get enough practice.

Thorne's position with the Crimson Fang had been tenuous

ever since his dysfunctional initiation. He never should have been a member at all, let alone working high-profile jobs like the ones Sadiq had started putting him on. But he'd gotten saddled with the job of following Erion around ever since their first trip to that damned nuraghi. Ever since then, the leaders of the Crimson Fang decided wherever Erion went, so did Thorne. The stoneburner was getting Thorne into all kinds of trouble, lately.

Much as Thorne liked the man, it was hard to trust him. Erion's loyalties were divided. He tried to hide it, but Thorne could read him well enough.

Erion was hiding more than the Crimson Fang tattoo up his sleeves.

"*Anyone* like the *baron.*" Erion crumpled the paper in his hands. "I can't remember the last time Niklas actually did his job. There's no chance he'd go."

"Thorne doesn't think the baron gets out much. Wouldn't worry about him."

"What do I have to do to get you out of here?" Erion leaned against the wall and crossed his arms.

"Hiding something?" Thorne asked.

"Hiding plenty. What's that?" Erion pointed to the sword hilt jutting over Thorne's shoulder.

"Oh! Thorne forgot."

"You forgot about a bloody great sword you lugged all the way here?" Erion's eyebrows rose, and Thorne sensed a current of amusement ripple through his emotions.

"Sadiq sends his regards." Thorne unstrapped the hand-and-a-half sword and held it out to Erion. "And good riddance. That thing weighs more than Thorne does."

Erion accepted the sword with a tangible sense of misgiving.

"Pays to get in good with the boss, doesn't it?" Thorne said.

Erion drew the sword. Sunlight refracted off the steel. He ran his finger down the blade's fuller, and his eyes gaze sharpened. "It's a stoneburner blade."

"Well, yeah. It's yours. And you're a stoneburner." But Thorne knew what Erion meant. Sadiq had gone out of his way to find a craftsman specializing in Land Magic—steel manipulated by majea with special properties.

"I'm going to be paying this off for a lifetime," Erion groaned, but admiration danced in his eyes and pulsed off him in subtle waves—the simple pleasure of one specialist recognizing another's mastery of their craft.

"Sadiq must like you. Better not sit too close." Thorne grinned.

"Send my thanks," Erion said, still scrutinizing the blade. Thorne knew he was going over every inch of it with his own majea, listening to its secrets.

"'Thanks' doesn't seem like the right word," Thorne said, feeding off Erion's returning misgivings.

"Get out of my head, Thorne."

"Hey. Just because Thorne *can* know things doesn't mean he abuses his power."

"Are you in my head?" Erion sheathed the blade.

"Maybe a little?"

Erion snorted. "Are you even going back to meet with Sadiq tonight?"

"Thorne's all yours for the night. He's supposed to bring you with him in the morning. Make sure you don't sneak away in the night."

"So they still don't trust me?"

Thorne shrugged.

"And I'm stuck with you all day? Isn't that suspicious?"

"Thorne is but a humble gate guard." He paused, wondering whether he should tell Erion he wasn't here on orders. "And also, he's bored."

Erion hesitated. "You want to go to steal some mail?"

CHAPTER TWENTY-THREE

RECONNAISSANCE

Erion led Thorne into the manor, through the main hall, then down a narrow side corridor. With a quick glance to make sure the hall was empty, he pushed Thorne into a storage room. It was little more than a closet. He tapped the hinges and willed the iron to heat up. The hinges sizzled softly and melted together. Nobody would be able to open the door until Erion fixed them.

Thorne raised his brows. "Flattered and all, o Sexually Frustrated One, but Thorne's heart is spoken for."

"Shut up," Erion grinned. "Spoken for?"

"Well. No. But you're not exactly Thorne's type."

"The sentiment is mutual. Move over." Erion pressed his hands against the back wall, listening to the familiar stonewhisper and urging it to shift. After a moment, the wall split along the mortared seams between the blocks of stone. The individual blocks folded in on themselves in a geometric twist until an archway opened into the wall, revealing a gaping passageway.

"Not bad," Thorne whistled. "See many chambermaids in the bath?"

"I'll leave the peeping to you." Erion clapped his hands together, sealing a small pocket of air there. A wisp of flame flickered above his palm, then died. Erion ground his teeth and repeated the gesture. It took him three times, but he finally managed to summon a serviceable sphere of light. The struggle was aggravated by the simplicity of the spell. Edric wasn't the only one who needed instruction from a proper kurios.

"You make this?" Thorne asked as they crept into the tunnel.

"*Shh.* Echoes like mad in here."

The passages long predated Erion. He'd discovered them by accident years ago—when stone had first started whispering its secrets to him. Since then, he'd played his part in expanding the warren of tunnels. They served a greater purpose than spying on maids. Erion had used them to spy on his father.

They reached a narrow, spiraling staircase that led to the guest quarters. Slits of light split the wall at intervals, showing the outside corridors and then, near the top, guest chambers.

Erion paused at a small landing and worked his fingers into the mortar. A horizontal seam widened there, just enough for him to peek into the room beyond. He blinked as his eyes adjusted to the light pouring through the open curtains.

The room beyond was empty. The duke's advisor had unpacked, but several bags were clumped in one corner and his writing satchel lay open on the desk. Erion put his palms flat against the wall. It seemed to breathe as it parted for him.

They padded into the room. Erion crossed to the door to ensure it was locked, then joined Thorne at the writing desk by the windows.

"Lots of good stuff here," Thorne said appreciatively as he sifted through the papers.

"I can't take any of it now... But it looks like I'll need to intercept the carrier tonight." Erion pointed at the topmost letter, addressed to the duke. It seemed innocent enough—a brief summary of their arrival, a note about the baron's apparent seclusion. *That's a nice word for it.*

The letter was clearly unfinished—doubtless the adviser was waiting for further details about the conditions of Rijeka, and the barony at large, before sending his report on to Duke Jesper.

"Sounds like you got the easy job. You just jump the messenger on his way out the gate?" Thorne asked.

"It's a little more complicated than that."

Erion took a small piece of clay from his pocket and rolled it in his hands until it was pliable and flat. After a moment's fishing in the writing satchel, he pulled out two signet rings. He stamped the marks into the clay, then carefully returned the rings.

Thorne was poking through the wardrobe. Erion grabbed the back of his belt and pulled him back to the gap in the wall.

"Thorne was just looking," the man protested as Erion pushed him back into the passage.

Erion hushed him and willed the stone wall back to its original shape. He left a single crack between two stones—a marker for later. Once satisfied there was no evidence of their incursion, he turned his attention back to the small discs of clay. One, a stylized "L," the other a hare.

A hare? Erion squinted at the animal, but there was no doubt. *Some family sigil.*

Erion blew gently on the clay. It hardened, solidifying the imprints. He'd have them for reference later, but could easily smash it to avoid incrimination if necessary.

"This place gives Thorne the creeps." Thorne's whisper could have woken the dead.

"You give *me* the creeps, but you don't hear me complaining."

Erion grounded his awareness into the stone beneath his feet, listening for footsteps in any of the exterior rooms. Once, he'd been lucky and caught his father stealing jewelry from a visiting lady's bureau—though it had only been lucky insofar as it enabled Erion to return the necklace before it could be missed. There was no reason to add theft from a noble to the list of

Niklas's transgressions.

The cadence of the old manor's stone lilted through Erion's body. The sound was comforting—until it wasn't. Erion froze as a discordant note entered the familiar stonewhisper. Thorne crashed into him and they both stumbled down several stairs.

"Watch it, Stoneburner!" Thorne grumbled.

"Wait a moment."

Erion tapped the wall to his left, where several feet of solid construction should separate them from the receiving chambers. Three stones down, Erion tapped into a hollow in the wall.

A shiver trickled down his spine as the stone's voice lowered, changing until it was a sinister hiss of warning. His majea slicked off the wall, struggling for purchase as he tried to sense the structure of the hollow beyond.

Erion's heart thudded in his chest. He knew that oily, resistant strain of magic, though he'd only encountered it once before.

"Thorne has to use the privy."

Erion resisted the urge to bash Thorne's head into the wall. He felt a burning need to investigate the chamber, but breaking into it with Thorne's skull probably wasn't the most efficient way to do it. Malice seeped through the manor's stones.

The hateful awareness was an exact echo of the spite he'd felt at the nuraghi near Lake Zagretsk—the same hellish place Isak had said he was taking Amelie to. Almost sentient in its intensity, the taint of it pulsed through the wall. Erion withdrew his magic, but not before the menace of it turned his stomach.

Thorne poked him.

Erion swallowed his trepidation and hastened down the remaining stairs. He fixed the door hinges with record speed, and the door opened with a click.

"Erion?"

Shit.

Edric stood a pace down the hall, staring at the door. Erion shot his brother a hasty grin and slammed the closet door on Thorne's face. He heard a muffled curse from the other side.

The two brothers stood in awkward silence for a moment, then both tried to speak at once.

"About earlier—" Erion said, just as Edric blurted, "I need your help."

"Anything. But…" Erion glanced back at the closet. "Later, all right? Please?"

Edric's shoulders slumped with resignation.

"I want to help," Erion assured him. "Now's just… not a good time."

"Sure." Edric turned without another word.

The door started to open and Erion leaned against it, forcing it closed again. He pinched the bridge of his nose and scrunched up his eyes, forcing himself to take deep, measured breaths.

Why could it never be just one problem at a time?

Edric rounded the corner, and Erion waited several heartbeats before he let Thorne out. He couldn't bring himself to throw his awareness back into the stone, for fear the nuraghi's taint might overrun the whole place.

Thorne burst across the threshold. "What was *that* about?"

"I guess he'll tell me later." Erion shrugged.

"No, on the stairs. Thought you'd seen a ghost or something."

Or something.

"I thought I heard someone behind us on the stairs," Erion lied.

Thorne narrowed his eyes. "No, you didn't. You and your stoneburner trick. You'd know if someone was behind you."

Erion didn't love it when Thorne was so perceptive. "When are we supposed to meet Isak and the others?"

"Dawn. The witching hour."

"I thought the witching hour was midnight."

"Depends on the witch."

"Uh, sure… Look, do you need anything else? I've got to catch up with—" He jerked his thumb over his shoulder, gesturing to the passage where Edric had disappeared.

"Just don't be late. Isak will blame Thorne, and Thorne will blame Sadiq, and everything will just get ugly from there."

"We wouldn't want things to get ugly." Erion rolled his eyes.

Erion ushered Thorne out of the keep and found Edric in the kitchens several minutes later. His brother was perched on a stool at the end of a long counter, chopping vegetables.

"You giving up life in the stables?" Erion asked, taking a seat across the counter and popping a tomato into his mouth.

"I like it in here." Edric glanced around the busy room and lowered his voice. "I want to dig up that body."

"You *what?*" Erion hissed. He copied Edric's scan of their surroundings. The cook and his assistants were making more than enough noise. They could probably speak freely.

"There was something weird about her. I *did* something weird to her."

"You said she was already sick. I still don't believe that was you." *Please don't let it have been him.*

"I need to understand what happened."

"What you need is to stay the hell away from that clearing." Erion sighed. The next time Edric tried to slip away, he'd find his sabotaged tack. His brother wasn't stupid—he'd know where to lay the blame.

"Something's changed, though. If I'm ever going to understand how this works..." He lowered his voice. "My majea. I have to practice."

"That's what the academy is for. Don't kill yourself before you can get there, kid."

"I'm not a kid," Edric bristled.

Erion lifted his hands in surrender. "I know that. I'm sorry. Look. I told you I'm close. I'm *so close*. You don't have to take any risks like this. Please."

"You take risks all the time."

"Let me be the dumb one."

"What if I do it to someone at the academy? Shrivel them up?" Edric's face was painted with lines of defiance. Erion could tell he'd been thinking about this for a while. Once Edric set his mind to something, dissuading him was almost impossible.

Must run in the family.

"What else is going on?" Erion had been away for too long. There was no way of knowing what other madness Edric had gotten up to in his absence.

Edric's defiance fizzled some. He turned back to the vegetables on the cutting board. "There's been weird creatures in the woods. Near the clearing. And…"

"And?"

"Someone told me about a kidnapping. And a monster."

"Daemanon is lousy with monsters, Edric." Erion would know—he'd killed plenty of them.

"A Human monster."

"You're not going to tell me unless I help you, huh?" Erion asked. He hoped Edric couldn't see how unsettled the news made him. Human monsters, kidnappings—a girl in the woods who'd never sought for help at the guard station like she was supposed to.

And icho dens and assassinations and Crimson Fang tattoos.

Too many secrets. Erion felt himself starting to break under the weight of them.

"This doesn't have anything to do with the Manifestation Festival, does it?" Erion asked after a pause.

"I don't think so." Edric looked thoughtful. "But if I was a healer, you could be my test dummy. I'll hire someone to beat you up and you'll have to sit there and look pathetic while I fixed you up in front of the crowd."

"I'm not sure that would be a crowd-pleaser. The real winners are always something flashy." *Don't encourage him, you idiot.*

"I need to go back. If you don't help me, I'll dig her up myself."

"It will take you forever." Erion had made sure the grave was deep.

"That would give you time to change your mind and come help me."

"Let me think about it?" Erion asked.

"I'll be really busy until the duke's men leave. I have to take care of all their horses," Edric said. "That gives us a few days."

Erion tried to look uninterested in the trip the duke's men were preparing for—one they wouldn't return from.

"I have a bounty tomorrow. I'm leaving early," the lie slipped from Erion's tongue easily. If he thought about the job as a bounty, maybe he'd get through it with his conscience intact.

Maybe.

"What this time?" Edric asked, brightening.

"What?" Erion dragged his mind back to the conversation with difficulty.

"What are you hunting?"

"Oh. Big flock of hate geese."

"Come on, tell the truth."

"Bhirtas'Drada nest. Little bastards are popping up all over the place."

"They should really send a Life Mage to do that one," Edric said. "Your magic isn't much good against them. If I didn't have to take care of the horses..."

"You'd still be staying here." Erion stood and ruffled his little brother's hair. "Be patient. Be *careful*. I'm going to turn in early."

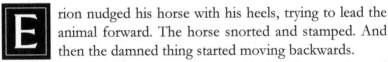

CHAPTER TWENTY-FOUR

AMBUSH

Erion nudged his horse with his heels, trying to lead the animal forward. The horse snorted and stamped. And then the damned thing started moving backwards.

"Thorne is going to leave you behind!" Thorne shouted from the path up ahead.

The woods were still in the soft pre-dawn light. Rare frost clung to some of the branches and leaves, a testament to the storms and unusually low temperatures that had been plaguing the barony the last few weeks. The occasional horse snort or halter jingle were the only sounds marring the quiet morning.

And Erion cursing at his horse. He kicked it in the ribs more fiercely, and the beast jolted forward to catch up with Thorne, who was fighting laughter.

"You gave me this one on purpose," Erion grumbled.

"It's not Thorne's fault you don't know how to ride a horse," Thorne said.

It wasn't worth the argument. A knot of tension had formed between Erion's shoulder blades. It tightened the closer they got to the ambush point, and he couldn't shake the nagging warning in his mind. He was about to cross a line, and he knew it. There was no way out but down. Getting entrenched with the Crimson Fang was supposed to fix his problems—now, the complications were piling up.

Edric would get out, but Erion never would.

Erion and Thorne caught up with the rest of the Crimson Fang. Isak and Sadiq headed the small group. There were two others from Isak's crew—Arent and Roan—but only one other from Sadiq's. Erion exchanged a nod with the latter. He knew Gerard in passing, though they'd never worked together. Erion *had* worked with Arent and Roan before. It wasn't an experience he'd ever hoped to repeat.

"On foot from here. Follow the plan and this will be quick." Isak signaled, and Arent and Roan ran on ahead of the group, unwrapping strings for their longbows as they went.

Erion dismounted and considered the crossbow strapped to his saddle.

"Better have it and not need it," Thorne muttered at his elbow.

"The crossbow?" Erion asked.

"What?" Thorne turned around. His hands were comically full of an array of throwing knives.

"Where do you *keep* all those things?" Even as Erion voiced the question, the blades started to disappear—up Thorne's sleeves, on a bandoleer across his chest, in boots and pockets and gods only knew where else. Erion had to admit it was impressive.

But Thorne was right. Erion took the crossbow and slung it over his back. It was cumbersome, but he could always drop it if necessary. Maybe Sadiq would replace *that*, too. A spelled crossbow was probably hoping for too much.

Isak appeared at Erion's side and handed him a scarlet tunic, trimmed in blue.

"I thought I was posting up ahead?" Erion asked.

The plan was simple enough. Isak, Thorne, and Sadiq would

attack the duke's men from the rear, chasing them across the fields and back onto the road—north, toward the border.

The longbowmen would post atop a ridge at the edge of the fields. They'd handle the first wave of the duke's men as they ran for cover. Erion and Gerard would wait for any stragglers at the choke point further down the road.

If Arent and Roan did their job right, there wouldn't be any survivors. A mercy, if only for Erion. If the duke's men were already dead, Erion wouldn't have to kill anyone.

"Change of plans. You're coming to the fields with me and Sadiq. Thorne's going with Gerard," Isak said.

"Why?" Erion and Thorne asked at the same time.

"Someone might recognize me," Erion said. "That's the whole point of putting me up ahead."

"Do your job right, and it won't matter whether anyone recognizes you," Isak said. "Put that on."

"Gerard smells funny," said Thorne.

Erion ignored both men and looked at the tunic Isak had thrust at him. He didn't recognize the sigils stitched on the breast, but he didn't have to. "Elarazii?"

Isak nodded. "And cover your face."

Erion exchanged a dark glance with Thorne as he slipped the tunic over his head and readjusted his weapons. The new bastard sword rested easily on his hip. The magicked steel hummed when he wrapped his hand around the hilt.

The forest ended abruptly. The growth had been brutally cut back to make room for the agriculture necessary to feed the Barony of Caraz. But instead of rice or cassava in the field beyond, brilliant buds of faint purple shrouded the ground. In some places, the v'deru plant was already blossoming, petals opening to soak in the early morning sun.

"Are they in season?" Erion wondered aloud.

"How should I know?" Sadiq asked.

Erion shrugged. Edric liked to talk about planting seasons and growth schedules. Erion would have thought it was too cold to grow the leech petals, and these were freshly sprouted.

Life Magic. Someone was helping the plants grow by adding nutrients to the soil, encouraging the tiny buds to open and the roots to dig deep.

What was the field doing *here*, and why had the baron arranged for the duke's men to visit this site? Erion ran over a list of uses of v'deru in his mind—it was short, and none of the applications pleasant.

Erion touched Sadiq's elbow, and they fell behind Isak.

"Tell me what's going on," Erion said hoarsely. Too many things weren't lining up. "First you tell me you need to plant me inside the baron's house. It looks like you already have someone there."

"I knew you weren't stupid," Sadiq said with a twisted smile.

"Who is it? What are we doing here?"

"Defending the v'deru. Nobody can know about it."

"*Then why bring them here?*" Erion hissed.

"The Ithynon wants them dead. What he wants, he gets."

Several things clicked into place in Erion's mind. "And we're claiming the icho is being imported from Elarazii."

Proximity to the border between the two duchies had its advantages. The more attention the Crimson Fang could draw away from Rijeka, the better. If they were careful enough, they could slip drugs over the border and split the suspicion between the two duchies. It would take longer for the dukes to collaborate on solutions to the trafficking.

"How much of it is in Elarazii?" Erion had always been so focused on the crisis at hand, he'd never considered the scope of the icho ring outside of his city, let alone neighboring duchies.

"We're expanding, but the dens haven't really taken hold in the cities yet. Mathieu has footholds all over the south banks of Lake Zagretsk. The actual v'deru is processed across the border, then brought upriver. You must have noticed that."

Erion had been on plenty of the smuggling routes, he'd just never really noted where the smugglers were coming from. Most of the time he didn't even know what the caravans carried. He'd always figured that the less he knew, the better.

How things have changed.

"So, who do you have working in the baron's estate? Is it Halek?" The baron's manservant had access to the manor and all of the baron's personal effects and ledgers.

"No." But Sadiq didn't deny there was someone pulling strings.

"What's in it for me if I agree to become the next steward?" Erion asked.

"You'll prove we can trust you."

Erion didn't miss the unspoken *or else.*

"Keeping my silence about the girl wasn't enough to prove you can trust me?" Erion finally broached the subject he'd been avoiding for so long. Sadiq was up to something, but he wasn't sure he wanted to be involved in whatever it was.

"Later." Sadiq pointed down the road. A small group of riders approached the v'deru field from the south.

Erion tightened his grip on the hilt of his sword. The extravagant blade felt more like a bribe now than ever. It was clear Sadiq was intent on buying him, but why?

The only thing Erion could do was wait. He'd do what he came here to do. If it finally gave everyone the proof they demanded, maybe they would stop breathing down his neck.

I'll do penance later. Somehow, Erion would make up for it. Someday, he'd repay his dues.

Isak and Sadiq fell into crouches and covered their faces as the duke's men followed the worn path around the field of v'deru. Nine riders approached at a quick trot. Erion shaded his eyes with his hand, squinting at the approaching party. His heart sank into his gut.

He'd known it was coming, but nothing could have prepared him for the jolt he felt as he recognized two of the riders. Durant Vinke was tall, sallow, his pale complexion stark even from this distance. He'd been working with Erion's father as the steward's assistant for nearly two years—ever since Erion had rejected the prospect himself.

And Hugo, the gate guard who'd gone out of his way to

make sure Edric got his own key to the stables, so the boy could go see the horses whenever he wanted.

Erion closed his eyes.

A tree exploded a few paces behind the contingent's horses. Erion dropped to his stomach and covered his head as shards of wood flew in every direction. The horses in the back of the group reared and bucked. Swearing filled the air as the men struggled to regain control of their mounts.

Erion hadn't been briefed on *this* part of the plan. He looked around wildly. Isak was holding a small ceramic disc. The duke's men formed into a tight group. One of the riders nudged his horse toward the tree line.

Isak drew a line onto the disc. Another tree blew apart, sending its foliage and splinters out in a wide arc. The riders broke, urging their mounts down the path, straight toward Erion.

Isak hefted a boar spear and leapt to his feet as the first rider reached them. He hurled the spear. It struck the oncoming man low in the chest, and the rider slumped sideways in his saddle.

And then it was chaos. Erion lost track of the baron's men as horses bolted down the path.

One of the mounted knights bore down on Erion, sword held aloft. Erion parried. The two blades sang as they glanced off one another.

Erion reached into that song of steel and pulled on it. The knight's sword wrenched from his hand. Erion scrambled to recover the fallen weapon.

The blade was notched where the two swords had clashed. Erion touched his hand to the broken edge and tapped into his majea once more. The blade snapped in two at the weak spot.

"Watch out!" Sadiq shouted.

Erion dropped the broken sword and rolled to the side before another horse could trample him. He scrabbled backwards, digging his mind into the earth as he retreated. Stone burst up behind the horse's hooves, cracking and showering debris on rider and horse alike as they barreled down the path—

towards Arent and Roan's waiting longbows.

Isak and Sadiq had the other riders on a hard retreat. Two men were dead, another slumped low in his saddle as they charged down the road. Erion came up to his knees and cranked back the string on his crossbow.

He dropped the lever in the dirt as he slipped the bolt into place and aimed.

Fired.

The bolt took one of the retreating riders high in the shoulder. Erion tried to ignore the familiar gray cloak as he drew another bolt from the quiver.

Crank. Bolt. Aim.

Fire. The bolt struck the retreating horse's flank, and an animal shriek of pain filled the air. Droplets of dark blood rained on the ground behind it.

Hugo fell.

"Take care of him," Sadiq yelled at Erion. He and Isak ran after the remaining riders, leaving Erion surrounded by bleeding men. At least one of the duke's knights was still alive. His breathing was interspersed with wet, gurgling sounds. There was blood in his lungs. He wouldn't last long.

If he didn't kill Hugo, Sadiq or one of the others would come back and finish the guard off.

If Erion didn't kill Hugo, the Crimson Fang leaders would know he couldn't be trusted. A man who might intentionally botch a job was a man who'd wake up with a blade in his chest. If Erion didn't kill him, Isak or Sadiq would come back and finish him off anyway.

But if Erion *did* kill him... He lifted the crossbow to his shoulder, heart pounding in his chest. He didn't want to see the light fade from this man's eyes.

Hugo looked up at Erion, and their eyes met. For one fleeting moment, hope flared on the man's face. Bile rose in Erion's throat.

The crossbow bolt tore through Hugo's neck.

CHAPTER TWENTY-FIVE
GROUNDWORK

Sadiq cut Duke Jesper's sigil off one of the fallen knights' tunics and handed it to Thorne, along with the others he'd collected. "Burn these before we get back to the city."

It wasn't the kind of thing they could afford to leave lying around. The bodies would be incriminating enough. To the casual observer, this had to look like a random attack by bandits. If anyone got close enough, they'd find empty purses and ransacked gear. With luck, it would be nightfall before the baron would send anyone to investigate. The Crimson Fang would be well away by the time anyone actually found the scene.

"Can Thorne keep this?" Thorne held out a long silver chain with an amethyst the size of his thumb dangling from it. A token from some lady, no doubt. A woman waiting at home for a man who would never return.

"Most of us would just shove it in our boot and pretend it didn't exist," Sadiq pointed out. He never could get a read on Thorne—but he suspected that was exactly the way Thorne liked it. It was enough incentive for Sadiq to keep him under close watch.

Thorne shrugged.

"Shove it in your boot, and let's get out of here," Sadiq said.

The plan had gone off without a hitch. Not even Isak's men, Arent and Roan, had managed to screw up the ambush. Sadiq wasn't convinced they weren't very small, hairless trolls. But they could shoot, and that was all that mattered.

He'd chafed when Mathieu told him that he'd be splitting the job with Isak instead of taking the whole bounty for his own crew. If things went sideways, the bounties would be Sadiq's problem, and he had too much at stake to go underground now. Sadiq had spent years watching Mathieu. The man's caution had given the Crimson Fang the upper hand in Rijeka, and now he had his mind set on moving his crew into Elarazii. Fresh territory, new opportunities, less oversight.

The only question was which of his lieutenants Mathieu planned on bringing with him on his climb.

"Where's Erion?" Sadiq asked Thorne.

"The stoneburner went back to check the fields. Something about trees?"

Sadiq nodded, understanding. Isak had been so proud of the detonators he'd bought from a Line Mage in the market. He'd insisted they'd spook the horses and ensure the duke's men ran straight into their ambush. In the end, Sadiq hadn't been able to talk him out of it. He hadn't bothered to tell Isak how much he'd overpaid for the spells—watching the brute get swindled was free entertainment.

As Sadiq had predicted, the fallout from the spells was astronomical. Maybe Erion had come up with a way to minimize the damage. Sadiq climbed into his saddle and nudged his horse down the road, where he found Erion sitting with his back against a tree trunk.

"It's done," Erion said when Sadiq reached him.

"Clear up ahead, too. What's done?"

"I buried the trees, did what I could to get all the pieces out of the road. What *was* that?" Erion asked.

"Bit of clever idiocy Isak picked up in the Empori District. Line Magic." The two discs had been linked. Isak had embedded one deep into the tree's trunk and kept the other with him. Once he completed the spell on one of the ceramic discs, the other had burst apart, shredding the trees from the inside out.

Sadiq followed Erion's gaze to a body in the middle of the road. The man wore Baron Voloy's gray livery.

"You knew him," Sadiq said.

Erion nodded. He opened his mouth as though to speak, then shook his head and held his silence.

"It was cruel of Mathieu to send you." Sadiq walked to the fallen guard and crouched down to inspect the body. A bolt from Erion's crossbow stuck out from the man's neck. The ground beneath him was marred with hoofprints and dark, dried blood.

"Can the bolt be traced back to you?" Sadiq asked.

Erion shook his head. Sadiq took a corner of the guard's cloak and covered the man's face with it, then stood and joined Erion.

"You did well," he told Erion.

"How much is this job worth?" Erion croaked, refusing to meet Sadiq's gaze.

"For you? Two hundred."

A shadow of rage flickered across Erion's face.

"You knew him well?" Sadiq asked.

"Well enough." Erion let out a ragged breath. "When do you tell me what's going on?"

"When you earn it."

"How many more innocent men do I have to kill before I get to stop worrying about a knife in my back? We both know Isak would be happy to do it. What happened to the protection Mathieu promised me?"

Sadiq worked to keep a satisfied smile off his face. Erion was almost ready.

"What do you want out of this, Erion?" Sadiq took the reins

of his horse and gestured for Erion to walk with him. They started their way back up the road toward Isak and the others. The two walked in silence until they reached the break in the road where the rest of the gang was waiting for them.

"I just want what I was promised. My fair cut. I'm not a second-rate cutthroat anymore. I'm *blooded*."

"Thorne would like to go home now!" Thorne's voice rang out.

"You're not going home, you lout," Sadiq called back.

"You mean Thorne still has to go back to that murder-dungeon? Make the new guy do it."

"Not the nuraghi?" Erion's face went a few shades paler. "What's going on?"

"I'll explain it to you when we get back to the city. Do you like the sword?" Sadiq nodded at the blade at Erion's side.

Erion didn't fall for the change in subject. "I can count, Sadiq. Eight bodies. *Eight*."

It hadn't taken Erion long to realize which body was missing. Sadiq waited for the accusation.

"Just how long has Durant Vinke been working for the Crimson Fang?" Erion asked.

"That doesn't concern you."

"Like hell it doesn't! You've already planted Vinke in the manor. Why do you need me?"

"Have you made up your mind about taking the job, then?" Sadiq asked. He needed to be sure he had Erion well in hand before divulging his plans—he couldn't afford any leaks.

"Are you joking? After *that*?" Erion wiped a hand over his mouth, looking like he was going to be sick. He glanced over his shoulder at the bodies in the road. "I'm in."

CHAPTER TWENTY-SIX
MORE POTENT THAN BREATH

Drazan Voloy paced the protective circle in the bowels of the nuraghi. A ring of torches encircled the stone altar, casting ghostly shadows on the ground. Cedivar hovered by the altar, the only audience to Drazan's outrage.

Well, *almost* the only audience. A body lay tied to the altar. The man was unconscious, and a poor sounding board.

The latest experiment had failed fantastically. At first, it was almost enough to give Drazan hope. He was close—he could practically taste the victory. The girl had come back; heart pumping, nerves firing, lungs expanding. She could even speak, after a fashion. Cedivar's newest recruit, a Love Magician named Petyr, had managed to bring back a glimmer to the girl's eye, and enough sense of self to arise terrified. She'd been stricken by her sudden awakening in the dark of Drazan's labs.

But then she, too, had fallen silent, and then after a few fleeting minutes, died.

The efforts had drained Drazan's energy. His own, and the last of the majea he'd stored in the zomajea crystals recovered from the Reinholdt ruins.

Drazan had need of two things. More power, and to find the girl who'd gotten away—the one they'd thought had died, but somehow evaded the diggers and escaped. He'd used the exact same formula twice now, with disappointing results.

There had been something different about the girl who'd escaped. Drazan had a sneaking suspicion he knew what it was, but he wouldn't voice the idea until he'd had a chance to research it. If they found her—*alive*—he might have his answers.

Hang on a little longer, my love. I am doing all I can.

"Why have your scouts not found her?" Drazan ceased his pacing and rounded on Cedivar.

"It could be that the girl is dead, my lord." Cedivar hesitated. "Again."

"The formula would still be in her veins. They still have her bones. They still have her *scent*." That wouldn't have changed even if the body had fallen apart completely. Drazan grimaced. That had happened before. The memory still haunted him.

"Perhaps she's found a way to mask her signature."

"You assured me that wasn't possible. All the time you've spent tinkering with those damned hounds—*wasted*." It was a simple enough equation. The bone scouts had failed.

"We will keep looking, my lord."

Drazan moved to the foot of the altar, where the grooves in the stone table met the carved basin at one end. "Do it now."

Cedivar bowed his head and moved to the body on the altar. He withdrew his dagger, a blade spelled with symmajea of Cedivar's own making. As always, Drazan's feelings about the mage flickered. He needed Cedivar, and was often impressed by him, but he tired of the constant promises that fell short of their mark.

Drazan centered himself as Cedivar's blade slashed the unconscious man's throat. It was easier when they were unconscious—Drazan couldn't handle the screaming, the look in their eyes that mirrored his own pain.

He was so close.

Blood spurted then sank into the altar as though pulled down by a lodestone. It streamed through the grooves carved in the stone and trickled into the basin. Cedivar leaned across the body and sliced into a second artery.

Drazan held his hands over the zomajca crystals in the basin. The thirst in them radiated through him. Steam rose in whirls above the basin as the blood pooled around the stones. Drazan seized the blood with his majea. Vitality surged through his hands, and he directed that power into the stones. His palms tingled where they made contact with the artifacts as Life Magic—the purest form of all majea—raged through him.

For precious heartbeats, Drazan *was* power. He was drunk on the raging force that swept through him and into the ancient artifacts that he'd bent to his will.

The artifacts devoured the energy from the sacrifice's blood with eternal hunger. The vortex crept to the edge of Drazan's power, prodding at his life force when the majea in the blood was gone.

Drazan's mind and his majea melted into the torrent of power. He teetered on the brink of that seeking void, caught in a current that threatened to carry him away.

"*I* am the master!" The words tore from Drazan's throat as he threw his will at the stones. He snapped his connection with the seeking tendrils of energy. Flaring heat scalded his palms. He pulled them away from the crystals with a gasp.

Drazan slumped and cradled his hands in front of him. The higher the energy transfer, the stronger the pull from the crystals.

"Are you well, my lord?" Cedivar knelt beside him.

"Fine," Drazan snapped, heaving as he tried to catch his breath. It had been close, that time. He closed his eyes and pressed his palms against them, wondering at the ocean of energy that had passed through his body and into the waiting stones. It was so much simpler than the mess of siphoning drops of majea from icho crystals—and there was no comparison at all to the returns.

Blood was magnitudes more potent than breath.

"What kind of mage was he?" Drazan asked after long moments.

"Gekurios, we think."

"We?"

Cedivar bristled. "Naturally, I have informants who alert me to potential candidates."

"Why did you bring me a sacrifice if you weren't certain he was a mage?" Drazan demanded. There wasn't enough time to leave this to chance. Once he had the missing girl, he'd have the right equation—he knew it in his bones and his heart.

He just needed enough power to charge the final spell.

"There was a collective of them, working in tandem on a logging crew. We wanted the Life Mage, but my informant wasn't sure which was working the trees and which the currents. I instructed him not to get too close and seize whichever he could most easily get."

"We need more."

"I have plans for that."

"See that they work. And quickly."

"By the Kuriositar, my lord."

That gave Drazan a little time—time for the bone scouts to recover the girl, hopefully. Time for him to test a few more subjects. Whether it would be before Pelinon decided to rain its helpful oversight down on the barony was yet to be seen.

A Guardian could be dealt with.

Drazan Voloy had come too far to be stopped by a Guardian of Pelinon now. A glimmer of light at the end of this trial started to form in his mind. Duke Jesper's men were handled, and Cedivar was cutting ties with the Crimson Fang—though that part was a detail Drazan needn't worry about.

Once he healed Jolie, they'd leave Caraz behind—and Drazan would finally have his peace.

CHAPTER TWENTY-SEVEN
THE PRICE OF SURVIVAL

Erion woke in a cold sweat. He struggled upright, fighting the blankets twisted around his chest. His hand shot to his belt—but his sword was hanging on the back of his chair several feet away. Erion let out a ragged breath and collapsed back onto his small bed in the baron's estate.

The only monster in the room was him.

His gaze drifted toward a bottle of whiskey near his chair. Unopened. Just out of reach.

Erion swallowed and averted his gaze, choosing to stare at the ceiling instead. Sadiq's words echoed through his mind as he stared at the wooden planks. He'd counted them over and over before falling asleep. Tracing constellations in the knots that mottled the wood with his eyes.

Tried, and failed, and tried again to forget that glimmer of hope in Hugo's eyes.

Just before Erion had killed him.

"When you earn it," Sadiq had said.

Erion didn't want to earn Sadiq's trust.

Looking back, Erion couldn't believe his naivete. He'd rationalized that joining the Crimson Fang was a viable solution to his problems, fooled himself into believing it couldn't be worse than what he was already doing for them. He'd trusted himself to find a way to be a good person.

Blood spattered from Hugo's neck, brilliant against the dusty road.

Erion scrunched his eyes against the memory. *Edric. Remember Edric.*

"It was cruel of Mathieu to send you."

Night had fallen, but more sleep would be a long time coming.

Nine men in the contingent they'd ambushed today, but only eight bodies. There was no way they thought Erion was that stupid. They'd meant him to see Durant at the head of that column of men.

Being the baron's steward would be dull, repetitive work—but it was better than the killing.

"Erion!" A fist banged on Erion's door as Edric shouted at him. "Come quickly!"

Erion shot a look of regret at the unopened whiskey. He waved his hand at the door and cast a thread of majea at it. The bolt lifted and Edric burst across the threshold.

"Durant Vinke is dying."

Blood pounded in Erion's head. "I just saw him."

"Wha—no, he's been gone all day. But he just got back." Edric's eyes were wide with panic. He paced back and forth across Erion's small room.

"Calm down, everything's going to be fine. So he's still alive?" Erion's mind reeled. How long had he been asleep? Durant had escaped—he should have returned hours ago.

"The physician says he can't be saved. I thought if you could get me to him…"

"Don't even think about it," Erion snarled. He didn't want Edric within fifty feet of Durant, alive *or* dead. "If Gian says he can't be saved, he can't be saved."

"But they don't have a lifeweaver. They've sent for one, but he won't make it that long. I could tell." Edric's voice was thick with emotion.

Erion buckled his sword to his belt and pulled on his boots. "Stay here."

Still, Edric followed him down the corridor and into the small medical quarters where the baron's healer resided.

The rooms had never been intended to hold so many people. Men and women clustered around the door, craning their necks to get a look at the healer as he worked. Erion barged through them, heedless of their hisses of displeasure and the disgruntled looks he received from the servants.

Durant Vinke lay on the physician's table. His eyes were closed, but his chest rose and fell with weak breaths. His clothes had been cut away from his chest, the strip of his shirt indiscernible from the bloody rags used to clean his wounds. The physician, a short, wiry man named Gian, grimaced at Erion as he pushed into the room.

The smell overwhelmed Erion at once—acrid, coppery-tinged blood, and the sickly, malodorous stench of a pierced abdomen. He pulled his tunic over his mouth and nose. It was a wonder the physician could stand to stay in the room.

Gian held a blood-soaked cloth against Durant's side. He lifted it away and dropped it into a basin. A single, razor-thin cut ran horizontally across one side of Durant's chest, just beneath his ribcage. Gian pressed another rag against it, determinedly applying pressure to an injury that refused to stop bleeding.

One blade, one cut. Deadly precision. Edric was right—Durant was dead. His body just hadn't accepted it yet.

"What happened?" Erion asked.

Gian shot him a dirty look, and Erion took a step back on instinct. He had no authority here, no reason for Gian to answer to him. And Erion already knew what had happened. Durant had survived the ambush, but not the day.

Erion had finally agreed to take Durant's place as their man inside the baron's household. In doing so, he'd made Durant unnecessary. Now Mathieu had gone out of his way to send a powerful message: Nobody was safe.

CHAPTER TWENTY-EIGHT

SANCTUARY

Edric pushed through the crowd pressing against the healer's ward, trying to get a glimpse inside. His shoulders had broadened over the last year, and most people moved out of his way without complaint. Erion was in hushed conversation with Gian. They both looked up warily when Edric reached the front of the huddled servants.

"You don't need to see this," Erion said tersely.

"What happened?" Edric forced himself to look at Durant's body. Dried blood crusted his abdomen, leaking from a single wound just below his ribs.

Life wasn't pretty, Edric reminded himself. He'd spent his life in Erion's shadow, letting his brother shelter him from the worst of their father's addiction and the things Erion had done to keep the family out of debt. Edric resisted pressing a hand to his churning stomach as he looked at Durant's injury. Erion wouldn't be around to protect him forever.

Gian frowned at the body on the table. "He was attacked."

"Obviously." Erion closed his eyes and pinched the bridge

of his nose as though pained. "Edric, please."

"I want to see." There was so much unearthed potential in Edric's abilities—skills he'd never practiced. That would have required revealing his talent, and Erion wouldn't hear of it.

If a lifeweaver had been here when Durant arrived, maybe he would still be alive. And if Edric was a proper lifeweaver, that woman in the forest might still be alive, too.

Erion's face was gaunt. There were dark circles under his eyes, and that new, enormous sword hung from his waist. It had been years since Edric had seen his brother so on edge. He didn't think Erion had known Durant very well. Besides, in Edric's experience, anyone who *did* know Durant well didn't like him much.

So why was Erion so upset about his death?

Edric stepped closer and touched Durant's hand. It was clammy. He reached out with his majea, searching for a spark. Any sign that Durant might be saved.

Erion smacked his hand away. Edric glared at his brother. They were nearly of a height, but where Erion was all slender, corded muscle, Edric's work in the stables and fields had broadened his shoulders and built heavy muscle. He wasn't so much smaller than his brother anymore.

"Stop that. Let's go." Erion ushered Edric out of the healer's room. Edric glanced over his shoulder to see Gian watching them leave with narrowed eyes.

"What were you thinking?" Erion hissed when they were out of earshot from the others.

"I could have helped him."

"You could *not*." Erion heaved a sigh. "What was it you wanted to tell me yesterday?"

"You won't like it," Edric said.

"Tell me something I don't already know."

"Something weird is going on."

"Yeah?" Erion didn't even try to hide his sarcasm. "Actually, no. Not here. Do you still have your hideout? Can we go there?"

Edric's shoulders dropped. He'd wanted to warn Erion

before they got there, but now he worried Erion would never go if he knew what was going on. "Yes, but—"

"Great. Let's go now."

When they reached the stables, Erion took an unfamiliar bridle off its hook and handed it to Edric.

"Uhm…" Edric tried to hand it back, but Erion set his jaw and shoved it into his hands.

Edric glanced at his brother sidelong as he turned to his own tack. A quick inspection showed damage to bridle and saddle. He turned an accusatory glare onto Erion.

"It's a long story." Erion grunted.

"*You* did this? Why?" Edric demanded.

"For your own damn good. Just goes to show half-baked plans never survive first contact."

"First contact with what?" Edric wasn't sure whether he was more furious or confused.

"We're wasting time." Erion turned away to saddle his horse.

Edric's temper rose as he inspected his tack. All of it was ruined.

"Here." Erion threw a bridle at him.

"This isn't mine," Edric protested.

"I thought you wanted to get out of here?"

Edric gritted his teeth. He didn't want to press Erion more than necessary today. There was too much at stake. He saddled Caz and left the stables without waiting for Erion to catch up. They rode in silence until they reached the wall of plants that guarded Edric's hideout.

"I'm not letting you in until you listen to what I have to say," Edric said.

"What's so important it can't wait until we're inside?" Erion swung down from the saddle. "Actually, if it's so important, we really should be talking about it *inside*, because—"

"Erion," Edric snapped. "Shut *up*."

"Make it quick." Erion's eyes darted around the woods, and Edric knew he would be searching through the ground for—for what? Was someone following them?

But he had to warn Erion before they went into the clearing. Before—

Erion stiffened and turned toward the wall of glodis vines. "Go back. Someone's in there."

"That's what I've been trying to tell you!" Edric exploded. "I've been trying to get you out here because I need your help, but you're too thick-headed and self-important to give a damn what I have to say!"

"What's going on?" Erion's voice was calm, but his eyes glittered dangerously. Erion didn't lose his temper often, but when he did...

"A friend is in there. She needed help. Someone hurt her, and I'm trying to help find out why."

"How do you know we can trust her?"

"*We?*" Edric almost laughed. "I had to decide on my own, since you never talk to me anymore. But I thought you already knew her. She had your cloak and said you—"

"Not *Amelie?*" Erion gaped.

Edric nodded.

"Get us inside. *Now.*"

Edric bristled at the order. Erion had no idea what was going on, no right to tell Edric what to do. Erion wasn't his father—he was barely around anymore.

But Edric still needed his help. He summoned his dignity and put a hand out to the barrier. The flora parted, creating an opening just big enough for the two brothers to lead their horses into the clearing.

"I knew you'd come back," a soft voice said as the barrier closed behind them.

"I promised I would," Edric said, looking over at Amelie. Edric had tried to get her to stay at a nearby inn, but she'd refused to leave once he'd brought her to the clearing. She didn't believe that anywhere else was safe. Instead, he'd stolen fresh clothes and woven tree boughs into a shelter to keep her out of the rain.

"Not you. Him." Amelie gestured at Erion with her chin.

"Someone better start explaining," Erion said.

"What do you mean? You sent her to find me," Edric said.

"I sent her to *Captain Talbot*. He said she never showed up."

"*She* is standing right here!" Amelie shouted. "And she's just as confused as you lot!"

"Fine. Everybody calm down." Erion lifted his hands in a pacifying gesture.

"Don't tell me what to do," Edric snapped.

Amelie rounded on Erion. "I did exactly what you told me to. Went to the guardhouse and asked for Talbot. Then I met the *steward's son*. How was I supposed to know there were two of you?"

Erion opened his mouth as though to argue, then screwed up his face with frustration. "*Shit.*"

"I thought you wanted me to help her." The fight went out of Edric all at once when he realized what must have happened. Part of him had believed that Erion was finally trusting him with something important. Amelie had been looking for *a* steward's son—and she hadn't known enough to realize she'd found the wrong one. She may have believed Erion had intended for Edric to help her, but it was clear Erion had fumbled his instructions.

He didn't trust Edric with much of anything. Why should this be an exception?

"She *did* need help but…" Erion pinched the bridge of his nose as though pained, then turned to Amelie. "How much have you told him?"

"Only that you helped me escape."

"Did Isak hurt you?" Erion asked.

"Who?" Edric was lost already. Amelie had insisted on waiting for Erion to explain what was going on. All Edric really knew was something terrible had happened to her.

"The blond guy? No." Amelie shook her head and looked at Erion. "You helped Mira get away, that night in the alley."

Erion grunted.

Edric glanced back and forth between the two, totally lost. "Helped who?"

"Don't worry about it." Deep frown lines creased Erion's forehead into an expression Edric recognized too well. He wouldn't be getting any more information out of his brother on the topic.

"Erion, we need to dig up the body," Edric said, forcing the subject back to his original concern.

"What does that have to do with *her*?" Erion raked his hands through his hair until it practically stood on end.

"It has to do with *this*." Amelie raised a heavily bandaged hand. Erion just stared.

"They cut off one of her fingers," Edric said quietly. "She won't tell me why."

"He did *what*?" Erion asked.

"Not your friend. The... the other one."

"Isak isn't my friend," Erion hissed. "Explain—everything. Now."

Amelie's eyes flickered to Edric. He gave her an encouraging nod. Erion was being a pain in the ass, but if they couldn't trust him, they couldn't trust anyone.

"After that night in the alley, those men—I don't know their names—brought me to a prison cell and left me."

"Where?" Erion asked.

"I was blindfolded. I don't know." Amelie took a deep breath. "A man fed us—there were two others. And then he used a chisel and mallet to... to cut off a finger. From each of us."

"What did he look like? Red hair?" Erion asked.

Edric stared at his brother. He'd had his suspicions that Erion wasn't just taking up bounties and killing monsters—he'd been bringing in too much coin for that. But how had he managed to get caught up in something like *this*?

"Not red, white. Long. He wasn't old, though." A furrow formed between Amelie's brows as she thought. "He took the other two women away. And I heard aw—awful things. Screaming. And the smells... like rotting flesh and ash but I... And then I knew I was next and—"

Her chest rose and fell with rapid breaths. Edric touched her shoulder and led her to a nearby tree. They all sat. Amelie drew her knees up and hugged them to her chest. Her eyes were open, but she was staring at something far away—some horror only she could see.

"Sorry," she said weakly. "They said they needed to move me. That's when they gave me to your friend. Isak?"

"Not my friend," Erion repeated.

"And then you found me." Amelie shivered and dropped her eyes. A weighted pause filled the air.

"So… I really need to look at that body again." Edric turned a pleading look on his older brother. "That woman was probably being chased by the same people who took Amelie."

"It's not your fight, Edric. The important thing is that she's safe now."

"*Erion.* It might mean I didn't do… whatever it was… to her. Somebody else…" Edric faltered. He'd spent weeks living in fear of his powers, terrified that something he'd done had inadvertently killed the last woman he'd tried to help.

There was no imagining what Amelie had been through, or how much strength it had taken for her to run away. After everything that had happened, it was amazing she had even trusted Erion enough to follow his instructions to find help.

"It's not your fight." Erion was practically pleading now.

"How can you just sit back and watch something like this happen?" Edric demanded. What had changed in his brother? Edric felt like he was arguing with a stranger.

"No—look, there's more going on here. Things you don't understand. The plan hasn't changed. We're getting you out of here next term. All right? I've saved up enough."

"Where are you getting all this money?" Edric asked. "And how do you know the people who kidnapped her?"

Edric couldn't believe that Erion was involved in trafficking—Erion, who was so quick to condemn their father for his addiction. He'd always stressed how important it was to do the right thing. So what in Kalistar's name was going on?

"Not your fight," Erion breathed. "I won't help you dig her up."

"If you don't, I'll find somebody else who will. I'll go back to the estate right now and get a crew to help me dig. I swear it."

Edric was prepared to lead the whole estate to the hideout if it meant getting to the bottom of this evil—to get justice for Amelie and the others like her. He crossed his arms and glared at Erion, who glared right back.

Amelie's head rested on her knees. She let out a muffled sob, then took a shaky breath. "You're both idiots."

"*Fine.*" Erion got to his feet. "On the condition that you don't tell anyone about this until I agree to it. Deal?"

"Deal." Edric said coolly. That much he could handle—for now.

CHAPTER TWENTY-NINE
DECAY

Erion wrinkled his nose as he peered into the open grave. A thin layer of damp earth still covered the body he'd gone to such lengths to hide. Sickly tendrils of rot and stale air wafted up from the grave's depths. "This is disgusting."

"This is *necessary*." Edric crouched by the hole, squinting down at the figure below. "Be careful."

"I'm always careful." But even as Erion said it, he had to admit it wasn't true. Most of the time he was about as subtle as a warhammer with his gemajea. Mindlessly scooping a grave out of the earth was one thing—flinging dirt indiscriminately was something he could handle. This would require finesse.

His mind sifted through the layers of dirt and clay, trying to lift them all as a single unit, but there were too many pieces of sediment to keep track of. Erion gritted his teeth. *Fine, new strategy.* He willed the dirt under the body to harden, compressing the sediments together until they formed a mostly solid layer. It took more energy than he'd expected, but a moment later the earth beneath the corpse began to move upwards.

With a snarl, Erion yanked the fragile slab of compressed earth upwards. The woman's body barreled toward the surface. Loose dirt spilled over the sides of the grave. With a final force of will, Erion shoved the earth away from the grave.

The woman's body tumbled and rolled several feet before coming to a stop face down on the grass.

"*Daemonshite*, Erion." Edric hurried around the hole and knelt beside the body. Gently, he rolled the woman's body onto its back.

"Disgusting," Erion said again. He dropped to the ground and dangled his legs over the edge of the grave, breathing heavily.

"Research." Edric's tone was lofty, but Erion noticed his brother wipe his hands on the grass after he'd moved the body.

The decay had spread, but not in the way Erion had expected. He leaned forward to get a closer look despite himself. The decomposition hadn't so much turned the body squishy as it had hardened it somehow. Instead of falling apart and putrefying, the woman's body was rail stiff. Darkened skin stretched across her bones, emphasizing her cheekbones and the hollow of her eyes.

It was almost like she'd been mummified. But they'd just pulled her out from under ten feet of damp, dense soil, waterlogged by the winter rains. It wasn't possible. She should have been worm food by now.

"The same finger is gone." Edric almost looked triumphant, but then the color drained from his face as he seemed to remember what they were doing. He sat back on his heels. Peering down at the body, he mused, "What *happened* to you?"

Erion wanted the answer to that, too. He glanced over his shoulder at Amelie, who hadn't moved from her tree at the edge of the clearing. He couldn't blame her.

"What are you hoping to get out of this?" Erion asked Edric.

"I just need to know I didn't do this."

"I thought we'd already decided that."

"She must have been taken by the same people who took Amelie." Edric's brow furrowed, and he looked up at Erion. A shadow of doubt crossed over his face.

Erion took a deep breath and wondered how much he could tell Edric and still keep him safe. Now that his brother was tangled up in this, it would be hell trying to get him out of it.

"I don't know what's going on. But I'll find out." Erion settled on not telling Edric anything. *The less he knows, the better.*

"You're lying to me," Edric accused.

"You're not a heartbender," Erion said, deadpan.

"I'm your brother."

"All the more reason for you to trust me."

"I don't, though." Edric's gaze turned to frost. "I know you've been lying about the bounties you're collecting. You're making too much coin. You like to think I'm blind to everything going on—to father's addiction and how close he is to getting sacked, to everything. But I'm not stupid, and I'm not buying it anymore."

"You don't want to know," Erion tried.

"What do you know about all this? How did you run into *her*?" Edric gestured at Amelie. "And who's Isak?"

"A pain in my ass, that's who. I was on a job up north when I found Amelie. Not far from here, actually." The truth. "And one of the men I was working with helped her to escape." Also truth.

"You just conveniently ran into them in the woods?" Edric clearly didn't buy it.

"More or less."

"And what happened to the guy who was moving her? Isak."

"He got away."

"Tell me you're not a part of this," Edric said.

"I'm not a part of this." Erion answered on instinct—too fast. Edric clenched his fists.

"Why won't you tell me what's going on?"

"To protect you."

"*Stop protecting me.*"

"Once you go to Saritu'e'Mere, you won't need my protection. Better? Then we'll both be happy."

Edric stared at him in disbelief. "You're mad if you think I'm taking any of your coin. Blood money from trafficking or murders or who knows what else? No. Never."

"You—"

"I'll do it myself. I don't need you."

Erion sprawled back in the grass and stared up at the gray sky. He was tempted to tell Edric everything—about the deal he'd made with the Crimson Fang years ago, and how everything he'd done since the gang had come to collect Niklas's debt had been to protect Edric.

Edric would never understand. Erion rubbed his eyes, too tired to think. Everything he'd done flashed before his mind's eye in a blur. Hunting atlas cobras and ikunem with Thorne. Guarding smugglers' caravans. Murdering Hugo.

He'd give Edric some time to cool off. He would come around. He had to.

Erion closed his eyes, listening to Edric murmur to himself as he poked and prodded the body. What he was looking for was anyone's guess—healing was one skill he knew Edric hadn't studied. Who would he have practiced on?

A howl rose on the breeze.

Erion bolted upright, his hand on his sword hilt. Edric's hideout was secluded, and they weren't all that far from the city. Wolves didn't usually come this close.

The sound repeated, closer this time.

"Can animals get through that wall?" Erion asked.

"Animals?" Edric dropped the woman's hand and looked up.

"Are we safe in here?" Erion asked.

"I think so? And I think I'm done with her. There's something wrong with her blood. And her lungs. And..." Edric took a step back and waved a hand at the corpse. "All of her, really. Signatures of magic that I don't recognize. I only know what *living* people feel like. It's... almost like she's still alive. But she's also been dead a long time."

Erion blinked.

"I know it doesn't make any sense. I don't know what I'm doing."

It was the perfect opportunity for Erion to push the question of the magic academy. Edric was going to that school—Erion didn't care if he had to send him in a crate addressed to the Chancellor. Whatever it took.

Snarling joined the haunting howls. The animals were closer.

"Go to Amelie," Erion told Edric. "Now."

Edric darted a glance toward the source of the sound, then ran across the clearing.

Erion crept to the barrier, where the dense foliage was rustling. An animal chuffed with frustration on the other side of the wall. Then the air stilled. Erion held his breath—the thing would move on once it realized there was no opening.

Growls vibrated through the ground, reverberating through Erion's head and his majea. The sound was deep, guttural—and only a few feet away.

He realized too late that he should have asked Edric to strengthen the wall. Claws shredded through a wave of glodis vines. A paw nearly as big as Erion's head pierced through the living barrier. Something orange glimmered in the gap. Erion drew his sword as the creature swiped at the foliage once more. And then it was through.

The animal moved faster than Erion could react. It sprang at him through the hole it had clawed open. It barreled him over, one massive paw smashing into his chest. Erion landed flat on his back, and the breath went out of him. The wolf leaped over him and landed lightly just a few paces away from the corpse.

Erion rolled to a crouch with his sword held ready, but he was prepared for an attack that didn't come. The wolf stood stock-still, alert, but with his back to Erion.

And it wasn't a wolf at all, but a hound. Erion squinted at the thing. Probably a hound. It was nearly five feet tall, with sleek gray fur and pointed ears that swiveled as it took in the clearing. The hound circled the corpse, sniffing it thoroughly. Then it turned its attention skyward and howled—a grating, unearthly sound that shook Erion to his core. He dropped his sword and clapped his hands over his ears. Daemanon had conjured some new breed of monster.

The hound turned fiery orange eyes to him, and leapt.

Erion threw himself to one side. He narrowly dodged the fangs that were as long as his hand, but the hound's shoulder slammed into him, sending him flying. Erion landed on the flat of his back. He scrabbled for the dagger at his belt.

The beast lunged again. Erion kicked the creature's snout. The hound snapped at him, and its jaws clamped down on his ankle. White-hot pain seared up Erion's leg as the fangs pierced through the leather of his boots and into skin.

Erion swore and slashed at the hound with his dagger. The blade tore through the fur and flesh of its muzzle.

The fiery orange of the hound's eyes flared as it snarled around a mouthful of boot. It thrashed its head side-to-side, jerking Erion around like a rag doll. White streaks flared across his vision.

"Hey!" All at once Edric was shouting from nearby, and the hound yelped in pain. It dropped Erion's foot and rounded on Edric with a menacing growl.

Edric didn't run. He wasn't even *armed*. He just stood stock-still with his hands lifted in front of him as though the pacifying gesture would ward the creature off.

No. Erion pushed through the haze of pain and rose to his knees. He seized his sword and tried to rise, but the injured ankle gave out beneath him.

The hellhound bounded at Edric.

Erion's scream caught in his throat. Ropes of sickly looking glodis vines surged up from the ground at Edric's feet. The slimy plant slammed into the hound, catching it in midair and winding around its torso like snakes.

"Run!" Erion shouted at Edric. His brother didn't spare him a glance. Edric scowled in concentration as more and more glodis vines wound around the monstrous hound. The beast strained against the bindings, growling and snapping. It bit through one and dropped it in disgust; the slick, blue slime coating the vine probably tasted just like it smelled—fetid and dead.

Relief flooded across Edric's face. Erion dragged himself to his feet and limped to the trapped animal. He hefted his sword and drove the tip into the beast's neck, severing its spinal cord. The creature collapsed with a choked growl.

"Erion!" Edric paled as the eerie orange light faded from the hound's eyes.

"We're getting out of here. Where's Amelie?" Erion said.

" '*Thanks for saving my life, Edric. It's a good thing you've been practicing your magic all this time,*'" Edric said bitterly. "You're so welcome."

"Thanks," Erion spat through gritted teeth. He sighed as he wrenched his sword from the hound's neck with a twist. "Thanks. Really."

"Did you have to kill it?" Edric voice quavered.

"It tried to eat me, E." Erion found himself calling Edric by the old nickname on instinct.

"I guess… Are you all right?"

"It tried," Erion repeated through gritted teeth, "to *eat* me." He risked a glance down at his ankle.

It was worse than he'd expected. The hound's teeth had savaged through his boot, nearly tearing the heel off. His breeches above the ankle were in tatters. Erion dropped to the ground with a groan. He'd have to cut the boot off to assess the damage.

The shock from the injury wore off. Panic started to crowd around the edges of his mind. He started tentatively pulling back his pant leg, fighting against blacking out. When he'd pulled the fabric back, Erion slid his dagger under the top of his boot. He used his majea to heat the blade and began slicing the leather away from his foot.

Edric hissed in sympathy as the boot fell away piece by

piece. Erion's calf had taken the brunt of the injury. If his boots had been any thinner, he probably would have lost the foot. Blood oozed from deep puncture wounds in his skin, and his ankle twisted at an odd angle.

Erion's mind went blank. He was on the verge of unconsciousness, and he suddenly wished it would come. Anything to get away from the pain—and the horrible feeling that this might just be a crippling wound.

That's just what the Crimson Fang needs—a bounty hunter with one foot.

"Hold still." Edric materialized at Erion's side. His hands were full of shredded, burnt orange petals. Edric frowned down at the flowers. They stitched themselves together before Erion's eyes, forming a long strip of dark orange material almost like cloth. Edric wrapped the makeshift bandage around Erion's leg, then wound it around his ankle like a brace.

"What the..." Erion's question died as his injuries began to sting under the petals. He hissed a sharp intake of breath.

"I said hold *still*." Edric pushed down on Erion's knee to keep him from flinching as he finished tying off the last of the bandage. He bit his lip and looked up expectantly a moment later.

Erion opened his mouth to swear, but shut it again as a soft cooling sensation replaced the stinging. The petals were leeching the pain out of his injuries.

"What the hell?" Erion asked.

Edric let out a shaky laugh. "It worked?"

"It—" Erion moved his foot experimentally. Still painful— but tolerable. "Damn. I think it did."

"That's what I've been doing here. Breeding athis flowers."

"So this is your secret genius?" Erion knew the flower was often used by mundane healers in poultices.

"It's going to get me a sponsor." Edric said it with conviction, and Erion was too exhausted to fight him.

"Really impressive, E," Erion said, honestly. The idea of Edric trying to win over a sponsor at the Kuriositar Festival still set Erion's teeth on edge, but Edric had probably just saved his life. He'd definitely just saved his leg. The argument could wait.

"What *was* that thing?" Amelie was walking across the clearing toward them. Her face was chalk white.

"No idea. But let's go before another one can find us." Erion hauled himself up and tested his injured foot. He stifled a groan and put all his weight on the uninjured leg. Too soon to tell how lasting the damage would be.

"Let's move then." Edric looked over at Erion. "You good?"

Erion grimaced, but nodded. "Just tell that damned horse to take it easy on me."

"No promises. She doesn't like me. Is there a plan? What about Amelie?"

Erion hadn't thought that far ahead. It probably wasn't safe for her at the manor. They could put her up at an inn, but he couldn't see her agreeing to that.

"I know someone who can help," Erion said at last.

CHAPTER THIRTY

A SMALL FAVOR

Vandra let herself into the back room of the small bakery on the ground floor of her building. The scents of freshly baked bread and spiced fruits filled the air. One of the benefits to owning the building was having her choice of tenants. There were worse things than living above a bakery—and an incredibly fine one, at that.

Haral, the mastermind in the kitchen, gave her a toothy grin when she walked in. He didn't know Vandra was both neighbor and landlord, which was how she liked it. As far as anyone in the building knew, she was a contracted agent for the Hunter's Guild earning a modest income.

"Orange today?" Vandra tried not to drool as she peered into a large bowl of preserves.

Haral nodded. "And pomegranate."

Vandra fished a dakkari from her pocket and held it up. "Anything leftover from the day?"

Haral laughed. "For a full dakkari? Take your pick. There are fresh sugar buns on the cooling rack. We're taking them to family tonight."

Vandra put the coin on the counter next to Haral and wrapped two of the delicacies in a napkin. Dinner.

"You've missed company, by the way," Haral said.

"Sorry?" Vandra froze with a third pastry halfway to her mouth. Unexpected company was happening a lot lately.

"Some guy came in asking for you. Dark hair. Big sword."

"What did he want?" she asked.

Haral shrugged. "Seemed upset."

"He would be," Vandra muttered. Erion was always upset about something.

"Should I tell him to bugger off if he comes back?"

"He's trouble for sure, but nothing I can't handle." Vandra grinned and winked.

Haral snorted and went back to the dough he was working. Vandra bade him good night and took the back stairs up to her rooms to find scorch marks outside her door. She rolled her eyes. Some people never learned.

She let herself in. Two people, barely more than kids, sat in front of a merrily crackling fire. *Her* fire. Erion looked up at her from the table. She'd expected mischief, but his face was drawn and haggard.

"I didn't know you had kids." Vandra looked pointedly at the two sitting by the fire. The boy, maybe sixteen, had to be Erion's brother. They had the same angular features, and something reminiscent of Erion's intensity flickered in his eyes. The girl, though...

"I need a small favor," Erion said.

"Have you eaten?" Vandra handed the two sugar buns to Erion's brother. The boy glanced at Erion for approval before accepting the food with a curt nod of thanks.

"You—back here. Now." Vandra pointed to her bedchamber. Erion rose stiffly to his feet, and she gasped when she saw his bloodstained breeches. He was only wearing one shoe. "What happened?"

"Funny story." Erion winced and limped across the room,

then sunk onto her bed.

"Do I even want to know?" Vandra shut the door and leaned her back against it.

"I'm fine, by the way. Thanks for asking. How much *do* you want to know?"

Vandra narrowed her eyes at him. "Is she pregnant?"

"Very funny. She just needs a place to stay for a little while."

"Why? Does it have anything to do with that?" Vandra pointed at his leg. "*Are* you fine?"

"I think so." Erion's brow furrowed. Far from looking relieved, he seemed almost disturbed by the idea. "You remember how you said there might be someone working for the Fang at the baron's estate?"

"My memory is excellent."

"It was Durant Vinke."

How had she missed *that*? It was painfully obvious, in retrospect. Niklas couldn't be relied upon, but Mathieu needed somebody with access and influence.

"Vinke," she mused aloud. "Thank you. I'll put someone on him."

"Sure, if you mean on his *grave.*"

"He's dead?" Vandra shook her head when she realized her voice betrayed her shock. She took a steady breath and fought to rein in her emotions. "Tell me what happened."

Erion gave her a brief summary of the attack at the v'deru fields, ending the story with his suspicions about Vinke's death.

"And now *I'm* supposed to be Niklas's new apprentice." Erion held out his hands, putting his frustration on display.

"That sounds *fun.*"

"You're hysterical today. Really."

"So what's the girl's deal? I can't help unless I know."

"Can't or won't?"

Vandra waited him out.

Erion groaned and put his head in his hands. When he finally spoke, it was in a rush. "She was abducted for some kind of... experimentation. I don't know. Twisted stuff. They cut off one of her fingers. She escaped."

"Escaped how?"

"Sadiq… may have helped. It's complicated. Isak had her."

Vandra shivered involuntarily. She'd already guessed this was the same girl Thorne had told her about. "Just Sadiq, huh?"

"I may have been involved. A little. It doesn't matter. We don't know who's after her, and nobody in Mathieu's circles can know she ended up with me. I have to find a safe place for her."

"This isn't a small favor," Vandra said.

"I know."

Vandra tapped her fingers on her lips, considering him for a moment. She sympathized with Erion—he was trying so hard to be a decent person. The Crimson Fang was making it next to impossible, and it was obviously eating away at him.

But he was asking her to lie to one of the most powerful men in the city about this.

No, not lying, exactly. She could hold her silence. There wasn't any reason for Mathieu to ask her about this specific girl.

"What did Isak want with her?"

"He said he was taking her—to Reinholdt's ruins. To the nuraghi." That last word was almost a whisper.

Vandra's blood ran cold, her suspicions confirmed.

"This is the Ithynon's work, then. He's dangerous."

"So is Mathieu."

"Not like this."

"How long can you keep her?" Erion asked.

"How long do you need?"

Erion rubbed his neck and stared at the ceiling for a moment. "Until after the Manifestation Festival. I'll be able to get Edric out by then, but he won't leave unless he knows she's safe."

"Ah. A white knight."

"Clearly doesn't run in the family. Will you help?"

"What do you mean, 'get Edric out'?"

"Away from here. He's not safe with Niklas. Look at what happened to me. He has to go to school somewhere. To make something of himself." Erion averted his eyes as he spoke.

Vandra could tell there was more he wasn't telling her. She supposed everyone was entitled to a few secrets. She'd let him keep this one, for now.

Vandra crossed the room and sat down next to him on the bed. She'd been steeped in the Duchy of Razhari's criminal underground for so long, she'd almost forgotten what it was like to be around someone with a good heart. For all the trouble he was causing, Erion's pull was magnetic.

"I just need to... to sort this out," Erion said. "If I'm working for the steward, I'll be able to figure out a more permanent place for her."

"I'll help. On one condition."

"Anything."

"Take me for drinks."

CHAPTER THIRTY-ONE
WIDOWER'S WALK

D razan Voloy paced the long wall that bordered his estate. No matter the chaos of the world below, he had always found solace above the gardens his Jolie had so loved. Of late, that small peace was more and more elusive. The darker the world below, the more important these walks became.

Dearest Jolie, what things I've done. What things must still be done.

Drazan stopped by a stone bench and stared out over the grounds. The white blooms of winter roses stood out starkly in the moonlight, giving the garden an ethereal, ghostly air.

He didn't care what Cedivar said; he was close. He could taste it. Jolie still lived. If Drazan could unlock the secret to that kind of stasis, he would find the key to bring her back to him. The memory of her laughter in this very garden warmed him. If he could have but one more smile, see one more twinkle in her dark, shining eyes…

If he could have even one more moment, it would have been worth every ounce of blood and grief.

And others will benefit. Drazan had taken what Duke Reinholdt had tried so many years ago, twisted with his malice and craving for power, and turned the force into something *good.* Something useful. Something that would help people.

There were sacrifices—but what was worth fighting for that came without sacrifice? The gods knew Drazan had lost enough himself.

He was so very close.

Drazan paced the walk until his fingers grew numb from the winter wind. He slept little these days, and ate less, and felt he would be at risk of withering away and drifting off into the breeze if his plans didn't come to fruition soon.

Everything for *after* was arranged. If nothing else, the icho rings had been a brilliant financial success. He had more than enough to whisk Jolie away, and they could live out the rest of their natural days unburdened by the responsibilities of running a barony.

Tonight, he would try again. He was convinced the formula was right, and his timing nearly so. Tonight, the next girl they killed would come back when he summoned her. Most importantly, this one wouldn't escape.

Drazan's lips twisted with distaste at the thought of another woman tied to his table, her eyes wide and afraid as Cedivar drove a blade into her heart. There would be no more of that after tonight. There would be no more blood, at least outside of the nuraghi's confines.

Drazan straightened his spine and adjusted the clasp at the neck of his cloak. He'd sacrificed this much for his peace. There was no turning back.

Soon, my love.

CHAPTER THIRTY-TWO
FOUL PASSAGES

Erion hadn't been ordered to kill anyone in over a week. If Sadiq never gave him another execution order, it would be too soon. He tried to remind himself how lucky he was to be in his new position as steward-in-training as he went about his new duties. Each was more dull and depressing than the last.

He drifted down to the stockrooms in the eastern basement, where Niklas used to send him to inventory supplies. It had been years since anyone had been down there, and Erion wasn't in any particular hurry. He wouldn't be surprised if his father was intentionally giving him the meanest of jobs to try and drive him away from the position. Niklas had made it clear that he'd prefer to train Edric—or anyone that wasn't Erion.

The sentiment was mutual. Erion already missed bounties from the Hunter's Guild. He hadn't realized how satisfying ridding small pockets of the barony of pests like Bhirtas'Drada and otterwraiths had actually been. Starved of any company but his father's, Erion even found himself missing Thorne.

To make matters worse, Edric had been avoiding him ever since they'd left Amelie in Vandra's care. Everything seemed to have unraveled at once. Edric was particularly sour that Erion still forbade him to go to the festival—even after his new athis flower had worked so well to heal his foot.

Erion couldn't even argue with him on that front. The rudimentary bandage Edric had conjured was nothing short of miraculous. After two weeks, Erion was almost completely healed from an injury that should have crippled him for life.

The door to the storeroom creaked and protested when he pulled it open. The crates were draped in a thick layer of dust, the labels had been worn off most of them. Erion pried one of the crates open and jumped back when its putrefied contents were revealed. He thought it was some kind of vegetable, but... Erion pinched his nose and leaned over the contents. No, whatever it was had been in teardrop shaped glass vials, most of which had been smashed.

Erion pushed the lid back on and shoved the crate into the hall. He'd get some of the baron's laborers to dispose of the spoiled goods when he was done with the room.

Hours later, Erion had cleared about half the room. He'd salvaged a few things. A shipment of iron and smithing tools had been delivered and forgotten about at some point. The blacksmith would be delighted when he saw the equipment.

Erion hated the work, but he hated the inefficiency of everything more. His father's neglect long predated the baron's extended period of mourning.

His fingers twitched toward a sword hilt that wasn't there. What he wouldn't give to be throttling an atlas moth right now.

He gave the next two storerooms in the abandoned corridor a cursory review. He'd lived in the estate most of his life, but he'd never been down here before. Not a surprise, since apparently nobody else had, either.

The hair on the back of Erion's neck stood up as he reached the last room. He stopped dead on the threshold. Every muscle in his body tensed with anticipation.

The dust in this room had been disturbed, and recently. Erion took a hesitant step forward, into a radiating sense of hatred. He fought against the sudden urge to run. This was the second time he'd encountered the taint in the manor.

Ignoring it wasn't going to make it go away. Erion blew into his hands, charging the air until it ignited and formed a small sphere of light hovering over his palm. This time, the sphere came effortlessly. He held it aloft as he entered the room, careful to step only where the dust had already been disturbed. He laid a hand against a precariously piled crate. It wobbled under his touch. Erion prodded another. They were all empty.

Fine, I'll play. Erion followed the trailing footprints to the back of the room, where a semicircle of scrape marks marred the dust. He squinted at the wall—it was obvious there was some kind of door there, but it wasn't one that could be seen by a casual observer. With a whisper of will, his majea snaked forward and into the wall.

Erion's senses slicked off the wall like it was made of slime, or the repulsive glodis vines Edric favored to camouflage his hideout.

Erion squared his jaw and threw a dart of magic against the wall, splitting the mortar between the stones. He fought off nausea as he forced a way through the wall and into the passage beyond. He slipped through quickly and closed the wall behind him. Someone had gone to great lengths to hide this passage. It wouldn't do to give away his presence if they came calling.

Unease radiated through Erion as he walked down the passage. It had been years since he'd explored the bowels of the manor, but he'd have remembered this kind of presence in his childhood home. This was something new.

Erion knew without a doubt that this hall was connected to the passage he'd discovered when spying on Duke Jesper's men. The malevolent whispers increased the further he went. His majea pulsed through the stone, guiding him forward until he sensed a wide opening—a room at the end of the short hall.

Air and earth were silent here, no signs of life ahead. Still,

Erion proceeded with caution. He blew on the sphere of fire in his hand and held it aloft. The flickering light cast shadows into the four corners of the room, revealing three doors on the far wall.

A long table dominated most of the area. Scales, scrolls, and an array of tools covered the workspace. A wide stone basin—common quartz, Erion could sense at once—took up a full third of the table.

A smaller table was tucked away in an alcove to his right. Erion glanced at it in passing, then froze and turned back. Chains wrapped around the table, affixing leather cuffs to its four corners. Blood crusted over the leather.

Erion's gut wrenched. Some of the evil in the air explained—but there was still the matter of the nuraghi's signature taint. A suspicion nagged at him, bringing with it a memory of a cracked cliffside and emerald light radiating from somewhere deep within the waters of Lake Zagretsk. A memory of stones that weren't stones, and the magic he'd awakened beneath the Reinholdt ruins.

Don't be stupid. This doesn't have anything to do with you.

Perhaps he'd stumbled on one of Cedivar's workshops? Absent Baron Voloy's oversight, had the Line Mage sunk himself into black arts, taking advantage of the baron's resources to do so?

Erion swallowed his trepidation and crossed the strange workshop. He willed his heartbeat to quiet as he focused on the stones beneath his feet, making sure the areas beyond the doors were empty before he opened each one.

The first opened into another corridor, vast and dark. He closed that door and moved on to the next, revealing another storage area.

No, it was more of a laboratory. It resembled the back rooms at Quill's apothecary more than anything else. Crowded shelves lined the walls, filled with vials and labels of ingredients and items Erion had never heard of before. Something glittered in the corner when the light touched it; chains, saws, and chisels hung on the wall in neat rows. They were clean, with one exception—a pair of what looked like tongs had dark stains on the ends.

More blood.

Erion turned away from the tools. He steeled himself before entering the final chamber. That now-familiar sense of dread permeated the air here. It clawed into Erion's mind, forced itself down his throat until it threatened to choke him.

Defiant, Erion swung the door open.

He stepped back as soon as it opened, half expecting some ancient evil, long forgotten, to be lurking just beyond the threshold.

A soft, bluish-green glow emanated from the chamber. Erion peeked around the corner. A glimmering cocoon, nearly six feet long, lay on a stone ledge.

Spurred by curiosity, Erion pushed through the sense of wrongness weighing on him. He'd never heard of anything like the object on the ledge, let alone seen its like. Atlas moths were sometimes as large as a man, but there was no way one of those monsters had made its way all the way down here.

And this one was glowing.

The cocoon was made up of thousands of fine, woven strands. The delicate material recalled the lace the baroness's seamstress used to make. Intricate and fragile. He reached out and pressed his fingertips against the surface. It was hard as stone, but not made of any material he could name. His majea slipped over and around the substance like it wasn't even there. This was something that, at one time or another, had been alive.

Might still be alive. The thought shot shivers down his spine.

As Erion withdrew his hand, the cocoon's light strengthened. The top of the long object shifted, bubbling like something underneath the surface was trying to force its way through.

Erion took a step back and drew his dagger, ruing the choice he'd made to stop carrying his sword around while going about his steward's duties.

The bubbling concentrated near the top of the cocoon. Then the woven filaments parted and split back from the center like pages in a book. A face peered out from the opening. Erion jumped back, then hesitated when the figure remained motionless.

It wasn't looking at him—the eyes were closed. Erion chided himself and sheathed his dagger with a shaking hand.

Not a cocoon. A coffin.

Erion took a closer look at the face—a woman's face, high cheekbones and a narrow chin framed by locks of chestnut hair. It was Baroness Jolie Voloy.

It's not.

She'd been dead more than a year. He looked closer. There could be no denying it. The late baroness lay within a living cocoon of light, her cheeks still tinged pink. Erion couldn't tell whether or not she was breathing, but he wasn't about to get close enough to find out.

He had to get out of here.

Erion stumbled into the wall, tripped back to the main room, and slammed the door shut behind him.

He took in the laboratory with new eyes. The basin at the end of the table drew his attention. A box by the quartz was full of hexagonal stones. Erion took a hesitant step forward. Icho crystals.

The quartz basin was inscribed with rings of copper. Symbols and Line Magic he couldn't read encircled two depressions in the basin. One depression held three icho crystals. They were clear, almost white in the light from Erion's fire sphere. Their signature resonated with Erion when he reached out to them with his majea—familiar, if foul.

But three ink-black stones rested in the second depression.

Bile rose in Erion's throat. He didn't have to inspect them with his magic to know what they were. He wouldn't feel anything if he tried. He didn't have to look closer to see the inverted-V symbol carved into the stones, either.

Stones that weren't stones. Stones that had no business

being here, in the bowels of Baron Voloy's estate.

Stones that Erion had dug up at the Reinholdt ruins. The artifice of a madman who'd meticulously recorded experiments and majea so vile Erion's stomach turned just thinking about them.

Footsteps pulsed through the ground, warning Erion that someone was coming down the same corridor he'd entered from.

Pull yourself together. Erion threw himself at the only other way out of the laboratory, not bothering to check whether anyone was in the hall beyond. It didn't matter—if someone was there, he was caught either way.

It was mercifully empty. He ran down the dark corridor, passing several alcoves that had been barred off as he did so. Cells.

The hall ended in a small, winding staircase. Erion bolted up the steps two at a time. He didn't stop until he reached a narrow landing. He rested his forehead against the cool stone, mercifully void of the nuraghi's taint. When he'd caught his breath, he started tapping out the stone, searching for a familiar corridor where he could slip back into the estate's sunlit halls.

Erion couldn't leave his magic behind, but he wanted nothing more than to close his connection to the taint of the nuraghi's blood magic in the dungeons below. He'd never been so eager to get away from stone in his life.

CHAPTER THIRTY-THREE

HEALING

Edric sat on a rafter high above the stable floor with his legs dangling over one side. He'd been trying to draw the attention of the horses with his majea, with little success. It wasn't really a surprise. Every mage ultimately specialized in one or two things.

A Life Mage—*zokurios, that's what they call them at the academy*—might be good with plants or crafting or healing, but they almost never had an affinity for all the skills within their stream of magic. Edric was good with plants—great with them, in fact. He was good with animals, too, but he'd spent half his life working in the stables.

Dead things—byproducts of organic materials used in crafting—barely resonated with him. He'd tried his hand at spelling leather and wood. The outcomes had been pitiful. Edric would never be a craftsman.

But sensing the vitality of the people around him was like breathing. If he brushed shoulders with someone, or shook their hand, their energy jumped out at him like sparking coals. A shiver slipped down his spine as he remembered the moment he'd known Durant Vinke was dead on his feet. He'd sensed Vinke's life force seeping out at an unsustainable rate. His end had been as obvious to Edric as the blood staining the man's tunic and cloak.

The stable door opened, and Edric crept off the rafter and back into the hayloft. It was Erion.

Edric thought about going down the ladder to talk to him. He wanted to ask about Amelie, and whether she was safe. He wanted to ask about the woman in the lower city that Erion had taken them to, and how he knew people who could secret a girl away without a trace.

He wanted to demand that Erion tell him where all his money was *really* coming from—but he was scared of the answer.

He decided against a confrontation. If they talked, they'd fight, and Edric didn't have the energy for it. He watched his brother saddle his horse, his interest piqued by the heavy saddlebags Erion loaded onto the animal.

Where was he going? Erion never rode unless he had no other choice, and it looked like he planned on being away for a while. *Good riddance*, Edric thought. At least he wouldn't have to worry about running into his brother for a few days.

As soon as Erion left, Edric ran back to the estate. He was stepping into the hall near the sickrooms before he could think too much about the repercussions. He'd had enough. Erion was making his own plans—Edric was finally going to do the same.

The sickroom was mercifully empty, but he found Gian in the wide workspace that connected his bedchamber to the sickroom. Edric wrinkled his nose as he considered that. Being a healer would be useful—noble, even, but he didn't relish the idea of living next door to a bunch of sick people all the time.

"How can I help you?" Gian looked up from a large leather-bound journal, worn from use. He put his quill aside and frowned slightly at Edric. "Are you well?"

"Do people only visit you when they're unwell?" Edric

asked. His eyes took in the room, really looking at it for the first time. He'd spent his fair share of time in the sickroom, but he'd never had reason to visit Gian in his office before. Chagrined, he realized Gian probably *didn't* get visitors unless they were unwell. It sounded lonely.

"Not generally speaking." Gian's smile was warm.

"I was wondering…" Edric hesitated, suddenly unsure of how to voice the question. Gian was busy all the time—he probably wouldn't be interested in helping anyway. Then word would get out that the stable boy was suddenly trying to apprentice to the keep healer. That might garner unwanted attention.

"Yes?" Gian prompted when the silence stretched too thin.

"Is it difficult to be a healer?" Edric asked.

"Sometimes." Gian put his quill down and scratched his chin, looking thoughtful.

"And… other times?"

"Other times it's greatly rewarding to return people to full health. From the brink of death, even."

Edric nodded. He liked the sound of that. Helping people. Doing something *good*.

"I'm trying to go to school," Edric said, hoping this was vague enough to avoid undue suspicion. "But it's expensive."

Gian's eyes lit up. "You find yourself interested in the healing arts?"

Edric nodded.

He'd made the decision when he was going over the dead woman's body. There had been a strange sense of life in her— not flourishing or sparking, like a real live person. She'd also been undoubtedly dead. No heartbeat, no breath, no pulses or sparks in her brain that were all requisites for life. It was like an infection had seeped into her and then clung stubbornly, even after she was long dead.

He didn't understand it, and he needed to. That had almost been Amelie. The two kidnappings, the missing fingers—they had to be connected.

"Healers are in high demand everywhere. You could work in a great city or with traveling merchants. See all of Daemanon, if you wanted."

"How do I learn?"

"Are you certain you want to? It's not for the faint of heart." Gian wrinkled his nose. "Well, naturally. You saw Durant Vinke."

"It was just blood." A *lot* of blood.

"But alas, it wasn't the blood loss that killed him," Gian said. He steepled his fingers together. "Do you know what happens when the breath is constricted?"

"It—you die." Edric wasn't sure what the question really was.

"Air is a crucial element for all living things. Plants, animals, man. As is water. But air circulates through the body," he made a circular motion with his hand, "enriches the blood. Strengthens the humors."

"But Durant was sliced open." Edric had *seen* the cut in Durant's side. A single, long wound beneath his ribs. Precise, deep. Deadly.

"His windpipe was crushed. It was a miracle he made it to me at all."

"That's why he couldn't talk," Edric mused. He bit his tongue to distract himself from a woozy sensation that swept through his head at the thought. If he was going to be a healer, he'd have to get used to blood.

"And why his body was dying, faster than he could even bleed out."

"Could you have stopped it, if you got to him sooner?"

Gian paused to consider the question. "A lifeweaver could, perhaps."

"But you aren't one."

"It is a beautiful gift, but rare."

Edric balled his hands into fists and took a deep breath. "I want you to teach me."

CHAPTER THIRTY-FOUR
SUSPICIONS ON TRIAL

Erion neared the ridge above Lake Zagretsk when he and Thorne heard the riders. They exchanged glances and froze, listening carefully to the sound. Thorne stood up in his stirrups, trying to see further down the trail. Erion, on foot and leading his horse, threw his senses as far forward as he could, trying to pinpoint how many riders approached. Their ears hadn't lied—at least two horses were coming straight toward them at a measured pace.

"Another one?" Thorne mouthed the words. Erion nodded. Together, they led their horses off the trail and into the woods.

Mathieu had forbidden any of his thugs from crossing into Elarazii after framing the duchy for the murder of Duke Jesper's men—but what Mathieu didn't know wouldn't hurt him.

As usual, though, Mathieu's instincts were spot on. This was the second patrol that Erion and Thorne had come across, and they weren't even that far across the border.

Erion watched as four soldiers, heavily clothed against the rain and even more heavily armed, trotted past them. He'd wondered what kind of idiot put their soldiers in yellow livery to patrol the woods, but these men weren't trying to be discreet. Their presence was more message than militant—Elarazii wouldn't be caught with their trousers down if Razhari was trying to start a war, and the increased border patrols were a testament to that.

Thorne moved to go back to the path, but Erion stopped him. A few moments later, the second half of the patrol appeared. Two soldiers wore the same yellow garb as the others, but the other rider surprised him.

A tall, dark-haired woman clad in well-worn, well-cut travel leathers accompanied the Elarazii guards. She rode with her hood down, a long, dark braid pulled over her shoulder. A long flexible case was slung over her back, along with a bristling quiver of arrows, and an elegant, curved saber rested across her lap. Like her garb, its scabbard was simple but sturdy. Even so, the simplicity couldn't hide the obvious worth of the blade it contained. Even from a distance, Erion could make out the weapon's intricate cross guard.

The woman's seat in the saddle was casual, but her dark eyes scanned the road with a hawkish intensity. Erion was seized by the irrational sense that she'd seen him. He slunk back on instinct and waited with bated breath until she had passed out of sight.

"Let's go," Erion said as soon as he was sure the riders weren't going to circle back.

He'd informed Mathieu, via Sadiq, that he'd be away from the estate for a few days to visit some of the baron's tenants. He hadn't waited for permission—or any response at all—before leaving Rijeka. He'd just needed an excuse to leave the city for a few days. He'd visit the tenants when he was done with more pressing matters.

Erion and Thorne didn't stop until they reached the ridge overlooking the Reinholdt ruins, though for now, the decaying hold was invisible in the dark and fog. Erion crouched near the cliff's edge, staring out over the dark water of Lake Zagretsk with growing foreboding.

Somewhere far below, Nuraghi Uzhastik lurked.

Behind him, Thorne swore as he fought with a patch of brambles, making a poor attempt to hide their equipment in the thicket. Erion watched Thorne suck his finger where a thorn had pricked him. He hoped the man didn't miss the irony.

Thorne kicked the offending bush, to little effect. It occurred to Erion that having Edric around would be useful for this bit of camouflage, but he dismissed the thought just as quickly as it had come. Edric hadn't spoken to Erion since they'd left Amelie with Vandra.

He'll get over it. Edric couldn't keep a grudge for long. Even so, Erion knew things were changing. A chasm had grown between them, where once there had only been a small fault line.

"Thorne kinda thought we hated this place," Thorne said over their dinner of soft cheese and cold bread.

"Sure do."

"So are you gonna tell Thorne why he's freezing his arse off, or what?"

"I don't even remember inviting you," Erion said.

He hadn't really been surprised when he'd found Thorne waiting for him, geared up for a journey. What had surprised him was *where* Thorne was waiting. He hadn't been on the northern road where Erion was supposed to be going, but at the western fork. Like he'd known exactly what Erion was up to.

Thorne sniffed. "Still trying to figure you out, Death Wish."

"Is that what you've decided on, then? Death Wish?"

"Fits more often than not. Doesn't roll off the tongue as nicely as *dumbass* though. Don't push it."

Erion chuckled. "How did you guess where I was going?"

"Sadiq told Thorne what you were up to."

Erion's pulse quickened. How could Sadiq possibly know?

"Relax, Backstabber. Thorne knew you were lying. Remember?"

Erion popped an especially large piece of bread into his mouth to avoid answering. Thorne's majea seemed to be most useful when it was inconveniencing someone else.

"But here?" Erion asked finally.

"This place gives you the creeps. You heard Isak talking about it with the girl. You know what's going on with the Ithynon... and by now, Thorne figures you're in with Sadiq enough to know what's going on here."

"What *is* going on here?" Erion leaned forward, suddenly intent on Thorne's every word. It was hard to get a read on the man, but Erion had started to pick up some of his mannerisms after all the time they'd spent together. Thorne made a good show of acting the fool, but Erion knew better.

"Are you really saying you don't know?" Thorne asked through a mouthful of cheese.

"What do you want, Thorne?"

"More cheese." Thorne popped another wedge into his mouth.

Erion waited him out.

"Thorne just keeps his head down. Stays out of things. Out of trouble. But it's hard when some idiot keeps running around like a bear sticking its head into every killer beehive it runs across. Especially when Thorne is assigned to watch that particular bear."

"So you *have* been assigned to watch me." It wasn't exactly a revelation, but Erion was glad to have it out in the open.

"If you didn't know that, you're more of an idiot than Thorne thought."

Erion regarded his companion for a moment, his mind whirling with possibilities. If Thorne was only following him around because he was reporting everything back to Mathieu or Sadiq, he was about to make the biggest mistake of his life.

"I think I know who the Ithynon is," Erion said.

Thorne spluttered. "Say *what?*"

"Does Mathieu know?"

"That you know?"

Erion rolled his eyes. "No, who the Ithynon is."

"Oh, that. No. And it makes him angry." That seemed to

amuse Thorne.

"I'm just here for more information," Erion said. "It's not a coincidence this all started after we dug up Reinholdt's treasury."

Thorne grunted. "Kinda figured."

"Unless you're going to help me, you should go back." Erion wanted to trust Thorne, but he wasn't sure he could afford to.

"Gods, you really believe you did this, don't you?" Thorne's eyes widened.

"Kalistar's truth," Erion swore.

"Fine. Thorne already tried to get out of this and couldn't. Might as well help. Talk."

Erion took a deep breath and launched into an explanation before either of them could change their minds. Thorne listened intently as Erion told him about the girl in the woods, her sudden decay, and the creatures that came after her. Then he added the horrors Amelie had relayed, and how she and Isak had come to run into them in the cave after they'd fought the aster mole. He was careful to leave out any mention of Edric—no reason to risk dangerous questions if he could avoid it.

"And I think I found the laboratory where it was happening. Where she was being held." Erion held his breath when he finished, waiting for Thorne's reaction.

The man had sat still during Erion's tirade—unnaturally still, for someone was fidgety as Thorne.

"So it *is* the baron, then," Thorne said after a thoughtful silence.

"You knew?"

"Everyone thinks Thorne is stupid, you know? They forget he's around, sometimes. They forget what he can do."

Erion nodded. Thorne had a knack of melding into the background. If he was involved in serious conversations at all, he spent them making offhand jokes or rambling about unrelated issues. He always seemed to be in his own world.

Thorne was certainly in his own *head*, but it was one that Erion suspected was in constant motion. He knew far more than he let on.

241

"How did you know?" Erion pressed.

"Thorne *guessed*. He went with Isak once to a drop down there." He waved a hand vaguely toward the lake. "Recognized the guy making the exchange."

"And Isak didn't?" Erion found that hard to believe.

"Not *him*, him. His *brain* him. Sure. Thorne remembers stuff like that. And someone that cold... hard to forget."

"The baron?" Erion felt the blood drain from his face. It was one thing to suspect heinous acts by someone in power, but another entirely to have it confirmed.

"Nah," Thorne shook his head. "Creepy guy. Ponytail."

"*You* have a ponytail," Erion said.

"Mage. Silver hair. Freaky eyes."

Understanding dawned on Erion. He didn't know Cedivar well. The symkurios was rarely seen in the halls of the estate, and he was the type who didn't lower himself to consort with lowly servants.

Even so, Erion should have suspected Cedivar from the moment he'd discovered the laboratory in the dungeons.

"Wait, so Cedivar is the Ithynon?" Erion asked.

"What a stupid name," Thorne said nonchalantly.

"Stupider than *Thorne*?" Erion couldn't help it.

"The crystals have Line Magic under the cap, Rude One. That's how they make their version of the icho so potent. But the stones from the Reinholdt ruins were full of Life Magic."

"How do you know *that*?" Erion burst out. The final piece of the puzzle slammed into place, and horror bloomed in his stomach.

"Thorne read Vandra's reports. You didn't think she just handed those stones over without knowing what they were?"

"She told me it wasn't anyone's business."

"Vandra isn't just anyone."

Erion had to admit that was true. A wheel turned in his head. "The baron... Baron Voloy is a Life Magician."

Wasn't he? Erion wracked his brain, trying to remember. He knew that Voloy was a low-level talent—it was part of why Edric thought the baron might sponsor him to the academy. Was it really Life Magic, or was Erion trying to force pieces into place in order to make sense of what he'd seen? Nobody ever talked about Voloy's majea, and as far as Erion knew, he never used magic for anything—and he'd certainly never advertise the skill.

But it made sense. Cedivar didn't have any use for a zomajea artifact like the ones Erion had discovered in the laboratory. Cedivar didn't have any personal reason to keep the baroness's body in a cocoon deep within the bowels of the estate. Baron Voloy certainly did, and he had all the resources and power he needed to build up a drug empire.

"Thorne knows. He keeps it quiet."

Thorne's interjection broke Erion's focus. Erion wasn't sure whether that meant Thorne kept the knowledge quiet, or the baron did. He hoped it was both.

It was no wonder Baron Voloy hadn't rallied the city watch to fight the icho dens and the Crimson Fang's rising tide of corruption. Voloy was the one behind it all—the icho *and* the kidnappings. They were sowing Human misery like it would grow into a harvest ripe for picking.

And it had something to do with the baroness's body, secreted away in the estate's depths.

Erion wouldn't have believed it possible, but Reinholdt's ruins were in even worse repair than the last time he'd laid eyes on them. The ghosts of time had finally claimed the last tower. Rubble crushed the entrance to the basement where Erion and Thorne had ventured into the old duke's treasury over a year ago.

"Good thing we're not going down there again." Thorne glanced at Erion and squinted at him. "Right?"

"We're going down *there*." Erion pointed out at Lake Zagretsk, where the nuraghi was waiting for them.

"Maybe *you* are."

"Suit yourself." Erion started pacing the ground. He stretched his majea as far down into the cliffs as he could, about twenty paces or so. He needed more practice—more power.

There had to be easy access to the nuraghi somewhere. Erion wasn't keen on entering the way he had last time—sucked down by a whirlpool in Lake Zagretsk. Even in summer, the water's icy depths had stolen his breath and frozen his blood. In January, it would be madness.

Erion spent most of the morning scanning the ground near the ruined Reinholdt keep, but his search eventually brought him back down to the lake's edge. Thorne followed him, keeping himself busy by alternately napping and throwing stones into the water. The ripples marred the black, glassy surface of the water.

"If you wake up a murker, I am not coming in to save you," Thorne muttered.

Erion turned to his companion with a grin.

"What's got you in such a good mood?" Thorne's eyes narrowed.

"I found it."

The entrance to the nuraghi wasn't far from the tower of black stone that jutted from the waters of Lake Zagretsk. It was masterfully hidden—next to invisible to anyone but a Land Mage. Erion slipped into a craggy recess at the base of the cliffs. The stone cut at a sharp angle several feet in. From the outside, it looked like a dead end, but Erion's majea had snaked through the gap and found the passage beneath.

Erion conjured a fire sphere when he reached the heavy door that barred passage. It was one of his longest-lasting spells, probably because it was also one of the simplest. He could hear Thorne grumbling behind him as he put one finger to the heavy padlock. It had two internal devices—under normal circumstances it would take two keys, turning in opposite directions, to open.

He didn't want to melt the lock. With an effort, Erion split his concentration into three parts, prodding at the iron's makeup with his majea to manipulate the internal levers.

Erion shifted a lever aside, careful not to use too much force and snap any of the pieces. The key needed to work the next time someone came.

Not just someone—Cedivar and Baron Voloy. Erion grimaced. He nudged the upper half of the lock at a right angle, straining to keep the lower lever in place. After a moment, the lock popped open.

At least all those years of breaking into the cook's cupboards weren't in vain. Who said crime didn't pay?

"Are we sure we want to go down there?" Thorne asked.

"Shut the door behind you," Erion said.

Their breath misted in front of them as they wound deeper into the depths of the earth.

"Stay close," Erion instructed when they reached the end of the staircase.

Erion stepped out of the passage and into a nightmare. The all-too-familiar malevolence of the nuraghi seeped into his bones, seized his throat, and threatened to choke him. He took a moment to steady himself, then made the painful decision to withdraw his magic from the stone.

He didn't like it. Earthwalking had saved his life more than once—but it wouldn't do him any good if he was too sick to fend off any attackers.

Dense, frigid air pressed against Erion's skin as he moved forward. The darkness closed in around them like a living thing, dampening the light from the fire sphere and swallowing the sounds of their footsteps. Erion had the impression of being in a vast chamber, but there was no echo from their footsteps.

The floor sloped gently downward as they crept forward. The scale was just as staggering in life as in memory. Even without conscious use of his earthwalking, Erion couldn't contain his awe—or unease.

"Thorne would like to know what exactly we're looking for, Dead Man."

"You're counting me out already?" Erion wasn't sure what to look for. Whatever "it" was, he'd been hoping it would be obvious when they came across it.

"We'll both be dead men if Mathieu finds out we came here. If this hellscape doesn't kill us first," Thorne muttered.

He was right. Erion did his best to fend off the misgivings lurking around the edges of his mind. If he gave in to them, the fear wouldn't be close behind, and he had to get to the root of what was going on.

They walked on for what might have been an eternity until they finally hit a wall. Erion steeled himself, then reached out with a sliver of his majea to carve an "X" into the stone. It wasn't much of a marker, but it was better than nothing. He was reasonably confident that he could navigate their way out of the nightmare with his earthwalking if he had to, but he wanted that to be a last resort.

Erion kept his left hand on the wall as he followed it. Where it ended at a sharp right angle, he marked the corner with another "X," fighting nausea as his magic made contact with the stone. Listening to stonewhisper was so natural to him, he'd almost come to think of the earth as a friend.

The taint in the nuraghi felt like a personal betrayal. The hatred was so vile it bordered on tangible. And yet... the whispering stone here was something *more* than any other element he'd encountered. The malice was almost... *sentient,* the muttering nearly a language Erion understood. Erion cringed, then sunk himself into the magic that made up the dungeon.

Blood... power... control. The nuraghi radiated with a fierce desire for dominance. Erion had never encountered its like.

"What's that?" Thorne asked.

Erion wrenched his attention away from the sentience, grateful for the distraction. Thorne was pointing out into the darkness, where a soft light glowed in the center of the cavernous space.

Erion quenched his light to get a better look, and Thorne followed suit. They exchanged an uneasy glance before moving forward. Erion's senses hit a wall when it reached the source of the light. He reached the line a moment later and frowned down at the strange barrier. Two circles of runes—Line Magic, Erion had no doubt—had been carved into the stone. He tried to scratch one of the runes, but his majea slipped off the surface.

He hesitated, then stretched out a hand. The runes were cool to the touch, the grooves of each symbol carved deep in the stone.

Erion held his breath, then stepped across the line of runes.

Nothing happened. Erion looked around, confused but relieved. He'd been prepared for the wards to zap him—like the ones on Vandra's door—or at least stop him from entering the circle.

"Thorne will stay here, thanks."

Erion couldn't blame him. His majea drew him to the center of the wide circle, where stone jutted up from the ground to form an enormous table. There were no seams where the base of the table met the ground. The transition into the floor was flawless, as though something had scooped the ground out from around the table and carved it directly from the native rock. Something—or someone. Like a Land Mage.

Or a Giant?

Erion recoiled from the thought. There was no way. Giants were a fable—a tale that was long-tired, too old to be believed. He pressed his palms against the stone and forced himself to sink his mind into it. Grooves covered its surface, and the whole thing crawled with malevolent intent.

Erion moved away from the stone and circled it, pitifully grateful to end the contact. The table he'd run afoul of in the baron's estate was an obvious replica of this monstrosity. Suspicions confirmed, he returned to Thorne. "Let's get out of here."

"Thorne's ahead of you there. Let's never do this again."

Erion nodded. He wished he could believe it was the last time he'd find himself in this nightmare of a legend, but he suspected this place wasn't finished with him yet.

CHAPTER THIRTY-FIVE

A DYING CITY

Lars Talbot glanced over his shoulder as he stole down the moonlit street. The air was more fog than true drizzle, lending the night a silvery sheen. Icy droplets clung to his oiled cloak, slithered under his collar, and down his back.

The Empori District was far from the waterfront and the worst of the city's criminal activity. But Talbot was a captain in the Rijeka watch, and he knew of few places that were truly free of crime these days.

"You're punctual," a voice said from a shadowed doorway.

Talbot's hand went to the hilt of his sword on instinct. A cloaked figure slunk into the road.

"Were you followed?" Her voice was sharp with authority. Here was a woman used to issuing orders and seeing them carried out without question.

"Of course not." Talbot bristled. He'd left early and spent more than an hour wandering the city before heading to the meetup with this woman. There was too much at stake to risk being followed.

She nodded. "Good. There is much to do."

"It's about time one of your lot showed up." Talbot winced at his own words. *So much for being cordial.* It wasn't every day that someone got to meet one of Pelinon's own Guardians. Or ever. He should be honored.

But Captain Talbot was just outraged. Rijeka—the city he'd been raised in, his *home*—was rotting from the inside out. One by one, his comrades had fallen into trenches of indifference. Talbot had watched the city sink with the baron into mourning, and then into squalor.

The city that he loved was dying, and Talbot had nowhere else to turn.

"Your Duke sent a contingent," Aleria syn'Duvar said.

She lowered her hood when she reached Talbot. He'd been prepared for a battle-hardened, weather-beaten warrior. Instead, a wild beauty stood before him. A number of scars accented her high cheekbones and sharp jawline. Aleria was of a height with him, with dark hair tied in a braid nearly down to her waist. The hilt of a fierce-looking saber was visible beneath the folds of her cloak.

"He's sent two now," Talbot said. "It went over well for the last ones. Dead, all of them."

The words had their intended effect. Aleria had been on the road. By the look on her face, she obviously hadn't heard about the attack near Elarazii yet.

"Who?" she asked.

Talbot shrugged. "A dead man wearing Elarazii leathers was found with the bodies, but it smells like a setup to me. No word from Elarazii yet, but they'll deny involvement.

"Besides, Duke Jesper has more concerns than just Rijeka. Or haven't you heard about the Nissrans?" Talbot pushed.

"Impertinence won't get you far, Captain. I'm here to fix things. You don't have to be a part of that equation."

"You'll have a hard time finding anyone else willing to help." Talbot knew she was right, though. Aleria had far more resources than he did. She didn't need him any more than he needed another crooked lieutenant taking bribes from the Crimson Fang.

Be civil. She was here to help.

"Let's go somewhere we can talk freely," Talbot said.

"You read my mind." But rather than wait for Talbot to lead the way, Aleria turned down the road, clearly expecting him to follow her.

Fine, we'll do it your way then. Like he had any choice.

Aleria led with the confidence of a woman not only comfortable on the streets, but familiar with them. The Wharf District greeted them by scent before sight, the stench of rotting fish and refuse rising on the breeze as they approached.

Talbot wrinkled his nose. When he'd received Aleria's invitation to meet, he'd expected just that—a *meeting.* She led him practically to the river's edge, finally stopping in the shadows of a decrepit warehouse. Clearly there was more on her mind than talking.

That was fine by Talbot—action was good. He fended off a sense of foreboding. The Guardians were fine warriors all. It would be a mistake to underestimate her. He only hoped he could keep up if things got dangerous.

"How long have kurioi in your city been going missing?" Aleria stared out across the water, taking in their surroundings with a critical eye.

"Kurioi?"

"Your magic users."

"I know what it means." But how did the Guardian know it was almost exclusively mages that were going missing? Talbot took a deep breath through his nose and sighed. "The disappearances started about two years ago. There was a cluster near this time last year, then things went quiet for a while. But now they're getting worse. Women, mostly."

"That cluster last year—women?" Aleria asked.

"Kids. Four of them, all around the same time. Late February." Talbot didn't have to think about it. Agony had been a tangible presence in the city. Frantic parents had practically been knocking Talbot's door down—in one case, a man had succeeded. The blacksmith who'd managed it had been muscled like an ox. His apprentice, a promising lad by all accounts, had been among the missing.

Missing—now presumed dead, just like the others.

"And Ilfar Hovert? Tell me about him."

"A logger." Talbot was taken aback by the question. They hadn't connected his disappearance to the slew of other missing persons in the city. The Drakunem was a dangerous river. It was presumed, even by Hovert's brother, that he'd been snagged by a dashelfin or ikunem.

"Productive, though," Aleria said.

Talbot wrinkled his nose. "Are you suggesting he was a kurios?"

"Not suggesting. He was. I'd be curious to know how many more of your missing persons were the same."

"At least one of them. I'll look into it." The blacksmith's apprentice had been a gifted, if novice, gekurios. Rare enough for any youth, and especially valuable to a blacksmith hoping to strengthen his steel and spell his weapons.

"There's a drop point here, where most of your drug trade is being exported to the north." Aleria pointed at the warehouse.

Talbot gritted his teeth. She must have other contacts in the city. He knew about the warehouse, but admitting as much would mean admitting that he'd willfully done nothing.

"Shall we take a look?" Aleria started for the downtrodden building without waiting for an answer.

The windows of the decrepit warehouse were well above Talbot's line of sight—built for ventilation more than light or a view of the street. Talbot eyed the trash-lined walk. With a view like that, who would want one?

Aleria skirted the building's perimeter until she found a rickety staircase that led to a second-story landing with access to the workshops above the main floor. The stairs trembled and shook under their weight as they crept upward.

"*Ah*," Aleria said with a satisfied grin as she peered through the nearest window.

Talbot followed her gaze. A mountain of crates and refuse had been shoved against the walls to form a clearing in the center of the room. Lanterns stood on makeshift tables, illuminating four armed men sitting in a loose circle. Two rows of large, iron-bound crates sat just outside the glow from the lanterns.

Talbot leaned forward, squinting. Not crates. Cages. Six of them with thick metal bars, each practically large enough to hold a small horse.

Human figures occupied the cages. Finally, here was incontrovertible proof that the Crimson Fang was behind the disappearances. Talbot's hand tightened on the sword-breaker at his hip.

"They haven't even set up a perimeter." Aleria laughed. "Amarassa knows I love a stupid criminal."

Talbot chuckled despite himself. He didn't need to ask Aleria what she was planning to do next as she tugged on the door leading into the lofts. It opened on mercifully silent hinges.

The lofts were in no better condition than the warehouse below. Puffs of dust dampened the sound of their footfalls as they navigated piles of discarded carpentry equipment and broken shelving. They crouched at the top of the stairs. Talbot did a quick check of the area. As far as he could see, Aleria was right; the four guards hadn't set a watch, though there was always a chance there were men outside that they hadn't spotted.

"I can pick locks." Talbot kept his voice low.

"Once they're dead, that won't matter. But I plan on sending a bit stronger message." Aleria stayed low as she crept down the stairs. Talbot unsheathed his rapier and loosed the shorter sword-breaker in its scabbard in case it was needed.

It wasn't.

Aleria burst into the circle of warm light with a fierce shout. One of the Crimson Fang's men actually yelped as she drew her saber. It flared with a fiery light of its own as she whirled it through the air. The man gaped and dropped the bottle of spirits he'd been clutching. It shattered on the stone floor as he scrabbled for his sword. Aleria skewered him before he could reach it.

Another guard turned tail. Talbot sprinted after him, grateful that he hadn't let age turn him to seed like so many of his contemporaries had. He caught the man easily. His quarry whirled, producing a curved dagger, and slashed wildly at Talbot's face.

Talbot parried the slash with his rapier. The thug lunged again, and this time his blade caught on the reinforced stitching of Talbot's leather jerkin. The swing had overbalanced him, though, and the man staggered forward.

It was enough. Talbot sidestepped his attacker and raised his sword. His foe was dead before he could take another step. He would happily have spared the man's life so they could question him, but mercy and self-preservation weren't always compatible.

Talbot turned back to assist Aleria, but the fight was already over. The Guardian had moved beyond the circle of light, her fiery sword now illuminating the figures curled inside the cages. The bodies of the three men she'd so neatly dispatched were heaped into a careless pile. Following her lead, Talbot grabbed his attacker's body by the collar and dragged him across the floor to join the others. His mouth twisted with distaste as he dropped the body. He hated cleaning up corpses almost as much as he hated the killing.

Aleria whispered something to the occupant of the first cage, then put the tip of her saber to the bars. The sword sliced through the iron bars like they were made of warm butter.

Now that he had a moment to truly appreciate the blade the Guardian wielded, Talbot looked on in wonder. He'd never thought to meet a Guardian of Pelinon, but it wasn't so outlandish in itself. But a true firebrand—because there was no doubt that's what Aleria syn'Duvar wielded—was a rarity few had the privilege to see in action.

Talbot jumped to help the prisoners from their confines as

soon as the bars from the first cage were removed. Aleria moved on to the next while Talbot led the first woman to a crate and sat her down. She was shaking uncontrollably. Talbot handed her his water skin, then turned to help the others.

Five captives were soon released. All women. Talbot shuddered to think what their intended purpose was.

"Thank you," Talbot said to Aleria.

"An absolute pleasure." A fierce light burned in Aleria's eyes, mirroring the light from her sword.

Talbot echoed the sentiment. Five fewer missing persons reports to file, but more importantly, five lives saved. He knew all too well the ripple effect of such tragedies. Thanks to Aleria, countless people would be spared the agony of not knowing what had happened to their loved ones.

Aleria turned to address the women, all of whom showed signs of mistreatment at the hands of their captors.

"We will assist you in returning to your homes, for those of you who wish it. If you don't, I will ensure you find safe passage out of Rijeka. Captain?" She turned to Talbot. "If you'll ensure there aren't any rats outside waiting to ambush us? Then I think we should return to the guardhouse to arrange returning these women home."

"What about them?" Talbot toed the nearest corpse.

"Leave them." Aleria tossed one of the iron bars onto the pile of bodies. "Like I said—we're sending a message."

CHAPTER THIRTY-SIX
UNEXPECTED ARRIVALS

E rion lurked at a corner table in the Crimson Fury, the most notorious tavern in the Apothiki District. It wasn't far from the Maw, where Mathieu made his official home and did most of his business. Sympathizers of the Crimson Fang—people either indifferent to the gang's corruptive influence or keen to avoid its wrath—were eager to curry favor with Mathieu. The owner at the Crimson Fury was no different. The Fury served the Crimson Fang almost exclusively.

For once, Erion was here to drink. He was making good on his promise to buy a round for Vandra, but he'd come early to prepare himself for the conversation they needed to have. A friendly evening wasn't in the cards, much as he wished things could be different.

Erion finished the last of his mead, caught the barkeep's eye, and ordered two more. Vandra would be there soon.

When she arrived, it wasn't for drinks. She threw herself down on the chair next to him, not bothering to remove her cloak.

"What are you doing tonight?" she asked. Her hair was falling out of its long braid and she had dark circles under her eyes.

"Is that a bruise?" Erion touched two fingers to her cheekbone.

Vandra winced at his touch. "Probably. I've been looking into a few things. What are you doing?"

"Having drinks with you," Erion said. "What's going on?"

She didn't reply, but grabbed his hand and dragged him out of his seat.

"What the..." Erion tossed a dakkari on the table by the two full tankards and followed her out into the street.

Vandra's hand was warm in his as she practically dragged him into the Empori District. At last, she stopped outside a small inn. Five-point antlers were painted on the hanging wooden sign, above the inn's name—*Wilder's Keep*. Modest enough for the Empori District, but practically royal compared to Erion's usual haunts.

Vandra stopped under the awning and took out her braid. She drew her fingers through her hair, combing out the snares. Erion eyed the gargoyles at the corners of the steeply sloping roof with suspicion. They were artfully disguised rain gutters, but they wouldn't be the first Bhirtas'Drada he'd seen masquerade as the small stone gargoyles.

"Not sure I can afford this place," Erion said as he watched Vandra plait her hair again.

"I've seen your bounties, we both know you can."

"What's going on?"

"You'll see. Act natural." Her expression was grim as they entered the inn.

"*Naturally*, I wouldn't be here." Erion smiled at a serving maid standing at a low counter near the entrance. "Just two."

Vandra took off her cloak and hung it on a line of coat hooks near the door. Beneath, she wore the fine red dress he'd seen her in once before. She looked like she belonged here.

Erion's clothes were clean, but far from the level of finery Vandra had arrived in. He looked more like a stray she'd adopted off the street than her escort for the evening.

Erion shucked his cloak, but refused to remove his sword when Vandra nudged it. They may be in the Empori District, but he wasn't willing to part with it. The serving girl frowned at the weapon but made no comment, instead gesturing for them to follow her through the foyer.

A small sitting room opened to their right, full of comfortable looking armchairs and a crackling fire that guarded against the winter chill. The walls had fine wood paneling, but the place was absent lavish decorations. A bar of polished quartz ran the length of the room. They were early for the dinner rush, but a few of the inn's patrons and some local merchants were already seated around the bar.

The serving girl led them to a table near the center of the room.

"Perhaps something more private." Vandra pressed a coin into the girl's hand, then wrapped an arm around Erion's waist suggestively.

The girl pursed her lips, but she looked more amused than scandalized as she indicated a table in the corner. "Dinner is honeyed rabbit with mushroom pasties and roast potatoes, if it please you."

Vandra ordered dinner and drinks for them both. Erion didn't want to know the price.

"*Now* will you tell me what's going on?" Erion asked.

"Soon," Vandra said. She'd positioned herself so that she could see the whole room. Her eyes narrowed when two women entered the dining hall, but she sat back with a sigh after a moment.

"We need to talk," Erion said. If this wasn't a social call, he had questions he needed answered. "About Amelie. And…"

"Not now."

Erion ground his teeth. "Is she safe?"

"I told you she would be."

"Answer the question."

Vandra tilted her head, her eyes meeting his with a calculated look. "She's safe."

"Is she in the city?"

"She'll be safer if you don't know the answer to that."

Erion ceded the point. As long as he could honestly tell Edric that she was still safe, that was enough. He had lied about so many other things—he wanted to be honest about *something*.

"I found something," he told Vandra, not sure how to broach the subject. He'd only returned from the nuraghi that morning. The taint of the place still lingered in his bones.

"Not. Now."

Two glasses of white wine appeared on the table before them. Erion raised a questioning brow.

"We might as well enjoy ourselves if we have to be here." Vandra shrugged.

"And here I thought you wanted my company." Erion masked his irritation by taking a sip of the wine—he had no idea whether or not it was any good.

"I do." Vandra rested her hand on his. "But you need to see something."

Erion nodded, trying not to look at their hands.

"You're not exactly inconspicuous with that bloody great sword," Vandra said after a moment. "What is it with men and their constant need to show off?"

Erion grinned and twisted his hand under hers so their palms were touching. He squeezed her hand quickly, then pulled away. "I've got to keep your attention somehow."

Jokes aside, Erion hoped Vandra would get to the point of their detour soon. He hadn't liked taking Thorne into his confidences about the baron and his discoveries at the manor. Now he had to step outside of his comfort zone again, and pray he wasn't asking Vandra to stick her neck out too far this time.

Their dinner arrived. Erion tucked in, thoroughly enjoying the sticky-sweet honey sauce that the rabbit had been roasted with. Vandra picked over her food. Her hawkish gaze darted to the doors every time someone new entered.

"Are you watching?" Vandra asked.

"Watching for *what?*"

"Try something for me—anything unusual in the room?"

He glanced out over the tables. The room was more than half full now, and busy enough that they weren't likely to be overheard. Several soldiers sat in the corner across from them, one eyeing Erion's sword with obvious suspicion.

Erion followed the others' gazes to the only other armed person in the room, a woman with dark hair tied in a casual knot on the back of her head, her back turned to them. She shifted as he watched her, bringing her face into profile and moving just enough that the great saber buckled to her waist came fully into view.

Erion's brows shot up. He should have recognized her immediately. The casual manner in which her hand dangled by the hilt of the saber was unmistakable. This was a woman ready to fight, and fight well. She'd been patrolling the Elarazii border just days before, and now Erion was just outside her sphere of awareness once more.

He chewed his rabbit slowly, thinking.

"Maybe," he hedged. What would Vandra find unusual? Two Delvers sat at the bar—that was unusual, but probably too obvious.

Vandra lifted her wine to her lips but didn't drink. She was watching the armed woman closely.

Erion frowned. Following a growing suspicion, he tapped into his majea. His bastard sword practically thrummed at his side, reverberating with the soft drumbeats he'd come to associate with the weapon's unique makeup. He still had no idea what he was looking for, but he stretched his senses further— something he'd been practicing.

His majea zeroed in on the woman's blade immediately. He could all but see magic bleeding out of the weapon, radiating with a white-hot energy.

Vandra tapped him on the arm, and Erion realized he'd been

staring. He lifted his brows. "Like magic sword, unusual?"

Vandra set her jaw, looking grim but satisfied. "I thought as much. It looks like we have a visitor from Corsia."

Erion choked on the mushroom turnover he was eating. He took a drink and cleared his throat. "You can't mean…"

Vandra nodded grimly. "Aleria syn'Duvar. A Guardian of Pelinon."

Erion looked down at his food, suddenly petrified of accidentally catching the Guardian's eye. When he'd seen her in Elarazii, he'd suspected she would bring new complications… but this? "I know her."

"No, you don't," Vandra said.

"Fine. But I've seen her before. She was with one of the Elarazii patrols when Thorne and I—" Erion hissed in pain as Vandra kicked him in the shin.

"Later." Her eyes were wide with panic, an expression he'd never seen on her face before.

"There are easier ways to get a point across," Erion growled. "What's she doing here?"

"Isn't it obvious?"

Erion tapped his fingers against the table. There were plenty of things going on in Rijeka that might merit a visit from the highest enforcing body in the country—but surely if King Sarren III was going to send someone, he would have done it months ago.

"Something big is about to happen, isn't it?" Erion asked.

Vandra pressed her lips together into a thin line. "Let's go. I have to take care of something."

Erion reached for his coin purse, but she shook her head. "I have a tab here. They'll handle it."

"A tab?" Erion asked. Vandra was so entangled with the Crimson Fang he sometimes forgot that she did plenty of legitimate business on top of enabling kidnappers and smugglers.

They retrieved their cloaks in the foyer. Erion stood with the door open while Vandra made a fuss tying her cloak. A hooded man hurried up the steps and pushed past Erion into the inn, bumping into Vandra in his haste to get into the dining hall.

Vandra made a face at the man as he rushed past, but he didn't seem to notice. Erion eyed the man, and was surprised when he stopped at the Guardian's table and lowered his hood. It was Captain Lars Talbot.

Erion did a double-take. Vandra was already halfway down the stone steps leading to the street. Biting back a frustrated sigh, he followed her out the door.

"Are you going to tell me what's going on?" Erion asked as he caught up with Vandra on the street.

"There's a piece of this that Mathieu hasn't told me. Something he's brokered with the Ithynon on his own."

"What does that have to do with a Guardian being in the city?"

"He's taking risks and he isn't consulting me. He's going to get caught."

Erion shrugged, trying to look indifferent—but something in him flared to life at the thought. With Mathieu out of the equation, he might be free from the Crimson Fang for good.

A gust of icy wind blasted down the street, ruffling their cloaks. Erion tapped Vandra's shoulder and drew her under the eaves of a nearby shop. "You do *all* of Mathieu's deals?"

"The big ones. As far as I know."

Erion puffed out a breath. He wasn't sure whether he should be amused or disturbed that Vandra was so upset at being left out of deals involving kidnappings and murders.

"I thought he didn't know who the Ithynon was?" he asked, proceeding with caution.

"*I* certainly haven't told him."

So she did know. Erion threw caution to the frigid wind. "It's the baron, right?"

Vandra's calm, collected facade shattered. "How do *you* know that?"

"Nice to have the suspicions confirmed." Erion ran a hand over his face. A headache was building in his temples.

Of course, Thorne had already agreed with his theory, but

Erion had harbored a small hope that they were wrong. If it was Voloy, all of this had been happening right under Erion's nose. He'd been so focused on hating his father that he'd never noticed the rot in his own basement—literally.

"This is madness," Erion said finally.

"This is *business*," Vandra argued, but misgivings flickered across her face.

Erion rolled his eyes. "We're just going to sit back and watch this?"

"I don't like it any more than you do."

"How much money are you making off all of this misery?" The words snapped out of Erion, whip-quick and bitter.

"At least I'm not wielding the sword."

"So what *I'm* doing is wrong, but you're in the clear," Erion said flatly.

"We all make our choices."

"I didn't *get* a choice," Erion said.

"You could have left the city."

"You actually made it quite clear that that was a death sentence for me *and* my brother." It was the first time Erion had ever been tempted to tell someone about Edric's magic. Vandra knew how dangerous the situation was—surely she'd sympathize with his need to get Edric as far away as possible. But he couldn't tell her. It was too risky—and it wasn't his secret to give. "The situation is… complicated. It's not what you think."

"What I *think* is that you're a spoiled, self-centered, narrow-sighted servant's boy who's never had to worry about anything but himself. I *think* you've tried to make the best of a bad situation, but every single decision you've made since joining the Crimson Fang has made things worse. For yourself, for *me*—and don't get me started on what you've done to Thorne."

"Thorne?" Erion sputtered. The turn in the conversation was as bewildering as her sudden burst of temper. "What does Thorne have to do with this?"

"Do you know how hard he's worked to stay in Rijeka? How hard it was for him to come back here?"

"I have no idea what you're talking about," Erion said, truthfully.

"Of course not. Why would you care about anyone else's problems when your own are so very pressing?"

"You don't understand." Now Erion definitely wasn't going to explain the truth of his predicament.

"I understand that a Guardian is nosing around the city, and if Mathieu goes down, he's taking all of us with him."

"So your concern is all self-interest." Erion shouldn't have been surprised.

"We're all on our own, in the Fang."

"With Mathieu gone, maybe it wouldn't have to be that way."

"Or *maybe* a dozen petty crime lords in the city will start a bloodbath over who gets to be the next king of the sewers."

Erion couldn't argue the point. He was all too familiar with choosing the known evil over the unknown.

"So what are you going to do, tell Mathieu? Let him kill a Guardian of Pelinon?" he asked.

"Because *that* would go over so well."

"Then what are we talking about, Vandra?" Erion's irritation bled out of him. The night had been so promising, and now they were having a full-fledged argument over who was more at fault for the city's decay.

"Nothing," Vandra snapped. The cold fury in her eyes stung, but not more than her determination to write off Erion's own good intentions.

"Goodnight, then." Erion lifted his hood and stomped away from her. Vandra didn't follow him.

He could find information about the Guardian back at Voloy's estate. While he couldn't discredit Vandra's concerns about Mathieu being exposed, he couldn't sympathize with it.

If Aleria *could* bring down the Crimson Fang, if she *could* stop the kidnappings and the madness... Erion trudged down the road with his head bowed against the chill. He needed more information.

Erion approached the guardhouse from a narrow alley. He wanted to speak to Talbot, but he couldn't afford to get caught by that Guardian if they came back here. It wasn't too late. He could afford to wait a while.

He tapped the back wall of the guardhouse and, with a thought, loosened the mortar in the wall. A handful of stones pushed out toward him, forming footholds and hand grips. Erion scaled it easily. Each stone slid neatly back into place after he climbed it. With the slightest prompting, the mortar re-sealed once Erion reached the roof.

He lay on his stomach, brooding as he watched passersby on the street below. The sun fell, and traffic waned as the night's chill grew. He'd almost resolved to go home when Talbot came down the road, accompanied by the Guardian Aleria syn'Duvar.

She cut an imposing figure. Nearly as tall as Talbot, she walked with a confidence that made the sword on her hip seem an extension of her body rather than a weapon. Erion tapped into the wellspring of his majea and was once more overwhelmed with the power in the saber she carried. He itched to learn more about it, but didn't think he'd get a chance.

If he ever got close enough to inspect the weapon, the Guardian would probably be skewering him with it.

Aleria syn'Duvar was here to make an end of the Crimson Fang, and Erion was caught in the storm. He scowled when Talbot and Aleria entered the guardhouse together. He'd waited here for nothing. He didn't dare approach Talbot while the Guardian was with him. But maybe...

Erion crawled forward until he reached the edge of the roof. He had a general idea of where Talbot's office was. Erion slipped his fingers between two roof tiles. They whispered of stone quarries and split shale, a fractured song that contrasted the warm, sturdy feeling of the brick from the fireplace a few paces to his left. Erion gripped the two tiles and urged them to part, but ran into timbers of wood beneath the roof.

No good. He tried again near the window, leaning over the edge of the roof and cutting carefully into the mortar that joined the uppermost stones together. The mortar melted away under his prompting. Voices drifted through the small opening.

Grinning, Erion split the seam wider, then pulled aside a few more roof tiles until he could see through the small gap. It wasn't much of a view—just Talbot's elbow resting against the arm of his chair—but he could hear, and that was all that mattered.

"...the dates line up perfectly." A woman's voice, strong and authoritative, drifted up through the stone. Erion let one arm hang over the side of the roof and pressed his hand flat against the stone wall. It reverberated each word slightly, enhancing his hearing.

"Where are you going to send the others?" Talbot asked.

"Two have requested passage out of the city. That's being arranged. We don't have any reason to think they were targeted specifically, but..."

"They were all of an age, all reasonably healthy," Talbot argued. "They must have other things in common."

"None of them had magic, if that's what you're asking," Aleria said after a pause.

"Two clear groups, then."

"We can't delay the Kuriositar Festival," Aleria said.

Erion's brows knit together. *That* was a subject jump. He wasn't following the connection.

Talbot snorted. "Even if we wanted to, the baron would never authorize it. He rarely responds to petitions anymore."

"I've arranged an audience with him."

"That's a feat in itself."

"His steward wasn't in a position to argue. I found him in a... compromising position."

Stoned out of his mind, probably. Niklas hadn't scribed anything about an audience with a Guardian, though. After an initial wave of irritation, Erion realized it was better that way. He didn't have to report Aleria's arrival to Mathieu if he didn't officially know she was here yet.

But when was her meeting with the baron, and what did any

of it have to do with the festival?

Erion had almost a thousand dakkari squirreled away in his rooms at the estate, and perhaps another eight hundred waiting at the Hunter's Guild for him to sign for. He thought over his recent jobs for Sadiq. Maybe another two hundred credited to him, once his father's most recent debts had been subtracted.

Two thousand dakkari. It was enough to get Edric started at the academy in Saritu'e'Mere, at least for a term or two. The boy would have to find work—and Erion would probably never sleep again if he was going to keep the funds flowing to sustain Edric's education.

He needed more time—something there was never enough of.

Voices drifted toward him again. Erion refocused on Aleria's words.

"…completely out of hand."

"I've been doing what I can—but I have no idea who to trust. How do you get rid of corruption that's gripped every other official in the whole damned barony?" Talbot was saying.

"By banging heads against the wall, one at a time." Erion could practically hear Aleria grinning. "Starting at the top."

"If anyone needs a good shake, it's Voloy," Talbot replied. "His steward isn't much better."

"I've seen worse."

"I'll start juggling our rosters, make sure the watch is doubled over the next few weeks."

"With men you trust?"

Talbot laughed bitterly. "The ones I mistrust least."

"We all do what we can. I've got my eyes on another hot spot in the city, I'm hoping you can give me some information. A tavern in the Apothiki District."

"You could widen that to the whole district, and the Wharf District, and you've just about found the whole territory of the Crimson Fang. The worst of their dens are near the docks, but the biggest one is actually up north. Wealthier clients."

"And the tavern, the Crimson Fury? They aren't exactly

trying to hide."

"No need. I don't have enough men to take the place. It's right in the center of Mathieu Sifet's holdings."

Erion's interest piqued. Talbot was better informed than he'd suspected—and Mathieu wasn't being as careful as he thought.

"It's enough to be getting on with, I suppose. I'll be in touch about that," Aleria said.

"You're not *going* there?" Talbot asked, sounding shocked.

"Only if other plans fall through."

"Alone?"

"They already know who you are." Aleria laughed faintly. "Cheer up, captain. There are worse places to get into a bar fight than a tavern full of drunken criminals."

"Like a tavern full of sober ones?"

"Exactly."

"Amarassa's blessing follow you, Guardian. I'll keep you updated about the watch. Should I contact you at Wilder's Keep?" Talbot said.

Aleria must be staying at the inn where Vandra had taken Erion. He made a mental note to avoid the area for the foreseeable future.

"No, I'll come here. Better nobody makes a connection between us, for now."

A few moments later, Aleria appeared on the street outside the guardhouse. Erion held his breath as he watched her figure disappear into the night. If one good thing had come out of the conversation, at least Erion knew he'd made the right call in trusting Talbot to help with Amelie, even though the girl had never reached him. If the guard captain was this willing to help a Guardian, then Erion could trust him too.

CHAPTER THIRTY-SEVEN

ATHIS

E dric sat back in his chair and rubbed his eyes. He'd spent hours bent over the workbook Gian had given him. The candles in the workshop were burning low, and sunlight was beginning to fade beyond the windows.

A growl in his stomach reminded him he hadn't eaten dinner. It had been worth it. He looked over his notes with grim satisfaction, then glanced at the vials of sunset-orange-tinted oils by the window.

It wasn't a showy trick—not unless someone who was bleeding out came to him during the Kuriositar Festival. But once people realized he'd successfully bound zomajea into the athis bandages… If that wasn't enough to get him a sponsor to the magic academy, nothing would.

The door to the workshop opened. Gian escorted a kitchen worker, Moura, into the sickroom. Her hand was wrapped in bloodstained linen. Edric hopped up from his chair and followed them. He'd known the cook's assistant since he was a boy— Moura had calloused hands, a kind smile, and no hesitation over smacking him with a spoon when he got too close to the soup.

She sat on a bench, keeping her hand elevated above her heart as Gian directed. She couldn't have been too badly hurt because she smiled as Edric approached.

"Butchering another pig?" Edric asked her.

"Cutting one of them damned onions!" A pink tinge of embarrassment rose in her cheeks. It made her look younger. "My eyes water something fierce and I nearly chopped off my own finger. Silly thing."

Gian took the rag away from her hand. Edric's head spun when her wound was revealed. It was *not* a silly thing. Moura hadn't exaggerated her wound, her left middle finger was sliced almost all the way through at the second knuckle.

Edric bit down on his tongue. Erion's injury had been far worse than Moura's, and he'd gotten through it. He couldn't afford to be squeamish.

"Everyone thinks working in the kitchens is a soft job," she said as Gian inspected the injury. "I've had worse."

"You have not," Gian scolded her. "I might not be able to save it. Hold this."

Gian put the rag back over her hand, and Moura pressed it around the wound obediently. Gian turned to a shelf and started collecting ingredients. He upended a healing tincture into a small bowl.

"Edric, would you help me? I'm going to clean the wound. Add a sealing agent to that and make a salve of it, please. Something thick, we'll need to make sure it adheres to her finger."

Edric obeyed, taking over the small array of ingredients that Gian had laid out. He added the sealing agent, meant to stop bleeding, to the tincture Gian had already prepared, then paused with his hand hovering over several small clay jars.

As soon as Gian turned his back, Edric slipped a vial of his own orange-tinted mixture from his pocket, an oil derived from his athis flowers. He added several drops to the small bowl, then set to mixing all of Gian's ingredients together into a thick salve.

Edric frowned at the bowl as he brought it to Gian. Was the color off from what Gian would expect from this mix, or was he imagining the soft orange tinge?

"What did you use?" Gian threaded a fine bone needle with a thread of treated sinew. Edric winced as the needle pierced Moura's skin. Tears formed in her eyes, and she bit her lip as Gian put careful stitches into her calloused skin.

"The eranthus clay," Edric said. "It shouldn't move much, once it sets, right?"

"Good choice." Gian's eyes never left his work. Moura winced when he tied off the last stitch. Edric forced himself to look more closely at the work. The stitches were so tiny they were all but invisible. Gian claimed he wasn't a lifeweaver, but to Edric, that made what he did even more impressive.

"Go ahead," Gian said, taking a step back.

"You should take a break, after this," Edric told Moura. He dabbed the salve gently on her finger. Tears were streaming down her cheeks now, but she managed a chuckle.

"You just tell Runan that, lad," she joked.

"I will." Edric met her eyes. "I'll talk to him. You need rest."

The athis flower had powerful healing properties on its own, but Edric's spellwork had heightened their potency. In doing so, he'd also heightened the stinging sensation of the treatment— and the energy-sucking properties that made it such an unpredictable reagent in healing.

Edric closed his eyes and called his majea forward. Moura's life force danced where his hand rested on her wrist. Tendrils of energy slipped down her arm, stopping to congregate and pulse around her injured finger.

The athis salve practically glowed with a soft energy of its own, intermingling with Moura's natural wellspring of life. The athis wasn't actually healing, in a magical sense—not like how Edric had used his own energy to heal Erion after he'd been kicked by that colt, or even how the raw poultice had helped to heal Erion's leg. Instead, the oil derivative was redirecting Moura's own energy, encouraging her body to quicken the healing process.

Confidence and excitement burned in Edric's chest as he watched Gian wrap Moura's finger first in bandages, then a soft cast. She already seemed more at ease, more calm, and the sense of shock and distress in her life force was waning rapidly.

It's working.

He couldn't go around the festival cutting people open and forcing his bandages onto them, though. There had to be a better way to show off the skill. He just needed to find it.

CHAPTER THIRTY-EIGHT

REVELATIONS

rion went straight back to the guardhouse to meet with Talbot the next morning. Any way Erion looked at it, trouble was brewing. It was time to decide what side he was on.

He took a deep breath before tapping on Talbot's door. It opened almost at once. Talbot was unshaven, and his disheveled clothing and dark circles under his eyes led Erion to think the man had slept in his office.

"Erion?" Talbot's eyes darted around the hall. "Who's seen you?"

"Just Josef, at the desk." Erion jerked a thumb over his shoulder.

"Come in." Talbot rushed him over the threshold, then closed and locked the door. "What do you need?"

"Where's the fire?" Erion asked, trying to act casual.

"The entire damned city." Talbot slumped behind his desk. "Unless this is important, Erion, I really don't—"

"It's about the kidnappings."

Talbot's jaw slacked. "How do you know about that?"

"Everyone knows." Erion tried not to snap. He had to be as forthright as possible to get the information he needed. He'd been up half the night thinking over the conversation he'd overheard between Talbot and the Guardian.

In truth, Erion didn't want to know what was really going on. He wanted to hide under a rock somewhere and believe he'd come to a madman's conclusion about the whole thing. It was a great plan—except he suspected Edric was still planning on going to the Kuriositar Festival. Where Edric was concerned, Erion couldn't afford to play deaf and dumb.

"I sent a girl to you a few weeks ago. Her name was Amelie."

Talbot ran a hand across the stubble on his jaw and frowned. "Young girl? Someone might have mentioned it. She didn't give her name, but I was told someone was asking for me. She ran out before I got back. You sent her?"

"She was one of the kidnapping victims. She escaped."

Talbot narrowed his eyes at Erion. "And how did it come about that *you* spoke with her?"

"Chance," Erion said, honestly. "I knew you'd be discreet about helping her."

"I don't know what happened to her. I'm sorry."

"She's safe," Erion said. "Look, I know about the missing women. And about the warehouse breakout last week. I need some information, and I think I can give you some in return."

Talbot closed his eyes. "You're about to tell me something I really don't want to hear, aren't you?"

"Only if you make me." Erion had been careful not to tell anyone outside of the Crimson Fang that he'd become a blooded member. It was safer this way. The fewer people knew, the less likely Edric was to find out.

Things were coming to a point past which there would be no return, though. Talbot's meeting with a Guardian of Pelinon confirmed that Erion could trust him to do the right thing. The real question was whether Talbot would trust *him* once he admitted to being a member of the barony's most dangerous gang.

"Sit." Talbot gestured at the chair across from his desk, which was littered with crumpled parchments and a small pile of confiscated icho crystals. "Tell me what you know."

"The primary icho supplier for the city's lounges has threatened to pull out. I'm pretty sure it's the same man behind the disappearances."

"I'm going to need something more concrete than that."

"The drugs are being ferried through Elarazii, but most of it is actually being produced here. Some of the v'deru plants are cultivated on the baron's lands. Would you be interested in their locations?"

Talbot leaned forward. "How do you know?"

"I've taken over some of my father's duties as steward. He's not... well. And I know the fence who brokered the deal for the Crimson Fang. Their supplier calls himself the Ithynon."

"Ithynon... Fine, I'll bite. But first, tell me how you know all this. The truth."

Erion bit the inside of his cheek and unlaced the bracer on his left arm to reveal the fang tattoo. All he could do was pray Talbot wouldn't arrest him. *No going back now.*

Talbot blew out a deep sigh and nodded at the mark. "That recently?"

Erion ran a hand over the intertwining ridges of white scars on his inner arm, his fingers lingering over the two blood-red drops at the point of the mark. He nodded.

"I'm sorry, lad. I know it hasn't been easy for you."

It had been a while since someone had called Erion *lad.* Coming from the watch captain, it rang of pity.

"It was..." Erion trailed off, not knowing where to start. He might trust Talbot with this, but he still couldn't tell anyone about Edric's magic—especially after what he'd overheard the night before.

"Complicated?" Talbot suggested.

Quiet relief washed over Erion, and he nodded. "For me— but especially for my brother. It may be the only way out for him."

"How involved are you?" Talbot's serious, grey eyes bore into him over steepled fingers.

"Too much," Erion admitted. "They seem to like having me around."

"They trust you?"

"Sort of."

Talbot snorted and put fingertips to his temples as though warding off a headache. "We knew about the v'deru. It was too risky to destroy the fields without knowing who we were really dealing with. Mathieu seems to have a stranglehold on half the city."

"He can't know I'm here." Desperation tinged Erion's words. Talbot would know the consequences Erion faced if he was caught, but he had to make sure they were on the same page.

"They won't get it from me. But a full quarter of my men are taking bribes. I suspect another quarter, but can't prove it."

"These kidnappings. The women. They're being taken by the same supplier."

"You don't know who this Ithynon is?"

"As it so happens, I do," Erion said, slowly. He wouldn't be doing the captain any favors by giving him that information right now.

"The tiniest bit of blood on your arm, and they trusted you with that information?" Talbot actually looked impressed.

"I figured it out."

"You're not dumb, lad, I'll give you that." Talbot fixed him with a hard, calculating look. "But you're not going to tell me, are you?"

Erion shook his head. "There's still too much I don't know, and I don't want to put you in danger. You already know about the warehouse in the Wharf District. I hoped… you'd be able to keep an eye out for more problems, there. They're not doing very nice things to those girls."

"I didn't exactly think they were being taken for tea."

"I need any information you can give me about the other disappearances."

Talbot's brows raised.

"I know there have been a few that don't fit the typical profile."

Talbot's gaze flitted across the room and rested on a map of Rijeka tacked to the wood-paneled wall. He stared at it for a weighted moment. Silence stretched between them, the tension palpable.

"Please," Erion said. "I'm trying to help."

"You've got a funny way of showing it, you know?"

"I know a lot more than I let on," Erion said cautiously. "Like how you probably had help clearing out that warehouse and getting those girls away."

Talbot actually laughed. "I guess being up there in the manor has its perks. Nothing gets past you... no wonder you were recruited."

"Like I said, it's complicated." Erion hesitated. "I do want to help. I haven't told Mathieu anything he doesn't already have from other sources."

"Oh?"

"How long has she been here?"

Talbot drummed his fingers on the table. "You're putting me in a tough situation here. Aleria syn'Duvar... I'm not sure. Just met her."

"It's getting serious if a Guardian is involved."

Talbot stood and motioned for Erion to follow him to the map on the wall. Blue and green pins dotted its surface. "There's not much more to lose at this point, and if your lot are behind it, it's not like I'm giving away any information."

"I wouldn't exactly call them *my lot.*" Erion curled his shoulders defensively. He was on the wrong side of the fence and knew it—but he didn't have to like it.

Talbot ignored him and jabbed a finger at two pieces of parchment tacked up to the right of the map. Erion skimmed Talbot's untidy scrawl: one, a list of women's names, followed by locations or places of employment. A few didn't even have surnames. In one case there was no name at all, only *"laundress; Psari District."*

Women of no family or position to speak of; notable enough for someone to report their absence, but not well known enough to warrant a name of their own.

Vague descriptions accompanied each line item. That was their legacy. Lifetimes of struggle, hopes, and community, reduced to a line item on the watch captain's wall. The list was longer than Erion had hoped.

The second list was shorter, but far more disconcerting.

Merthin Oxnard; blacksmith's apprentice; 15
Laila Kirstsdotir; apothecary; 17
Gerome Morrow; trawler; 15

He wrenched his gaze away from the names.

What in Gallantyr's name is going on? The disappearances had to be related. Erion followed Talbot's attention to the map, where two sets of colored pins were scattered across the city.

Erion pointed to a cluster of pins around the town square bordering the Empori District, where there wasn't usually much crime. "So what are these?"

"This first list is green. That's been going on longer."

Erion did a double-take. That meant the second list—*kids, they were just kids!*—was marked with blue pins. "This is where they were living?"

"Where they were last seen."

"Talbot… when did this start?"

"The women? A year and a half or so ago. The kids—just a little over a year."

Erion felt the blood drain from his face. The disappearances had started around the time of the Kuriositar Festival… youth disappearing, just when Rijeka's talented were putting their newly cultivated majea on display for the whole city to see.

"I went back and realized there might be one from last winter that I'd missed. Otherwise… all around the same time, with a few exceptions. These—" he pointed to a third list that

Erion had missed, half-covered by the map "—we didn't immediately associate, but they seem to fit."

"To fit *what*?" But Erion could feel the blood draining from his face again. There weren't any immediately obvious similarities in the last list. Men and women, all of differing ages.

Talbot hesitated, grimaced. "Kurioi—almost all of them."

"So if this started around the time of festival... those kids... People are still going missing and the festival is *next week*," Erion said, trying to ward off panic. Signs of preparation were already springing up all over the city. Arrangements of greenery, garlands—a few early vendor stalls had even been erected near the town square.

"If you have a solution, I'm happy to hear it," Talbot snapped. "Maybe you can get rid of Mathieu, save us all some grief."

Erion fell back into his chair. The icho crystals weren't just drug paraphernalia. That much had been clear from their presence in the baron's dungeon workshop. His *laboratory*. If the so-called Ithynon had threatened Mathieu with cutting off the Fang's supply of crystals, it could only mean one of two things: either the baron had gotten what he wanted from the arrangement or, more likely, he'd found a better way to accomplish what he needed.

He thought of Jolie Voloy's body in its hellish chrysalis, the bloodstains on the worktable and the nuraghi's altar. The finger they'd cut from Amelie's hand. The hellhounds, magically altered until their size and tracking abilities far outstripped that of any normal hound.

Whatever the baron was up to, he'd been using huge quantities of magic to do it.

"Talbot." Erion was afraid to know the answer to his next question, but he had to know. "Is the baron a kurios?"

Talbot looked surprised at the question. "Not many people know that. He doesn't have a lot of formal training—nothing like Cedivar. But he's a Life Magician."

"Gods protect us." Erion stared up at the map, not seeing it through the horror that seized him.

He should have seen it the moment he'd discovered the baroness's body. Baron Voloy was trying to resurrect his late wife—and he was experimenting on women and young mages to get power and experience enough to do it.

CHAPTER THIRTY-NINE

THADDEUS

E rion left Talbot's office through the back wall, opening a doorway through the stone directly onto the street.

"Nice and discreet," Talbot said wryly as the stones folded away to create the opening.

"If I'm lucky, everyone will forget I was here," Erion said. "I'll do what I can for you."

"That's a dangerous spot to be in," Talbot warned. "Be careful. I'd hate to arrest you."

"I'll try not to disappoint." Erion forced a grin.

Erion broke into a run as soon as he'd sealed the wall back up. It was still early, and the freezing air chapped his skin as he turned to run back to the baron's estate.

An obstacle in the shape of Thorne leapt out at him as soon as he rounded the corner.

Erion's arms windmilled as he tried to avoid the man, but their collision was inevitable. His feet knocked Thorne's legs out from under him and they crashed onto the cobblestones.

"What do you want?" Erion practically screamed at him.

"Shut up and follow me." Thorne grabbed Erion by the forearms, hauled him to his feet, and started dragging him down the road.

Erion was too stunned by Thorne's use of "me" to argue. He followed, half-dazed. He was overwhelmed with the news he'd gotten from Talbot, and lacked the presence of mind to fight back.

They didn't go far. Thorne marched Erion through a warren of merchant stalls in the Lower Empori District, down a side street, and onto a street of modest row houses. They stopped at one with blue shutters. Thorne unlocked the front door and shoved Erion inside.

"Are you *trying* to get killed?" Thorne slammed the door shut.

"Where are we?" Curiosity momentarily won out over Erion's other concerns. The home was neatly furnished. Simple but comfortable furniture was laid out on colorful woven rugs. The tantalizing scent of fresh-baked bread wafted out from the small kitchen at the back of the home.

"Not your business. What are you doing meeting with that guard?"

"I'm getting really sick of you following me all the time, you know?"

"Thorne knows. Doesn't care. He didn't say anything when you went to that damned nuraghi against orders, or when you hunted down that Guardian, or when you let that girl go, but this is too much."

"Vandra found the Guardian," Erion argued before he could stop himself. "Wait, how did you know about that?"

"Thorne will be having plenty of words with Vandra later. What did you say to the guard?"

"He's an old friend." Irritation bubbled in Erion's gut. He didn't have to explain himself to Thorne—he had to get out of here. He grabbed the door handle.

A soft thunk and a tug of pressure drew Erion's attention to his hand. One of Thorne's throwing knives was embedded in his sleeve, pinning him to the door.

Erion turned a cold glare on his companion. "I'm leaving, Thorne. Stop following me."

"If Thorne stops, you're going to get us both killed."

"Tell Mathieu I ran away, I don't care." The Crimson Fang didn't matter anymore. He'd lost sight of his goal in all the madness of his reluctant criminal life, but Talbot's revelation had brought everything home in astounding clarity. If he left, Mathieu would probably follow Erion to the Wyrm Wall and back. But that was a problem for the future.

Erion just had to get Edric out before the festival.

"Explain." Thorne's tone was calm, but another throwing knife danced in his fingers.

"Hello?" A woman's voice floated down from the floor above. Thorne's eyes widened with panic. The floorboards overhead creaked; someone was coming down the stairs.

In a blink, Thorne's knives—including the one nailing Erion to the door—vanished. "You don't talk," he hissed at Erion.

A cheery looking woman appeared on the landing. She beamed when she saw Thorne.

"It's about time you lugged your sorry carcass here." Her black hair, knotted neatly at the top of her head, was graying at the temples, and the crinkles around her eyes didn't fade when her smile did. She embraced Thorne when she reached the bottom of the stairs.

"I do wish you wouldn't bring all that in here." She poked the hilt of Thorne's butterfly sword, then put her hands on his shoulders and held him at arm's length. She was several inches shorter than him, but he seemed to shrink in her presence. "You're filthy."

Thorne grumbled something inaudible.

"Who's your friend?" The woman turned bright, inquisitive eyes on Erion.

"Nobody," Thorne said. "Just needed a place to talk."

"You can talk and wash dishes at the same time. I'm Saara, love. Welcome in," she added as an aside to Erion. She bustled them toward the kitchen.

"Take that off, will you? Both of you. Amarassa bless me, no weapons at the table. Who raised you?" She laughed at her own joke, then shoved a clean rag into Erion's hand.

"We don't really have time—" Thorne protested.

"Wash." Saara thrust a rag at Thorne and pushed him toward a basin in the corner. She pointed at Erion. "Dry."

"Yes, Mother." Thorne slumped, defeated.

Thoroughly amused, Erion followed Thorne to the basin. "*Mother?*"

"Did you think Thorne sprouted out of the ground?" Thorne growled.

"I hadn't ruled that out."

"Just needed a quiet place to talk. They know not to come here." Thorne poked at a large bread pan floating in the basin.

"The Fang?" Erion asked.

Thorne nodded. "Special privileges for people who don't court disaster. But you watch your mouth. What Mother Saara doesn't know about Thorne's life could fill several books, and he'd like to keep it that way."

"I'm not a snitch." Erion understood better than most the importance of keeping certain things quiet. Like Edric, the less Thorne's mother knew about his involvement with the Crimson Fang, the better.

"Start talking, Traitor."

Erion sighed. "I just needed some questions answered. About that girl."

"You mean the one you traitorously released?"

"The one Sadiq let go," Erion corrected. "And yes. Drugs are one thing but Amelie... she didn't deserve that."

"But the addicts do?"

"They made their choices."

"Some of them." Thorne forced the clean bread pan at Erion. "Others..."

Erion started drying the pan automatically, distaste filling his mouth. He knew what Thorne had stopped himself from saying.

Sometimes people were pressed into their first dose of icho. That first taste was usually enough to bring them back for more. It was reprehensible—and lucrative.

"I just wanted to know—" Erion began, but Thorne interrupted him.

"Do you know what Isak would do if he'd seen you? If *Mathieu* had seen you?"

"They didn't." But Erion was far from sure. Thorne had found him easily enough. Erion was slipping.

"They *did.*"

Erion froze mid-drying.

"And Thorne saved your sorry ass so you're *welcome* for that."

Erion finished the pan and set it aside. "You don't want to get involved."

"*Duh.*"

"You're not going to report me?"

"Yet to be determined."

"I think I'm about to do something stupid."

"Thorne figured."

"Thanks for the vote of confidence."

"What's new?" Thorne menaced Erion with the bread knife he'd just washed. "Thorne doesn't like it any more than you do, but he's worried we're stuck. Whatever you're into, Thorne is into."

Erion eased the knife from Thorne's hand. Thorne had him cornered in more ways than one. Erion couldn't shake the man, and lying wouldn't do him any good. For the second time that day, he had to trust someone.

"I have to get my brother out of the city. I've been saving every dakkari since I started doing jobs for Mathieu to pay for tuition."

"To where?"

"Somewhere... not here. Anywhere. A school in Saritu'e'Mere."

"A magic school?" Thorne shot Erion a sidelong glance.

"No." But Erion answered too fast.

"Hmph. Thorne figured." Thorne nodded sagely. "It runs in families sometimes. Does the young Skala knock down walls, too?"

Erion glanced over his shoulder. Thorne's mother had gone back upstairs. He dropped into a chair, defeated. "Life Magic."

"So he talks to plants. Not crazy at all."

"You're one to talk." Erion put his head in his hands. Everything was unraveling.

"Your father throws you to the wolves, fine. You join up to protect someone. Normal. You want to get the boy out— tricky."

"Mathieu would do anything to get him if he knew Edric's abilities had manifested. Just like me."

"And fool that he is, young Skala would do anything to save your idiot self from yourself."

"Something like that."

"Then what happened?" Thorne sat down across the table from Erion and squinted at him. "What's the rush?"

"You swear you won't tell?"

"Can't do that, Dead Man."

Dead Man. Erion didn't like that one. He put his hands on the table and looked at the lines on his palms, the bloody tattoo dripping down from his wrist. "A bunch of kids went missing last year. And a few of the people lately... they think they're all kurioi. The icho—whatever they're using it for—wasn't enough."

"You're not telling Thorne everything."

"I don't have to," Erion growled through gritted teeth.

"You do if you want Thorne's help."

"Are you offering it?"

"Not yet."

Erion thumped a fist lightly against the table. "The baron's wife died. Well, I thought so. Everyone did."

Thorne just stared at him.

"Remember that day we broke into the guest chambers to

spy on the duke's men?"

"Intimately."

"Right… Well, there was something wrong that day. With the stone, the sounds…" Erion paused, wondering how to describe the malice he felt every time he tapped into the nuraghi's hateful stonewhisper.

"It's evil and probably alive and wants to murder you, Thorne's on board. Go on."

"The baron's wife is down there. Below the dungeons. They're experimenting on the women they've been kidnapping. I think the baron and Cedric are going to use the altar in that nuraghi to bring Baroness Voloy back to life." Erion said it in a rush, barely believing he was confiding in anyone, let alone Thorne.

Then again, Thorne was probably the closest thing Erion had to a friend these days. He shot a glance at the man and tried to gauge his reaction. Thorne's face had gone noticeably whiter, his chipper veneer all but shattered.

"Those scrolls in the Reinholdt place. We delivered it all right into his hands." An undercurrent of genuine worry carried Thorne's words.

Erion nodded. "My fault."

Thorne drummed his fingers on the table, casting his gaze around the modest kitchen as he thought. "Sadiq let the girl go."

Erion waited for the rest of the thought to manifest.

"So either he's in on it. Or he's not in on it," Thorne said.

"Uh… sure," Erion said, exasperated.

"So what are you gonna do about it?" Thorne asked.

Erion stared up at the ceiling. What *could* he do about it? He didn't have a plan past forcing Edric to leave the city. He didn't even have a plan to keep Edric out, once he'd gotten that far.

"If anything happens to Edric because of my mistakes, I could never live with myself," Erion said.

"Well you're not gonna live with Thorne, that's for sure."

"Thanks," Erion said wryly. "But I'm just trying to get Edric out."

Erion turned to the next dish to dry and realized a knot had loosed in his chest. Talbot and the Guardian were watching the situation. He wasn't alone in this anymore. And for some twisted reason, he trusted Thorne.

That was a scary thought.

"Thaddeus?" Saara came back into the kitchen and scowled when she saw them both sitting at the table. "Did you come here just to eat my food and make a mess, or are you going to help?"

Thorne jumped to his feet.

"Go to the well and bring back some water for the kettle, love. I'll put on tea."

"Thaddeus?" Erion mouthed. Thorne shot him a black glare on his way out the back door.

Saara pursed her lips. "He doesn't visit often. I know he's grown. I shouldn't worry, but…" Saara looked Erion up and down as though taking in the measure of him. "You seem nicer than his other friends. I don't much like that Crimson Fang business he's up to."

Erion plastered a smile onto his face. Mother Saara wasn't as naive as Thorne thought.

"It's my fault, you know. Or didn't he tell you? Got myself into a spot of trouble with a man. Thorne was just a lad. He didn't have to do what he did." She wiped her hands on a rag absent-mindedly, her eyes far away. Soft frown lines creased around the corners of her lips.

Erion desperately wanted to know what Thorne had done, but couldn't bring himself to ask. If Thorne wanted him to know, he'd have said something.

The door opened and a murderous-looking Thorne reappeared with a bucket of water. He put it down next to the cast-iron stove.

"Brilliant." Saara wiped her hands unnecessarily on her apron. "I'll just put the kettle on and feed you boys."

Thorne shot Erion a significant glance as soon as Saara's back turned. "We're in it now, Death Wish. We'll talk about your crazy later."

"Thaddeus?" Saara sing-songed.

"Yes?" Thorne practically shook under her scrutiny.

"Finish those dishes."

CHAPTER FORTY

INCOMPETENCE

L ong shadows stretched across the Wharf District's muddy streets as Cedivar reached his destination. He paused once he was within sight of the decrepit old warehouse. His latest shipment of subjects should be here, but he'd never received notice they were ready.

Cedivar had more eyes in the city than anyone suspected. They'd alerted him of the problem before Isak had—finally—come to him to report the incident. The Crimson Fang had let the Ithynon's subjects escape.

Isak called it a mistake. Cedivar called it willful incompetence.

His meetup with Mathieu wasn't for another hour or more, but Cedivar hadn't risen so far in life by being unprepared. He looked for a street number to confirm the address of the building he stood outside, then sighed irritably as he took in the worn facade. If there had ever been an address posted, the paint had long since peeled away.

He entered the alley and stomped down several stairs to the

below-street entrance. Clutching a spelled dagger at his belt, he knocked.

The door opened at once, revealing a sallow-skinned man with bushy eyebrows and a deep scar running across his jawline. The damaged skin puckered one side of his lip, giving him the air of constant wry amusement. Cedivar knew the man—and Petyr was rarely amused.

"You're early," Petyr said.

"And you shouldn't be surprised. You need to see it before the meeting."

Petyr nodded and stepped outside, and Cedivar realized he hadn't caught him by surprise. Petyr was already cloaked, armed, and ready to leave.

"Do I need to reiterate the terms?" Cedivar asked as they made their way down the street to the warehouse.

Petyr grunted. "There's no money in telling the baron about this, runecaster. You don't have anything to worry about."

Cedivar scowled at Petyr's choice of words. "Or anyone else."

"Might be money in that," Petyr admitted, without humor. "Guess you'll just have to trust me."

Cedivar couldn't afford to trust Petyr. That was probably why they had a successful working relationship. Mutual mistrust led to cautious negotiations.

The warehouse had been abandoned until very recently, and it looked the part. Windows were boarded up by rotting planks and the south side of the roof was in danger of collapse. Cedivar wrinkled his nose. What he disliked most about the Wharf District was the smell. He'd have to send his clothes to the laundress twice to get the stench out.

Cedivar considered the heavy padlock on the front door for a moment. He drew the smaller of his two daggers, then a stylus from his pocket. He drew four precise lines on the blade of the knife. The majea flared gold in his mind's eye, though to anyone else it would appear that he was scratching the steel with nothing to show for it. He inserted the tip of the blade into the keyhole on the padlock.

The blade flared white hot. Cedivar turned his face away from the brilliant light. A wisp of smoke rose from the interlocking metals, bringing with it the acrid, steel-tanged scent of melting iron.

Cedivar dropped the dagger as the heat reached the handle. Lock and blade dropped to the ground as one, forming a lump of smoking iron at the base of the doors.

"Inconspicuous," Petyr said dryly as they entered the warehouse.

"I'm tired of being underestimated," Cedivar said. And he was. Baron Voloy saw him as no more than a means to an end, and the Crimson Fang thought he was no more than the Ithynon's messenger boy.

Cedivar had contented himself with biding his time, but his patience was wearing thin.

The warehouse was a warren of broken crates and dusty, discarded fishing equipment. A rough path had been created through the refuse. The dying sunlight filtered through missing tiles in the roof. Its rays highlighted puffs of dust under Cedivar's boots as he navigated his way through the mess of useless things.

Cedivar loathed useless things—and it looked like Isak had just crossed into that territory.

A wide space had been cleared in the center of the warehouse. Six cages, not unlike the ones Cedivar kept for his bone scouts, had been brought in to fill the space. This was where Cedivar's specimens were held before the Crimson Fang brought them to him.

Except there were no women imprisoned here for experimentation, and no mages for harvest. Instead, a pile of bodies lay in the center of the floor. They'd been killed quickly—there was plenty of blood, but only one of the corpses had been dragged from outside the circle of cages. The idiot Isak hadn't even posted a lookout—his men had all been lumped in one place, waiting for death like fish in a barrel.

It was *sloppy*.

Even though he'd known what to expect, Cedivar was disgusted. Moving past the murdered men, he turned to inspect the first of the cages. The front bars had been cut away. He ran a finger across one of the stubs of metal. It came away black with ash.

Petyr followed him silently, and Cedivar had to remind himself to take care not to drop his guard. He wore a precautionary ward against the man's ermajea—Cedivar would know whether Petyr tried to read or manipulate his emotions, but he hoped the man wouldn't try. He didn't have time to kill him and find a replacement for Voloy's experiments.

"What do you think?" Cedivar asked. All four cages bore the same marks—the bars had been cut out, enabling the prisoners inside to escape.

"Smells like magic," Petyr said. His eyes were grave. "Are we here to intimidate these men, or kill them?"

"The former, unless things go poorly." Mathieu and his crew hadn't completely run the course of utility just yet.

"Land Magic, do you think?" Petyr asked, gesturing to the cages.

Cedivar frowned and didn't reply. Surely a gekurios would find a simpler method. Shearing the bars seemed an unnecessary use of energy. He stored away pondering the means of escape for later consideration.

"When he arrives, you're not to speak until I give you the signal," Cedivar instructed. "Do whatever you can to put the fear of Giants into his bones. I want him shaking."

The scar on Petyr's jaw twisted as he smiled.

CHAPTER FORTY-ONE
ONE LAST DEAL

Sadiq swaggered into the dingy warehouse like he owned it. This was the first time Mathieu had brought him to one of the Ithynon's meetings. It was critical he made a strong impression. The Ithynon may think their working relationship was over, but Sadiq knew better. Nobody with so much blood on their hands would be able to make a clean break.

Sadiq glanced sidelong at Mathieu. The big man's gaze darted around the warehouse, no doubt looking for traps and making backup plans in case the meeting went south.

Two men waited for them near the ruined cages in the center of the warehouse. One tall and thin, the other shorter, broader in the chest and shoulders. They were both hooded and cloaked, with masks covering the lower halves of their faces so that only their eyes were visible.

"Right on time." There was a touch of a sneer in the slender man's voice.

Mathieu crossed his arms and straightened, taking advantage of his not-inconsiderable height. Sadiq, slender and dark where

Mathieu was wide and sturdy, settled himself with looping his thumbs into his belt.

Mathieu was used to being the predator, and now his territory and power were being threatened. He was responding to the situation in kind with a show of aggression. It was predictable—and, Sadiq thought, a little pathetic. Sadiq preferred being underestimated. It wasn't hard to shrink into the bigger man's shadow. Mathieu's time would come. It was better to let him think he was in control.

"What happened here?" The slender man pointed to the cages.

"Are you the Ithynon?" Mathieu demanded of the shorter man.

"No preamble, I see. You so desperately wanted to meet the Ithynon. I assure you his terms haven't changed, but…" The slender man made a grandiose gesture toward his companion.

"We've done right by you," Mathieu said. "Done everything you asked. I want to know why you're ending our agreement."

"It no longer suits my needs," the Ithynon's voice was a harsh growl.

Sadiq swallowed against a lump forming in his throat. He didn't like this man, though he couldn't quite explain what exactly was putting his back up.

"What about my business needs?" Mathieu asked.

"I suggest you fill them elsewhere."

"I want *your* supplier," Mathieu said. Sadiq was impressed with his boldness, but he supposed Mathieu had little to lose at this stage in the negotiations. They couldn't force the Ithynon to provide them with a steady supply of icho crystals—and the Ithynon knew almost everything about the Crimson Fang, already.

"I'm afraid that's impossible."

"Are you?" Mathieu asked, lowering his voice. "Afraid?"

"Are you?" the Ithynon whispered.

Sadiq's hands tightened on his belt. Suddenly, *he* was very much afraid. He glanced around the warehouse. The large room was cloaked in shadows, with too many hiding spots to count. The Ithynon and his lapdog had promised to come alone—but so had Mathieu and Sadiq, and they had a half-dozen cutthroats posted at various points around the neighboring streets.

"I want what was promised me." Mathieu pursued his grievances doggedly, but Sadiq didn't miss a faint quaver in his voice.

"We never agreed on a time frame. My work here is done," the Ithynon said.

"The hell it is." Mathieu's voice had fallen almost to a whisper.

"I did warn you," the tall man added.

Sadiq frowned. He'd heard that voice somewhere before, but couldn't quite place it.

"I'll see to it you don't receive support from any of the gangs in Caraz," Mathieu said. "In the whole duchy."

"And you have that much power?" the Ithynon's mocked.

Fear cut to Sadiq's bones at the words. He found himself wanting nothing more than to run—to be far away from this man.

"Try me," Mathieu said.

"Tempting," the Ithynon said dryly. "But the icho has run its course. On that, I won't waver."

Was there a hint of reconciliation in his tone? Sadiq's gaze flitted toward Mathieu, wondering whether his boss had also sensed the shift. A weighted silence settled upon them. Mathieu glowered openly at the two men across from them.

To his horror, Sadiq's hands trembled slightly. An interminable pause stretched between the four men.

"You have proved yourself more than useful, Mathieu Sifet." The Ithynon spoke slowly, as though reconsidering something. Sadiq's growing fear ebbed.

Mathieu grunted. A faint sheen of sweat glistened on his forehead.

"I wonder whether you might take one more bounty?"

Sadiq's eyes narrowed to slits. His suspicions were

confirmed—the Ithynon had planned for this. There was always more work to be done.

"A bounty rich enough to make up for the gap in my supply? I'm going to have a lot of addicts tearing down the walls of my operations when they don't get their fix." Mathieu's words were bold, but his voice rang of false heartiness. He was clearly on edge, maybe even as much as Sadiq.

"You'll raise prices. I'm not worried about you. Call this a bridge between profits. A peace offering. Are you interested?"

"Tell me the job first."

"So you *are* interested. Very well. Despite this despicable failing—" the Ithynon swept his arms towards the damaged cages that were conspicuously free of the captives the Crimson Fang had been meant to deliver "—I think you should be able to learn from it. I need one more delivery of subjects."

"You'll have whores this time," Mathieu said. "I won't risk my men taking highborns. Too risky."

Sadiq rolled his eyes. Anyone with reputable employment or a whisper of a title was *highborn* to a wharf rat like Mathieu.

"Not women. The Kuriositar Festival approaches, as you must know. I require mages."

Satisfaction bloomed in Sadiq's chest, momentarily throttling his unease. He'd been waiting for just such an opportunity.

"I wouldn't exactly call those kids mages." Mathieu's eyes narrowed. He wasn't balking at kidnapping kids—Sadiq didn't think anything would make Mathieu flinch. No, the man's accountant-brain was trying to see how much coin he could squeeze out of this transaction.

"Six hundred a head, and you let me worry about their potentialities," the Ithynon said.

Sadiq snapped his teeth together to keep from gaping. The pay was generous—almost too much so. "What's the catch?"

"It would be remiss of me to tell you how to do *your* work," the Ithynon's invisible sneer was all but audible. "Bring them to the usual drop point at the ruins."

"And the icho?"

"Your last shipment will be waiting for you, along with the bounty."

Mathieu flexed his fingers, curling and uncurling his hands into fists. Pretending to consider, but Sadiq suspected they all knew he was going to agree to the job.

The pay was too good to turn it down—and Mathieu's earlier threats aside, the Ithynon wasn't a man they could afford to cross.

"And Mathieu? Let's keep that little wench, the Hunter's Guild girl, out of this."

"She has my full confidence," Mathieu said.

"But not mine." The Ithynon's voice was frosty. "Are we in agreement?"

"Fine." Mathieu lifted his left hand to shake hands with the masked, gloved Ithynon. His Crimson Fang tattoo, inked in deep red almost to his elbow, was prominently displayed.

The Ithynon ignored the gesture. "I'd say meeting you was a pleasure, but it wasn't. Don't disappoint me."

There was little to discuss by way of arrangements. The job and the drop point weren't new—and how hard could it be to kidnap a couple of kids? The fee the Ithynon was offering was almost laughably high.

Which meant there was a catch, whatever the Ithynon suggested.

The Ithynon and his companion left, leaving Sadiq alone with a stewing Mathieu. The doors to the warehouse scraped shut, leaving them in the cool semi-dark of the rotting building.

CHAPTER FORTY-TWO

A ROLL OF THE DICE

T hey weren't exactly shaking," Cedivar reprimanded Petyr. A putrid tang of rotting fish and refuse tainted the breeze as they approached the heartbender's quarters.

"Anything more would have been too obvious."

"Do you think they'll do it?"

"Mathieu's too proud not to. Can't be sure about the other. He's not as submissive as he pretends to be."

Cedivar filed that away for future consideration. He'd have to get more information about the slender, dark-eyed man. He might be useful.

"You have the map to the ruins?" Cedivar asked Petyr when they stopped outside the dingy boardinghouse.

"Destroyed. Got it up here." Petyr tapped his temple.

"We'll need you tomorrow night, but I expect it's the last time. We won't be getting any more specimens."

"He's ready, then?" Petyr looked skeptical.

Cedivar pursed his lips. He'd known from the beginning that

what Voloy was attempting was impossible. Once dead, a man *stayed* dead. That the Baroness Jolie Voloy was only *mostly* dead made no difference in his eyes. Cedivar was no zokurios, but he was formally educated. Life's natural processes couldn't just be reversed.

But... Drazan had proven him wrong, not just once but three times now. Since they'd added Petyr to their spell casting, the formula the baron had constructed finally seemed to be working. The last girl had been able to speak, and she'd retained enough of her senses through awakening to project true, abject terror when she'd risen from her death. She lived still—a decrepit husk of a Human. The baron was convinced Petyr would improve with practice, that a more refined touch of the mage's Love Magic would restore heart and spirit. That his beloved Baroness Jolie would return to him as she was in life.

Cedivar had almost started to believe that Voloy's experimentation would be successful, but they'd reached an impasse. A parting of the minds that Cedivar feared would be the end of this mad quest. If the baron's quest could be fulfilled, they didn't have time to perfect it.

"The whole ordeal is a gamble. But the Ithynon certainly thinks he's ready, so he won't be deterred," Cedivar said at last. "He'll succeed in his quest or he'll break in pursuit of it."

The baron was increasingly convinced that the key lay in harvesting enough life force from others to sufficiently bolster his own craft. Cedivar knew this to be folly—but Voloy wouldn't hear it.

Beneath the veneer of grieving widower, Cedivar feared true madness lurked.

Regardless of whether the venture would succeed, the time was ripe. They'd avoided the worst of Duke Jesper's speculation, but their time was running short. The murder of the duke's retinue was too suspect. There would be an inquest.

And to make matters worse, Corsia finally had the Barony of Caraz in its sights. Cedivar had it on good authority that a Guardian of Pelinon was in the city. He didn't know which one, yet, but his spies would root the warrior out soon enough.

It was time to act. The baron would harvest every last drop of life force they could after the Kuriositar Festival, and enact the final ritual deep within the nuraghi's heart.

Baron Voloy would be successful, or he wouldn't. He'd survive, or go mad, or his pursuit would kill him. No matter how the dice rolled, Cedivar would be ready.

CHAPTER FORTY-THREE

PREDATORS

Erion scattered the scrolls on his father's desk, his fingers scrabbling for the rare missives Niklas had actually bothered to open. The baron's meeting with the Guardian wasn't listed in the steward's appointment book, but he couldn't imagine Aleria had lied to Talbot about it. Far more likely Niklas had botched the records.

But if the appointment had been secured, at some point a note had been answered—which meant a letter had been *opened,* surely. He could only pray Niklas hadn't disposed of it.

He flipped through the scrolls, peering at wax seals and glancing over signatures. He'd reached the dregs of the pile before his gaze finally rested on the king's seal. The Guardians of Pelinon.

Aleria syn'Duvar.

It was all the confirmation Erion needed. Guardians didn't strike him as the type to sit around waiting for an audience. If she was in the city, she'd be meeting with the baron soon.

Erion pocketed the scroll and left the office. The baron's

chambers weren't far, and he was known to linger over his midday meal. He rapped his knuckles on the door, biting the inside of his lip as he went over his scant excuse for interrupting.

The baron's valet, Halek, opened the door and looked out at him with mild curiosity.

"I need to speak with Baron Voloy," Erion said. "The steward sent me."

"I'm afraid he's not here." Halek oozed superiority.

"Where is he?" Erion asked.

"Aren't you in charge of his appointments?"

"You're in for some surprises," Erion growled. The valet was clearly under the impression things were functional in the manor. It would have been funny under other circumstances. "Where is he?"

"He and Master Cedivar are in council."

"The council doesn't meet today." Erion was reasonably sure that hadn't changed—not even Niklas could have screwed *that* up.

"In the baron's private reception chamber. He requested a tray be brought up from the kitchens."

"Thanks. Can you send a runner for me? Have them find Edric Skala, and ask him to meet me at his rooms in about an hour. He's probably in the stables." Erion hoped.

Halek sniffed and gave Erion a measuring look.

"Thank you," Erion said, preempting the man's refusal as he turned to leave.

"Fine. But the baron asked not to be interrupted. He wasn't exactly in a fine mood." The valet had to shout his final warning—Erion was already halfway down the hall.

"I'm not exactly, either," Erion breathed as he pounded down the stairs.

His footsteps echoed around the manor's receiving hall. Two guards were posted at the door at the far end of the room, blocking Erion's way to the baron's private reception chambers. He glowered at the men and their halberds. The weapons were shiny—impressive looking, until you realized their near-perfect condition was the result of disuse. These guards should be required to work with the city watch to scourge the city of cockroaches like Mathieu, but Erion would wager they hadn't seen anything resembling real work in months.

"Get going, Skala. Baron's orders," a blond guard said as Erion approached.

"He told you, specifically, to keep *me* out?" Erion planted his feet and crossed his arms, staring the guard—Niels—down.

"He told me, generally, to keep *everyone* out." Niels leered. "No disruptions. Important meeting."

"And they've got the mage with 'em." The second guard, Olivier, scowled darkly. "Don't like crossing him."

Niels smacked Olivier in the chest.

"They who?" Erion caught Olivier's eye.

"Some woman. That mage didn't say, did he? Just told us to watch the door."

The admittance earned Olivier another backhand. This time he shoved Niels back. "No reason not to say it. Erion's just doing his job, same as us."

Erion rolled his eyes and left the guards to their squabble. Maybe it was better this way. His excuse to speak with the baron had been razor thin—something about the v'deru fields, a slim explanation of his father being ill. *And would my lord please mind going over his schedule a moment so I can make sure it's all correct in the books?*

It might have worked—or it might have gotten him kicked out of the room on his arse. Erion didn't know Cedivar well, and despite growing up in the manor, he'd only spoken to the baron a half-dozen times in his life. Considering the havoc the baron and his pet mage were wreaking in secret, perhaps a competent steward-in-training would set the men ill at ease.

But it sounded like Aleria was already here. *Some timing.*

Another pair of guards opened the front doors. A rare beam of sunlight spilled onto the tiled floor, and a small crowd of harried-looking men followed. Erion started up the stairs to avoid them. These would be representatives and tax collectors from the lands that were in arrears on their rents. Niklas was supposed to be meeting with them later this afternoon. First, no doubt, the visitors would be given food and water and excuses as to why the steward would, inevitably, be late.

Erion did a double-take. He recognized one of them. Sadiq strolled alongside the other petitioners as though he, too, carried the weight of unfair taxation and ruinous criminals running unchecked on his lands.

Their eyes met. Sadiq gave him a wolfish grin.

What was he doing here? Erion nodded back, hoping he looked casual about it. It would be too suspicious to speak with him here. Sadiq lifted one hand and made a staying motion; *nothing to see here, Skala, get on with your business.*

Then the doors that Niels and Olivier had been guarding swung open. Baron Drazan Voloy, looking ill and more foul tempered than ever, exited. He was flanked by his silver-haired mage, Cedivar, and a tall, raven-haired woman armed to the teeth. Erion gave up trying to look inconspicuous and went back down the stairs.

It was the first time he'd been able to openly stare at the Guardian of Pelinon. He'd been dazzled by the magic radiating from the sleek saber strapped to her hip. Now, he took a proper look at her face. A prominent scar marred her bold features, crossing down from her temple and down one high cheekbone until it just touched the corner of her mouth. Her gaze swept over the room, calculating and sharp.

As Erion watched, Aleria angled her head to better hear something Cedivar was saying. She didn't reply but shot the man a look of such obvious disgust that Erion took a step back.

The man standing behind Erion grunted and tripped backwards, knocking over a pedestal, upon which stood a vase holding long-stemmed sundew lilies.

The pedestal crashed into the wall, and the man's flailing arms sent the vase flying towards Erion. Water splattered across his shirt. He fumbled the catch. Acting on instinct, Erion cast a line of majea at the falling vase. The raw components in the glass reacted to his touch. The vase slowed, then came to rest gently on the ground.

Erion undid the ties at his wrists and pushed his sleeves, soaked, up to his elbows. The water squelched beneath his leather bracers, but he couldn't very well remove those in the middle of the baron's hall.

He bent to pick up the vase, painfully aware that every eye in the room was fixed on him.

A gloved hand darted forward and plucked up the narrow vase before he could. Erion looked up to find Aleria syn'Duvar crouching beside him. Her eyes were so dark they were almost black, her gaze calculating and collected. The sounds in the chamber surrounding him faded as Erion locked eyes with her. Her gaze slipped down to his exposed hand.

Erion followed her attention to the blood-red ink on his wrist. He recoiled from vase and Guardian alike, nearly knocking it to the ground again in his haste.

"Lucky, that." Aleria returned the vase to the granite-topped pedestal, then stooped to pick up the burnt-red lilies. She stroked one petal gently. The tattered blooms brightened under her attention.

Erion averted his eyes and backed away with a muttered apology.

His surroundings came back into focus gradually, like all sound and movement hastened their return to normal at once. Baron Voloy and Cedivar walked past Erion without paying him any mind. They vanished down a side hall, followed by Olivier and Niels.

Two of Niklas's minor aides were corralling the new arrivals, collecting cloaks and giving them directions. One of them met Erion's eye.

"I'm looking for the steward?" the young man asked. He couldn't be much younger than Erion, but he bowed his head with deference when Erion turned his attention to him.

"Your guess is as good as mine," Erion shrugged. A flash of sympathy struck him. "I'll find him. Go ahead and bring them to the lower council hall when they're ready. He'll be there."

Aleria was still posted at Erion's elbow. "You work for the steward?"

"In a manner of speaking. My lady," Erion added, remembering himself at the last moment.

Aleria clicked her tongue. "I practically tore this place to the ground trying to find him. Heard he's not... reliable." She flashed Erion a predator's savage grin.

Erion crossed his arms, trying to hide the edges of his Crimson Fang tattoo. "Is there anything further I can assist you with, my lady?"

Aleria pulled his arm away and yanked at the laces on his bracer before he could stop her. The leather parted, revealing the ink on his arm.

Erion shoved his sleeve back down over the mark. He half-expected her to haul him out to the town square and execute him in front of dozens of witnesses.

"Your lot has done enough *assisting*, I think." She cocked her head at him with a thoughtful expression on her face. "Though I'll admit you've answered more questions than your baron did in almost an hour. How much did they pay the steward to take you under his wing?"

Erion chewed on the inside of his cheek. She didn't know as much as she thought she did. A deep-seated urge to tell her everything stirred in him. This woman was powerful. She had resources and connections that Erion could only dream of.

The last of the petitioners and landholders filed out of the room, ushered by the two young steward's aides. Sadiq, the last in the line, shot a dark warning glance at Erion as he vanished into the corridor behind the others.

Sadiq's look doused the hopeful embers in Erion's mind. Aleria's help was something Erion would only *ever* dream of. His best hopes lay in redirecting her attention as best he could—and anything he said now would only make the situation worse. Erion bowed his head obsequiously, the very picture of a contrite servant.

Aleria pressed something into his hand and leaned close. "You want to be on the right side of this one."

And then she was gone, sauntering down the hall and out the front doors with the grace and deadly confidence of a vellish.

Erion remained rooted to the spot long after the Guardian was out of sight. If the Crimson Fang's knife at his throat hadn't been enough, now Erion had a Guardian of Pelinon breathing down his neck.

CHAPTER FORTY-FOUR

AN INKED THREAT

Niklas Skala's hands shook as he looked out over the table full of angry landholders.

Well, *most* of them were landholders. Niklas had spent the better part of an hour trying to place the face of the man seated nearest the door. He had a slender fighter's build, not a farmer or logger's broad shoulders, and the sword at his waist was both well maintained and worn with use.

Niklas knew this bronze-skinned, dark-haired man. He was certainly no landholder. But who was he? He alone hadn't brought a complaint to the table.

The steward rested his palms flat on the table in an attempt to stop them shaking. The chills would come soon, and then the overwhelming anxiety that gnawed through his mind like a living thing.

There was an icho pipe in his chambers. He just needed this meeting to end *now*.

"We will adjourn," Niklas said. "Until tomorrow."

Waves of protests washed over him, with several men

jumping to their feet in outrage.

Niklas raised his hands, a silent plea for quiet.

The baron had demanded more funds—Niklas had overseen the tax increases. The baron demanded lands be converted to v'deru fields—Niklas oversaw replanting, destruction of carefully rotated planting schedules, and disruption of seasonal trade.

The baron demanded Niklas settle matters with these unhappy, mistreated people just trying to feed their families and make an honest living. And Niklas stood at the head of the table, knowing he had managed to fail them all.

"You will all be given quarters, and fed, and we will resume in the morning." Niklas strained to maintain an air of authority. A sense of hollowness ravaged his core, his craving growing with every second.

"We have to look to planting soon, steward. My hold won't replant mid-season again, you have my word. You'll have to send men to burn the fields and reseed themselves if you want v'deru growing on my lands. I won't have it." The man speaking was the youngest of the bunch, and had quickly asserted himself as spokesman. The others seemed keen to let this firebrand lead the way.

"The v'deru has been very profitable," Niklas argued. His knees were weak. "For trade with Elarazii."

"It doesn't feed my village. The taxes are criminal, and the damned plant ruins the soil." There was a whisper of agreement from the other petitioners.

"Tomorrow." Niklas waved a hand at one of the baron's guards by the door, who nodded and opened the door. One of Niklas's aides—he was always forgetting their names—started telling the villagers where they'd be spending the night.

A wave of exhaustion swept through Niklas, and he slumped back in his chair. He should have brought Erion to this meeting. The boy was smart. Why not put him in charge?

His eyes closed of their own volition. He'd put Erion through so much. The withdrawal was taking hold. Niklas was always at his weakest right before his first pipe of the day.

Erion didn't want his help. Why give it? Why bother?

Niklas forced himself upright and opened his eyes. A folded piece of parchment had been placed in front of him without his noticing. He hadn't fallen asleep, surely...

Someone coughed. Niklas paused with his hand resting on top of the parchment and looked around. The room was empty save for the bronze-skinned man, who leaned languidly against the door frame. Where were the guards?

The man coughed again, and nodded at the parchment. Niklas unfolded it with apprehension. A single, carefully scrawled depiction of a fang covered the page. His stomach curdled as he realized where he knew this man from.

Niklas looked up again, but the room was empty.

Chapter Forty-Five

HALF-ARGUED

Edric wavered outside the door to the small rooms he shared with Erion. He held the message sent via the baron's valet crumpled in one fist. He did not want to see his brother.

You can't avoid him forever. Though he had to admit the idea was tempting.

Steeling himself for a fight, Edric went inside.

The door to his room was open, and two bags lay on the floor, both half full. Erion's head poked around the door.

"Great, you're here. Look, I know you hate me. I don't care. Things have changed."

Edric reeled at his brother's clipped tone. "What's changed? What are you doing?"

"We have to get you out of here. And what exactly is *this?*" Erion tossed a notebook at him, then disappeared back into Edric's room. A cloak and two pairs of boots flew into one of the bags on the floor.

"My plans for the—*Erion.*"

It looked like a tornado had been through his room. Edric's scant possessions had been scattered as Erion went through everything, tossing apparently random articles of clothing and knickknacks into the bags.

"You're not going to the festival, Edric. It's too dangerous. Nobody can know—"

"*Why* can't anybody know?" Edric shouted. All his pent-up frustration rose to the surface and burst at once. "What's so important that you can't tell me? What has you sneaking around all the time? It's *my* majea, *my* talent, *my* life! I don't need your dirty money to go to the academy. I have a plan."

But Erion ignored him. He secured the straps on one of the bags, now full, and then went into his own room. He came back with two sacks full of coin.

"*What?*" Edric stared at the bags dumbly. It was more money than he'd ever seen in one place before.

"You'll take this to Saritu'e'Mere. I have someone who will meet you there, and your passage is already arranged." Erion shoved a sheaf of parchment at him. Bewildered, Edric glanced inside; ferry details.

"I'll send more when I can. You can start at the academy right away, or you can wait another term and work while you wait for the next installment. But the ferry leaves..." Erion glanced out the window at the sun. "Soon, so we have to go."

Edric didn't move.

"We have to go. *Now.*"

"Does Father know?"

"Father knows all the wrong things. He's the reason we're in this mess."

"Are you coming with me?"

Erion paused. "I can't."

"Why?" Edric demanded.

"It's not safe for you."

"Don't pretend like you're doing any of this for me," Edric snapped.

"There's something bad coming." Erion sat back on his

heels. A wrinkle formed in his forehead as he frowned. The dark circles under his eyes had never been more pronounced, and his shirt was disheveled, the ties at the wrists loose. It looked like someone had sloshed water all down his front.

"Worse than everything else going on in this damned city?" Edric asked.

"Much worse. Amelie was just a small part of it."

Edric crossed his arms, seething now. Erion hadn't even trusted him enough to tell him where Amelie was, let alone what had really happened to her. He was half-convinced Erion was responsible for the disappearances—that the woman he'd taken Amelie to was part of the kidnapping ring.

Not Erion. He wouldn't do that.

But Erion wouldn't talk to him, either. Edric had been left to stew in a myriad of worst-case scenarios.

"Even if I *wanted* to go, I can't. I promised Runan I'd help with his stall during the festival tomorrow." And Edric had plans of his own. His display wasn't as polished as he'd hoped, but…

It will be enough. He only wished he could share his plan with Erion.

"You're not to go near it, do you understand? *Please.*" Erion flipped from demanding to begging in a split-second. Genuine panic and fear glistened in his eyes.

"What's going on?" Edric sat down at their small table.

"You know about the disappearances—about what happened to Amelie? I think it's about to happen to a lot more people. To kids."

"Why?"

"I—someone told me."

"You're going to have to do better than that," Edric said.

"There's a Guardian of Pelinon in Rijeka, did you know that?" Erion asked.

Edric looked up, curiosity getting the best of him. "Really?"

"Really," Erion said. "It's not good news. Father's debts keep getting worse and… *please*, E."

"I can't believe you still don't trust me. I haven't told anyone about the clearing, you know. Or Amelie or those hellhounds, or any of it. I know how to keep my mouth shut. And I don't *need* your money!" Edric did his best to avoid looking at the sacks of dakkari. Where had Erion gotten it all?

Edric held up the notebook Erion had tossed at him. "I have a plan. I'll get a sponsor. Maybe even the baron, when he sees what I can do."

Erion's face clouded. "You *can't*."

Something in Erion's expression touched Edric, and his anger subsided against his better judgment. "School will be better for me if I have a sponsor, you know that. I won't be looked down on or forced to scrub floors, or…"

"There are worse things than menial work, Edric. I'd rather you scrub floors for the rest of your life than risk losing it if you stay here any longer. You want to be a mage bad enough, you'll do whatever it takes."

Edric was at a loss. "Lose my life? What are you talking about?"

"I've got some fun friends these days, you know?" Erion grimaced.

"Explain it to me," Edric deadpanned. He'd spent so much of his younger years practically hero-worshiping his brother. When his magic had manifested, he'd been sure it could only bring them closer—one more thing in common between the Skala brothers, who had once been inseparable. Instead, the discovery had done nothing but widen the gap between them.

Still, he wanted badly to believe Erion wasn't somehow involved in the horrifying things happening in the city. He wanted to believe Erion was a good man.

A succession of quick, irritated knocks rattled their door before Erion could answer him. Edric opened it by habit. A darkly tanned man with a wolfish grin stood in the hall.

"You must be Edric." The newcomer looked Edric up and down with a calculating eye.

Like a man about to buy a horse. The thought put Edric on edge. He clenched his jaw in distaste and nodded. No reason to be rude without cause, but…

"Just here to see—ah, Erion." The man pushed past Edric without invitation and looked around the small rooms. "Don't blame you for staying with Thorne, this place isn't exactly cheery, is it?"

"What are you doing here, Sadiq?" Erion addressed the visitor, but his eyes locked onto Edric's. He tilted his head the slightest fraction, his expression all but begging Edric to leave.

"Friendly visit. Can we talk?" the man asked.

"Later," Erion said.

Sadiq arched a brow, then glanced at Edric. Comprehension seemed to dawn.

"Now suits, actually," Sadiq said. "Perhaps…?"

"Not here. Edric—wait for me. *Please.*"

CHAPTER FORTY-SIX

DEFIANCE

rion shoved his hands into his pockets to stop them shaking as he led Sadiq to the nearest exit, the manor's main entry hall. "Get out."

"I'd expected a warmer reception, I have to admit." Sadiq crossed his arms and leaned against the wall. "I thought we had an understanding, you and I."

If by "understanding" he meant Erion accepted that Sadiq was moderately less malicious than Mathieu and Isak—sure. Erion glanced around the hall. They were alone, but he kept his voice low all the same. "What are you doing here?"

"We know who the Ithynon is."

A cold shiver lanced down Erion's spine. *How?* "Who?"

"Some bilge rat holed up in the Wharf District. Ostensibly."

"That's a big word, Sadiq. Are you going to tell me what's going on or not? What does Mathieu want?"

"To send a message."

"To the Ithynon?"

Sadiq nodded. "He needs to know we have the power

Mathieu keeps going on about. We need something big. A hit."

Erion's heart sank into his stomach. There was nothing of the heart-pounding anxiety he'd experienced when the orders to kill the duke's contingent had come down. Instead, a slow, insidious self-loathing crept over him. "You said I was done with that."

"You're uniquely positioned for the job. Mathieu needs Niklas Skala dead."

Erion put a hand out to steady himself against the wall. Sadiq had said it so casually, but his choice of phrasing wasn't lost on Erion. Not "we need you to kill *your father*." Sadiq had tried—and failed—to distance the job.

Not the job. Murder. Call it what it is.

Rage at the injustice flickered in his chest. He sensed, more than saw, Sadiq's stance shifting to a ready position.

Good. Erion was angry enough to murder. He held little love for Niklas—but *kill his own father?*

"What are you playing at?" Erion grunted when he regained control of his senses.

"Mathieu's my boss, too."

"I won't do it."

"I told him you'd say that." Sadiq actually grinned, and Erion had to quash a powerful urge to punch him in the face.

Mathieu ordered this. Not Sadiq.

"You said you knew who the Ithynon was," Erion said, trying to find the reasoning behind the order. Why bother with Niklas? Why not kill Cedivar? Niklas was a wastrel, but he was firmly under the Fang's control in more ways than one.

"Mathieu *thinks*. We just met with him this morning."

Erion ran his hands across his face. His mouth was dry. Should he tell Sadiq? Whoever they thought they'd found, it couldn't be the right man.

"Why Niklas?"

"You need to have a greater hand in things from now on. Mathieu needs better leverage with the baron."

If only you knew. Steel wormed its way into Erion's spine.

Useless and toxic as Niklas was, his death would ruin Edric. And what if Edric ever found out who'd wielded the blade?

"Tell Mathieu *nobody* touches Niklas. Nobody. I was promised protection. *Nissra's blood.* It's the reason I signed on to all this. The *only* reason."

"You're intent on that?" Sadiq asked.

Erion nodded.

"Mathieu won't like it—someone refusing a direct order."

"He doesn't have to like it."

"You'd challenge him so publicly?"

"Watch me," Erion growled.

Sadiq cocked his head to one side, narrowing his eyes as though trying to read Erion's thoughts.

"I'm not going to change my mind. And I'll kill anyone who tries to touch him," Erion said.

"You might remember—the law of succession prevents that. It's written in blood."

Erion's lip curled. He hadn't remembered—and Sadiq obviously knew it. "Tell Mathieu."

Sadiq pursed his lips. "You have until tomorrow morning to decide. Mathieu will probably send someone else if you refuse. But you have that long."

Erion rubbed his neck and looked away. Was Sadiq giving him a way out? Could it be so easy? If they were to run, all of them...

Niklas would never go. Erion wasn't sure he could even convince Edric to go.

But he had to try.

"Meet me at daybreak at the Wharves' End, with your decision. *Think* about it, Skala. I know you're not stupid."

"Goodbye, Sadiq." Erion turned away without a dismissal.

"Think about it," Sadiq shouted at Erion's retreat.

Like hell, I will.

There was no sight of Edric when Erion returned to their rooms. The doors were locked, and the two bags he'd packed were still on the floor where he'd left them. No note. No indication of where he'd gone.

Damn.

> *Edric,*
>
> *I'll be back later tonight. I'm going to tell you everything, but it has to be in person. You're right—you deserve to know what's going on.*
>
> *Don't go anywhere until we've talked.*
>
> *I'm sorry.*
> *Erion*

He left the note on Edric's bed before leaving. Erion searched the kitchens and stables, with no luck. As a last resort, he slipped into the hidden passage behind the store cupboard and crept through the walls.

Erion had memorized the warren of passages years ago, and soon found himself at the familiar stretch of wall behind his father's chambers. Holding his breath, he spelled the mortar at eye level and peered through the narrow crevice that split between the stones.

The gray light of dusk illuminated the room, casting everything in skeletal hues of silver. A single candle burned on Niklas's desk, warding off the ghostly hues.

Niklas Skala slumped over the desk. Erion's chest constricted. Was he breathing?

Erion dug his fingers into the stone. In his haste, it practically melted under his touch. He lurched forward as soon as the opening was large enough to fit through.

Sadiq said Mathieu would wait until morning. *Hours. I still had hours to decide.*

The candle had nearly burned down to its base. Pooling wax spilled onto the table by Niklas's hand.

Erion reached out and seized his father's shoulder, then pressed shaking fingers into the junction where his jaw met his throat. His skin was still warm. A moment later, the soft thrum of a pulse pattered against Erion's fingers.

Slow, sludgy, but there. Erion fell back into the chair next to Niklas. The panic screaming through his body was slow to subside.

How had it come to this? He was supposed to be protecting his family, broken though it was. And now…

"You miserable bastard," Erion whispered. He wasn't sure whether he was talking to himself or his father.

Erion walked across the room and opened the door that joined the study to Niklas's bedchamber. He sent a pulse of his majea through the stone floor as he checked the room for intruders. Once he was satisfied it was empty, he went back to the study and slung one of his father's arms over his shoulder.

A small icho pipe rolled onto the floor as Erion pulled him out of his chair. Reaching the bed, he shoved aside the quilt and heaved his father onto the mattress. With a sigh, he tugged off Niklas's boots and covered him with the blanket. The steward began drooling onto his pillow almost at once.

Erion looked down at his father's sleeping form with mingled fury and regret—for the life that might have been, had icho not overshadowed Niklas's senses. For the pain Erion might have avoided if he'd managed to get Edric away from the city before the Crimson Fang had cornered him into joining.

Kill Niklas Skala. Erion recoiled from the thought. Weak willed and shiftless as he may be, Niklas was still Erion's father.

It was time to set things to rights.

CHAPTER FORTY-SEVEN
VALIDATION

Sadiq had been planning on following Erion, but he realized it wasn't necessary. He'd seen something break in Erion's eyes when he'd delivered the false order—and the fierce protectiveness he had for his brother, Edric.

Erion was unbalanced and desperate—a piece of white-hot steel ready for the final, deciding blow.

Sadiq settled himself at the window of a tavern on High Street, overlooking the manor's gate. If there was news about Erion, he wanted it quickly. He was expecting an important dinner guest later that evening. He wanted to be able to report that he'd garnered enough support for the venture he was proposing.

He was confident he'd have Erion's support—it was only a question of how long it would take Erion to realize Sadiq was a much better leader than Mathieu. Sadiq's guest would be pleased when he heard there was a spy already placed within the baron's household.

Sadiq looked up expectantly when Gerard joined him some

time later with the news that Erion had left the manor.

"You have men following him?" Sadiq swirled the remnants of his ale, thinking. Who would Erion trust? Thorne, most likely—Sadiq already had men watching his home.

Gerard scowled. "Liam lost him in the markets."

Sadiq slammed the tankard onto the table. "What did I do to warrant such incompetence? The man's a stoneburner, not a ghost. *Find him.*"

CHAPTER FORTY-EIGHT

INTERVENTION

andra had never been so angry to see Erion on her doorstep. "What do you want?"

"I need help."

"When don't you?" she said coolly.

He put his hands up in a conciliatory gesture. "Just let me explain?"

Vandra rolled her eyes, but stepped back to let him in.

"Mathieu wants me to kill Niklas." The door had yet to swing fully shut when Erion blurted the admission.

Vandra clapped a hand over her mouth. It went against everything she knew about Mathieu's system. If anything within the Crimson Fang was ironclad, it was guaranteed safety for family members.

"Sadiq says they want to send a message. To prove to the Ithynon they have enough control to ruin anything he does in the future," Erion said. "They think they know who he is."

"You're not *considering* it?" Vandra leaned back against the wall. Maybe Erion wasn't the man she'd thought he was.

"If I say no, Mathieu would have me killed." Erion collapsed into her armchair and glared into the fire.

"Mathieu isn't that stupid. He knows how valuable your position is." Vandra was still having a hard time wrapping her head around the order. Why not force Niklas to retire? If Mathieu wanted to send a message, Baron Voloy had plenty of other high-ranking servants for him to kill.

But she had to admit Erion was right. If he was telling the truth, Mathieu would have him killed if he refused.

"I'm supposed to give my answer to Sadiq in the morning. I don't think he would..." Erion wavered.

"You have an understanding with him?" Vandra asked, wary.

Erion shrugged. "It's hard to tell with him. But... I think so."

"Then Mathieu will kill you himself. Or he'll have Isak do it."

"Not if I kill them first."

"You can't," Vandra said. He couldn't attack any superior officers in the Crimson Fang. She'd inked the spell herself. "The symmajea—"

"I know. I need you to change it."

Vandra stilled. What Erion was suggesting was suicide for both of them.

"The alternative is sitting vigil at my father's bedside until the end of time, waiting for someone to attack me so I can claim self-defense."

"So you're not going to do it?" Vandra asked sharply.

"Nissra's blood, Vandra. No. What kind of monster do you think I am?" Erion turned the full force of his glare on her. Relief coursed through Vandra's body.

"I'm not drunk enough for this conversation." She crossed to the liquor cabinet and added two fingers of whiskey to a pair of tumblers, then handed him one. "You can't be serious about the symmajea."

"Dead serious. If you can't do it, I'll find someone else who can."

"Nobody in the city can out-spell me." Vandra sniffed and finished her drink.

"So you *can* do it." Erion's characteristic crooked smile was gone. The news of Mathieu's order had killed the humor that usually danced in his eyes.

"That doesn't matter. I won't. I have—"

"Too much at stake?" Erion snapped.

"We all do. There's got to be another way."

Erion pulled a stiff envelope from his breast pocket and handed it to her. "A letter to Aleria syn'Duvar. Explaining *everything*."

Vandra dropped the envelope like it was white hot. "You *wouldn't*."

"Watch me. And this is a copy, so don't bother trying to destroy it."

"Erion… Why?"

"I have Edric to think about."

"You're both better off without Niklas." Not that she wanted their father dead.

"So I should just kill him—that's the answer?" Erion roared.

Vandra shrunk away. In the few years she'd known him, she'd never seen Erion's temper so close to the brink.

"If I have to get the Guardian to help, I will. She's already working with Talbot, and he'll vouch for me. I'll leave the city and all this daemonshite behind."

"They'll follow you."

"Once Edric is safe, I don't care."

Vandra smoothed her palms flat against the table, considering the envelope like it was a viper. The spells she'd worked into Erion's skin would enable Mathieu to track him to the shores of the Paekkomore Sea and back. If Erion went with him, Edric would never be safe.

"I won't encourage you to go against Mathieu's orders. They're monstrous. But…" Her mind was blank. There wasn't a satisfactory answer.

"Gallantyr's bones, Vandra, why do you put up with this?"

"It's my job."

"We both know you could work with anyone in the city. You could work for the baron if you wanted to."

"Because he's so much more benevolent."

They glared at each other for a heated moment. Vandra could see the calculations behind Erion's eyes as he hunted for an escape that didn't exist. He seemed to make up his mind and stood to leave.

Vandra jumped up between him and the door. "You can't go to Aleria."

"Isn't that why you let me know she was in town?" Erion squared his shoulders in a combative stance.

Vandra leaned her head back against the door and scowled up at the wooden timbers overhead. Why *had* she brought Erion to see Aleria? She'd been deeply disturbed by the Guardian's presence in Rijeka—though not, she had to admit, surprised. Someone should have come to intervene ages ago.

No... Vandra had been wondering whether it was *her* time to pack up shop. Leave Rijeka and the Crimson Fang behind once and for all. But, like Erion, she was stuck unless Mathieu deigned to release her.

Erion wasn't the only one with secrets.

Empathy welled within her as she looked up into his dark eyes. He was a good man who'd fallen far—but he was still a good man. Erion was always trying to find the loophole, the path that led to the least amount of harm. He'd helped that girl Amelie escape, and it wasn't the first time he'd toed his orders from the Crimson Fang.

He was a fool, but a fool whose actions had sent a gentle wind that stoked the embers of Vandra's own dying conscience. She reached out and took his hand in both of hers. She couldn't let him directly defy this kind of order from the Fang any more than she could bear to see him kill his own father.

"You said Sadiq is expecting you in the morning. Stay. Have a drink. Let's talk it out. I could even try to talk to Mathieu."

"I have to go find Edric."

But she could tell he was tempted. She laced her fingers through his.

"You can't talk me out of this." Erion pulled his hand away. "I'm not doing it."

"I don't want you to," Vandra said frankly. "One drink."

Erion groaned. "Fine. But this is my problem. If you won't help with the symmajea, at least don't tell anyone I was here."

"If you're about to do something this monumentally stupid? I wouldn't dream of it. The last thing I need is you dragging me down with you, Skala." Vandra handed him the whiskey again. He tossed it back in a single gulp.

"Thanks. Bye." But he didn't move.

Vandra rolled her eyes. "Sit."

To her surprise, he did. Vandra turned to the counter and hesitated as she considered a small vial at the back of the cabinet. She glanced over her shoulder at Erion. He stared at the fire with the blank expression of a man totally resigned to his fate.

Why Niklas? If they really knew the baron was the Ithynon, what was Mathieu playing at? Voloy wouldn't spare a sigh for his steward if he died—so why bother?

Maybe if he missed his arranged meeting with Sadiq, they wouldn't kill Erion. Maybe, if he was delayed, they'd send someone else to kill Niklas before Erion could throw himself in front of an arrow meant for a selfish bastard who wouldn't do the same for his own children.

Decided, she grabbed the bottle and slipped two clear drops into his cup. If Erion wasn't going to save himself, she'd have to do it for him. Whatever Erion thought, Mathieu could be reasoned with.

CHAPTER FORTY-NINE

THE KURIOSITAR FESTIVAL

dric tapped his fingers idly on the table in Runan's stall. He'd been attending the Kuriositar Festival for as long as he could remember, and he'd been helping Runan prepare and sell his meat pies, kolaches, and fruit tarts for nearly as long. It was usually his favorite event of the year, but today his stomach clenched with nerves.

After months of careful preparation—years, really—it was finally time to prove he deserved a spot at the magic academy in Saritu'e'Mere.

A tray covered in steaming sugar buns dropped onto the table, missing Edric's hand by a hairsbreadth. He snatched his hands back from the hot tray with a soft yelp. At his elbow, Runan chuckled.

"I've never seen you more distracted," the cook said.

Edric shrugged. He was defying Erion enough already by going through with his plans for the festival. It wasn't worth the risk to tell *anyone* about his plans.

"Why don't you go off and enjoy some of the contests?"

Runan suggested, patting the top of the buns to test their readiness. He nodded with satisfaction. "I've done this plenty of times, lad. Go enjoy yourself."

Edric tried to keep the relief off his face. He'd been wondering how to get leave to slip away to the demonstrations. He glanced around the stall. There was one more thing he might need. His eyes fell on a paring knife sticking out of a carving board.

"How has it gone today?" he asked Runan as he tried to appear casual, sidling up to the carving board. "Everybody— doing well?" Edric felt his cheeks redden at the awkward question.

"Well enough." Runan arched a wry eyebrow and snapped a rag at Edric. "I mean it, be off with you."

Edric dodged the washcloth with a chuckle. "Thanks, Runan," he said earnestly.

The cook waved a dismissive hand, his attention already back on the tray of sweets. When Edric was sure Runan wasn't paying attention, he snatched the paring knife off the chopping block and slipped it inside his belt pouch.

Edric glanced at the sun overhead and decided to make his way to the demonstration area at the center of the green. A woman with ink-spattered hands looked up at Edric with beady eyes when he approached.

"Name?"

"Edric Skala." Edric wiped his sweat-slicked hands on the inside of his tunic as he looked out over the areas set up for magelings at the Kuriositar Festival. He'd spent most of the last year preparing for this moment—*dreaming* of this moment. But now that the opportunity was staring him in the face, all he felt was sick.

"Your place of residence?"

"Baron Voloy's estate."

The woman sat straighter at that, and when she addressed him next, her tone was kinder. "And your stream of magic?"

"Life Magic." The pronouncement was strange on his

tongue. It was the first time Edric had ever said it aloud to anyone but Erion.

"Entrants are assembling at the tents over there." The woman pointed with the tip of her quill. "And you'll be called by name when we're ready for you. Do you need anything?"

"I..." Edric swallowed, wondering how insane his request would sound. "Has anyone been hurt today?"

"I'm sorry?" The woman blinked politely at him, as though he'd been speaking a foreign language.

"Anyone injured. I'm... it's healing." Heat rose in Edric's cheeks. It wasn't like he could go around slicing people open to demonstrate his invention. He'd been hoping one of Runan's kitchen hands would sustain an injury during the morning rush—something he was ashamed to hope for, but had hoped anyway—but the morning had been unfortunately free of burns, cuts, or bruises.

The scribe narrowed her eyes. "I'll ask around, but you'll need to come up with a backup plan." She gestured at the tent again.

It was a clear dismissal, and Edric shuffled out of the line obediently. He looked over the crowd and the tent full of other hopeful magelings carefully, alert to see any recent bandages. People traveled for days just to attend the festival. For some, it might be their only chance to show off their skills and earn a better life for themselves and their families. Travel in Daemanon could be risky at the best of times, but nobody he saw sported any obvious injuries. It had probably been too much to hope for.

Edric's sense of time warped as he paced his small corner of the mageling's tent. It might have been hours or mere minutes, but he finally heard his name called. He clutched his pack with quivering hands and followed the announcer from the tent.

A small area had been cleared away for the official demonstrations. Edric immediately picked out three or four obvious mages in the crowd—robes could be a dead giveaway, but these were paying closer attention than most. His gaze swept the crowd again—and he realized he was looking for Erion.

Whenever Edric had imagined this moment, Erion had been here cheering him on. Even while they'd been fighting, Edric had somehow been sure he'd talk his brother around.

When it really mattered, when Edric really needed him, Erion would be there.

But he wasn't.

Edric shoved the pain of it away as he reached the table in the center of the staging area and opened his bag. He laid out the three wooden boxes he'd carefully prepared for this moment.

The onlookers' eyes seemed to burn into him as he took the lid off the first box. The athis vine he'd carefully re-planted into the box would be hard to see for anyone not in the front rows—for now.

Here goes nothing.

Edric pressed his palms against the sides of the box, closed his eyes, and summoned his majea. The tiny seedling shot upward at his prompting. A vine curled over the side of the box and sprawled onto the tabletop. Edric exhaled, trying to maintain control over the spell. He opened his eyes. The vine trailed down to the ground now. He prodded again.

Two deep orange athis flowers budded, then bloomed, as quickly and easily as unfolding a piece of parchment. Edric dropped the spell and chanced a quick look at the crowd. A few looked bored, but most looked on with bright interest.

"Is—does anyone have any injuries? That need healing?" Edric was grateful his voice didn't crack or shake. He'd never spoken in front of so many people before. A quiet murmur ran through the crowd.

Edric opened the third box and took out two rolls of reddish bandages. They were the same as the slapdash one he'd used to help Erion's ankle heal, but far neater looking. He'd crushed the athis petals and used his majea to weave them together with the vines. They were strong, flexible, and suffused with healing majea.

The third box held vials of the tincture he'd perfected in Gian's workshop. He'd never have even thought to make a concentrated athis oil if he hadn't seen how the healer worked his craft.

"Any burns, cuts?" Edric looked around hopefully. A few people shook their heads, but most just looked wary. He supposed he couldn't blame them—he wouldn't want to take the chance at being an unknown mageling's experiment, either.

"All right. Um." Edric lifted the bandage and held it up. "This species of athis has concentrated healing properties that staunch blood flow much quicker than common varieties. I used fibers from the vines to weave these bandages and infused them with Life Magic and…"

But Edric was losing them, he could tell. He bit his lip, thinking fiercely. There was only one way he could *show* them how it worked, how useful it could be. He'd just wanted to avoid it at all costs.

With a deep breath, Edric reached into his pouch and took out the kitchen knife he'd filched from Runan's stall. A last resort. He held it up.

"I'll just…" For a moment, Edric couldn't see anything but sunlight shining on the blade's surface.

Now wasn't the time to be squeamish. He shook himself—and drew a long, shallow cut running the length of his forearm. A current of curious whispers rippled across the crowd. Several of the mages Edric had noticed in the crowd stepped closer to the ropes separating the demonstrations from the onlookers.

Edric shook off a fresh wave of nerves and focused on his demonstration. Sharp pain trailed down his arm where droplets of blood swelled and ran down his skin. The wound was just large enough to be visible—to prove to the crowd that he'd really cut himself. He pressed his hand against the wound, then walked to the nearest group of onlookers and held out his arm. It was stained red, and blood had smeared across his skin.

He bit down hard on the inside of his tongue as he wound one of the bandages around his forearm. The second he handed to a woman wearing a jade-green robe and a curious expression. She unwrapped and examined it with a practiced eye. Edric glanced at the identifying marks on the collar of her robe. A lifeweaver.

"I'll just… give it a few minutes." He felt stupid just standing there, though, so he raised one of the vials. "The oil from my athis flower, even without being treated by majea, is much stronger."

Edric was no great orator, and he squirmed under the crowd's attention. They were passing around the bandage now. Some people looked for a long time; others barely glanced before passing it along. A few started to drift away.

Now or never. Edric wiped his hands on a cloth and unwound the bandage on his arm.

He'd needed the cut to be minor so the athis had a chance to work in a short amount of time. His flesh hadn't healed completely, but the bleeding had already stopped. A faint pink line had replaced the torn flesh. Feeling foolish again, he held his arm up. "Uhm, so. Any questions?"

The second half of his presentation flowed better than the first. Some of the spectators had faded away when they realized he was done performing any actual magic. The woman in the green robes pushed forward as the crowd thinned, accompanied by a balding man with crooked teeth. They asked pointed questions about how Edric had bred the athis, how he'd created the serum, what he'd done to infuse the bandages with the flower's essence.

Faced with direct questions about the process he'd spent so much time perfecting, Edric found himself answering their questions easily. This was something he understood—something he was passionate about. Talking to two people was far less intimidating than trying to project to an entire crowd.

"We'll find your information on the registry then, I assume?" The man held his hand out to shake. "What's your name?"

"Edirc Skala." Edric shook the man's hand, feeling lightheaded. The woman nodded appraisingly, a small smile curving her lips.

* * *

Edric was lightheaded with relief when he finally returned to the tent with the other hopeful magelings. It seemed far friendlier this time than it had been last time. He cheerfully agreed when a boy named Dmitrii and a few others asked him if he wanted to find some food. He'd been too nervous to eat anything that morning.

Edric was steering the other magelings—Dmitrii, Telia, and Laurel—toward Runan's stall for celebratory meat pies when something tugged at his belt. He put a hand to his purse.

"That bastard just stole my coin!" The girl Telia turned around and started racing after a lone figure pushing through the crowd, away from the green. Edric and Dmitrii followed her at a sprint.

The cutpurse was quick. In a matter of moments, he burst through the crowd and took off at a run down an alley. Telia rounded the corner on his heels, Edric and the others pounding behind her.

A piercing scream tore through the air as soon as Telia was out of sight. Edric skidded around the corner, heart pounding with alarm. A stick shot out at him from a shadowed doorstep and tangled his feet. Edric crashed to his hands and knees, and the momentum flopped him over onto his back.

Dazed, Edric looked up from the ground to see a man tying Telia's hands behind her back. Before he could scramble to his feet, rough hands seized his shoulders. He glimpsed a tattoo on his captor's forearm before someone forced a bag over his head.

CHAPTER FIFTY

BETRAYED

E rion groaned and covered his eyes to ward off splatters of sunshine. The light was digging through his eyes into his head, intensifying a throbbing headache. It was like someone had drilled holes into his temples.

He rolled over and groped blindly for the waterskin he kept hanging by his bed. His hand slid over impossibly soft covers. Erion sat up with a jolt that set his head throbbing all over again and looked wildly around the room. Groggy and disoriented, he hadn't realized where he was.

Vandra's apartments. Vandra's *bed*.

Erion ran a hand across his jaw, trying desperately to recall why he was there. Surely they hadn't...

No. He was fully clothed save for bare feet. Vandra was nowhere in sight, but his sword belt, boots, and gear were neatly laid out on a plush armchair in the corner of the bedchamber. Memories flooded back to him with a sickening lurch.

Mathieu's twisted order. His meeting with Sadiq. The Kuriositar Festival.

Edric.

He bolted from the bed and tugged on his boots. A handwritten note rested on top of his neatly folded cloak.

> *It was for the best.*
> *-V*

Erion crushed the note, grabbed cloak and weapons, and raced out the door. He buckled his sword belt as he thundered down the stairs. Vandra couldn't be trusted—he should have known better. How many times now had he come to her for help, only to be rejected?

Blood of Nissra, did she want him dead? What had she done to him? With her contacts, any kind of drug was available to her. He'd made an easy target.

Damn, damn, damn.

His footsteps pounded on the cobblestones as he ran up the street toward the manor. Festival-goers crowded the streets, which were closed to carriage and equine travel to make way for the heavy foot traffic. Merchant tents and food stalls spilled over into the road.

Erion swore as the crowds jostled him. There seemed to be a bard at every corner, each surrounded by a larger knot of revelers than the last.

If Edric bore Erion any goodwill, he'd still be at the manor. But Edric would be furious with him. Erion had disappeared again—Edric was done waiting. The boy would be here somewhere.

Erion glanced up at the sun. It had to be nearly noon. He'd slept away the most precious hours of the day. He waded into the crowds, and the sea of celebration engulfed him. Curses followed him as he elbowed his way to the village green, heedless of the men and women he knocked aside in his rush.

Runan's stall was mercifully quick to find. The baron's cook headed a long, canvas-covered stall at the north end of the green. Scents both savory and sweet wafted from the makeshift kitchens, making Erion's stomach growl and reminding him that he hadn't eaten since the night before. He pushed the hunger aside—that was a problem for later.

"Runan!" Erion spotted the cook overseeing half a boar roasting on a spit.

"Erion, lad. Pleasure. Pasty?" Runan held out a tray covered in perfectly browned beef pasties. Erion gave in to his hunger, nodding his thanks as he took one.

"Did Edric come with you today?" Erion wolfed down the turnover in three quick bites, and accepted a second gratefully.

"Try not to choke on it, there." Runan handed Erion a flagon of cider. "I thought he told you. He's been helping me most of the morning. I sent him off a little over an hour ago. Why?"

"Where did he go?" Erion heard the quaver in his own voice. *Keep it together.*

Runan shrugged. "He said something about watching the demonstrations, but I didn't pester him. He's worked hard enough. He deserves to have some fun for a change."

"Which way did he go?" Erion asked.

"I've just told you—the demonstrations were at the south end of the green. Saw a hail of fire all the way from here. I doubt the city watch was happy with that one. Why?" Runan shouted the last word after Erion's retreating form. Erion was already bolting down the green.

I should have tied him up and thrown him onto the first cargo ship out of Rijeka. If anything happened to Edric, it would be his fault.

How had it come to this?

Erion skidded to a halt at the roped-off area set aside for the magelings. Twin girls stood back-to-back in the center, each blindfolded. As Erion watched, one girl formed a small ball of light in her hands, not unlike his own fire spheres. Her lips moved, forming an inaudible spell, and the sphere darted from her hands. It arced in a wide circle before flying straight at her sister's face.

Her twin threw her arm up just in time to encase the fire sphere within a ball of ice. Steam showered from the abruptly doused light as it dropped to the ground. Appreciative applause broke out among the crowds.

Erion tore his eyes away from the twins, though part of his mind wondered at their control. The ground began stirring beneath the girls' feet, no doubt for an earth magic display, but he couldn't afford to stay and watch.

"Excuse me." Erion grabbed the sleeve of a passing mage, obvious by his ostentatiously flowing robes. "Have all the candidates gone already?"

The man's brows furrowed. "Most of them."

"Where are the rest? Did you see a Life Mage?"

"Several." The man offered no more information.

"He has light brown hair, broad shoulders."

"What was his skill?"

Erion ground his teeth. He hadn't the faintest clue what Edric had settled on. Maybe if he'd spared his brother the time of day, Edric would have told him. He shook his head.

"Most of them are in that tent over there." The mage pointed toward a canvas of brilliant scarlet.

"Thanks." Erion edged his way around the crowd and pushed into the tent. Several hopeful magelings turned when he entered. Erion's gaze darted around the space. No Edric.

"Are they ready for us?" The boy's face was pale—he looked like he was about to throw up.

"Has anyone seen Edric Skala?" Erion looked around at the occupants desperately. "He's a lifeweaver—lives at the baron's estate. Probably showed off—a plant or…"

"I think he run off with Telia." A boy with enormous ears said. A wicked grin split his lips. "Looked like they was—"

"Oh don't be gross, Antony," a girl with fiery red hair rolled her eyes. "They were with Dmitrii and Laurel. I think they just went to get food."

"How long ago? Which direction did they go?" Erion asked.

"Is he in trouble or something?" the girl asked.

"Just tell me!" If Erion had Thorne's magic, maybe he could just pull the information out of her head—though that probably wasn't the way it worked.

"They went out the back, that's all I know." She jerked her thumb over her shoulder, indicating the opposite side of the tent.

Erion tore past the magelings. This was getting ridiculous.

⬠ ⬠ ⬠

Erion was barely away from the crowds when the attack came. Two pairs of hands seized him from a doorway, yanking him backwards and forcing him against the exterior wall. His head smacked against the stone. Stars blinded him as one of the men slipped a hood over his head.

The assault was quick and efficient—and the men had come prepared to deal with Erion's majea. They lashed his hands together with strips of leather. He couldn't sense any signs of metal weapons, or even coins, on their bodies.

"Try anything funny, and I'll knife you. I don't care what Mathieu says." Erion recognized Gerard's voice, and his blood ran cold.

Somewhere in the city, Edric was probably being dragged away for sacrifice—and his only crime was being related to Erion. Because Erion had resisted one of the most dangerous men in the city by refusing to kill his own father.

All the kid had wanted was to demonstrate his new powers.

Erion's earthwalking senses kept him from stumbling as his captors jostled him along down the road. Thanks to his majea, he knew the streets of Rijeka intimately, even with a hood over his head. They were heading to the Apothiki District.

They had to be taking him to Mathieu at the Maw. Erion wanted nothing more than to confront the Crimson Fang leader, even though any hostility would likely result in his own death. He followed obediently and tried to work out a plan. His head ached and his body was still weakened by the aftereffects of whatever Vandra had drugged him with. Erion was at a clear disadvantage—outnumbered, blind, and weaponless.

Erion's captors had come prepared to avoid the worst of his majea, but they couldn't take his abilities away from him altogether. The man trailing behind them carried Erion's weapons—not so far away. Not impossible. The pulse from his gemajea-spelled sword was just distinct enough for him to lock onto its signature with ease.

He might have a chance.

They had to be close to the Maw now. Gerard's grip on his elbow had loosened, his vigilance tempered by Erion's compliance.

Erion jerked his chin upward, yanking at the cobblestones under Gerard's feet. The man's grip on his elbow jerked, then released, as Gerard's feet were pulled out from under him.

"What the—" The man behind Gerard swore.

Erion yanked away from the captor who held his other arm. Freed, he ran down the road. He focused every ounce of his concentration into the ground ahead of him. Until he could get the hood off, he'd need to be extra cautious.

Something whizzed past his ear. Erion veered to the side, but another projectile struck him and lodged itself beneath his shoulder blade. He bit back a cry. The wooden shaft, sharpened to a point to form a crude, if effective arrow, was resistant to his majea.

Erion inhaled deeply and seized the cobbles lining the road between himself and the man chasing him. The stones shot at his assailants like dozens of self-propelled missiles, their speed fortified by a furious gust of wind.

Another arrow grazed his upper arm, tearing shirt and skin as it whizzed past him.

Erion gritted his teeth against the pain. He needed to focus properly if he was going to get out of this. Erion turned and ran back towards Gerard, letting his earthwalking guide him toward the vibrations of his movements on the cobblestones. Two paces later, he skidded to a stop and channeled the forward momentum into his majea. A wave of earth thundered down the road. Gerard and the others scattered, their footsteps resonating through the ground.

"Erion!"

Erion recognized Sadiq's voice at once. Where had he come from? Against his better judgment, Erion froze.

"Gerard, you bastard. Stop this. Immediately," Sadiq ordered.

An uneasy silence settled over the road, marred only by the shuffling footsteps of Erion's assailants.

Then the black hood was pulled from Erion's head. He winced as the sudden sunlight stabbed into his eyes. Sadiq moved behind him and cut the straps binding Erion's wrists, then yanked the crude arrow from his back. Erion gasped in pain and relief. He felt a trickle of blood slip down his back.

"Mathieu's orders." Gerard looked sulky.

"You're on *my* crew." Sadiq shot Gerard a scathing look, then turned his attention to Erion. "Where were you this morning?"

Erion glowered. He didn't owe Sadiq an explanation— besides, he could hardly admit he'd let his guard down enough for Vandra to drug him.

"We've got to get to the Maw," Sadiq said. "Mathieu's ordered for you to be brought in after…"

"After I refused to murder my own father." The words were ash in Erion's mouth. Sadiq had just confirmed all his suspicions. So much for the protection the Crimson Fang had offered.

"That's where we were taking him!" Gerard snapped. Erion rubbed his wrists, trying to analyze the situation. They'd come to a dead standstill in the middle of a small alley linking two residential streets. Something about Gerard's protests struck him as insincere. He found himself wishing Thorne was around to help him interpret whatever the hell was going on here.

"The Fang's sent a messenger," Sadiq said. A muscle in his jaw twitched. "Nothing Mathieu ordered matters anymore. We've got bigger problems."

Erion stared at him, nonplussed. "What?"

"*The* Fang," Sadiq snarled, emphasizing the first word. "In Vhalla? He's sent a delegate to look into the icho problem."

Erion blinked. The head of the Crimson Fang had sent someone all the way from the ducal seat? Erion hadn't given much thought to the wider world of the underground he'd joined. Who had time to worry about Mathieu's boss in Vhalla when things were so bad at home?

He wanted to think that anything preoccupying Mathieu was a good thing—anything to buy Erion more time to find Edric— but this had trouble written all over it.

"So?" Erion was done trying to play both sides of the street. "I have shit to do, Sadiq. Are you going to turn me in or not? If not, stop wasting my time."

He fixed Sadiq with an obstinate glare. He had no intention of going down without a fight.

"You don't know," Sadiq mused. It was more statement than question.

"I imagine there's a lot I don't know." Erion channeled invisible vortexes of air into his hands. He charged the energy with every ounce of his rage, prepared to shove Sadiq or any of the others away if they grabbed him.

"The festival this morning. They have your brother," Sadiq said.

Erion's heart crashed into his stomach. He'd expected the worst already, but Sadiq's confirmation was a death sentence.

It was going to be so easy. Join the Crimson Fang. Collect ludicrous bounties. Fund Edric's school.

"Where?" The single word was all Erion could manage. His knees threatened to give out on him.

Erion's punishment. It hadn't been enough that Mathieu ordered Erion killed. He had to suffer, first. This game was meant to hurt.

"I'm not sure how far they've gotten. Isak's crew was in charge of rounding them up. Mathieu…" Sadiq faltered. He gestured to Gerard and took Erion's sword, then unsheathed it. Sunlight glinted off the finely tempered steel.

Sadiq sheathed the sword and held it out to Erion wordlessly.

"What are you doing?" Erion stared at the sword hilt with suspicion. Just minutes ago, Sadiq's men had been dragging Erion off to his death. He'd suspected from the onset that Sadiq was trying to buy him, but the full extent of the crew leader's plans eluded him.

"Things are out of hand. The icho shortage has Mathieu in a panic. He's tripping up, getting sloppy. Not treating his people right."

Erion's eyes narrowed as he realized Sadiq was far more ambitious than he'd ever guessed.

Sadiq leaned toward Erion, a fierce light glimmering in his eyes. He spoke in the barest of whispers.

"I need your support, Erion. I need men I can trust."

CHAPTER FIFTY-ONE
THE WRONG SEWER

Thorne and Isak skulked in a doorway a few blocks away from the festival green. Distant chords of music and revelry drifted on the breeze, but Thorne was hardly enjoying the festivities. He scowled at Isak and handed over a tightly rolled scroll. Vandra had sent it the previous evening, but he hadn't found it until late that morning. He was sharing it with Isak as a last resort. The situation was insanity made flesh.

The note detailed the orders Erion had received, his refusal to comply—even that she'd drugged him to keep him from meeting with Sadiq and doing something stupid. Isak's brows contracted as he reached the end of the script.

"This is a joke," Isak said.

Thorne snorted. The stoneburner was up to idiocy again. Vandra had done her part to save him from himself, and now it was Thorne's turn. He'd been skulking around the festival green on Vandra's request, but he hadn't seen hide nor hair of either Skala brother. Instead, he'd found Isak. It wasn't even close to a fair trade.

Isak's mouth thinned into a grim line. "I can't believe I'm saying this, but I need your help."

"Thorne thinks—"

Isak cut Thorne off with a savage gesture. "None of that. We've got to move fast. There's company from Vhalla. Mathieu's been holed up at the Maw ever since the Fang's messenger arrived."

Thorne grimaced. The only news that ever came from Vhalla was the bad kind.

Isak went on in a rush. "We never ordered a hit on Niklas. Even Skala should have seen through that, but the idiot is too easily manipulated."

Thorne squinted at the big man and reached out with his majea. Isak's calm was tense as a drawn crossbow. He could go off at any second.

But… Isak was genuinely worried. Thorne decided he must be telling the truth.

Thorne bit his tongue as he considered the situation. He'd been wary of Sadiq ever since he'd let the girl escape in the woods. Suddenly the man's careful currying of Erion's favor, the ends he'd been trying to meet, snapped into sharp relief. How long had he been working against Mathieu?

"So… So you're going to…" Thorne faltered. "Whose side are *you* on?"

"I'm going to find that bastard Sadiq before he talks Skala into doing something *really* stupid."

"Thorne is skeptical you're trying to help the stoneburner do anything, actually."

"It's not for him." Isak shoved the note back at Thorne. "Destroy that. We need to get to the Maw and figure out what the hell is going on."

Thorne could believe Isak was worried about the balance of power, but he was still skeptical that the big mercenary actually wanted to help Erion. "You hate Skala."

"Damn right I do. Someday he's going to botch a job so

badly he'll get us all arrested—maybe killed. But I don't trust Sadiq." Isak took a deep breath, looking like he was going to regret what he was about to say. "Besides, Skala's about to step right into the middle of it and muck up everyone's plans… they've taken his brother."

"What?" Thorne's mouth dropped open of its own accord. Isak was right—if Erion found out, the stoneburner *was* about to do something monumentally stupid.

"I saw Sadiq's men myself. I was supposed to be doing the job, but…"

"But?" Thorne prompted.

"But nothing. I always thought Skala was the rat. Turns out I was looking in the wrong sewers."

"You came here to stop Sadiq." Was Isak that loyal to Mathieu, or was there something more at play?

"I was too late," Isak growled.

It was too late for Thorne to run. If the leader in Vhalla— the Fang himself—was involved, there wouldn't be another faction of the Crimson Fang anywhere that would risk harboring him.

Erion's brother. Little Skala was probably the only thing Erion really cared about on all of Daemanon. It was time to choose a side.

"Dammit," Thorne said.

"Let's go. Sadiq will be taking Erion to the Maw." Isak was moving before he finished the sentence. Thorne trailed behind him. Isak's hulking shoulders rose above most of the festival-goers—at least he was easy to follow.

Isak took off down a side street. Thorne cursed and rushed to keep up with him. If they were lucky, they might beat Sadiq and Erion to the Maw.

Thorne just wasn't sure which side Erion would be on by the time they got there.

CHAPTER FIFTY-TWO

RIGHT OF CHALLENGE

hey've taken Edric.

Erion's majea shattered the lock on the door leading to the leadership's private chambers in the Maw. The doorknob exploded outward, leaving a charred, smoking hole in the door.

There were no courts in the Crimson Fang. In Rijeka, Mathieu was judge and executioner alike. He hadn't ordered Erion to be brought here to mete out justice. Mathieu intended to make an example of him.

Just as the head of the Rijeka Fang was intent on punishing Erion's alleged treason, Erion was intent on bringing an end to the whole bloody mess.

"Where are they?" Erion entered the chamber buoyed by a blast of frigid air. The small crowd in the room beyond fell silent as every head turned to stare at Erion. Sadiq and his men crowded the doorway behind him.

Mathieu lounged in a plush chair in the center of the room. A stout man in a garish red cloak sat beside him. That had to be the messenger from Vhalla. Lucius Nishka, a representative of the Fang himself. The man's head was shaved bald. Beady black eyes looked out over a squashed nose that had undoubtedly been broken more than once.

Mathieu jumped up from his seat. "Get out of here, Skala."

"Where are they?" Erion demanded again. He centered his focus on his palm, and a ball of fire ignited there. The flames flickered and sparked, fueled by his barely contained rage.

"What the hell are you talking about?"

"The kids from the festival. My brother." The flames soared higher. A wave of heat rippled across the room.

Mathieu's brows knit together. Erion could almost believe he had no idea what was going on. Before Mathieu could reply, the door slammed open again. Erion turned to see Isak storm into the room, Thorne hot on his heels. In his peripheral, Erion noted Sadiq's stance shifted almost imperceptibly at the intrusion.

Mathieu nodded with grim satisfaction. "Take care of him, Isak." He turned his malice onto Erion. "I don't answer to you, Skala, in case you've forgotten."

Erion shifted, prepared to smash the sphere of fire into Isak's face if the man came near. His arrival brought memories of Amelie—terrified, injured, and huddling in the cave Isak had dragged her to. Erion wouldn't be surprised to learn that Isak had kidnapped Edric himself.

The flames in his hand crackled.

"Mathieu—" Isak began, but Mathieu cut him off with a severing gesture.

"Later."

Isak stood stock-still, and the air in the room pulsed with tension.

Erion's gaze shifted to Thorne. He willed every ounce of venom he could muster into the glare. Trusting Thorne had been his own mistake, like so many others he'd made, but the man's betrayal cut to the bone all the same. Thorne widened his eyes and shook his head a fraction, but his meaning—if there was any—was inscrutable as ever.

"What have we here?" The red-cloaked man's eyes glimmered with greedy intensity as he looked between Mathieu, Isak, and Erion. "More evidence of your ineptitudes, Mathieu. You can't even control your own men."

Mathieu's face purpled. He took a menacing step toward Erion.

"You swore my family would be protected!" Erion shouted. A shock wave of air blasted at Mathieu, tearing at his clothes and shoving him back a step.

"What the hell are you—"

"Mathieu, he's right," Isak interrupted. "They took the younger boy this morning. He's with the others."

Under any other circumstances, Mathieu's double-take would have been comical. Erion looked at Isak in shock. Was Isak… standing up for him?

Mathieu's gaze darted around the room. His focus finally fell on Sadiq. "Is this true? You were responsible for the grab. How did this happen?"

Sadiq stepped up to stand shoulder-to-shoulder with Erion. He lifted his chin imperiously. "Lying doesn't become you, Mathieu."

The Fang's messenger stood. Mathieu's head twitched around as he tried to keep Nishka and Sadiq in his sights at the same time. The fire in Erion's palm shrank. He was no longer sure where to direct his rage. His hopes of provoking Mathieu into a confrontation were dashed. Instead, Sadiq's greasy smile was twisting his guts into knots.

"Sadiq's been taking contracts from the Ithynon directly," Isak accused.

"No. I ordered him to take the magelings." Mathieu had the frantic look of a drowning man desperate to be thrown a rope. "Just not Skala. I—"

"He's taken a half-dozen women without your knowledge and delivered them directly to the Ithynon, right under your nose. And he's been stockpiling icho," Isak interrupted.

Erion's fireball died.

"I had a higher directive. It's not my fault Mathieu wasn't capable of filling the Ithynon's orders. Besides—you weren't exactly doing your part, either," Sadiq snarled.

Isak rounded on Sadiq, murder burning in his eyes. He was easily head-and-shoulders taller than Sadiq, and he towered over the other man. "Kids?" he snarled. "It's not right."

Erion's heart pounded. He took several steps back from Isak to take in the room, finally seeing the den of vellish he'd landed himself in. He'd let his dislike of Isak blind him to the real threat. Erion turned to Nishka just in time to see him give Sadiq an almost-imperceptible nod.

A blade flashed in Sadiq's hand, and he lunged at Mathieu.

Erion saw through the careful attack at once. Sadiq's arm swung intentionally wide. It was a feint never meant to hit the mark—the same technique Erion had planned to deploy.

Chaos erupted.

Isak snarled and lunged for Sadiq, but Sadiq's small crew moved like lightning. Gerard and Bryant wrestled Isak to the ground before he could take two steps.

The sudden decisiveness of the attack took most of Mathieu's men unawares. Erion narrowly dodged a wildly flailing blade as the coup erupted around him. He slipped away from the brawl. Sadiq's men took no notice of him—they must have received orders to leave Erion be for the moment. Sadiq was still counting on Erion's loyalties.

In the Crimson Fang, forcing a superior to strike first broke Vandra's spellwork. Sadiq couldn't attack Mathieu outright, but he could act in self-defense. Mathieu, bewildered and under siege, couldn't see through the theatrics. He sidestepped Sadiq, seized his collar, and slammed him into the back wall. A meaty fist landed on Sadiq's jaw. Erion could practically feel the threads of Line Magic that bound Sadiq snap.

Sadiq rammed his forehead into Mathieu's nose. Erion winced—he'd been on the receiving end of a blow like that more than once.

Only a handful of men attended Mathieu in the Maw. He wasn't a man to trust easily, and Erion saw immediately that it would be his downfall now. Mathieu's skeleton crew was made up of dead, dying, or bound men within moments. He was alone—at the mercy of Sadiq's ferocious attack.

Blood fountained from Mathieu's nose, but he didn't cry out. His fingers found Sadiq's throat, and he reached for his dagger with his other hand. Sadiq kneed Mathieu in the groin. Mathieu's grip slipped and he slumped bonelessly to his knees.

In two quick gestures, Sadiq seized a fistful of Mathieu's hair and stabbed his dagger into the side of his neck. Bright blood spurted from the juncture between Mathieu's neck and jaw.

It was over.

Sadiq kicked Mathieu onto his side and stepped over the body. Erion looked away. He couldn't be accused of harboring fondness for Mathieu, but that didn't mean Erion wanted to see the light die in his eyes. A tension as dangerous and latent as a drawn bow filled the room.

"What are you doing, Sadiq?" Isak snarled from where he was pinned to the ground. "Kidnapping and torturing innocent women for pleasure not enough for you anymore?"

"I knew you were the one getting in the way of that." Sadiq moved toward Isak, a madman's glimmer in his eye. Isak held a stony silence. Gerard's boot was still planted on his back.

Sadiq crouched next to Isak and pressed the tip of his dagger just under Isak's jaw. "I've got to decide who I can trust. So, that night in the woods. What were you doing with the girl?

"Been going against orders this whole time, I expect. Every time a girl got away, you were behind it, weren't you? Weren't you?" Sadiq put just enough pressure behind the dagger that a single bead of blood welled on Isak's neck.

Erion caught sight of Thorne in the far corner. Thorne jerked his head to the side, urging Erion to join him. After a wary glance at Sadiq and Isak, Erion did so. Out of anyone, Thorne was most likely to have a read on the room.

"What the *hell*—" Erion began in a rough whisper, but

Thorne shook his head. He watched Sadiq with a fixed intensity, eyes narrowed.

"I worked too hard to get those subjects to the Ithynon to have someone sabotaging my every move. Mathieu couldn't trust you, Isak, and I sure as hell can't, either," Sadiq continued.

"Let's get on with it, Sadiq," Nishka interrupted. The Fang messenger had settled into Mathieu's abandoned chair. He looked almost bored. "I'm not interested in your personal revenge. Your job was to seal business with the Ithynon."

Sadiq grimaced and stood. "Let him go," he told Gerard and Bryant. The two men exchanged a glance but released the big man. Isak pushed himself to his feet with a grimace.

"Thorne's confused," Thorne said quietly.

"Like that's new," Sadiq rolled his eyes. "Isak was supposed to be rounding up those subjects for the Ithynon. Mathieu was too slow to realize that he didn't have the guts, so I had to do it."

"It wasn't right," Isak repeated.

"Sadiq," Nishka said again. Sadiq rolled his eyes and ignored the messenger completely.

"You're not in a line of work where you can afford morals, Isak. Ask Erion." Sadiq turned to Erion with a half-smirk. He extended the dagger hilt first. "Kill him."

The weapon dropped into Erion's palm like lead. Thorne stirred at his elbow but held his silence. Not for the first time, Erion wished he could see Thorne's Love Magic at work. If there was ever a time to use it...

"They took your brother. As punishment for failing to kill your own father. What kind of sick bastard puts out that kind of order?" Sadiq whispered.

Erion swallowed against a lump in his throat.

"They've been using you," Sadiq urged.

They'd all been using him.

"That's a lie." Isak said it softly, earnestly. He wasn't acting like himself at all. It had to be stress—Isak had been Mathieu's right-hand man for years, and now his closest ally lay in a pool of his own blood mere feet away.

A murder in cold blood, no matter how carefully Sadiq had twisted the Fang's own laws in his favor.

"There was no order. Mathieu never wanted Niklas dead. Why bother?" Isak's eyes never left Sadiq.

"A test of Erion's loyalty, and a message to the Ithynon. The Crimson Fang won't be so easily double-crossed now that I'm in charge."

"Sadiq, get on with it." Nishka's voice held a note of warning; a master calling his dog to heel.

Erion had no idea what to believe. "Where's Edric?"

"On a boat to Elarazii," Isak said. "Where Sadiq put him, with the others. Kids."

"Kill him," Sadiq told Erion again. "Mathieu made them murder your brother to teach you a lesson. Kill the man responsible for your brother's death."

"The Ithynon wanted them alive," Isak protested again.

Erion's breath was shaky. The only thing he'd ever trusted Isak to do was to make Erion's life as miserable as possible. And Sadiq...

Sadiq had seemed genuinely sympathetic to the difficult decisions Erion had been forced to make. He'd even voiced objections to orders that compromised Erion's divided family loyalties. He'd replaced Erion's sword and helped Amelie escape.

But why? Was Sadiq really behind the worst of the disappearances?

Erion glanced at Thorne. He'd never had much confidence in the man's abilities. Once, he'd tried to smooth out a particularly unfortunate situation with a bouncer at a tavern in Elarazii. Instead of calming the giant man, Thorne had somehow managed to make him fall asleep. Even so, he had to rely on the erkurios now. Did Thorne know who was telling the truth? And could Erion trust him?

Thorne's eyes flicked to Sadiq and back, then shook his head in an almost-imperceptible motion.

"We'll go get your brother as soon as this is done," Sadiq

urged.

"You told me he was dead."

Sadiq flinched. It was all the confirmation Erion needed. Edric was alive.

Impossibly, Isak had been telling the truth.

The Guardian's arrival in Rijeka must have finally forced the baron's hand. Erion knew what he'd find at the nuraghi: the baroness's body in her otherworldly cocoon, a line of aspiring mages waiting to be sacrificed, and a relic from an age beyond measurable time.

Erion tightened his grip on the dagger. Every act he'd taken since the Crimson Fang had raided his home so many years ago seemed to flash before his eyes.

They made me. I had no other choice.

He'd badly miscalculated. He should have known that Edric would never be safe as long as Erion was mixed up with the Crimson Fang. Surely some small part of him had known that. He'd been hiding behind the excuses for too long.

"I was promised my family would be protected. That oath has been compromised." *And you did it on purpose, you absolute bastards.*

Erion took a deep, steadying breath, willing his anger away. He couldn't afford to lose control. Control was everything. "I claim the right of challenge."

CHAPTER FIFTY-THREE
LAW OF SUCCESSION

adiq clapped Erion on the shoulder and leaned in to whisper in his ear. "He feints to the left. Get in close where those damned simiot arms can't abuse their length."

"I'm challenging *you*." Erion watched the grin slide off Sadiq's face with bitter satisfaction.

Sadiq's hand dropped from Erion's shoulder, his eyes narrowing.

Erion permitted himself a small smile. In hindsight, the recruitment had all been too obvious. Clumsily handled. Sadiq had mistaken him for an easy mark because Erion was out of his depth.

Erion was desperate, but he wasn't stupid.

You might be a little stupid, actually. He should have seen it sooner—not Isak's actions, perhaps, but Sadiq's ham-fisted attempts to recruit him. His actions had gone beyond a crew leader looking out for the new guy.

"After everything I've done for you…" Sadiq's voice was

venomously soft. "This is your repayment?"

Erion took a shaky breath. The whole situation was beginning to feel unreal—the worst of nightmares come to life. But time wasn't a luxury he could afford. Edric might not have much longer. *If he's still alive at all.* Erion forced the intrusive thought away.

It was time to choose a side.

"You took Edric," Erion said simply.

Sadiq actually laughed. "You believe *Isak*?"

Gods save me, but I think I do.

Erion pushed past Sadiq, choosing to ignore his taunt. He looked around at the small scene of carnage. Three of Mathieu's men were dead—the others had fled. Sadiq's crew—six men in all—hovered around the corners of the lounge like hellhounds waiting for their master's order to pounce.

"Help me out here," Erion whispered when he reached Thorne.

"What are you doing, Death Wish?" Thorne mumbled.

Erion stared at him, momentarily panicked. "You—I thought—Isak was telling the truth?"

"I am." Isak was still glaring at Sadiq. "Don't mistake that for any fondness for you, Skala. This is a right mess you've got us in."

"*I've* got us…" Erion sputtered. "Why didn't *you* challenge him?"

"You beat me to it."

Erion clenched his fists to keep from punching Isak in the face. He didn't know exactly how Vandra's symmajea prevented that kind of violence, but he was sure it wouldn't be pleasant if he struck first.

"What do you plan on doing with him?" Isak gestured toward Nishka, who was in hushed conversation with Sadiq.

Erion had all but forgotten the messenger was there. Sadiq may have been power hungry for Mathieu's position, but he'd been worried enough about the takeover that he'd cut a deal with someone over Mathieu's head. Erion had no idea what

Nishka—let alone the Fang—would do if Erion immediately upended that new balance of power.

"Deal with that later," Thorne advised. "If you're not dead."

Erion nodded, grateful to ignore the messenger for now. "How does this work?"

"Formality. You challenged, so Sadiq gets to choose the weapon," Isak said.

"That's not how it worked with Mathieu," Erion argued.

Isak shook his head. "Mathieu attacked him. Self-defense is different."

"Great." It didn't matter the weapon. Erion would do what needed to be done.

"No weapons." Sadiq's voice rang out from across the room. Fluttery whispers filled the air at the pronouncement.

Isak looked grim. "Less chance you'll use your magic."

Erion nodded—it made sense. Naming any weapon with iron would give Erion the upper hand. Even when he didn't explicitly employ his majea, he could usually sense the element and, when he was lucky, anticipate blows. Sadiq didn't have magic. There was no reason he'd let Erion use his to gain an advantage.

Just get to Edric.

The men of the Crimson Fang cleared tables and chairs from the center of the room and formed a small circle around the two combatants. Erion left his sword and dagger with Thorne with a small twinge of regret. It wasn't an easy thing to kill a man with bare hands. *Or at all.*

Erion never thought he'd regret his inexperience with killing.

"If there was ever a time to be ruthless..." Isak nodded at Sadiq as though reading Erion's mind. "This is it."

"You just get more and more interesting, don't you?" Just when Erion had thought he'd figured out the Crimson Fang's more nuanced politics, Isak had to hit him with... kindness? Sympathy?

Erion puffed out a breath and turned to face his opponent. He wanted nothing more than a drink and a soft bed. His muscles and head ached from the night before—*Damn Vandra and her meddling*. He cracked his neck side-to-side, his joints protesting the motion.

A deathly silence filled the room. Erion turned his attention to the manipulative bastard in front of him. Sadiq's malevolent grin forced all hesitation out of his mind. Without any formality or warning, Sadiq lunged.

Erion barely had time to dodge. Sadiq followed with a punch to Erion's stomach that knocked the wind out of him. He summoned all his fury and threw it into his attack.

Erion rammed his forearm into Sadiq's throat, then curled his hand around the back of his head and grabbed a fistful of Sadiq's long hair. He yanked hard, wrenching Sadiq's head around. The man hissed in pain.

With a strangled grunt, Sadiq kicked the heel of his boot into Erion's shin, then looped his leg around Erion's and shoved him. Erion's knee gave out, but he kept a tight grip on Sadiq's hair and dragged the man down with him.

Sadiq grabbed Erion's arm and dug his fingers into his wrist. Erion twisted away before he could exploit the pressure point. They fell into a flurry of strikes and tangled limbs.

Erion's energy began to flag almost at once. In his condition, all Sadiq really needed to do was wear him out. This had to be quick.

Erion's hands slicked with sweat. He fumbled his grip. Sadiq slipped away and lashed out with a fury. A barrage of blows struck Erion's temple, his jaw, his gut. When Erion finally succeeded in catching Sadiq's arm, he grabbed for his thumb. Sadiq threw himself forward and smashed his elbow into Erion's jaw.

A sickening crack split the air around them as Sadiq's thumb snapped. He screamed and jerked away, though whether it was more from pain or rage, Erion couldn't tell.

Sadiq cradled his injured hand close to his chest. There was no time to think—no time to catch his breath. Erion tackled him round the middle. Sadiq slipped to the side. He seized Erion and snaked an arm around his neck.

Pressure built in Erion's head. His fingers scrabbled at Sadiq's forearm as he tried to twist away. The headlock tightened.

Erion's vision started to tunnel. The well of majea bubbled inside him without thought. He forced back the instinct to clap a mask of dense air over Sadiq's mouth and nose.

No magic.

Instead, he scrabbled for Sadiq's injured thumb again. Sadiq snarled and recoiled.

Erion curled onto his side. Sweet air rushed into his lungs, clearing his head and easing the ache in his chest—just in time for Sadiq to kick him in the ribs.

Erion gasped at the sudden, sharp pain. He was ready for the second blow. He watched for Sadiq's boot out of the corner of his eye and grabbed for it just before contact. He wrenched Sadiq off his feet and lunged.

Sadiq rammed his head into Erion's face. Blood, hot and metallic, filled his mouth.

Erion spat and drove his knee into Sadiq's side. He finally managed to trap Sadiq's arm and neck in a lock. In control now, Erion grabbed Sadiq's hair at the base of his neck and rammed the man's face into the floor.

Once. Twice. Blood flowed freely from Sadiq's nose and smeared on the floor beneath him. He thrashed against Erion's hold, twisting and bucking with increasing desperation.

Erion's muscles screamed from the effort of holding him. He tightened his grip. Sadiq's breathing was labored, wheezy. Erion pushed down on Sadiq's head, forcing his neck forward, shoving his face into the floor. He was gasping for every breath, his arms shaking from prolonged exertion.

Sadiq's body went slack. Erion waited for several pounding heartbeats. Sadiq didn't stir, but his chest still rose and fell with desperate breaths.

Erion glanced up at Thorne and Isak. His grip on the Crimson Fang crew leader eased as he looked to them for direction.

I don't want to kill him.

The hesitation cost him. As soon as the hold loosened, Sadiq surged to his forearms and knocked Erion's hands away.

"*No!*" The word ripped from Erion's throat of its own accord. Sadiq rolled onto his back, gasping for air.

"Rot in hell, Skala," he wheezed.

Erion smashed his fist into Sadiq's windpipe.

His heart threatened to pound out of his chest. He fought off Sadiq's hands, locked out one of his arms, and rolled until his crew leader was face down once more.

Forgive me.

He didn't know who the prayer was for—the gods, his brother, or himself.

Erion slammed Sadiq's face into the floor, again and again until Sadiq's form went limp.

Blood pounded in Erion's head. As soon as the muscles in Sadiq's neck relaxed, Erion grabbed the man's head with both hands. He eased Sadiq's jaw back and forth slightly, making sure his old crew leader didn't have the strength to resist anymore.

Erion shoved Sadiq's neck around and forced his chin up. Sadiq's cheek slammed into the floor, and Erion glimpsed his wide-eyed panic. He closed his eyes and yanked Sadiq's chin upward with another twist, harder this time.

A strangled sound, more animal than Human, escaped Sadiq.

SNAP.

Sadiq convulsed once, then stilled.

Erion dropped Sadiq's body and recoiled. *Snap.* The sudden end of the fight took him by surprise as much as the ease at which he'd broken Sadiq's neck. Thorne and Isak pulled him away. Erion flinched and wrenched himself from their grip. He didn't want anyone touching him—not ever again.

Shaking, Erion wiped his mouth with his hand. He winced. His hand came away bloody. One or more of his teeth had gone clean through the skin when Sadiq had rammed his face, leaving a bloody gash on his lower lip.

The sounds of the small crowd rushed back all at once as Erion came back to himself. Sadiq lay face down on the scuffed floorboards, blood smeared around his head like some kind of cursed halo.

Erion's stomach curdled at the sight.

He turned away. Just like Mathieu's corpse, Erion didn't want to see the blank eyes—the shattered nose, the fractured cheekbones. The last thing he needed right now was puking. He couldn't afford to show weakness in front of these men.

His men.

Someone was clapping. Erion wrenched his gaze from the body and looked up into Lucius Nishka's black eyes.

"Well *done*." Nishka said it like a father commending a favored son for executing his first hunt. "What was your name?"

"Erion Skala." Erion's body trembled from the sudden release of adrenaline and violence. He watched Nishka warily. There was no strength left in him for another fight.

"We should talk, you and I," Nishka said.

"I'd rather not." Erion sagged into a chair, too tired to care that it had been Mathieu's only a few minutes before.

"You've caused quite the upset. Impressive, really. I could ensure you power and wealth beyond your wildest dreams."

"Thought you were just a messenger." The gouges in Erion's lips made speaking an agony.

"*Erion.*" Isak's voice carried a soft warning.

Nishka grabbed Erion's hand and pushed his sleeve up. He scoffed at the leather bracer, took out his dagger, and sliced the laces away. His eyes widened as he took in the form and colors of Erion's tattoo, and Erion knew what he must be thinking. The mark was still more white scar than true ink. He was barely blooded.

"Who *are* you?" Nishka asked.

"I'm the leader of this faction." The words sounded unreal in Erion's ears. "And I don't want trouble."

Thorne put his face in his hands and groaned at the words. Erion ignored him.

"You've caused a fair amount of that, lad."

"Do we have a problem?" Erion didn't have time to deal with this. He didn't have the stomach to kill Nishka, and he couldn't afford the mire it would land him in with the head of the Crimson Fang if he did.

Nishka sucked on his teeth. After a weighted pause, he sheathed his dagger. "I don't believe we do. But make no mistakes, Erion Skala. We'll be watching you."

Without further threat, Nishka wove through the small crowd of Sadiq's men and left the Maw.

Erion could only feel relief at the man's exit. He couldn't summon the energy to think about the situation. He glanced sidelong at Thorne, willing the man, for the first time, to dig into his head. If he ever needed strength, it was now. Thorne shot him a single sideways glance, but said nothing. Erion thought he saw the man's nose twitch, but couldn't be sure. Steeling himself, he turned back to Sadiq's remaining men.

Every eye in the room was fixed on him, and murder was painted on several faces that glared back at him. Erion straightened his stance. If he looked weak now, he only risked another challenger. He took a deep breath.

"Go get as many crews together as you can in the next half-hour. We're going to the nuraghi."

CHAPTER FIFTY-FOUR

DEAD MEN

T horne stuck to Erion's side like a barnacle after he killed Sadiq. He'd been keeping a close watch on his friend's emotions ever since he'd first walked into the Maw. Thorne had never seen anyone so strung out—though Erion had good enough reasons.

Erion had worked hard to hide his brother's secret, but the goblin was out of the cage. Or the lifeweaver was. The lifeweaver was out of *something*.

Little Skala had magic, and now everyone knew it.

And he probably *was* in a cage somewhere.

Thorne didn't find that thought encouraging.

He narrowed his eyes at Erion. At first, Thorne had worried Erion was going to pass out. He hadn't been in good condition after whatever Sadiq had done to him, and everyone knew Skala didn't have a stomach for killing.

Erion Skala—the new leader of the Crimson Fang.

But Erion had pushed through his obvious fatigue—and the scrambled fear and anxiety that colored his emotions—and started snapping orders. He pulsed with a ruthless, unpredictable energy.

Erion gestured to Fenris, one of the Crimson Fang's newest members. The gangly youth was all legs and nervousness. He actually tripped over his feet in his haste to join Erion.

"Give this to a runner and have it delivered to Wilder's Keep. Pay whatever it takes to get it there immediately." Erion handed a sealed envelope to the boy, along with a handful of dakkari. Fenris burned a deep red, then *bowed* before running out the door.

Well, that's not going to go to his head at all. Thorne didn't care if Erion tried to bash his face into the floor like he had Sadiq's. He wasn't about to start *bowing*.

The room was suffused with a buzz of shock and unease, a tangible cloud of emotions that Thorne's majea was struggling to cut through.

It took some serious stones to pull a trick as bold as Sadiq's play today. Whatever could be said about the man's ambition, he'd gone out with flair.

And then Erion—blessed, ignorant fool that he was—had outstripped them all with his own special brand of idiocy.

Thorne turned his attention to Isak. The big man was hovering at Erion's elbow, offering quiet advice when questioned and providing names and information about resources as Erion needed them. Thorne could feel the subtle compulsion of Vandra's carefully worked symmajea in their tattoos. The spellwork urged Thorne to aid Erion, and he knew the same must be working on everyone else in the room.

The soft urge was new—some delicate working of the spell meant to come into play only in the event of a change in power. It couldn't just be a game Thorne's mind was playing. The delicate balance of players in Rijeka had just been upended.

"So now we're all dead men, huh?" Thorne said to Isak out of the corner of his mouth. Erion slumped into the plush chair once occupied by Mathieu. He'd wanted to leave immediately, but Thorne and Isak had managed to convince him to remove the bodies—*Amarassa help us, two bodies*—and call for a healer before heading to the docks.

With Erion's approval, Isak dispatched men from his own crew to carry out the orders: ready the boats, call all hands, fetch the lifeweaver.

"Yeah, probably all dead men," Isak agreed.

Erion's vengeance was going to send them all to an early grave.

Erion stood up, still looking shaky, and buckled on his sword belt. "Have the healer meet us at the docks. I want him with us."

"Uhm," Thorne said.

"What?" A flicker of Erion's old uncertainty crossed his face.

"Well. It's Quill," Thorne said.

"*What?*" Erion's mouth hung open.

"And he's not blooded, so he can't be compelled," Isak added.

"But he'll still meet you at the docks," Thorne said, trying to be helpful. Quill wasn't exactly ancient, but he was in no condition to go storming a Giant stronghold and chasing necromancers around.

"Well that's new. Anything else I need to know? The little old flower lady on the corner is secretly fencing v'deru?" Alarm painted Erion's features. "Actually, don't answer that. We're leaving."

Thorne thought about voicing his misgivings. Erion's tumultuous mental state was cause enough for concern, but what he was suggesting was almost literally a suicide mission. Thorne didn't want to go back to that nuraghi, and he *really* didn't want to die.

"Do we have to?" he found himself saying instead.

Erion blinked at him, and a wave of uncertainty slipped through his emotions. He looked around the room as though seeing it for the first time. It was empty, now, save for Isak and Thorne.

"Only if you don't want to piss off the boss," Isak told

Thorne. He folded his arms with an air of distaste. Mistrust and resentment roiled beneath his relatively calm surface. Thorne cocked his head to one side. Actually, Isak was handling the sudden upheaval fairly well. He'd hated Sadiq so much, he was willing to put up with taking Erion's orders—at least for the time being.

"The Ithynon has gone to ground because of the Guardian in the city. He can't afford to wait anymore."

"And are you going to tell us what he's been waiting *for*?" Isak asked. "Some of us are more in the dark than others."

"He's going to kill those kids," Erion said. "And use their magic to try and bring back his wife."

"Huh?" Isak said.

Thorne glanced at Erion, silently asking permission to speak, and Erion nodded grimly. "It's Baron Voloy. He's been using Mathieu this entire time."

"Did Mathieu know?" Isak asked. Thorne frowned and tried to sort through Isak's mind. The news caused a faint ripple of concern across the smooth waters of his calm, but not much else.

A dangerous man.

"I don't think so. I only figured it out because of the work I was doing for Niklas." The last of the color drained from Erion's already pale face. "Niklas. Is he…?"

"There wasn't ever a hit on him. Sadiq lied," Isak said.

A muscle twitched in Erion's jaw, and he headed toward the door without another word.

Things were about to change, and Thorne wasn't sure it was for the better. He'd suddenly found himself in a position of confidence with one of the most dangerous men in the duchy. Erion himself probably didn't even realize the power his actions had just amassed.

"Dead men," Thorne whispered again.

CHAPTER FIFTY-FIVE

THE DRAKUNEM

E rion stood at the prow of the boat as it surged downstream. He forced down another piece of the dried jerky that Quill had pressed on him after healing. Erion knew he needed to eat to keep up his strength, but his stomach revolted against the food all the same.

He was exerting all his self-control not to throw his majea into the current. They were already heading downstream at a quick pace, the river's flow bolstered by the steady rains of the last few weeks. They were going as fast as he could have hoped. Besides, he wasn't near strong enough to hasten both boats, and he needed all the men and majea he could get. In the span of twenty-four hours, Erion had done enough idiotic things for a lifetime, but even he wasn't fool enough to hope Baron Voloy wasn't lurking in the nuraghi without at least a dozen guards.

Erion turned his attention to the thirty-odd men behind him on the boat—anyone in the Crimson Fang they'd been able to hunt down on such short notice. Most had been enlisted on the oars. Others wandered the deck while they waited their turn to row.

My men.

"You got a plan, Dead Man?" Thorne appeared at his side as though conjured.

"Still going with that one, are we?" Erion deflected. "Don't I get some kind of new title now?"

"Thorne didn't think you'd like that."

"No," Erion admitted. "I wouldn't. How many men do you think Voloy will have?" Erion asked.

Thorne stuck out his tongue and grimaced. "Depends on how many kids. Three, four to carry the body. Five or ten to round up the sacrifices…"

Erion's heart skipped a beat at the word. He glanced up at the sky—the sun had long since set. They had to be getting close.

"Plus Cedivar," Erion said. They couldn't afford to discount the Line Mage.

Thorne nodded in acknowledgment. "Say at least twenty."

"Carrying the kids, it would have taken them a lot longer to get down there." Was it too much to hope Erion would reach Edric before the depths of Nuraghi Uzhastik claimed them? He cringed at the thought of descending into those depths again. "How long ago do you think they left?"

"Nobody's seen Voloy or his dog all day. A group of Sadiq's men took the kids a little after midday… Thorne forgot you weren't awake yet."

"Great." Erion ground his teeth. It had been hours. "What's going on with Isak?"

"Isak?" Thorne wrinkled his nose.

"He's… helping."

"Ah," Thorne said, nodding. "Self-preservation."

"Maybe." Erion couldn't afford to let his guard down. The last time he'd done that… The thought made him want to kill Sadiq all over again.

It felt like an eternity before they reached the mouth of the river. Silver ripples danced across the black expanse of Lake

Zagretsk in the boat's wake.

Erion ordered the men to dock as close to the Reinholdt ruins as they could. The faint outline of a plan had sketched itself into his mind as they'd traveled, and now the details were beginning to manifest.

Erion had almost forty men with him, but no idea how to give them orders—and no idea who he could really trust. The symmajea in their tattoos was supposed to encourage, if not exactly compel, obedience. He wanted to rely on that as little as possible, even if he did trust Vandra's spellwork.

The thought of Vandra sent a frisson of betrayal down his spine. *Later.*

"No lights." Erion hopped down from the prow and waded through the final few inches of Lake Zagretsk to the shore. Thorne splashed behind him, swearing.

The men from Isak's crew followed more slowly. Erion had elected to leave Sadiq's men in Rijeka after they'd gathered as many other members of the Fang as they could. He didn't need any more reasons to watch his back tonight. There was foul blood between the crews now.

"I don't know who I can trust. Can you..." Erion turned to Thorne, but floundered for the right words. He knew little about Love Magic, and even less about Thorne's actual capabilities.

"Sort of." Thorne answered Erion's unfinished question. "If they're shifty, Thorne knows."

"Shifty?"

"Uneasy. Guilty."

It would have to do—though Erion had no doubt everyone was already plenty on edge. Proximity to the nuraghi alone would have been enough. Nobody *wanted* to storm a Giant fortress held by a mad necromancer and his goons.

Good thing they didn't have much of a choice.

"Line up by rank," Erion said to the gathered men. "Marks out."

Erion paced down the line, feeling like a charlatan as he inspected the men's tattoos. They ran the spectrum from fresh scars—a grizzly man who looked at least thirty years older than Erion—to the deep, blood red that went almost all the way up Isak's forearm.

After nodding at Isak, Erion pulled Thorne aside. He didn't have to be an erkurios to sense the tension. Erion's plans and his leadership were an unknown quantity, and most of them didn't have the slightest clue what they were about to do.

"Anyone I need to watch for?" Erion asked. He could practically feel the minutes slipping past him, but Edric would be just as dead if Erion rushed into the nuraghi's depths without some kind of planning.

Thorne closed his eyes and scrunched up his nose in concentration. After a moment, he rattled off a handful of names.

"We'll leave them to stand watch at the door when the rest of us go down," Erion decided.

"Can I trust Isak to come with us?" Erion asked.

"He's a bastard, but Thorne doesn't think a sneaky bastard."

Erion had to admit there was something to be said for working with a brute like Isak. You got what you expected from him. He gestured for Isak to join them, then laid out his plan.

"You're proposing to undo everything Mathieu's been working on for over a year," Isak said.

"They have my *brother*," Erion snarled. "And in case you've forgotten, Mathieu's dead."

"You're asking for a mutiny," Isak said.

Erion bit back a caustic retort. After years of being bullied by Isak, Erion finally had the standing to unleash his fury on the man—and couldn't afford to do it.

"Let them mutiny." Erion threw his hands up. "*After* we get Edric. It's not like the Ithynon is going to be sending more work our way after tonight, anyway."

Us. Gallantyr's bones, I'm talking like one of them.

"Let's get this over with, then. We'll have words when this is over, you and I," Isak said.

"Looking forward to it," Erion said.

"So… what are we waiting for?" Thorne asked.

"Backup," Erion said darkly.

Edric's alive. He has to be.

CHAPTER FIFTY-SIX

UNLIKELY ALLIES

Aleria syn'Duvar jumped from the deck of the boat she'd hired in Rijeka. It was a small vessel, but manned by gekurioi guiding the currents and the winds. They'd traveled the distance from the city to Lake Zagretsk in record time. She landed lightly in the shallows, and the boat glided silently away. She'd made it clear that the crew didn't want to be anywhere near this shore after they'd dropped her off.

The cold, clear air was invigorating. Shafts of silvery moonlight played through the trees on the shoreline. She could just make out two distinct groups huddled by the cliffside.

Aleria ran a hand over her gear, checking that her blades, bow, and firebrand saber were securely clipped to the leather bandoleer worn across her chest. She owed the fashion to a fellow Guardian, Rellen Falcoria—though she'd never admit to mirroring him intentionally. The ingredients she occasionally used in her zomajea were close at hand in water-tight packets affixed to the belt.

Everything about the letter she'd received from Erion Skala felt like a trap. Aleria had seen more than her fair share of insanity in her days serving the King of Pelinon. Even so, the note's contents had been almost too ludicrous to believe. Kidnapped magelings was one thing—but the local gang going on a rescue mission?

Other Guardians would condemn her recklessness in going alone, as the letter had requested—but the danger was part of the appeal.

One man broke off from the group as she approached. She recognized him at once as the man she'd encountered at the baron's estate. Aleria stopped and made an obvious show of looking him up and down. He was broad-shouldered and lean-muscled, with a hint of mania glittering in his hazel eyes. "Erion Skala, I take it?"

The man nodded. "I need your help."

"Say I'm not inclined to give it?"

"You can't afford not to."

"Talk," she ordered, folding her arms across her chest. His letter had raised more questions than it had answered.

"You're here to investigate all those disappearances, right? The baron is killing kids. They're down there right now, and if we don't—" Erion bit down on the rest of the sentence with an obvious effort.

"I met the baron. He doesn't seem like he's up to much." But she was playing Nissra's advocate. She'd sensed the vile majea that swirled around Baron Voloy the instant she'd stepped into his council room. Whatever experimentations he'd undertaken, the man had twisted his own life force almost beyond recognition. His majea was amateurish and sloppy—and all the more dangerous for it.

"He's had a lot of help."

"Like you and your men?" The tattoo on this man's arm was barely blooded. Who was this man? When she'd run into him at the baron's manor, she'd thought him an interesting piece of the puzzle—at best, a possible weak link she could crack open to dig into what the Crimson Fang was up to. But he was obviously in charge here… She cocked her head at him, considering. "You're young."

"Will you help or not?" Erion closed the distance between them. Rather than trying to be menacing, he seemed to be pleading with her.

"How many kids?" she asked. "And how do I know you're not storming down there to help him—and kill me for my majea, too?"

"We think five kids." Erion hesitated. "And the man in charge before—died."

Aleria quirked her brow at his stumble. There was a story there, but perhaps one for another time. "And *your* trustworthiness?"

"One of them is my brother." The cold fury in his voice rang of truth, and something clicked. This was a man on a quest for vengeance.

"Your brother is a mageling?" Aleria didn't miss Erion's flinch. "What stream?"

"He's a lifeweaver. He wants to go to the academy in Saritu'e'Mere. And he'll never get to if you don't help us." Erion's words were choppy, every word drawn out with effort.

"And you—you're a mage?"

"Does that matter?" Erion asked. Aleria held her silence. "Land Magic. But it doesn't do me much good."

Aleria nodded. "Honesty will get you a long way with me. So how does the leader of the Crimson Fang manage to get his own brother shepherded for sacrifice?"

Erion didn't answer. She decided to let him have that silence. She'd get to the crux of the matter soon enough.

"Well—sounds like fun." Aleria grinned. "I'm in."

He sagged with visible relief. "The entry is here. We think he'll have about twenty men, and at least one mage in addition to himself."

Aleria followed him back to his crew, frowning as he detailed what he knew about the nuraghi they were about to storm. She'd never been inside one before, and had always wondered how exaggerated the other Guardians' stories about them were. Rellen was supposed to have gotten his falchions in a nuraghi. Supposedly he never told the whole story because of how horribly wrong the mission had gone. He'd been the only one to return.

Nothing like personal experience to slake her curiosity.

"One last question." Aleria joined Erion in facing the motley group of criminals gathered by the shore. Thirty-odd men of varying age and status. The only thing they all seemed to have in common was their readiness; they were all armed to the teeth. "What's the baron's end game?"

"He's trying to bring back his wife."

"What do you—*bring back*?" Aleria's voice fell to a shocked whisper.

It went against every tenet she had studied and grown to respect and love over her years as a zokurios. It went against laws of nature that superseded those of Humans and Giants alike.

What was dead stayed dead.

"It's not possible," she pressed. "You can't—she *died*."

"Well, you're about to get your chance to tell him that. There's something in there—some altar or artifact, I don't know what it is—that he's using to enhance his powers. It's *evil*. Like ancient evil."

Aleria shook her head and tried to compose her thoughts. How brazen a man must Drazan Voloy be to try and conquer death? A corpse might be animated—she'd seen it before—but in the way of a carefully manipulated taxidermy. At best, a puppet. Nothing more.

To actually reclaim someone from the cloak of death? Impossible.

A dozen more questions chased each other through her mind, but Erion was already leading his crew to the cliffs.

Impossible, she thought again. *We should have known about this sooner.*

Baron Voloy had shown disgusting competence at hiding his tracks. The kidnappings, the icho rings, Duke Jesper's murdered representatives—it had gone on for too long.

A frisson of excitement overtook her. Stamping bastards like Voloy back into their place was why she had become a Guardian. She flexed her fingers on the hilt of her firebrand as she followed Erion and his gang to the nuraghi's entrance.

Let's dance.

CHAPTER FIFTY-SEVEN

DESCENT

Erion crouched outside the narrow fissure in the cliffs that led to the nuraghi's entrance. His majea sensed the weight of two people just outside the door, but it didn't take a stoneburner to know there were guards there. The soft scent of smoke lingered near the opening. Erion rested his palm against the ground and sent a wave of vibrations through the passage. A soft tremor—just enough to spook the guards—shuddered beneath their feet.

Voloy's men stumbled out of the passage, wide-eyed and unprepared for an attack. An arrow whizzed over Erion's shoulder. It had scarcely struck its target before another followed, skewering the second guard's throat.

Erion glanced over his shoulder to see Aleria lowering her bow. She was *fast*. "Remind me not to piss you off."

"We'll see how things wash out on the other side of this, Fang."

"Don't call me that," Erion said automatically. He grabbed one of the guards by his pauldrons and dragged him out of the crevasse. They wore the familiar gray livery of Baron Voloy's watch. Mercifully, Erion didn't recognize either man.

"If you survive this, we'll talk," Aleria said.

"I've heard that a lot tonight." Erion chose to ignore her unspoken threat—if she *let him* survive. He noticed she didn't question whether or not *she'd* make it out alive.

The guard's armor fit tightly over a frame of muscle that had long since gone to seed. He was heavier than he'd looked. Too late, Erion realized he could have ordered one of the men in his crew to move the bodies for him.

This was going to take some getting used to.

Aleria watched him closely, lips pursed. Her eyes shone dangerously. All hints of her earlier humor were gone, replaced with a razor-sharp scrutiny that made Erion want to shrivel up. He turned away, but still felt her lingering gaze piercing his back. Erion gestured for Brycen, one of Isak's men, to haul away the second guard.

Then Erion slipped into the crevasse. The baron's men hadn't added any additional security measures since his last trip. He melted the lock and swung the door open.

The nuraghi's rot assaulted him at once, more strongly malevolent than ever, as though feeding off the baron's twisted rituals.

He has to be alive.

Erion had waited long enough. The rancid breath of the nuraghi reignited sparks of panic within him. He started down the stairs, then skidded to a halt. He had men to order now.

Grinding his teeth at the burden of responsibility—he should be grateful for the support, for the power, but it was all he could do to keep the horror of what he'd done for it at bay—he went back up the stairs.

"Isak, send five of your men ahead to scout—just to the bottom of the stairs. Have them come back and report." Based on the lackluster security at the door, Erion didn't think it was likely that Voloy would have posted anyone at the stairs. But what was the point in having a crew of criminals at your disposal if you didn't use them? Erion could afford to be cautious.

"Thorne, can you come here a second?" Erion drew away from the others and dropped his voice to a whisper. "I need a favor."

Thorne lowered his voice theatrically to reply. "You don't need a favor. You get to order Thorne around now."

Erion rolled his eyes. He didn't know how to ask for what he needed. His nerves were on edge, every part of him tense and overwrought. He wasn't thinking clearly.

"When we were at that pub in the Psari District—the one with that girl who almost knocked you senseless—you did... something to her." That wasn't right. Erion sighed. "Calmed her down, or..."

He hadn't realized what Thorne had done to the girl until after they'd left the pub that night. Thorne had badly miscalculated her sense of humor, and one ribald joke had led to an impressive, curse-laden string of threats. She'd chucked a full tankard of ale at Thorne's head. Every sign pointed toward further violence, but then Thorne had rested a hand on her shoulder, muttered something, and walked out of the place without a scratch. The girl had simply sat down and blinked stupidly at them as they left.

"I need to be able to focus. Think clearly. Not..." Erion swallowed. He couldn't let his emotions lead him to something stupid. "Can you help?"

"Probably," Thorne said after a moment.

"Does it only work on drunk dock girls or something?"

"Shut up," Thorne advised. He reached out and put his palm against Erion's forehead, like a mother checking her child for fever. Erion flinched at the touch, but closed his eyes once his instincts settled. Thorne wasn't going to hurt him.

A cooling sensation seeped into Erion's head and slipped down his spine. It settled into his core, almost like he'd swallowed ice. The writhing tension in his chest melted away, and his heartbeat slowed.

Erion's breathing steadied. He let out a deep, measured sigh.

Thorne took his hand away and Erion opened his eyes. Thorne was looking at him warily.

"You're tied up in ten kinds of knots," Thorne said after a moment, confirming Erion's suspicion that the man was watching him closely.

Erion ran a hand over his chest, wondering at the change. "You don't get enough credit for that trick, mate."

"Thorne's never used it like that before."

"Really?" Erion constantly regretted his own lack of formal training—he knew he barely scratched the surface of what he could do with his majea. It only just occurred to him that Thorne was in the same position. Gifted with power; cursed to figure it out on his own.

Erion shook himself. He couldn't let his newfound calm take the edge off the urgency of the situation.

"Thanks." The word didn't do his gratitude justice, but it would have to do. Thorne messing around in his head was usually a source of discomfort, but Erion was grateful for it now.

One of Isak's men—no more than a boy, really—returned to the surface. "No guards posted at the bottom of the stairs. We heard... voices but..."

"What kind of voices?" Erion asked sharply.

"Arguing. Yelling."

"Screaming?"

"N-no, sir." The kid, Fenris, looked terrified at being addressed directly. Erion thought about telling him to snap out of it, but if he'd watched a man's face getting bashed in the way Sadiq's had at that age, Erion would have been petrified, too. He'd have to try and win his trust instead.

"Where are the other two?" Erion asked.

"Still down there."

Erion nodded. "Half of you ahead of me. Nobody moves past the stairs until I give the word."

Fenris paled. Erion couldn't blame him—even without his majea, the place radiated malice. A pang of doubt filled him. Fenris couldn't be much older than Edric. Erion hesitated, then tapped Fenris on the shoulder and drew him aside.

"I need your help," Erion said. Fenris's gaze darted toward the nuraghi's entrance. The boy gulped. "The magelings we're going after—they're going to need someone to explain things to them when they get out. I don't think they're going to trust any of us at first, but they might listen to you."

"What?" Fenris gulped.

"One of them is my brother, he's about your age. Would you stay here for me? I'll tell him to look for you, in case I don't make it back at the same time. You can let them know we're taking them back to Rijeka as soon as we can."

"I... I..." Fenris's face reddened.

Erion winked, doing everything he could to encourage the kid. "Thanks. Just stand here with the watch." He turned away from Fenris's stammering. Aleria leaned against the stone a few steps away, her eyes darkly appraising. She arched a brow at him when their gazes met.

"That was half-decent of you, Fang," she said when Erion reached her.

"Don't call me that." Erion glanced at Aleria, who was still watching him through narrowed eyes. "Let's just get this done."

Aleria's expression was impassive, but she made a tiny gesture toward the stairs, inviting him to go ahead of her. The meaning was clear: *I'm sure as hell not letting your lot get behind me.*

A sphere of fire flickered to life in Erion's palm. All around him, members of the Crimson Fang lit oil lamps or torches they'd taken from the boat. Erion exchanged a glance with Thorne, swallowed his misgivings, and turned to the nuraghi's entrance. He started running as soon as he hit the stairs. Twenty or so pairs of boots stormed down behind him.

Erion skidded to a halt as he struck level ground. Hesitant footsteps vibrated through the earth. Even with some light, the careful steps signaled the obvious unease of his men in the dark of the nuraghi.

Erion stretched his majea as far through the sickening stone floor as he could. Once he was confident that none of Voloy's men were in the vicinity, he gestured for everyone to close in around him. He'd already given the group the basic layout of the chamber—as far as he knew it—but wanted to reiterate the plan.

"Once we reach the central chamber, Isak will give orders and positions to take out the guards. I'll go straight to the magelings with Thorne and—" Erion glanced at Aleria. He let the question hang.

"You couldn't stop me," Aleria bared her teeth. "I'm not here for your grudge. I'm here for the magelings—to rescue them. Then arrest or end the bastards responsible for this."

Erion was overwhelmed with relief that, at least for the time being, this formidable warrior was on his side. She might arrest him the second they were out of the nuraghi, but it was a price worth paying. At least then he wouldn't have to worry about running the Crimson Fang after that.

He winced at every echoing footfall as they followed the wall, tracing his earlier path from the last time he'd visited the nuraghi. Erion's anxiety warred with Thorne's calming compulsion, and he was all the more grateful for Thorne's influence. He was sure he'd be a complete mess without the man's help.

An unearthly, rancid breeze raked through the passage. Erion gagged and heard several of the others do the same. Low chanting lilted toward them as they rounded the final corner.

A wide circle of torches lit the enormous cavern. The stone altar in the center drew Erion's eye immediately. It was larger and far more imposing than in his memory—a darkly menacing void that sucked life and light from the room.

Cedivar knelt at the base of the altar. The baron, stooped and haggard-looking, hovered several paces away.

Erion took in the details with growing foreboding. The crystalline cocoon that held Baroness Jolie Voloy's body rested on the ground to the left of the altar. A dark liquid filled the basin at Cedivar's knees. A fist of panic gripped Erion's heart as he scanned the rest of the room.

A handful of guards stood on the side of the circle closest to

Erion and his crew. Like their companions above, they were far from alert. Aleria's presence in the city may have spurred the baron to action, but he was confident that this place remained his own secret.

He should have been more selective of his friends. Joining his plot with the Crimson Fang had been a desperate measure. Not for the first time, Erion wondered whether the baron was completely sane. Losing a loved one—or nearly losing her; had she actually died?—had obviously wreaked havoc on the man's mind. He'd been a fair enough leader, once.

And I used to be an honest man.

There was no sign of Edric or the other magelings from the festival, but the enormous altar blocked his view of a sizable portion of the other side of the room.

Erion nodded at Isak—time to trust once more. He couldn't afford to oversee thirty-odd men, dispatch Voloy's guards, and cripple Cedivar—all his energies had to go to saving Edric.

He tracked his way around the circle, flanked by Thorne and Aleria. He eyed the circle of wards with unease. The symmajea marks seemed to flicker with cold light, but that might have just been his nerves.

Erion skirted around a colossal pillar of black stone. There were no seams of mortar or joining lines of any kind. Like everything else in this cursed place, it flowed seamlessly into the floor as though carved directly into the earth. Even thinking about magic on that scale was staggering.

Erion peered around the edge of the column, careful to stay out of the light—and his heart stopped.

A stake had been driven into the ground just outside the circle of wards. Five hooded figures hunched around it in a circle, manacles clearly visible on their wrists and ankles.

They weren't too late.

The cadence of Cedivar's chanting slowed, then halted. Erion's senses prickled as he watched the mage rise and incline his head toward Baron Voloy. The baron beckoned, and a third man Erion had mistaken for a guard joined their circle.

Aleria stirred at Erion's side. Broad strokes of disgust painted her face. "This is sick. There's all kinds of majea spelled into that thing. What is it?"

"An altar of some kind," Erion frowned. "It's carved right out of the stone, it had to be here before Voloy—"

"Not that. *That.*" Aleria pointed to the glowing white of the cocoon around the baroness's body.

"Baroness Jolie. I think she might still be alive. When I saw her…" *She looked like she was about to wake up any second.* To voice it aloud sounded mad.

"Whatever that thing is, it isn't alive." Aleria's mouth twisted with distaste. "We need a distraction."

Erion nodded. "Wait here."

He slipped back the way he had come, fighting the inherent sense of nausea that slicked his majea as he relied on his earthwalking to guide him through the near-pitch darkness. He tapped Isak's shoulder as he came abreast of the man.

"We need a distraction," Erion said. "Something big."

"Bigger than killing three of Voloy's guard?" Isak said in a coarse whisper.

"Already?" Erion delved his senses into the stone with his majea, searching… *there.* The weight of a body being dragged across the floor toward the stairs.

"A few doing perimeter rounds near the stairs. But nobody's noticed they're missing," Isak said.

"Let's be grateful."

"What kind of distraction?" Isak asked.

"You got any of those ceramic discs you used in that v'deru field?" Erion asked.

Isak's face split into a broad grin.

CHAPTER FIFTY-EIGHT

CHAOS

Erion watched two guards move toward the chained magelings outside the circle. They freed one and hauled the thrashing youth across the protective threshold.

It took all of Erion's restraint not to race out immediately. The prisoner was too slender to be Edric—but that became inconsequential when the boy started to scream in protest.

Aleria tensed beside him as the wail echoed around the chamber. She nocked a vicious-looking barbed arrow and shrugged her shoulders in preparation to draw her bow. On his other side, Thorne wrapped the chain of his scythe around one elbow, the weapon gripped at the ready in his left hand. His right hand flexed into and out of a fist, the only outward sign of his tension. For now, the short butterfly sword he carried stayed sheathed on his back.

Erion's grip on his own sword hilt tightened as the guards tied the boy to the altar. *Isak better hurry up.* The mageling writhed and kicked, but the manacles bound him to the stone all the same. Cedivar ushered the two guards out of the circle, then crouched down and pressed his hands to the ring of symmajea.

Light shot upwards from the wards. Erion threw an arm over his eyes to shield them from the sudden, dazzling column of white that encircled the altar. He blinked away the shock and peered back around the column.

It was as though he was viewing the altar and the three men surrounding it through a gauzy veil. The light shimmered, making his head hurt as he squinted at it.

The screaming soared to an inhuman pitch as Cedivar circled behind the altar.

Aleria tensed. "Enough." She drew and let her arrow fly just as Cedivar's arm jerked toward the boy's throat.

The arrow bounced off the curtain of light like it had struck a wall.

Aleria swore.

A final, heart-rending wail tore through the air. Then silence.

Erion fell back heavily against the column, unable to watch the grisly scene. His stomach heaved. What the hell was going on with that barrier? Aleria seemed just as shaken by its strange behavior as he was.

And what the hell was Isak waiting for?

The light around the altar flickered out. Guards removed the manacles from a second mageling, going down the picket line like animals for slaughter.

A resounding crash shook the cavern floor. Cedivar staggered into the stone altar, and the men carrying the mageling fell to crouches, dragging the fighting youth down to the ground with them. They hadn't made it inside the barrier before Isak's explosion.

Finally. Erion glanced at Aleria. Her mouth set in a line of grim satisfaction. Her arrow darted through the air, striking one of the guards in the shoulder. He stumbled, but didn't fall.

Shouts rang out across the cavern.

Aleria was gone in an instant, flickering into the darkness only to reappear at another column closer to the chained magelings.

Erion dug his palms into the stone floor and shot tendrils of his majea toward the source of the explosion. Isak must have found—or created—a fissure in the stone near the stairs and wedged one or more of his explosive ceramics into the stone.

The fracture line was almost outside the reach of Erion's majea. He ground his fingers into the stone and threw all his will at the fracture.

His majea snapped at the weak spot like a whip. Another fissure in the stone cracked open. The sound reverberated through the nuraghi like thunder.

A hail of arrows arced through the air. The guards who had been holding the mageling lay unmoving inside the circle, prickled with Aleria's arrows. Baron Voloy, Cedivar, and the third man Erion didn't recognize all crouched behind the stone table. Voloy was shouting something, but his voice was drowned out by the guard captain bellowing orders at his men.

Aleria moved again as Voloy's guards circled to flank her from both sides. Her arrows found their final marks before the men drew too close. Her speed and accuracy astounded Erion. It was all he could do not to stare.

"Go," Erion told Thorne. The man surged toward Aleria, moving far faster than Erion had ever seen him run.

Aleria drew her saber—and the remaining guards charging her faltered. Latent majea in the slightly curved blade flared to white-hot light. Angry tongues of flame licked the steel. It took Erion a moment to realize he wasn't the only one who could see the light—she carried a true firebrand. Erion gaped.

Thorne was the only one who didn't seem distracted by the flare of the firebrand. His silent footsteps carried him to the nearest guard.

Thorne took a flying leap. His boots struck the man squarely in the back. The guard staggered forward. Thorne kicked the man's knee out, landing with his knees pressed into the guard's back and his scythe buried in his neck. Even from a distance, Erion knew the man was dead. There hadn't even been time for him to cry out.

Confident those two could handle themselves, Erion shot his majea out toward the altar. His magic hit the slick protective barrier at speed, and Erion's sense of balance jolted as his spells bounced off the wards. *Fine.*

Then he saw Cedivar crawling back to the circle's perimeter. The mage lay on his stomach and pressed his palms against the carved symmajea. The white barrier dropped, and Cedivar grabbed the mageling girl, heedless of the bodies of the two guards around her. The girl kicked and screamed, struggling against him. Cedivar wasn't a big man—she might have a chance.

"No!" Erion ran to the altar, his heart threatening to explode in his chest. He closed the distance at speed, Cedivar didn't have far to travel. The mage shoved the girl across the circle, muttered something, and the barrier flew upward once more.

Erion tore up a slab of stone and threw it at the wall of light. It slammed over an invisible dome with all the effectiveness of a wave crashing into the cliffs.

Cedivar lifted something and struck the girl over the back of the head. She shrieked and fell back from him. He hit her again, crushing her hand this time. Her screams resonated through the chamber as though through a pane of thick glass.

Erion reached the shining wall and threw himself at it.

The energy sent him flying backward. A jolt of lightning tore through him as he crashed to the floor. Every muscle in Erion's body screamed for relief.

Erion rolled onto his forearms, gasping for breath. *So charging through the barrier isn't an option.* He should have guessed as much after it had so neatly repelled Aleria's arrow, but he'd needed to check.

The clashing uproar of a half-dozen skirmishes demanded Erion's attention. His sword had been thrown from his hand and lay several yards away. He scrabbled for the hilt, and his hand curled around it like it was an extension of his body.

Erion lurched toward the magelings still manacled to the ground a few yards away. Beyond the protective circle, the girl's screams had faded. He didn't turn to look.

It was time to focus on the living.

Erin fell to one knee next to the nearest captive and tore off the kid's hood. A boy, no older than fourteen, glared up at Erion through red-rimmed eyes. Lines of tears shone on his cheeks, streaking and smearing the dirt on his face and neck. Erion moved his hand to the manacles on the boy's ankles.

The mageling kicked Erion's hands with a shrill battle-cry brazen enough to shame berserkers. The kick jammed Erion's fingers into the chain. Erion jerked away, swearing.

"I'm here to *help*," he snarled through the throbbing pain in his fingers. He had to give the kid credit for grit, though. "Hang on a minute." Erion used a sliver of his majea to slice through the manacles.

Erion turned to the next captive and snatched off her hood. A girl with a badly bruised eye looked up at him sullenly as he removed her bonds, but he didn't stop to talk to her. The next in line was Edric.

Hood or no, Erion would have recognized him anywhere. Broad shoulders hunched over manacled wrists, Edric was tensed and prepared to face whatever horrors lurked beyond the hood blinding him.

An arrow skidded off the floor an inch away from Erion's knee. "*Hey!*" He jerked his arm upward and summoned a barrier of stone to shield himself and the magelings. The makeshift wall of dark stone rose reluctantly. A sinister stonewhisper slipped into his mind.

You are not welcome here.

Erion's hands trembled. *What was that?* The stone had felt sentient before but... now it was trying to *communicate* with him?

No, that was madness.

You are not welcome.

Erion gritted his teeth and forced away his nausea. He couldn't afford to dwell on it. The sooner they all got out of the nuraghi, the sooner he could put this horror out of his mind for good. Erion ripped the hood off Edric's head.

His brother exploded upward the moment he could see. The top of his head smashed into Erion's face, and they both fell back against the wall of stone Erion had conjured.

"Kalistar's blood, Edric!" Blood spewed from Erion's nose.

"Wha—*Erion?*" Edric's eyes were wide with shock and confusion.

Erion pinched the bridge of his nose with one hand and touched his fingers to Edric's manacles with the other. With a deft snap of the lever inside, the iron cuff snapped open. He tended the bindings at Edric's ankles while his brother babbled incoherently.

Dimly, Erion realized Edric was apologizing. "There's no time for that. Tell them I'm here to help, will you? That kid almost broke my fingers."

Edric turned to the two remaining captives, urging them to listen to Erion.

Two more arrows flew toward them. Erion just had time to raise another low wall of stone before they struck. The reserves of his magic were already ebbing. Widening the cracks Isak had blown into the stone had taken no small amount of energy.

A man jumped over the low wall, leading with his sword. Erion twisted and hurled his belt knife at the man. Wind and steel whispered as they carried the blade with expert precision toward their mark.

The dagger buried itself in the man's throat. He dropped to the ground like a stone.

Erion caught sight of Edric's face—the boy had gone white as a ghost.

"What about Dmitrii?" the girl at Edric's side demanded. She grimaced in pain as she spoke, and Erion saw that the bruising extended down from her blacked eye to her jaw and neck.

"He's—"

"And Telia?" she added before Erion could answer.

"You have to run. Get out of here."

The small boy poked his head over the low wall. His eyes widened at the chaos in the chamber. "Uhm... where?"

Erion winced. They were lucky Cedivar and the baron were cowering behind their barrier, but they wouldn't stay there forever.

He pointed toward the pillars where he, Aleria, and Thorne had waited for Isak's distraction. "Take one of those torches. There's a crack in the floor over there. Follow it to the wall, then put your right hand on the wall and walk until you reach the stairs."

"Where are we?" Edric asked.

"Somewhere you don't want to be. *Go*," Erion urged.

"You aren't coming?"

"I'm going to cover you guys when you run." Behind them, a man cried out in pain over the clatter of steel against steel.

"Then I'm staying with you," Edric said.

"Dammit, Edric, you're in this mess because you didn't listen to me. Take the others and go."

"What happens when we get to the stairs?" The other boy crouched over the body of the fallen guard. He took up the man's dagger and clutched it in a claw-like, almost feral grip.

"That's the exit. Just wait for me when you get up there. There's a kid—Fenris. He'll explain."

"Ok." The boy took a stick of charcoal out of his pocket and started scribbling on the dagger's blade. It glowed faintly when he held it up again. "Nobody can take it from me, now," he explained when Erion glanced at him quizzically. "It will burn anyone else who touches it."

"Nice," Erion said. At least one of them was taking this seriously.

From the corner of his eye, Erion saw figures approaching them from beyond the barrier. He glanced over to see Cedivar reaching his hands toward the symmajea.

"I'm not leaving without Dmitrii and Telia," the girl proclaimed.

"They're dead, Laurel," Edric told her. He picked up the guard's fallen sword and turned to Erion. "We'll go."

Erion peered over the top of the barrier, his stomach sinking at the sight beyond. Voloy had brought at least thirty soldiers, and the twenty or so Crimson Fang men Erion had trusted enough to descend into the nuraghi were falling back. Even though they were a bit rusty, the baron's men had all received formal training in combat. Once they'd recovered from the sudden attack, they'd fallen into rhythms born of hours in the practice yards. In comparison, most of the Crimson Fang were petty thieves and cutthroats. They weren't the type to back away from a fight, but they weren't really prepared to face well-trained men in full armor, either.

Aleria and Thorne alone seemed to be holding their ground. The Guardian's firebrand danced with her opponents like it had a life of its own, carving red-hot slash marks through the air as she swung it with deadly precision.

With her on their side, they might just make it—but there was still the matter of the mages to handle.

"Now," Erion said as soon as there was a break in their immediate line of retreat. He skirted around the wall, leading the three magelings to the back pillar. An arrow flew toward them from the far side of the cavern, but Erion saw the archer before he loosed. With a snarl, he sent a whirlwind of air and debris hurtling across the room at their attacker. The torrent caught the arrow mid-arc and whipped it upwards. The vortex tore into the guard, knocking him off his feet and sending him flying several feet through the air.

"*Whoa*," the small boy said appreciatively.

Who is this kid? Erion grabbed him by the shoulder to stop him gaping and hurried him to one of the enormous pillars.

"Follow this line." He pointed to the fissure in the stone again. "Then all the way to the stairs, you hear me?"

"Erion, I'm so s—" Edric began.

Erion pulled Edric into a fierce hug, cutting off his brother's words. He always seemed to forget how tall the kid had gotten.

"Later," Erion said, squeezing his relief into the embrace. If Erion never did another righteous act, Edric was going to get out of this alive—and that was enough. "I promise. I'll tell you everything. Now get out of here."

408

CHAPTER FIFTY-NINE

REINFORCEMENTS

C edivar tried to block out Voloy's babbling. The baron was alternately giving orders and cursing the interruption of his ritual. His thoughts, such as they were, came out in sputtered fragments of outrage.

"That Guardian. It's her. I'll kill Niklas when we get back, I swear—he failed to tell me—never was right again after the icho testing—what are they doing here? I *need*—"

They were safe behind the barrier for the time being. Moving quickly, Cedivar cut the leather bindings that held the mageling girl to the altar. Her blood splattered his face as he dragged her off the stone table.

"I need all of them, Cedivar! All of them!" Voloy shouted.

Cedivar glanced over at the picket where the other magelings had been chained. They were gone. He exchanged an irritated glance with Petyr. The erkurios had been maddeningly silent through the ordeal.

Outside the wall of light, figures grappled, weapons clashed. Men fell.

"That's not going to be easy," Cedivar told Voloy through gritted teeth.

"Send the guards after them." Voloy's courage seemed to have returned to him.

Cedivar's patience with Voloy was waning. They had rushed to perform the rite because of the Guardian's sudden presence in the city. They weren't ready—and Cedivar feared that even if they had some small success, the result was going to be ugly.

The Baron of Caraz wouldn't survive the night—it was only a question of whether he'd lose his life or his sanity.

Cedivar ran his foot over a length of the carved runes, muttering their names under his breath. A narrow opening split in the wall of light separating them from the rest of the room. He shouted at a nearby guard who had backed away from the main of the fighting.

The man turned, and Cedivar recognized him from the baron's estate. Olivier did a double-take, nearly tripped over his own sword, and narrowly avoided being slashed across the face by an unwashed-looking man who lunged at him.

Olivier fell to one knee and drove his sword into the man's gut, then jumped back from the blood as though terrified of it.

"Get over here—and bring him with you!" Cedivar yelled over the din. Olivier grabbed the man by the collar and dragged him across the floor. His sword, still embedded in the corpse's stomach, scraped audibly against the stone.

Under Cedivar's instruction, Olivier dragged the body into the circle. Cedivar raised the barrier behind him with a whispered word.

Petyr knelt by the body and inspected it. The dead man had a dusting of freckles and a mass of sandy, unkempt hair. It was nobody Cedivar recognized. On a hunch, he crouched beside Petyr and rolled up the man's sleeves.

An intricate tattoo of a fang had been inked in pinks and faint reds on his left forearm.

"*Mathieu*," Cedivar snarled with disgust. He didn't think Mathieu would have the stones to interfere on this kind of scale.

Cedivar cursed his own lack of foresight. He should have been prepared.

"The magelings!" Voloy screamed.

Cedivar looked at Olivier and nodded toward the nuraghi's exit. "Go get them. Take as many men as you can," he ordered.

"What, me?" Olivier spluttered.

"Do I look like I'm talking to myself?" Cedivar split the protective barrier again and practically kicked the man across the line. Once he'd recalled the runes, he opened his satchel and removed a small, leather-wrapped item. He pulled the covering off.

Cedivar had carved the whistle from the femur of a dead bone scout. It had a single hole bored through the center, and lines of red symmajea swirled and spread across its surface as he brought the bone to his lips.

The whistle's high, shrill call was without variation. Cedivar blew two blasts in quick succession, then wrapped the sensitive piece of artifice again before returning it to his satchel.

Beyond the barrier, Olivier and three other guards evaded the Crimson Fang's attackers and vanished into the darkness leading toward the stairs.

Baron Voloy might not survive the night, but Cedivar intended to.

CHAPTER SIXTY

IMPASSE

Erion waited until his earthwalking confirmed Edric and the others had reached the darkness of the far wall, then circled back to meet up with Isak. The battle had fallen to a stalemate of sorts. Baron Voloy's men had clustered near the barrier, backs facing inwards, half-shields raised against the vicious accuracy of Aleria's arrows. They seemed to be torn between protecting the baron and ferreting out the Crimson Fang's remaining attackers.

Erion tried to identify the fallen men as he counted them. More of the baron's gray-clad fighters were down, but at a glance, the Fang was outnumbered.

"We should run," Isak said. A bloodstained cloak was tied around his upper arm, and his eyes were glazed with pain.

"Can we?" Erion asked. His eyes flitted across the room toward Aleria, whose quiver of arrows must be nearly empty.

Most of the Crimson Fang had no interest in stopping Voloy from his ritual, but Aleria syn'Duvar was here *because* of it. She wouldn't retreat, and Erion had the feeling she'd make him pay for it if he tried to abandon her now.

"She won't like that," Erion said, jerking his chin toward the Guardian.

"So?" Isak hissed.

"*So*, can't exactly be picky with our allies," Erion snapped.

"Were you doing that before?" Isak asked.

A dozen or more of Voloy's guards were still alive. Most of the casualties were credited to Aleria's firebrand and deadly archery. The woman was a force to be reckoned with, and Erion hadn't even seen her deploy her majea yet.

Erion guessed he had ten men still in fighting condition. "So how do we break that barrier down?"

The circle was still resistant to infiltration by magical and physical means alike, but he'd seen Cedivar break the circle a few minutes earlier. They were going to have to trick the Line Mage into lowering the barrier.

Then the light split again, and a guard exited the circle. He yelled something Erion couldn't hear, and three more guards followed him. They took off at speed toward the nuraghi's exit.

Oh no, you don't. Erion raced after the men. Behind him, Isak hesitated, then Erion felt his bulk shift through the earth. Soon the big man was trotting at his side, his face stony with pain.

Edric and the others had a good head start. Erion told himself there was plenty of time to cut off the men pursuing the magelings down the passage. Still... he glanced over his shoulder as another scrimmage broke out between the Crimson Fang and Voloy's guards. Aleria's firebrand spun dizzyingly in the fray.

Erion quickened his pace and reached the far wall. The four guards had already melted into the darkness. He tracked their progress through the ground, his earthwalking measuring every step. With a whispered command to the resistant stone, Erion carved a disc of earth out from beneath the guards.

Four bodies tumbled on the newly broken ground. Erion moved closer, Isak trailing behind him with a string of curses. Erion shifted the displaced earth with an effort, shaping it into a sphere and preparing to crush the soldiers with it. The four men were scrambling in the dark, trying to find their feet, and—

Five bodies.

No. Erion drew himself to a halt and threw an arm out to stop Isak. The big man grunted as he collided with Erion's back.

Erion's arms began to tremble as the weight of the hovering stone stressed his control near to breaking. Five bodies meant somebody else had just come down the stairs.

With a grunt of effort, Erion dropped the stone into the center of the passage.

"Ow, dammit. Get off me!" Edric's voice was unmistakable.

Shit. What was he doing here?

But Erion didn't need to wonder. Edric was trying to help. That was all his little brother ever wanted—to help. And it was going to get him killed.

Erion snapped a fire sphere into life and clambered around the side of the rubble. His heart stopped. Olivier, the guard he'd spoken to outside the baron's chambers just days before, had Edric in an arm lock. Edric was bent almost double as he tried to relieve the pressure on his shoulder.

"Let him go, Olivier." Erion's mouth was bone dry. Edric looked up at him with panicked eyes. His lips were moving frantically, but Erion couldn't make out the muttered words.

Olivier's sneer was defiant, but Erion didn't miss the fear in his eyes.

"Orders," the guard whispered. The three men around him had found their feet, and they clustered around Edric like an honor guard.

"You don't want to do this." Erion stretched out a hand, palm up, trying to appeal to Olivier's better nature. Erion had never taken Olivier for cruel, but he knew all too well what a man following orders could be driven to.

I killed Hugo under orders.

Olivier let go of one of Edric's arms and drew his dagger. He pressed the blade against the side of Edric's neck. His brother hissed in pain and closed his eyes.

"Move," Olivier growled.

Erion backed away at once, terrified Oliver might do something stupid if he declined.

"Stay back," Olivier told Erion as they moved. "Or he's dead."

The guards half-dragged Edric back down the passage toward the ritual circle. Isak's hand twitched for his battle ax, but Erion put his hand on his shoulder, willing him to stillness. They stood, shoulder-to-shoulder, and watched Voloy's guards take Edric away.

"What are we doing?" Isak demanded. "Rescuing the kid was the whole point."

Erion barely resisted punching him. His calm was crumbling.

He waited until Olivier and his men reached the ritual chamber. Long enough that Olivier wouldn't twitch and spill Edric's blood just for the sake of making good on his threat. Then Erion bolted after the guards. If they succeeded in dragging Edric across the protective circle, his brother was dead.

Erion's heart pounded louder than his footsteps. The eerie white barrier pulsed over the central altar like a living thing. Across the cavern, he could just make out Aleria's firebrand.

The curtain of light around the circle parted as Olivier dragged Edric across the protective threshold. Erion sped up, heart pounding, arms pumping.

Cedivar swiped his foot over the line of runes just before Erion reached the ring of symmajea. He crashed once more into the wall of shimmering spellwork. Pain seared through his body as he slumped to the ground.

Erion rose to his knees, fending off the worst of the pain. Edric screamed, struggling against Olivier and Cedivar as they fought to get him on the stone altar. Mere feet away, Baron Voloy knelt by the basin at the foot of the table.

Olivier and his men held Edric down. Cedivar strapped the leather cuff around one of his feet, then cursed when Edric managed to kick his temple with his free leg. Cedivar's dagger flashed into his hands, silver and sinister, and slashed at Edric's calf. Edric howled, still fighting as they forced his injured leg against the altar and lashed him to it.

"Cedivar!" Erion shouted. The mage ignored him. He tied Edric's right arm to the stone, then circled to the other side of the Giant's cruel altar.

No. Furious, desperate, Erion beat his fists against the ground. Cracks spiderwebbed across the stone, releasing enraged stonewhisper from the nuraghi's depths. Feral whispers filled his mind, half-formed thoughts of revenge and retribution.

He struck again. The whispered threats sharpened with the deepening rift, a torrent of malignancy that lifted from the fissures in the floor.

Erion slammed his bleeding knuckles down once more, every scrap of focus and will he could summon focused on destroying the circle of runes. A deep, resonating boom echoed through the nuraghi.

Cracks chased each other across the carved symmajea encircling the altar. Erion was only dimly aware of movement through the ground around him. Several guards still scuffled with members of the Crimson Fang; Aleria's battle cries as she fought to join him at the circle's perimeter. Men screaming.

Quick, loping vibrations through the ground tugged at the back of Erion's mind. He pushed aside the distractions and sent another wave of force into the cracks in the stone.

The curtain of light wavered like a candle's flame under a soft wind. Erion's lips curled into an exhausted smile. He raised his head and met Cedivar's eyes.

The runes carved closest to Erion's hands exploded upward with an earsplitting roar.

The barrier fell.

The spellwork's cold white light faded to the disarmingly warm tones of torchlight. Aleria's firebrand flared up mere feet from Erion's left. A handful of Voloy's remaining guards crowded her—but the woman was smiling.

Baron Voloy wailed and scrabbled for the basin. His hands came out stained dark with blood, clutching three stones Erion recognized all too well.

Voloy tripped over the basin and fell to his knees at the side of the white cocoon.

Cedivar froze. Erion lurched to his feet and charged at the mage. As he watched, Edric reached out his free hand and grasped Cedivar's wrist.

The Line Mage hissed in pain and jerked away as though burned. Edric scrabbled at the leather ties binding his other arm to the table. He shouted, "*Loose!*" The straps fell away.

Cedivar lunged at Edric. Erion tackled him around the waist moments before he could slash Edric's back. The mage was tall, slender—and not at all built for fighting. He fell to the ground.

"Attack!" the mage shouted. The unexpected order stayed Erion's hand, and the hesitation cost him. He turned just in time to see the unearthly orange eyes of an enormous hound.

Claws raked Erion's back. The creature's weight barreled him over. Warm blood flowed freely from the cuts in his back.

A snarl of pain tore from Erion's throat. He raised the dagger meant for Cedivar and stabbed it into the hellhound's shoulder. The hound's teeth tore down along his forearm, slicing the ties on his bracer and ripping the leather armor away. Blood smeared down Erion's arm, mingling with the crimson droplets tattooed on his wrist.

Fully blooded.

Erion slammed his boot into the hound's muzzle. The beast didn't even flinch. One giant paw slashed at Erion's shoulder, knocking him aside like he was a ragdoll. Flaming pain flickered through his body.

Erion tucked his shoulder and used the momentum from the hound's attack to roll away. He clamped his jaw down against a scream; his back was on fire.

A fierce growl filled the air, rumbling in Erion's chest like a living thing as the beast bore down on him. Then the sound cut off with an abrupt yelp. Erion rose onto his forearms, looking up in time to see the hellhound veer off course. It twisted, its jaws snapping at a projectile sticking from its ribs. A second arrow followed the first, striking the beast in its flank.

Erion threw himself forward—he needed to strike while the hellhound was distracted. They collided. Erion's dagger sliced deep through the knotted muscles in its neck, and the hellhound thrashed. Knife-like teeth scored Erion's arm. Erion reached up, wrenched the dagger from the hound's flesh, and slashed again and again. With a final thrust, he drove the blade through the beast's eye.

The hellhound dropped with a whine, crushing Erion beneath its bulk.

"Edric!" Erion dragged himself out from under the hound's corpse. He left the dagger where it protruded from the hellhound's eye and reached for his sword, looking around desperately for signs of his brother. The stone altar was empty.

Another hound burst into the circle. Erion's sword took the monster in the neck. Bright red blood spurted from the wound, drenching Erion in sticky warmth. The hound snapped. With a grunt of effort, Erion severed the creature's head from its body.

Something moved in his periphery; Cedivar and Edric were locked together on the other side of the altar. The mage's long white fingers were wrapped around Edric's neck.

Edric croaked, obviously trying to speak. Erion threw himself into the fray, kicking Cedivar in the back. He wrapped his arms around Cedivar's neck, and the mage loosed his grip on Edric as soon as the headlock tightened. Edric seized Cedivar's hands. He gritted his teeth and gasped out, "*Pain.*"

The spell's raw force caught Erion in its wave. A jolt of fire rippled through his body. He fell to his knees. Blinded and shocked by the sudden agony, he dropped his hold on Cedivar. The mage's scream pierced to his core.

A pair of hands grabbed Erion and pulled him away from the altar.

"Thorne thinks it's time to go," Thorne's voice whispered in Erion's ear.

Erion blinked tears from his eyes and looked around for his brother. Where had Edric learned *that?*

Cedivar was crawling to Baron Voloy's side, where the third

mage still hovered. The three men crouched beside the strange, woven cocoon that bore Baroness Jolie's body.

Erion spotted Edric crouching behind the altar just in time to see the kid throw himself at Baron Voloy.

"Edric, *no!*" Erion shouted. Thorne and Aleria grabbed him by the arms and held him back. "Get off me!"

Edric pummeled Voloy wherever he could land a punch. Voloy dropped a flask of sludgy, green liquid. It cracked on impact and its contents trickled across the stone.

"Not now," Voloy gasped at the ground. He shoved Edric away with a snarl and drew his dagger. The blade slashed across Edric's chest, and the boy screamed.

Cedivar and the other mage seized Edric by the collar and hauled him off the baron. Despite his injury, Edric bucked and swore. He only stilled when Voloy pressed the tip of his dagger to the soft spot behind his ear.

"I'm sorry." Voloy's hand trembled, making the point of the dagger twitch against Edric's skin. "It must be done. There's no other way."

Voloy nodded at Cedivar. The mage moved to the cracked flask, unstoppered it, and leaned over the casket. Gently, he opened the baroness's mouth and filled it with the remainder of the liquid.

Thorne and Aleria's grips on Erion's arms slackened as a cold silence settled on the cavern. Cedivar massaged the baroness's neck. The muscles in her throat convulsed as though she was swallowing.

Cold wind slithered from the crevasse in the center of the circle. Rabid terror swooped through Erion, and he watched with growing horror as fear overtook Aleria and Thorne's faces. Thorne's eyes widened in understanding, then closed as he scrunched up his face in concentration. A measure of peace wormed its way into Erion's mind.

Damn heartbenders. The two warring magics were wreaking havoc with Erion's nerve.

He pushed through the fear. He'd leave Thorne to his work

battling the baron's Love Magician. Where the other could cast terror, hopefully Thorne would help them all keep their wits about them.

Whispers of revenge and retribution reverberated through the stone and slipped into Erion's mind on the frigid breeze. Latent power resonated through the ground, seeped through the cracks in the stone. Erion shifted his feet, sending his remaining magic as deep into the earth as he could while keeping his eyes fixed on Edric. Thorne had dropped his arm altogether, and Aleria's hold was cursory. He just needed the right time to strike.

"You killed those girls," Edric breathed, staring at Baron Voloy with blind rage.

"Actually, that was me." Cedivar shook Edric by the collar. "It gets easier with practice."

Baron Voloy rested his hands on his wife's forehead. "We have to wake you up now, my love. It will hurt." The man's voice broke. Dark circles ringed his eyes. "Only—only for a moment."

Erion pulled at Aleria's grasp. The Guardian rammed her elbow into his side. He wheezed and glared at her. Everything hurt enough already without her help.

"Wait," she said.

"I was waiting," he hissed. *Wait for what? Waiting any longer wouldn't stop Cedivar from killing Edric.*

"The timing has to be perfect," Cedivar told Voloy, unknowingly echoing Aleria's assertion. The mage seemed confident that they were at a standoff. As long as Edric lived, he needn't fear action from Erion or any of the others. As long as Edric lived...

"Petyr, stand there." Voloy pointed to the head of the casket. "Hold her head."

Baron Voloy rested one hand on the three zomajea stones at his side, his other on the baroness's chest.

"The potion will have spread through her body by now. It has to be now!" Cedivar said.

"I need the boy," Voloy hissed.

"When you raise her," Cedivar snapped.

Aleria tensed at Erion's side. Her fingers flexed on her firebrand. He tensed himself, preparing to follow her lead when she was ready to strike.

Erion's exhaustion was like a stone crushing his chest. His majea pulsed weakly as he reached deep into the earth. Something stirred in the depths below.

Baron Voloy frowned in concentration, his eyes fixed on his wife's face. The stones beneath his right palm glowed a soft red. His knuckles whitened as he strained to control power that was never meant to be wielded by man.

Baroness Jolie's eyes opened.

Chapter Sixty-One

STONEWHISPER

Silence cloaked the room as everyone stared, transfixed, at Baroness Jolie Voloy.

The baron reached for his dagger with shaking hands. Tears welled in his eyes—and he plunged the blade into her heart.

Erion recoiled in horror. The baroness's eyes fluttered shut once more, and Voloy's tears slipped down his own cheeks and onto hers. For a moment, Voloy slumped over the white cocoon holding her body, sobbing silently. After long moments, he pulled the knife from her chest. Dark blood seeped across the fabric of her dress.

Voloy picked up the stones with trembling hands and rested them atop the wound. "Petyr," he whispered.

The third mage knelt at the head of the coffin. He rested his hands lightly over the baroness's temples.

Aleria loosened her grip on Erion's arm. Her eyes were wide with shock. Erion thought he could see her straining to follow the majea that must be coursing through the zomajea stones, into and through Baron Voloy.

Power they had watched the baron leech from the blood of two aspiring mages, little more than children.

It had to be stopped.

Erion stamped his boot into the floor, and the earth rumbled. The barrier between Erion and burgeoning power he'd sensed growing there snapped.

Power tore through the earth, channeling through Erion's body. The surge re-energized him even as the sheer magnitude of it threatened to rip him apart. He glanced at Edric. One wrong move would mean his brother's death.

Erion fought to keep control of the rising tide of power within him as Voloy's soft chanting swept around the room. The spell rose and fell on the nuraghi's foul wind, setting Erion's teeth on edge. Then Voloy's voice fell to a whisper—and Baroness Jolie Voloy sat up.

Tangible shock rippled through the onlookers. Dark blood stained the baroness's bodice. Her spine was ramrod straight, unblinking eyes fixed straight ahead.

Voloy stood and pulled Jolie to her feet with him. An iridescent glow encapsulated her as she stepped out of the white cocoon. Voloy's eyes sparkled with unshed tears.

"Cedivar," Voloy said faintly. His gaze never left his bride.

The baron was too in rapture to see what was so clear to Erion. Though awake, Jolie had gone. Her eyes were blank, colorless. Everything about her seemed... shallow.

After all the destruction and malice, all Voloy had risen was an empty vessel—breathing, living. Utterly inhuman.

Cedivar gripped Edric by the nape of his neck and raised the dagger. The nuraghi trembled as Erion called more and more majea to him. Before Erion could act, Edric seized Cedivar's wrists. The Line Mage shrieked and dropped him.

Burgeoned by the nuraghi's strange sentience, Erion's majea threatened to burst through his skin. A wordless cry tore from his throat as he threw the power at Cedivar. A shock wave heaved through the earth. Stone rolled and pitched beneath them, throwing everyone but Erion off their feet.

Aleria recovered first. She pounced on Drazan Voloy with catlike agility. A spark of white light flared between them as they collided. They stumbled away from Jolie's body. The baroness held the side of the white cocoon, her expression vapid, almost serene.

"Here!" Aleria threw a small leather pouch at Erion. "Open that and give it to him!" The Guardian managed to gesture to Edric while she was dragging Baron Voloy away from the casket.

Erion skidded across the floor to Edric. Cedivar had grabbed him again. Neither were experienced fighters, and the two grappled clumsily. Erion loosed the ties on the pouch and pressed it into Edric's hand in a clumsy pass. He kicked Cedivar's knees out from beneath him, sending the mage and Edric to the ground in a flailing heap.

Cedivar's nails raked red claw marks on the skin of Edric's throat A measure of what might have been fine ash fell from the pouch into Edric's open palm. Without looking at it, he smashed a handful of the stuff into Cedivar's face. Erion turned his face and held his breath on instinct.

The mage had to go down.

Edric ground the powder into Cedivar's eyes, nose, and mouth with a vicious alacrity that took Erion by surprise. The acrid scent of burning flesh filled his nostrils. Cedivar gasped and choked.

"Edric, stop!" Erion finally succeeded in separating the two. He hauled Edric away from the Line Mage, horrified at his brother's aggression. "You're killing him!"

If he succeeded at nothing else, Erion had to stop Edric from stooping to the same levels he had.

He's not a murderer.

Edric's hands dropped at the words. "I didn't, I just…" He looked around frantically. A few feet away, Cedivar was curled into a fetal position, his hands tearing at a gooey substance on his face.

"Get the others out of here," Erion said.

"It's caved in." Edric buried his face in his hands.

Erion's heart pounded, circulating panic through his body with each frantic thump. Isak's distraction... the fractures Erion had added to the rocks... the cavern had fallen into an unsettling quiet. Thorne and Aleria stood over Baron Voloy, arguing heatedly about something. He couldn't hear them, but for now, he didn't care what they were talking about. The last thing he needed right now was another problem. "What happened to the other magelings?"

"They went up before the collapse. I don't... I don't know if they made it."

Behind him, Cedivar recovered enough to gasp out a throaty command.

A deep-throated growl announced the arrival of another hellhound. Without thinking, Erion tapped into the power source beneath the nuraghi. The unnatural energy surged through him. At his will, a barrage of jagged stone daggers flew up from the ground beneath the hound, skewering it like a boar.

Another rumble shook the cavern. The nuraghi was too large for Erion to search the whole thing for faults, but if the passage had collapsed, the rest of the dungeon might not be far behind. "Stay with me." He wasn't about to let Edric out of his sight again.

Erion shifted his stance as two more hellhounds pounded toward them. He lifted his sword with a snarl and hurled another hail of stone daggers at the animals. The nuraghi's stone bent under his command, malleable as clay. No longer resistant, it was almost eager to serve.

Eldritch mutterings, warnings of blood and death, slipped into Erion's mind.

Distracted, he didn't hear the last hound loping toward them until it was too late. The hellhound's jaws clamped down on his shoulder. Erion went down. Pain shocked down his arm, and his sword clattered from his grip.

Blood pounded in Erion's head as the creature's razor-sharp teeth dug into his shoulder, slicing through muscle and grinding against bone. He couldn't think, couldn't breath through the waves of pain.

Suddenly, the creature's jaws slacked. The sizzle of burning hair reached Erion's nose. The acrid scent snapped him back to his senses. Erion seized the hound's muzzle and sealed a pocket of moisture-dense air over its nose. Battling against a blackout that felt imminent, Erion wrenched the air from the creature's throat and lungs.

The hound let out a strangled grunt, spasmed, and tried to pull away. Its paws scrabbled weakly against the ground, and then it collapsed into heavy, dead weight on his injured back.

Erion's cheek pressed against the cool stone floor. Dimly, he was aware of Edric pushing the hellhound off him. A cascade of stone and rubble thundered somewhere near the back wall.

It's collapsed, he thought vaguely. *No way I can carve stairs out of here in this state.*

Not that he would have been capable to begin with.

Erion's vision started to blur.

"Hang on, you idiot," someone muttered. Warm hands pressed against the ruinous gouges in Erion's flesh, trying to stem the flow of blood. "Ugh."

It was Edric. Erion managed a smile. "Find Thorne. Tell him to get you out of here." But with the passage blocked, that was impossible. Erion fought to think through his fatigue.

"A thorn? You *are* hurt. Now shut up." Edric's fingers squeezed Erion's shoulder.

Erion let out an involuntary shudder. Heat dug into the wounds and spread to envelop his shoulder. He groaned as the pressure built up against his skin.

"Can you sit up?" Edric asked.

It was a moment before Erion realized the pain had subsided—not completely, but he no longer felt as though his arm had been ripped off. He rolled onto his back and looked up at his brother blearily. "Who the hell taught you to do that?"

"I'd have learned it a lot sooner if you weren't such an asshole." Edric didn't smile. Sweat matted his hair and soaked the collar of his shirt. He leaned down, grasped Erion's hand, and pulled him to his feet.

Erion staggered upright, prepared to be attacked at any moment, only to find the fight was over. The few of Voloy's guards who'd survived had been bound and dumped near the altar.

Baron Voloy was tied, weeping, next to his wife's body. Jolie Voloy lay prone on the floor, her limbs spread-eagle. A burnished copper film covered her eyes.

Either he'd lacked the power to complete the ritual, or Aleria was right—what was dead stayed dead.

Thorne sat crouched over the body of the third mage, who Voloy had called Petyr. Erion and Edric shuffled toward him. Petyr's body bore no visible signs of violence, but thin threads of blood dribbled from his ear. Thorne's expression was practically savage when he looked up at them.

"Where's Isak?" Erion asked.

Thorne pointed to the darkness beyond the circle. Two torches bobbed near the wall, led by Aleria's firebrand. "They're trying to find a way out."

Erion collapsed next to Thorne and leaned against the altar. A sense of unreality settled on him. It was over.

"You ok, Dead Man?" Thorne eyed Erion warily.

Erion closed his eyes. "That's *Lord* Dead Man to you."

An ominous grinding sound filled the air around them. Erion sent a tentative weave of majea into the stone. The alien sentience in the stone seized his consciousness. The whole of the nuraghi's will reared its ugly head. A magnitude of power pressed against Erion's mind, tugging at his majea and sucking his mind deeper into the stone's depths.

Erion sat upright with a jolt. He could feel Aleria and Isak's footsteps all the way across the hall, the disgruntled shifting of Voloy's guards a few feet away. Twelve more of the Crimson Fang had survived, their footsteps radiating from different corners of the nuraghi as they searched for exits. Cedivar, still crumpled in a ball outside the circle of runes, was alive, his breathing shallow and uneven.

The stonewhisper translated as clearly to him as words, feeding him information as easily as breathing. The hateful place became an extension of Erion's own mind; the slightest disturbances in the stone rippled through his earthwalking senses with unnerving clarity.

And he knew with a certainty that the cavern was unstable, the walls ready to collapse at the slightest provocation.

"Ok." Erion heaved himself to his feet. "We've got to go."

"Thorne could have told you that." Thorne rolled his eyes. He looked down at Petyr and kicked the man's body. He looked up at Erion and Edric defiantly. "What? He was looking at Thorne."

"Remember the first time we were here?" Erion asked.

"Thorne wished he didn't."

"There's another entrance."

"Oh no, you don't." Thorne shook his head vehemently. "No. *No.*"

"You can swim, can't you?"

"Thorne thinks you're missing the more important part of his objection."

"So you *can* swim."

Thorne crossed his arms and scowled. "There are too many of us."

Erion flexed his hands, testing the density and weight of the air around him. A breeze passed through his fingers at the slightest whisper. Exhausted though he was, the nuraghi responded to his slightest whim.

He'd awoken something in the depths. Even as he thought it, a feral presence slipped into the back of his mind.

Release, the stone whispered. *After so long.*

The thought was more sensation than words, a tendril of thought and emotion that leeched onto his mind and bled into his own tangled feelings. It was similar to the slippery sense of Thorne's interference in his mind but... stronger, more deliberate.

More malicious.

Erion had to get out of there.

"Isak! Aleria!" The lights on the far side of the cavern paused, then moved closer as the two returned to the center of the room. "There's another way."

"There's nothing, we've been all over this place." Aleria propped her fist on her hip and glared imperiously at him. "You look like shit."

Erion winced. He *felt* like shit. "There's an opening into the lake—I've used it before." *Sort of.*

He hadn't actually entered the nuraghi when the waters of Lake Zagretsk had swallowed him up. It had been enough to see the crevasse leading into the monolith open. Even then, there had been a siren call to enter its arcane depths.

"Thorne feels like we're losing sight of the real problem here," Thorne interrupted. "Like how you're going to keep Thorne from drowning."

"I'll cut stairs," Erion said, improvising. "Get everyone together."

"You don't have the strength for that." Aleria looked at him with a professional eye now. She reached out and pressed two fingers to his cheek. "You're half dead already. Although… an energy transference? Crude, but effective. Who helped you?"

"That was me." Edric looked sheepish.

"Well *done*, mageling." Aleria turned to consider him. "You're the brother, then?"

"Edric Skala." He fidgeted under her gaze.

"We'll see about you, young Skala." Her words seemed innocent, but Erion sensed the weight of a threat behind them. He took a protective half-step in front of his brother.

Another tremor rocked the nuraghi.

CHAPTER SIXTY-TWO

NURGAHI UZHASTIK

The tremors grew as Erion and the others rounded up the survivors. There was no time to trouble themselves with the dead. They had to drag Baron Voloy away from his wife's body as it was. Erion had been sorely tempted to leave Voloy and Cedivar both to rot in the nuraghi, but Aleria rebuffed the idea at once.

"He'll see the king's justice. That worm doesn't deserve death." Her tone was so powerfully vehement, nobody dared defy her.

Erion wanted to keep clear of the Guardian. He was still half-convinced she was going to arrest him. He dragged Cedivar to the far wall. The mage's face was raw and bleeding where it had come into contact with Aleria's ash powder.

"What was that stuff?" Erion asked Edric. They were practically dragging Cedivar behind them toward the nuraghi's back wall.

"Sulfur bark powder," Edric said. "Gian uses it to clean wounds."

"A healing ingredient did that?" Erion glanced back at Cedivar's face as they reached the wall. He could feel the dense weight of Lake Zagretsk pressing against the stone.

Edric winced. "It's acidic. In that concentration..."

Erion arched an eyebrow but didn't answer. Edric had clearly been doing his homework. Erion turned to Cedivar and shoved him against the wall. "*Stay.*"

Erion ran his hands across the wall's face. His majea slid over the fissures splitting the stone, searching for any weakness he could exploit. He prodded against one promising fault line.

The wall shuddered, then heaved Erion off his feet. He crashed heavily onto his wounded shoulder several feet away. Stars exploded in his vision. Erion rolled to his forearms and blinked away the light. Everyone had gone to ground, most of them curled with their hands wrapped over their heads for cover. The trembling rumbled to a halt a moment later.

"So what was this genius escape plan?" Aleria asked. Of the survivors, she seemed the least flustered.

Erion ignored her. He knelt, pressed his hands into the stone, and reached out to the sentience that lurked deep within the stone. He didn't know whether the power he'd tapped into was actually intelligent, or if he'd somehow disturbed a deeper working of ancient, latent magic in the stone, but they were out of options. Erion's strength was flagging—and he was the only hope they had of getting out of there alive.

I helped you. He felt foolish at once. He must be beyond exhaustion if he thought *talking* to it would—

You are not welcome here.

Horror trickled down Erion's spine.

Then get us out of here.

A panic-inducing malice seized Erion's mind. Ancient, primal rage seeped through him. Fury at being trapped for millennia. Gnawing thirst that would never be slaked. An unquenchable need for blood and retribution.

Power built up in the stone as the malice swelled. It spewed through cracks in the stone like magma surging toward the surface. The ground trembled.

A hand grabbed Erion's shoulder. He flinched, but it was only Thorne. His eyes were dark with apprehension. "Get us out of here, Dead Man."

"This isn't a power to be ignored," Aleria added.

Erion nodded grimly. Aleria sheathed her firebrand. "I might be able to channel some of it. And you." She jerked her head at Thorne. The man's brows lifted in silent questioning.

It took Erion a moment to understand. Of course— remnants of magic here might be of any one stream of power, or all of them. If he was overwhelmed by the rampant weaves of Land Magic, maybe she and Thorne were being assaulted by the same sense of power in their own streams of majea.

Madness.

Erion grimaced. "Hold on."

Aleria crouched down next to him and wrapped one hand over his. Thorne hovered at Erion's other side. He hesitated, then placed a bracing hand on Erion's shoulder. A soft course of warmth and reassurance pulsed through Erion at the touch. Thank the gods for Thorne.

With a steadying breath, Erion forced himself to sink into the well of alien majea that twisted his stomach and flooded his mind with feverish panic.

His skin under Aleria's hand warmed. Her power joined Thorne's, bringing with it energy and vitality that surged up Erion's arm and filled his chest. Erion envisioned a circle around the survivors. The floor cracked, causing several men to jump. The disc of earth that they stood on began to lift out of the ground.

The nuraghi's floor surged up beneath them, and the fissures in the wall cracked, revealing a gaping hole overhead. The disc of stone shuddered upward, Erion doing what he could to steady their ascent into the passage beyond, fueled by the streaming power filling him.

The earth built up beneath them like a living thing, pushing them into the darkness at an alarming speed. Soon it was all

Erion could do to keep from throwing up. The churning earth and nuraghi's intensity overwhelmed him.

It would be just as easy for the entity—demon? Whatever it was—to crush them into the bowels of the earth. Erion braced for impact as a deafening roar blistered his ears. He sensed huge sections of the cavern's ceiling break away beneath them.

Aleria's grip on Erion's hand tightened, bringing with it a renewed sense of strength. Just trying to steady their progress, to sense the seemingly unending chasm over their heads, he'd never burned through so much energy before. If this didn't kill him, surely nothing ever would.

The debt is repaid.

The message echoed in Erion's mind. His hold on the roiling magic slipped. Cold sunlight split the passage above. They tumbled into open air. Erion caught a glimpse of the crystalline blue surface of Lake Zagretsk as the nuraghi expelled them from its domain.

CHAPTER SIXTY-THREE

ACCORDS

Erion felt strangely disembodied as he walked through the entry hall at the baron's estate. Cloths of black velvet draped nearly every horizontal surface in the manor, dampening the sounds of the mourners and servants milling about the hall. Two guards he didn't recognize stood sentry at the door to the council chambers. He eyed them uneasily, but they parted without question and admitted him to the room.

An eclectic group waited for him there. Erion looked around—he'd only been expecting Aleria, but she was accompanied by Captain Talbot, Isak, Thorne, and Edric. They all rose as he entered the room.

They couldn't have assembled a more unlikely cohort if they'd tried. Erion caught Edric's eye. The boy was practically bouncing on his toes, obviously delighted about something.

Erion rolled his shoulders. The knotted scar on his right shoulder twinged. Between Aleria and Quill, it was mostly healed, but the wounds from the hellhound's savage bite—

Cedivar's specially bred bone scouts, they knew now—still itched and pulled when he least expected it.

"Sit." Aleria stood at the head of the table, and she pointed imperiously to the chair at her right. The group around the table returned to their seats.

Erion hesitated behind his chair. His run-in with the inhuman powers in the nuraghi had had lasting, unpredictable effects on his majea. At times, even the slightest whisper of gemajea was magnified ten times over. He stood a few inches away from Aleria's firebrand, and the spelled blade radiated power. She'd removed the tied canvas coverings that had disguised her firebrand for what it was while she'd been poking around the city unofficially. The sheath was made of intricately worked leather, the hilt skillfully—but practically—crafted.

"Edric?" Aleria said once it was clear Erion wasn't going to sit.

Edric's face split into a grin. "I'm going to Saritu'e'Mere."

Erion blinked at his brother while the reality of his words set in. *I'm going to Saritu'e'Mere.*

They'd done it.

"Edric, that's…" Erion's gaze flitted between the Guardian and his brother.

"Guardian syn'Duvar is sponsoring me. She says I have great potential." Edric drew himself up to his full height. The boy aged before Erion's eyes. Edric wasn't his kid brother anymore.

"I hadn't heard." Erion glanced sidelong at Aleria. She could have warned him in advance, but perhaps Edric had wanted to tell him the news himself.

"Your friend Quill here has helped me test Edric's zomajea. It's among the strongest I've seen in a mageling in some years."

Erion grasped Edric's shoulder and squeezed. "You deserve it. I know you'll make me proud."

The words set his heart to aching all over again. Erion set his jaw and lowered himself into the chair. It was all he had ever hoped for—so why did it pain him so badly? He looked around the odd collection of people sitting at the table. "What's this all about, then?"

Aleria slid a parchment across the table at him. Erion flipped it over and scanned the few scrawled lines there. It was a letter from Lord Vitas Kemez, claiming Baron Voloy's title and lands as regent.

"Well he didn't waste any time—though I've never heard of him," Erion said.

"The wax seals on the complaints against Voloy are barely dry," Aleria said. "Someone's been watching the barony closely."

"What does this have to do with me?" Erion couldn't lose anything by being blunt. It had been three weeks since the fallout in the nuraghi, two of which he'd spent abed, being plied by potions and salves and Nissra-only-knew what else by Quill. Vandra had sent him three letters in that time—none of which he'd opened. Her interference had almost cost Edric's life.

"We've been discussing the future of the barony, in light of recent developments." Aleria indicated Captain Talbot. Officials from Corsia would arrive shortly to escort Baron Voloy and Cedivar to the capital city for sentencing and judgment. *Good riddance to them.*

Erion said nothing.

"This Kemez is an unknown. The fate of the barony will remain undecided until I've spoken with the king and the other Guardians. Duke Jesper will doubtless have his own opinions on the matter. It must be handled carefully—but we need to decide the fate of more than one vacancy."

Erion's hand twitched to his left forearm. "I cede the title. I never wanted it. Thorne can—"

Thorne broke into laughter. Erion glared at him, which only made him laugh more.

"Isak, then. Anyone. Or disassemble the whole faction," Erion said loudly over Thorne's hysteria.

"Dismantling the Crimson Fang in Rijeka would mean chaos for the whole city. Any whisper of weakness will send the gang's leaders in Vhalla to desperate means. No." Aleria shook her head. "You disrupt that hierarchy and you have dozens, maybe hundreds of listless, itchy criminals with nobody to keep them in line."

"Funny, I thought that's what you were for," Erion snapped.

"Just because I haven't arrested you so far doesn't mean I can't change my mind."

"Hadn't occurred to me," Erion lied.

"We need to maintain some semblance of balance. The fall of the Crimson Fang would do nothing more than open a void for someone else to fill."

"Let them." Erion slumped back in his chair, well aware that he was sulking like a child.

"It's not a risk we can afford to take. This is just another opportunity to seize."

Erion glanced sidelong at Talbot, whose jaw was set in a grim line, then to Edric. His brother's bright demeanor had fallen into a crestfallen, stony expression. Their eyes met.

"I didn't want to believe it was true," Edric said. All traces of his earlier excitement had vanished.

"It's—complicated." Erion had kept his word and told Edric the story of how he'd gotten mixed up with the Crimson Fang to cover their father's debts, how he'd been pressed into joining officially when Mathieu had threatened Edric's life. He'd almost believed Edric had understood, sympathized with the choices Erion had been forced to make.

He'd been wrong. Edric's ironclad sense of right and wrong had widened the rift between them more than ever. After too many fights, Erion hadn't had the heart to tell his brother what he'd done to actually take over the Crimson Fang so he could order them into the nuraghi.

I only did what I had to do, Edric. Why can't you understand that? But Erion had sheltered his brother so well, Edric had never faced difficult choices. He couldn't understand stakes that held life and death in the balance.

"So?" Aleria asked.

Erion turned to Talbot. "You can't be on board with this."

"You're a sight straighter than Mathieu was. I'll never keep corruption out of my ranks. But you might help control some of the damage." Talbot's eyes shone with misgivings. "I'm sorry it has to be you, lad. But I won't lie and say I'm not glad of it."

"This is a joke." Erion shook his head, then caught Aleria's eye. He jerked his head toward Edric, then the door. *Get him out of here.* He needed a moment alone with his brother, but he got the impression Edric wouldn't be taking orders—or even requests—from him any time soon.

"Edric, I need your help with something," Aleria said at once.

Looking grateful for the distraction, Erion's brother snapped to his feet.

The Guardian handed him a thick sheaf of parchment tied with a yellow ribbon. "Take this to my contact at the gatehouse, please. They'll see to our passage north."

Edric hesitated. "How soon...?"

"Two days."

Edric swallowed, then made a small half-bow to Aleria before leaving the room. Erion jumped to his feet and followed his brother out of the council hall.

"Edric, I'm not going to do it," Erion said once the door swung shut behind them.

"Guardian syn'Duvar talked to me about it. She says you don't have a choice." Edric's cheeks were faintly pink.

"There's always a choice."

"That's not what you said when you told me you *had* to join the Fang. Did you have a choice when you killed that man—Sadiq?"

Erion's heart fell into his stomach with a sickly splash. "Aleria told you that?"

"She told me everything."

I was trying to protect you. But the excuse was tired, and Erion knew Edric wouldn't hear it.

"I never said I'd made the right choices. Just the best ones I could."

"I thought better of you, Erion."

Erion reeled. Edric might as well have slapped him. Everything he'd done had been for his brother—every terrible decision and poorly judged action.

But no such deeds—no matter how well-intentioned—could go unpunished. Erion put his hands on his brother's shoulders and looked into his eyes.

"I love you, E," he said. "I wanted so much better for you than this."

Edric held up the papers Aleria had given him. "I have to deliver these."

Erion dropped his hands, gutted. Edric turned to leave, but he paused at the end of the hall. "Brother?"

"Yes?" Erion's stomach churned.

"I know... I know you tried. That you did it for me. Thank you." Edric didn't wait for Erion's reply. He turned and exited through the guarded doors without a backward glance.

Erion stormed back into the council chambers. "What kind of sick joke is this, Aleria?"

"If it's a joke, it's not a very funny one." The Guardian leaned back and kicked her boots onto the table, peering at him. "I need you. Pelinon needs you."

"Does that line ever work?" Erion asked.

"Sometimes." Aleria cocked her head to one side as she considered him.

"You're asking me to lead a criminal underworld I never wanted to be a part of." Erion glanced at Thorne, silently begging for support. He'd even have welcomed an interjection from Isak, but none came.

"We all have to work with the hands we're dealt," Aleria said. "You don't have to like it."

"What if I refuse?"

"You won't," Aleria said.

"Humor me."

"Is arresting you and dragging you before the council in Corsia enough?"

Erion shrugged. He'd expected worse when he'd first tangled

his fate with the Guardian's.

"Say I pull Edric's name from the academy roll in Saritu'e'Mere." Aleria's voice was dangerously casual.

"You wouldn't." The words were out of Erion's mouth before he thought about it. "You said yourself he's talented. Or was that another lie to buy me?"

"Not a lie. Your brother has incredible potential. I'd be pleased to see him as a student there, perhaps even as my protégé. He'd go far."

"And you'd take that away from him? Edric hasn't done anything wrong. He's never hurt *anyone*. Not in his entire life."

"Commendable. Something that should be fostered. Rewarded, even. Perhaps somewhere far away from this barony, and the Crimson Fang."

The weight of responsibility—the love he'd harbored for his brother that had driven him to such terrible deeds—redoubled on Erion's shoulders. Aleria had told Edric the truth. Erion *didn't* have a choice.

"What do I have to do?"

Aleria beamed and laced her fingers together. "You've already started. Take over the Crimson Fang in the Barony of Caraz. Restore some order."

"And be your informant," Erion deadpanned.

"And try not to get killed," Aleria added. She lowered her feet from the table, stood, and proffered her hand for Erion to shake. "I'll be in touch after Edric is settled at school."

Aleria nodded at the men around the table and beckoned Talbot to follow her. Erion watched the door swing shut behind them with a sense of foreboding.

Take over the Crimson Fang.

For Edric.

What the hell am I supposed to do next?

Erion turned to Thorne and Isak, who were both staring at him expectantly.

"What are you two looking at?" he demanded.

"Thorne kind of figured you'd start to glow or something."

Thorne squinted. "Nothing yet."

"And you're fine with this?" Erion rolled up his sleeve and brandished his tattoo at Isak.

"You think I want that woman breathing down my neck for the rest of my life? Mathieu was bad enough." Isak stood up and considered Erion for a long moment, a scowl darkening his complexion. "Not sure how, but you've weaseled your way into a circle of powerful friends. You'll do—for now, Skala. Try not to muck it up."

Erion looked down at his own inked fang tattoo—the all-black, scrolling symmajea that marked not only his newfound seat of power, but a carefully painted target on his back.

All he'd wanted was to escape the maw of the Crimson Fang. Instead, he'd accidentally clawed his way to the top. The head of the most dangerous gang in the entire barony, backed and watched by a Guardian of Pelinon. A delicate balance of power had tilted unexpectedly in Erion's favor.

Now he just had to find a way to keep it there.

The End

Of

Stonewhisper

Continue your Eldros Adventure in the next book in the series:

Stealing the Storm

by

Aaron Rosenberg

Scan this QR Code to get it!

STONEWHISPER

ABOUT THE AUTHOR

H.Y. Gregor was born in Portland, Oregon, but she'll always call the mountains of Colorado home (where as a kid she was usually reading a book with a flashlight under the covers at night). In college she interned for congressional offices and law firms, and has a bachelor's degree in political science. She soon discovered  office life was not for her. This brought her full circle back to childhood ambitions of being a writer to bring new, fantastical stories to life. After narrowly avoiding law school, she now puts her international relations and government background to use creating intricate, colorful worlds to serve as backdrops for her fantasy fiction novels.

In 2022 her short story, "A Secret Spoken," received a Silver Honorable Mention from the Writers of the Future contest. Her short fiction can be found in *Animal Magica Volume 2*, by Tanya Hales, and *Particular Passages 4: South Wing*, by Knight Writing Press, with more exciting projects in the works. She can often be found at writing conferences with an overstuffed messenger bag and too many pens. When not writing, she laughs hysterically at the concept of "free time" and enjoys hiking and adventuring with her family.

For updates, free short stories, and photos of her dubious gardening attempts, you can check out her website or follow her here:

- hygregor.com
- Twitter (@toviahy)
- Instagram (@toviahy)
- Facebook (H.Y. Gregor – Author)

IF YOU LIKED...

If you enjoyed this novel and the world it's set in, then the creators of the Eldros Legacy would like to encourage you to don thy traveling pack and journey deeper into the mysteries of the world Eldros and all the myriad adventures set therein.

The mortal world of Eldros is coming apart. The Giants, who once ruled its five continents with draconian malice have set their mighty designs on a return to power. Mortals across the globe must be victorious against insurmountable odds or die.

Come join us as the Eldros Legacy unfolds in a growing library of novels and short stories.

You can find all the novels at:

www.EldrosLegacy.com/books

Our website is, of course:

EldrosLegacy.com

The Books by Series

Legacy of Shadows
by Todd Fahnestock

Khyven the Unkillable

Lorelle of the Dark

Rhenn the Traveler

Legacy of Deceit
by Quincy J. Allen

Seeds of Dominion

Demons of Veynkal

Legacy of Dragons
by Mark Stallings

The Forgotten King

Knights of Drakanon (Forthcoming)

Sword of Binding (Forthcoming)

Return of the Lightbringer (Forthcoming)

Legacy of Queens
by Marie Whittaker

Embers & Ash

Cinder & Stone (Forthcoming)

The Dog Soldier's War
by Jamie Ibson

A Murder of Wolves

Valleys of Death (Forthcoming)

Other Eldros Legacy Novels

Deadly Fortune by Aaron Rosenberg

The Pain Bearer by Kendra Merritt

Short Stories

Here There Be Giants by The Founders (FREE!)

The Darkest Door by Todd Fahnestock

Fistful of Silver by Quincy J. Allen

Electrum by Marie Whittaker

Printed in the USA
CPSIA information can be obtained
at www.ICGtesting.com
LVHW041125181023
761396LV00002B/24